Sophie Kinsella is a writer and former financial journalist. She is very, very careful with her money and only occasionally finds herself queuing outside the Whistles sale. Her relationship with her bank manager is excellent. She is the author of the bestselling 'Shopaholic' series: *The Secret Dreamworld of a Shopaholic*, *Shopaholic Abroad*, *Shopaholic Ties the Knot* and *Shopaholic & Sister*, as well as the bestselling *Can You Keep a Secret?* and *The Undomestic Goddess*, all published by Black Swan.

www.booksattransworld.co.uk

The Secret Dreamworld of a Shopaholic

Sophie Kinsella

BLACK SWAN

THE SECRET DREAMWORLD OF A SHOPAHOLIC
A BLACK SWAN BOOK : 9780552773461

First publication in Great Britain

PRINTING HISTORY
Black Swan edition published 2000

25 27 29 30 28 26 24

Copyright © Sophie Kinsella 2000

The right of Sophie Kinsella to be identified as the author
of this work has been asserted in accordance with sections
77 and 78 of the Copyright Designs and Patents Act 1988.

Set in 11/12pt Melior by
County Typesetters, Margate, Kent.

Black Swan Books are published by Transworld Publishers,
61–63 Uxbridge Road, London W5 5SA,
A Random House Group Company.

Addresses for Random House Group Ltd companies outside the UK
can be found at: www.randomhouse.co.uk
The Random House Group Ltd Reg. No. 954009.

Printed and bound in Great Britain by
Cox & Wyman Ltd, Reading, Berkshire.

The Random House Group Limited supports The Forest Stewardship
Council (FSC), the leading international forest certification organisation.
All our titles that are printed on Greenpeace approved FSC certified paper
carry the FSC logo. Our paper procurement policy can be found at:
www.rbooks.co.uk/environment

This book is dedicated to my friend and agent,
Araminta Whitley.

Acknowledgements

Many thanks to Patrick Plonkington-Smythe, Linda Evans and the Transworld team, Celia Hayley, Mark Lucas and all at LAW, Nicki Kennedy and Jessica Buckman, Valerie Hoskins and Rebecca Watson, and Brian Siberell at CAA.

Special thanks to Samantha Wickham, Sarah Manser, Paul Watts, Chantal Rutherford-Brown, my wonderful family and especially Gemma, who taught me how to shop.

Endwich Bank
1 Stallion Square
London W1 3HW

Ms Rebecca Bloomwood
Flat 4
63 Jarvis Road
Bristol BS1 0DN

6 July 1997

Dear Ms Bloomwood

Congratulations! As a recent graduate of Bristol University you are undoubtedly proud of your performance.

We at Endwich are also proud of our performance as a flexible, caring bank with accounts to suit everyone. We pride ourselves particularly in our far-sighted approach when it comes to customers of calibre such as yours.

We are therefore offering you, Ms Bloomwood – as a graduate – a free extended overdraft facility of £2,000 during the first two years of your career. Should you decide to open an account with Endwich, this facility will be available immediately.* I do hope you decide to take advantage of this unique offer and look forward to receiving your completed form.

Once again, congratulations!

Yours sincerely

Nigel Fairs
Graduate Marketing Manager
* (subject to status).

ENDWICH – BECAUSE WE CARE

Endwich Bank
FULHAM BRANCH
3 Fulham Road
London SW6 9JH

Ms Rebecca Bloomwood
Flat 2
4 Burney Road
London SW6 8FD

10 September 1999

Dear Ms Bloomwood

Further to my letters of 3 May, 29 July and 14 August, you will be aware that your free graduate overdraft facility is due to end on 19 September 1999. You will also be aware that you have substantially exceeded the agreed limit of £2,000.

The current balance stands at a debit of £3,794.56.

Perhaps you would be kind enough to telephone my assistant Erica Parnell to arrange a meeting concerning this matter.

Yours sincerely

Derek Smeath
Manager

ENDWICH — BECAUSE WE CARE

Endwich Bank
FULHAM BRANCH
3 Fulham Road
London SW6 9JH

Ms Rebecca Bloomwood
Flat 2
4 Burney Road
London SW6 8FD

22 September 1999

Dear Ms Bloomwood

I am sorry to hear that you have broken your leg.

When you have recovered, perhaps you would be kind enough to ring my assistant Erica Parnell and arrange a meeting to discuss your ongoing overdraft needs.

Yours sincerely

Derek Smeath
Manager

ENDWICH — BECAUSE WE CARE

Endwich Bank
FULHAM BRANCH
3 Fulham Road
London SW6 9JH

Ms Rebecca Bloomwood
Flat 2
4 Burney Road
London SW6 8FD

17 November 1999

Dear Ms Bloomwood

I am sorry to hear that you have glandular fever.

When you have recovered, perhaps you would be kind enough to ring my assistant Erica Parnell and arrange a meeting to discuss your situation.

Yours sincerely

Derek Smeath
Manager

ENDWICH — BECAUSE WE CARE

One

OK. Don't panic. Don't *panic*. It's only a VISA bill. It's a piece of paper; a few numbers. I mean, just how scary can a few numbers be?

I stare out of the office window at a bus driving down Oxford Street, willing myself to open the white envelope sitting on my cluttered desk. It's only a piece of paper, I tell myself for the thousandth time. And I'm not stupid, am I? I know exactly how much this VISA bill will be.

Sort of. Roughly.

It'll be about . . . £200. Three hundred, maybe. Yes, maybe three hundred. Three-fifty max.

I casually close my eyes and start to tot up. There was that suit in Jigsaw. And there was dinner with Suze at Quaglino's. And there was that gorgeous red and yellow rug. The rug was £200, come to think of it. But it was definitely worth every penny – everyone's admired it. Or, at least, Suze has.

And the Jigsaw suit was on sale – 30 per cent off. So that was actually *saving* money.

I open my eyes and reach for the bill. As my fingers hit the paper I remember new contact lenses. Ninety-five pounds. Quite a lot. But, I mean, I had to get those, didn't I? What am I supposed to do, walk around in a blur?

And I had to buy some new solutions and a cute case and some hypo-allergenic eyeliner. So that takes it up to . . . four hundred?

At the desk next door to mine, Clare Edwards looks up from her post. She's sorting all her letters into neat

13

piles, just like she does every morning. She puts rubber bands round them and puts labels on them saying things like, 'Answer immediately' and 'Not urgent but respond'. I loathe Clare Edwards.

'OK, Becky?' she says.

'Fine,' I say lightly. 'Just reading a letter.'

I reach gaily into the envelope, but my fingers don't quite pull out the bill. They remain clutched around it while my mind is seized – as it is every month – by my secret dream.

Do you want to know about my secret dream? It's based on a story I once read in the newspaper about a mix-up at a bank. I loved this story so much, I cut it out and stuck it onto my wardrobe door. Two credit card bills were sent to the wrong people, and – get this – each person paid the wrong bill without realizing. They paid off each other's bills *without even checking them*.

And ever since I read that story, my secret dream has been that the same thing will happen to me. Some dotty old woman in Cornwall will be sent my humungous bill and will pay it without even looking at it. And I'll be sent her bill for three tins of cat food at 59p each. Which, naturally, I'll pay without question. Fair's fair, after all.

A smile is plastered over my face as I gaze out of the window. I'm convinced that this month it'll happen – my secret dream is about to come true. But when I eventually pull the bill out of the envelope – goaded by Clare's curious gaze – my smile falters, then disappears. Something hot is blocking my throat. I think it could be panic.

The page is black with type. A series of familiar names rushes past my eyes like a mini shopping mall. I try to take them in, but they're moving too fast. Thorntons, I manage to glimpse. Thorntons Chocolates? What the hell was I doing in Thorntons Chocolates? I'm supposed to be on a diet. This bill *can't* be right. This can't be me. I can't possibly have spent all this money.

Don't panic! I yell internally. The key is not to panic. Just read each entry slowly, one by one. I take a deep breath and force myself to focus calmly, starting at the top.

WH Smith (well, that's OK. Everyone needs stationery)

Boots (ditto)

Specsavers (essential)

Oddbins (bottle of wine – essential)

Our Price (*Our Price*? Oh yes. The new Charlatans album. Well, I had to have that, didn't I?)

Bella Pasta (supper with Caitlin)

Oddbins (bottle of wine – essential)

Esso (petrol doesn't count)

Quaglino's (expensive – but it was a one-off)

Pret à Manger (that time I ran out of cash)

Oddbins (bottle of wine – essential)

Rugs to Riches (what? Oh yes, the rug. Stupid rug)

La Senza (sexy underwear for date with James)

Agent Provocateur (even sexier underwear for date with James. Huh. Like I needed it)

Body Shop (that skin brusher thing which I *must* use)

Next (fairly boring white shirt – but it was in the sale)

Millets . . .

I stop in my tracks. Millets? I never go into Millets. What the hell would I be doing in Millets? I stare at the statement in puzzlement, wrinkling my brow and trying to think – and then suddenly, the truth dawns on me. It's obvious. Someone else has been using my card.

Oh my God. I, Rebecca Bloomwood, have been the victim of a crime.

Now it all makes sense. Some criminal's pinched my credit card and forged my signature. Who knows where else they've used it? No wonder my statement's so black with figures! Someone's gone on a spending spree round London with my card – and they thought they would just get away with it.

But how have they managed it? I scrabble in my bag for my purse, open it – and there's my VISA card, staring up at me. I take it out and gaze at it. Someone must have pinched it from my purse, used it – *and then put it back*. It must be someone I know. Oh my God. Who?

I look suspiciously round the office. Whoever it is, isn't very bright. Using my card at Millets! It's almost laughable. As if I'd ever shop there.

'I've never even been into Millets!' I say aloud.

'Yes you have,' says Clare.

'What?' I turn to her, not particularly pleased to be interrupted. 'No I haven't.'

'You bought Michael's leaving present from Millets, didn't you?'

I stare at her and feel my smile disappear. Oh bugger. Of course. The blue anorak for Michael. The blue sodding anorak from Millets.

When Michael, our deputy editor left three weeks ago, I volunteered to buy his present. I took the brown envelope full of coins and notes into the shop and picked out an anorak (take it from me, he's that kind of guy). And at the last minute, now I remember, I decided to pay on credit and keep all the handy cash for myself.

I can vividly remember fishing out the four £5 notes and carefully putting them in my wallet, sorting out the pound coins and putting them in my coin compartment, and pouring the rest of the drossy change into the bottom of my bag. Oh good, I remember thinking. I won't have to go to the cashpoint. I'd thought that sixty quid would last me for weeks.

So what happened to it? I can't have just *spent* sixty quid without realizing it, can I?

'Why are you asking, anyway?' says Clare, and she leans forward. I can see her beady little X-ray eyes gleaming behind her specs. She knows I'm looking at my VISA bill. 'No reason,' I say, briskly turning to the second page of my statement.

But I've been put off my stride. Instead of doing what I normally do – look at the Minimum Payment Required and ignore the total completely – I find myself staring straight at the bottom figure.

Nine hundred and forty-nine pounds, sixty-three pence. In clear black and white.

I stare at it silently for thirty seconds, then stuff the bill back into the envelope. I honestly feel, at that moment, as though this piece of paper has nothing to do with me. Perhaps, if I carelessly let it drop down on the floor behind my computer, it will disappear. The cleaners will sweep it up and I can claim I never got it. They can't charge me for a bill I never received, can they?

I'm already composing a letter in my head. 'Dear Managing Director of VISA. Your letter has confused me. What bill are you talking about, precisely? I never received any bill from your company. I did not care for your tone and should warn you, I am writing to Anne Robinson of *Watchdog*.'

Or I could always move abroad.

'Becky?' My head jerks up and I see Clare staring at me. 'Have you finished the piece on Lloyds?'

'Nearly,' I lie. As she's watching me, I feel forced to summon it up on my computer screen, just to show willing. But she's still bloody watching me.

'Savers can benefit from instant access,' I type onto the screen, copying directly from a press release in front of me. 'The account is also offering tiered rates of interest for those investing more than £5,000.'

I type a full stop, take a sip of coffee and turn to the second page of the press release.

This is what I do, by the way. I'm a journalist on a financial magazine. I'm paid to tell other people how to organize their money.

Of course, it's not the career I always wanted. No-one who writes about personal finance ever meant to do it. People tell you they 'fell into' personal finance.

17

They're lying. What they mean is they couldn't get a job writing about anything more interesting. They mean they applied for jobs on *The Times* and the *Express* and *Marie-Claire* and *Vogue* and *GQ* and *Loaded*, and all they got back was 'Piss off'.

So they started applying to *Metalwork Monthly* and *Cheesemakers Gazette* and *What Investment Plan?* And they were taken on as the crappiest editorial assistant possible on no money whatsoever and were grateful. And they've stayed on writing about metal, or cheese, or savings, ever since – because that's all they know. I myself started on the catchily titled *Personal Investment Periodical*. I learned how to copy out a press release and nod at press conferences and ask questions that sounded as though I knew what I was talking about. After a year and a half – believe it or not – I was head-hunted to *Successful Saving*.

Of course, I still know nothing about finance. People at the bus stop know more about finance than me. Schoolchildren know more than me. I've been doing this job for three years now, and I'm still expecting someone to catch me out.

That afternoon, Philip the editor calls my name, and I jump in fright.

'Rebecca?' he says. 'A word.' And he beckons me over to his desk. His voice seems lower all of a sudden, almost conspiratorial, and he's smiling at me, as though he's about to give me a piece of good news.

Oh my God, I think. Promotion. It must be. He knows it's unfair I earn less than Clare, so he's going to promote me to her level. Or even above. And he's telling me discreetly so Clare won't get jealous.

A wide smile plasters itself over my face and I get up and walk the three yards or so to his desk, trying to stay calm but already planning what I'll buy with my pay rise. I'll get that swirly coat in Whistles. And some black high-heeled boots from Pied à Terre. Maybe I'll go on holiday. And I'll pay off that blasted VISA bill once and for all. I feel buoyant with relief. I *knew* everything would be OK . . .

'Rebecca?' He's thrusting a card at me. 'I can't make this press conference,' he says. 'But it could be quite interesting. Will you go? It's at Brandon Communications.'

I can feel my elated expression falling off my face like jelly. He's not promoting me. I'm not getting a pay rise. I feel betrayed. *Why* did he smile at me like that? He must have known he was lifting my hopes. Callous bastard.

'Something wrong?' enquires Philip.

'No,' I mutter. But I can't bring myself to smile. In front of me, my new swirly coat and high-heeled boots are disappearing into a puddle, like the Wicked Witch of the West. No promotion. Just a press conference about . . . I glance at the card. About a new unit trust. How could anyone *possibly* describe that as interesting?

'You can write it up for the news,' says Philip.

'OK,' I say, shrugging, and walk away.

Two

There's just one essential purchase I have to make on the way to the press conference – and that's the *Financial Times*. The *FT* is by far the best accessory a girl can have. Its major advantages are:

1. It's a nice colour.
2. It only costs 85p.
3. If you walk into a room with it tucked under your arm, people take you seriously. With an *FT* under your arm, you can talk about the most frivolous things in the world, and instead of thinking you're an airhead, people think you're a heavyweight intellectual who has broader interests, too.

At my interview for *Successful Saving*, I went in holding copies of the *Financial Times* and the *Investor's Chronicle* – and I didn't get asked about finance once. As I remember it, we spent the whole time talking about holiday villas and bitching about other editors.

So I stop at a newsstand and buy a copy of the *FT* and tuck it neatly under my arm, admiring my reflection in the window of Denny and George.

I don't look bad, I think. I'm wearing my black skirt from French Connection, and a plain white T-shirt from Knickerbox, and a little angora cardigan which I got from M&S but looks like it might be Agnès B. And my new square-toed shoes from Hobbs. And even better, although no-one can see them, I know that underneath I'm wearing my gorgeous new matching knickers and bra with embroidered yellow rosebuds. They're the best bit of my entire outfit. In fact, I almost wish I could be run over so that the world would see them.

It's a habit of mine, itemizing all the clothes I'm wearing, as though for a fashion page. I've been doing it for years – ever since I used to read *Just Seventeen*. Every issue, they'd stop a girl on the street, take a picture of her, and list all her clothes. 'T-Shirt: Chelsea Girl, Jeans: Top Shop, Shoes: borrowed from friend.' I used to read those lists avidly – and to this day, if I buy something from a shop that's a bit uncool, I cut the label out. So that if I'm ever stopped in the street, I can pretend I don't know where it's from.

So anyway. There I am, gazing at myself, thinking I look pretty good, and half wishing someone from *Just Seventeen* would pop up with a camera – when suddenly my eyes focus and snap to attention, and my heart stops. In the window of Denny and George is a discreet sign. It's dark green with cream lettering, and it says: SALE.

I stare at it, my heart thumping hard. It can't be true. Denny and George can't be having a sale. They never have a sale. Their scarves and pashminas are so coveted, they could probably sell them at twice the price. Everyone I know in the entire world aspires to owning a Denny and George scarf. (Except my mum and dad, obviously. My mum thinks if you can't buy it at Bentalls of Kingston, you don't need it.)

I swallow, and take a couple of steps forward, then push open the door of the tiny shop. The door pings, and the nice blond girl who works there looks up. I don't know her name but I've always liked her. Unlike some snotty cows in clothes shops, she doesn't mind if you stand for ages staring at clothes you really can't afford to buy. Usually what happens is, I spend half an hour lusting after scarves in Denny and George, then go off to Accessorize and buy something to cheer myself up. I've got a whole drawerful of Denny and George substitutes.

'Hi,' I say, trying to stay calm. 'You're . . . you're having a sale.'

'Yes.' The blond girl smiles. 'Bit unusual for us.'

My gaze sweeps the room. I can see rows of scarves, neatly folded, with dark green '50 per cent off' signs above them. Printed velvet, beaded silk, embroidered cashmere, all with the discreet 'Denny and George' signature. They're everywhere. I don't know where to start. I think I'm having a panic attack.

'You always liked this one, I think,' says the nice blond girl, taking out a shimmering grey-blue scarf from the pile in front of her.

Oh God, yes. I remember this one. It's made of silky velvet, overprinted in a paler blue and dotted with iridescent beads. As I stare at it, I can feel little invisible strings, silently tugging me towards it. I have to touch it. I have to wear it. It's the most beautiful thing I've ever seen. The girl looks at the label. 'Reduced from £340 to £120.' She comes and drapes the scarf around my neck and I stare at my reflection.

There is no question. I have to have this scarf. I *have* to have it. It makes my eyes look bigger, it makes my haircut look more expensive, it makes me look like a different person. I'll be able to wear it with everything. People will refer to me as the Girl in the Denny and George scarf.

'I'd snap it up, if I were you.' The girl smiles at me. 'There's only one of these left.'

Involuntarily, I clutch at it.

'I'll have it,' I gasp. 'I'll have it.'

As she's laying it out on tissue paper, I take out my purse, open it up and reach for my VISA card in one seamless, automatic action – but my fingers hit bare leather. I stop in surprise and start to rummage through all the pockets of my purse, wondering if I stuffed my card back in somewhere with a receipt or if it's hidden underneath a business card . . . And then, with a sickening thud, I remember. It's on my desk.

How could I have been so stupid? How could I have left my VISA card on my desk? What was I *thinking* of?

The nice blond girl is putting the wrapped scarf into

a dark green Denny and George box. My heart is thumping. What am I going to do?

'How would you like to pay?' she says pleasantly.

My face flames red.

'I've just realized I've left my credit card at the office,' I stutter.

'Oh,' says the girl, and her hands pause.

'Can you hold it for me?' The girl looks dubious.

'For how long?'

'Until tomorrow?' I say desperately. Oh God. She's pulling a face. Doesn't she understand?

'I'm afraid not,' she says. 'We're not supposed to reserve sale stock.'

'Just until later this afternoon, then,' I say quickly. 'What time do you close?'

'Six.'

Six! I feel a combination of relief and adrenalin sweeping through me. Challenge Rebecca. I'll go to the press conference, leave as soon as I can, then take a taxi back to the office. I'll grab my VISA card, tell Philip I left my notebook behind, come here and buy the scarf.

'Can you hold it until then?' I say beseechingly. 'Please? *Please?*' The girl relents.

'OK. I'll put it behind the counter.'

'Thanks,' I gasp. I hurry out of the shop and down the road towards Brandon Communications. Please let the press conference be short, I pray. Please don't let the questions go on too long. Please God, *please* let me have that scarf.

As I arrive at Brandon Communications, I can feel myself begin to relax. I do have three whole hours, after all. And my scarf is safely behind the counter. No-one's going to steal it from me.

There's a sign up in the foyer of Brandon Communications saying that the Foreland Exotic Opportunities press conference is happening in the Artemis Suite, and a man in uniform is directing everybody down the corridor. This means it must be quite big. Not television-cameras-CNN-world's press on tenterhooks-big, obviously. But fairly-good-turnout big. A relatively important event in our dull little world.

As I enter the room, there's already a buzz of people milling around, and waitresses circulating with canapés. The journalists are knocking back the champagne as if they've never seen it before; the PR girls are looking supercilious and sipping water. A waiter offers me a glass of champagne and I take two. One for now, one to put under my chair for the boring bits.

In the far corner of the room I can see Elly Granger from *Investor's Weekly News*. She's been pinned into a corner by two earnest men in suits and is nodding at them, with a glassy look in her eye. Elly's great. She's only been on *Investor's Weekly News* for six months, and already she's applied for forty-three other jobs. What she really wants to be is a beauty editor on a magazine. What I really want to be is Fiona Phillips on GMTV. Sometimes, when we're very drunk, we make pacts that if we're not somewhere more exciting in three months, we'll both leave our jobs. But then the thought of no money – even for a month – is almost more terrifying than the thought of writing about pension plans for the rest of my life.

'Rebecca. Glad you could make it.'

I look up, and almost choke on my champagne. It's Luke Brandon, head honcho of Brandon Communications, staring straight at me as if he knows exactly what I'm thinking.

I've only met him a few times, and I always feel slightly uneasy around him. For a start, he's got such a scary reputation. Everyone talks all the time about what a genius he is, even Philip, my boss. He started Brandon Communications from nothing, and now it's the biggest financial PR company in London. A few months ago he was listed in some newspaper as one of the cleverest entrepreneurs of his generation. It said his IQ was phenomenally high and he had a photographic memory. (I've always hated people with photographic memories.)

But it's not just that. It's that he always seems to have a frown on his face when he's talking to me. As if he knows what a complete fraud I am. In fact, it occurs to me, he probably does. It'll probably turn out that the famous Luke Brandon is not only a complete genius but he can read minds, too. He knows that when I'm staring up at some boring graph, nodding intelligently, I'm really thinking about a gorgeous black top I saw in Joseph and whether I can afford the trousers as well.

'You know Alicia, don't you?' Luke is saying, and he gestures to the immaculate blond girl beside him.

I don't know Alicia, as it happens. But I don't need to. They're all the same, the girls at Brandon C, as they call it. They're well dressed, well spoken, are married to bankers and have zero sense of humour.

'Rebecca,' says Alicia coolly, grasping my hand. 'You're on *Successful Saving*, aren't you?'

'That's right,' I say, equally coolly.

'It's very good of you to come today,' says Alicia. 'I know you journalists are terribly busy.'

'No problem,' I say. 'We like to attend as many press conferences as we can. Keep up with industry events.' I feel pleased with my response. I'm almost fooling myself.

Alicia nods seriously, as though everything I say is incredibly important to her.

'So, tell me, Rebecca. What do you think about today's news?' She gestures to the *FT* under my arm. 'Quite a surprise, didn't you think?'

Oh God. What's she talking about?

'It's certainly interesting,' I say, still smiling, playing for time. I glance around the room for a clue, but there's nothing. What's happened? Have interest rates gone up or something?

'I have to say, I think it's bad news for the industry,' says Alicia earnestly. 'But of course, you must have your own views.'

25

She's looking at me, waiting for an answer. I can feel my cheeks flaming bright red. How can I get out of this? From now on, I promise myself, I'm going to read the papers every day. I'm never going to be caught out like this again.

'I agree with you,' I say eventually. 'I think it's very bad news.' My voice feels strangled. I take a quick swig of champagne and pray for an earthquake.

'Were you expecting it?' Alicia says. 'I know you journalists are always ahead of the game.'

'I . . . I certainly saw it coming,' I say, and I'm pretty sure I sound convincing.

'And now this rumour about Scottish Prime and Flagstaff Life going the same way!' She looks at me intently. 'Do you think that's really on the cards?'

'It's . . . it's difficult to say,' I reply, and take a gulp of champagne. What rumour? Oh God, why can't she leave me alone?

Then I make the mistake of glancing up at Luke Brandon. He's staring at me, with a strange expression on his face. Oh shit. He *knows* I don't have a clue, doesn't he?

'Alicia,' he says abruptly. 'That's Maggie Stevens coming in. Could you—'

'Absolutely,' she says, trained like a racehorse, and starts to move smoothly towards the door.

'And Alicia – ' adds Luke, and she quickly turns back. 'I want to know exactly who fucked up on those figures.'

'Yes,' gulps Alicia, and hurries off.

God he's scary. And now we're on our own. I think I might quickly run away.

'Well,' I say brightly. 'I must just go and—'

But Luke Brandon is leaning towards me.

'SBG announced that they've taken over Rutland Bank this morning,' he says quietly.

And of course, now he says it, I remember hearing something about it on the news this morning.

'I know they did,' I reply haughtily. 'I read it in the

26

FT.' And before he can say anything else, I walk off, to talk to Elly.

As the press conference is about to start, Elly and I sidle towards the back and grab two seats together. I open my notebook, write 'Brandon Communications' at the top of the page, and start doodling swirly flowers down the side. Beside me, Elly's dialling her telephone horoscope on her mobile phone.

I take a sip of champagne, lean back and prepare to relax. There's no point listening at press conferences. The information's always in the press pack, and you can work out what they were talking about later. In fact, I'm wondering whether anyone would notice if I took out a pot of Hard Candy and did my nails, when suddenly the awful Alicia ducks her head down to mine.

'Rebecca?'

'Yes?' I say lazily.

'Phone call for you. It's your editor.'

'Philip?' I say stupidly. As though I've a whole array of editors to choose from.

'Yes.' She looks at me as though I'm a moron and gestures to a phone on a table at the back. Elly gives me a questioning look and I shrug back. Philip's never phoned me at a press conference before.

I feel rather excited and important as I walk to the back of the room. Perhaps there's an emergency at the office. Perhaps he's scooped an incredible story and wants me to fly to New York to follow up a lead.

'Hello, Philip?' I say into the receiver – then immediately I wish I'd said something thrusting and impressive, like a simple 'Yep'.

'Rebecca, listen, sorry to be a bore,' says Philip, 'but I've got a migraine coming on. I'm going to head off home.'

'Oh,' I say puzzledly.

'And I wondered if you could run a small errand for me.'

An errand? Who does he think I am? If he wants somebody to buy him paracetamol, he should get a secretary.

'I'm not sure,' I say discouragingly. 'I'm a bit tied up here.'

'When you've finished there. The Social Security Select Committee are releasing their report at five o'clock. Can you go and pick it up? You can go straight to Westminster from your press conference.'

What? I stare at the phone in horror. No I can't pick up a bloody report. I need to pick up my VISA card! I need to secure my scarf.

'Can't Clare go?' I say. 'I was going to come back to the office and finish my research on . . .' What am I supposed to be writing about this month? 'On mortgages.'

'Clare's got a briefing in the City. And Westminster's on your way home to trendy Fulham, isn't it?'

Philip *always* has to make a joke about me living in Fulham. Just because he lives in Harpenden.

'You can just hop off the tube,' he's saying, 'pick it up and hop back on again.'

Oh God. I can't think of any way to get out of this. I close my eyes and think quickly. An hour here. Rush back to the office, pick up my VISA card, back to Denny and George, get my scarf, rush to Westminster, pick up the report. I should just about make it.

'Fine,' I say. 'Leave it to me.'

I sit back down, just as the lights dim and the words FAR EASTERN OPPORTUNITIES appear on the screen in front of us. There is a colourful series of pictures from Hong Kong, Thailand and other exotic places, which would usually have me thinking wistfully about going on holiday. But today I can't relax, or even laugh at the new girl from *Portfolio Week*, who's frantically trying to write everything down and will probably ask five questions because she thinks she should. I'm too concerned about my scarf. What if I don't make it back in time?

What if someone puts in a higher offer? The very thought makes me panic. Is it possible to gazump a Denny and George scarf?

Then, just as the pictures of Thailand disappear and the boring graphs begin, I have a flash of inspiration. Of course! I'll pay cash for the scarf. No-one can argue with cash. I can get £100 out on my cashpoint card, so all I need is another twenty, and the scarf is mine.

I tear a piece of paper out of my notebook, write on it 'Can you lend me twenty quid?' and pass it to Elly, who's still surreptitiously listening to her mobile phone. I wonder what she's listening to. It can't still be her horoscope, surely? She looks down, shakes her head, and writes, 'No can do. Bloody machine swallowed my card. Living off Luncheon Vouchers at moment.'

Damn. I hesitate, then write, 'What about credit card? I'll pay you back, honest. And what are you listening to?'

I pass the page to her and suddenly the lights go up. The presentation has ended and I didn't hear a word of it. People shift around on their seats and a PR girl starts handing out glossy brochures. Elly finishes her call and grins at me.

'Love life prediction,' she says, tapping in another number. 'It's really accurate stuff.'

'Load of old bullshit, more like.' I shake my head disapprovingly. 'I can't believe you go for all that rubbish. Call yourself a financial journalist?'

'No,' says Elly. 'Do you?' And we both start to giggle, until some old bag from one of the nationals turns round and gives us an angry glare.

'Ladies and gentlemen.' A piercing voice interrupts us and I look up. It's Alicia, standing up at the front of the room. She's got very good legs, I note resentfully. 'As you can see, the Foreland Exotic Opportunities Savings Plan represents an entirely new approach to investment.' She looks around the room, meets my eye and smiles coldly.

'Exotic Opportunities,' I whisper scornfully to Elly and point to the leaflet. 'Exotic prices, more like. Have you seen how much they're charging?'

(I always turn to the charges first. Just like I always look at the price tag first.)

Elly rolls her eyes sympathetically, still listening to the phone.

'Foreland Investments are all about adding value,' Alicia is saying in her snooty voice. 'Foreland Investments offer you more.'

'They charge more, you lose more,' I say aloud without thinking, and there's a laugh around the room. God, how embarrassing. And now Luke Brandon's staring at me, too. Quickly I look down and pretend to be writing notes.

Although to be honest, I don't know why I even pretend to write notes. It's not as if we ever put anything in the magazine except the puff that comes on the press release. Foreland Investments takes out a whopping double-page spread advertisement every month, *and* they took Philip on some fantastic research (haha) trip to Thailand last year – so we're never allowed to say anything except how wonderful they are.

As Alicia carries on speaking, I lean towards Elly.

'So, listen,' I whisper. 'Can I borrow your credit card?'

'All used up,' hisses Elly apologetically. 'I'm up to my limit. Why do you think I'm living off LVs?'

'But I need money!' I whisper. 'I'm desperate! I need twenty quid!'

I've spoken more loudly than I intended and Alicia stops speaking.

'Perhaps you should have invested with Foreland Investments, Rebecca,' says Alicia, and another titter goes round the room. A few faces turn round to gawp at me, and I stare back at them lividly. They're fellow journalists, for God's sake. They should be on my side. NUJ solidarity and all that.

Not that I've ever actually got round to joining the NUJ. But still.

'What do you need twenty quid for?' says Luke Brandon, from the front of the room.

'I . . . my aunt,' I say defiantly. 'She's in hospital and I wanted to get her a present.'

The room is silent. Then, to my disbelief, Luke Brandon reaches into his pocket, takes out a £20 note, and gives it to a guy in the front row of journalists. He hesitates, then passes it back to the row behind. And so it goes on, a twenty-quid note being passed from hand to hand, making its way to me like a fan at a gig being passed over the crowd. As I take hold of it, a round of applause goes round the room and I blush.

'Thanks,' I say awkwardly. 'I'll pay you back, of course.'

'My best wishes to your aunt,' says Luke Brandon.

'Thanks,' I say again. Then I glance at Alicia, and feel a little dart of triumph. She looks utterly deflated.

Towards the end of the question-and-answer session, people begin slipping out to get back to their offices. This is usually the point at which I go and buy a cappuccino and browse in a few shops. But today I don't. Today I decide I will stick it out until the last dismal question about tax structures. Then I'll go up to the front and thank Luke Brandon in person for his kind, if embarrassing, gesture. And then I'll go and get my scarf. Yippee!

But to my surprise, after only a few questions, Luke Brandon gets up, whispers something to Alicia, and heads for the door.

'Thanks,' I mutter as he passes my chair, but I'm not sure he even hears me.

Still, who cares? I've got the twenty quid and that's all that matters.

On the way back from Westminster, the tube stops in a tunnel for no apparent reason. Five minutes go by, then ten minutes. I can't believe my bad luck. Normally, of course, I long for the tube to break down, so I've got an excuse to stay out of the office for longer. But today I behave like a stressed businessman with an ulcer. I tap my fingers and sigh, and peer out of the window into the blackness.

Part of my brain knows that I've got plenty of time to get to Denny and George before it closes. Another part knows that even if I don't make it, it's unlikely the blond girl will sell my scarf to someone else. But the possibility is there. So until I've got that scarf in my hands I won't be able to relax.

As the train finally gets going again I sink into my seat with a dramatic sigh and look at the pale, silent man on my left.

'Thank God!' I say. 'I was getting desperate there.'

'It's frustrating,' he agrees quietly.

'They just don't think, do they?' I say. 'I mean, some of us have got crucial things we need to be doing. I'm in a terrible hurry!'

'I'm in a bit of a hurry myself,' says the man.

'If that train hadn't started moving, I don't know what I would have done.' I shake my head. 'You feel so . . . impotent!'

'I know exactly what you mean,' says the man intensely. 'They don't realize that some of us . . .' He gestures towards me. 'We aren't just idly travelling. It *matters* whether we arrive or not.'

'Absolutely!' I say. 'Where are you off to?'

'My wife's in labour,' he says. 'Our fourth.'

'Oh,' I say, taken aback. 'Well . . . Gosh. Congratulations. I hope you—'

'She took an hour and a half last time,' says the man, rubbing his damp forehead. 'And I've been on this tube for forty minutes already. Still. At least we're moving now.'

He gives a little shrug, then smiles at me.

'How about you? What's your urgent business?'

Oh God.

'I . . . ahm . . . I'm going to . . .'

I stop feebly and clear my throat, feeling myself blushing red. I can't tell this man that my urgent business consists of picking up a scarf from Denny and George.

I mean, a scarf. It's not even a suit or a coat, or something worthy like that.

'It's not that important,' I hear myself mumbling.

'I don't believe that,' he says nicely.

Oh, now I feel awful. I glance up – and thank goodness, it's my stop.

'Good luck,' I say, hastily getting up. 'I really hope you get there in time.'

As I walk along the pavement I'm feeling a bit shamefaced. Maybe I should have got out my hundred and twenty quid and given it to that man for his baby, instead of buying a pointless scarf. I mean, when you think about it, what's more important? Clothes – or the miracle of new life?

As I ponder this issue, I feel quite deep and philosophical. In fact, I'm so engrossed, I almost walk past my turning. But I look up just in time and turn the corner – and feel a jolt. There's a girl coming towards me and she's carrying a Denny and George carrier bag. And suddenly everything is swept from my mind.

Oh my God.

What if she's got my scarf?

What if she asked for it specially and that assistant sold it to her, thinking I wasn't going to come back?

My heart starts to beat in panic and I begin to stride along the street towards the shop. As I arrive at the door and push it open, I can barely breathe for fear. What if it's gone? What will I do?

But the blond girl smiles as I enter. 'Hi!' she says. 'It's waiting for you.'

'Oh thanks,' I say in relief and subside weakly against the counter.

I honestly feel as though I've run an assault course to

get here. In fact I think they should list shopping under cardiovascular activity. My heart never beats as fast as it does when I see a 'reduced by 50 per cent' sign.

I count out the money in tens and twenties and wait, almost shivering as she ducks behind the counter and produces the green box. She slides it into a thick glossy bag with dark green cord handles and hands it to me. I almost want to close my eyes, the feeling is so wonderful.

That moment. That instant when your fingers curl round the handles of a shiny, uncreased bag – and all the gorgeous new things inside it become yours. What's it like? It's like going hungry for days, then cramming your mouth full of warm buttered toast. It's like waking up and realizing it's the weekend. It's like the better moments of sex. Everything else is blocked out of your mind. It's pure, selfish pleasure.

I walk slowly out of the shop, still in a haze of delight. I've got a Denny and George scarf. I've got a Denny and George scarf! I've got—

'Rebecca.' A man's voice interrupts my thoughts. I look up and my stomach gives a lurch of horror. It's Luke Brandon.

Luke Brandon is standing on the street, right in front of me, and he's staring down at my carrier bag. I feel myself growing flustered. What's he doing here on the pavement anyway? Don't people like that have chauffeurs? Shouldn't he be whisking off to some vital reception or something?

'Did you get it all right?' he says, frowning slightly.

'What?'

'Your aunt's present.'

'Oh yes,' I say, and swallow. 'Yes I . . . I got it.'

'Is that it?' He gestures to the bag and I feel my cheeks flame red.

'Yes,' I say eventually. 'I thought a . . . a scarf would be nice.'

'Very generous of you. Denny and George.' He raises his eyebrows. 'Your aunt must be a stylish lady.'

'She is,' I say, and clear my throat. 'She's terribly creative and original.'

'I'm sure she is,' said Luke, and pauses. 'What's her name?'

Oh God. I should have run as soon as I saw him, while I had a chance. Now I'm paralysed. I can't think of a single female name.

'Erm . . . Ermintrude,' I hear myself saying.

'Aunt Ermintrude,' said Luke thoughtfully. 'Well, give her my best wishes.'

He nods at me, and walks off, and I stare after him, trying to work out if he guessed or not.

Three

I walk through the door of our flat, Suze looks up – and the first thing she says is, 'Denny and George! Becky, you're not serious.'

'Yes,' I say, grinning from ear to ear. 'I bought myself a scarf.'

'Show me!' says Suze, unwinding herself from the sofa. 'Show-me-show-me-show-me!' She comes over and starts tugging at the strings of the carrier. 'I want to see your new scarf! Show me!'

This is why I love sharing a flat with Suze. Julia, my old flatmate, would have wrinkled her brow and said, 'Denny and who?' or 'That's a lot of money for a scarf.' But Suze completely and utterly understands. If anything, she's worse than me.

But then, she can afford to be. Although she's twenty-five, like me, her parents still give her pocket money. It's called an 'allowance' and apparently comes from some family trust – but as far as I can see, it's pocket money. Her parents also bought her a flat in Fulham as a twenty-first birthday present and she's been living in it ever since, half working and half dossing about.

She was in PR for a (very) short while, and that's when I met her, on a press trip to Guernsey. As a matter of fact, she was working for Brandon Communications. Without being rude – she admits it herself – she was the worst PR girl I've ever come across. She completely forgot which bank she was supposed to be promoting, and started talking enthusiastically about one of their competitors. The man from the bank looked crosser and crosser, while all the journalists pissed themselves laughing. Suze got in big trouble over that. In fact, that's when she decided PR wasn't the career for her. (The other way of putting it is that Luke Brandon gave her the sack as soon as they got back to London. Another reason not to like him.)

But the two of us had a whale of a time sloshing back wine until the early hours, and kept in touch ever since. Then, when Julia suddenly upped and ran off with the professor supervising her PhD (she was a dark horse, that one), Suze suggested I move in with her. I'm sure the rent she charges is too low, but I've never insisted I pay the full market rate, because I couldn't afford it. As market rates go, I'm nearer Elephant and Castle than Fulham on my salary. How can normal people afford to live in such hideously expensive places? I can never fathom it.

'Bex, open it up!' Suze is begging. 'Let me see!' She's grabbing inside the bag with eager long fingers, and I pull it away quickly before she rips it. This bag is going on the back of my door along with my other prestige carrier bags, to be used in a casual manner when I need to impress. (Thank God they didn't print special 'Sale' bags. I *hate* shops which do that. What's the point of having a posh bag with 'Sale' splashed all over it? You might as well splash 'Cheapskate'.)

Very slowly, I take the dark green box out of the bag, remove the lid and unfold the tissue paper. Then, almost reverentially, I lift up the scarf. It's beautiful. It's even more beautiful here than it was in the shop. I drape it around my neck and grin stupidly at Suze.

'Oh Bex,' she murmurs. 'It's gorgeous!'

For a moment we are both silent. We're communing with a higher being: the God of Shopping.

Then Suze has to go and ruin it all.

'You can wear it to see James this weekend,' she says.

'I can't,' I say almost crossly, taking it off again. 'I'm not seeing him.'

'How come?'

'I'm not seeing him any more.' I try to give a non-chalant shrug.

'Really?' Suze's eyes widen. 'Why not? You didn't tell me!'

'I know.' I look away from her eager gaze. 'It's a bit . . . awkward.'

'Did you chuck him? You hadn't even shagged him!' Suze's voice is rising in excitement. She's desperate to know. But am I desperate to tell? For a moment I consider being discreet. Then I think, oh what the hell?

'I know,' I say. 'That was the problem.'

'What do you mean?' Suze leans forward. 'Bex, what are you talking about?'

I take a deep breath and turn to face her.

'He didn't want to.'

'Didn't fancy you?'

'No. He . . .' I close my eyes, barely able to believe this myself. 'He doesn't believe in sex before marriage.'

'You're joking.' I open my eyes to see Suze looking at me in horror – as if she's just heard the worst profanity known to mankind. 'You are joking, Becky.' She's actually pleading with me.

'I'm not.' I manage a weak smile. 'It was a bit embarrassing, actually. I kind of . . . pounced on him, and he had to fight me off.'

The cringingly awful memory which I had successfully suppressed starts to resurface. I'd met James at a party a few weeks back, and this was the crucial third date. We'd been out for a really nice meal, which he'd insisted on paying for, and had gone back to his place, and had ended up kissing on the sofa.

Well, what was I *supposed* to think? There he was, there I was – and make no mistake, if his mind was saying no, his body was certainly saying yes, yes, yes. So, being a modern girl, I reached for his trouser zip and began to pull it down. When he reached down and brushed me aside I thought he was playing games, and carried on, even more enthusiastically than before.

38

Thinking back, perhaps it took me longer than it should have to twig that he wasn't playing ball, so to speak. In fact, he actually had to punch me in the face to get me off him – although he was very apologetic about it afterwards.

Suze is gazing at me incredulously. Then she breaks into gurgles of laughter.

'He had to fight you off? Bex, you man-eater!'

'Don't!' I protest. 'He was really sweet about it. He said, was I prepared to wait for him?'

'And you said, not bloody likely!'

'Sort of.' I look away.

In fact, carried away with the moment, I seem to remember issuing him a bit of a challenge. 'Resist me now if you can, James,' I recall saying in a husky voice, gazing at him with what I thought were limpid, sexual eyes. 'But you'll be knocking at my door within the week.'

Well, it's been over a week now, and I haven't heard a peep. Which, if you think about it, is pretty unflattering.

'But that's hideous!' Suze is saying. 'What about sexual compatibility?'

'Dunno.' I shrug. 'I guess he's willing to take that gamble.' Suze gives a sudden giggle.

'Did you get a look at his—'

'No! He wouldn't let me near it!'

'But could you feel it? Was it tiny?' Suze's eyes gleam wickedly. 'I bet it's titchy. He's hoping to kid some poor girl into marrying him and being stuck with a titchy todger all her life. Narrow escape, Bex!' She reaches for her packet of Silk Cut and lights up.

'Stay away!' I say irritably. 'I don't want my scarf smelling of smoke!'

'So what *are* you doing this weekend?' she asks, taking a drag. 'Will you be OK? Do you want to come down to the country?'

This is how Suze always refers to her family's second home in Hampshire. The country. As though her parents own some small, independent nation that nobody else knows about.

'No, 's'OK,' I say, morosely picking up the TV guide. 'I'm going to visit my parents.'

'Oh well,' says Suze. 'Give your mum my love.'

'I will,' I say. 'And you give my love to Pepper.'

Pepper is Suze's horse. She rides him about three times a year, if that, but whenever her parents suggest selling him she gets all hysterical. Apparently he costs £15,000 a year to run. Fifteen thousand pounds. And what does he do for his money? Just stands in a stable and eats apples. I wouldn't mind being a horse.

'Oh yeah, that reminds me,' says Suze. 'The council tax bill came in. It's three hundred each.'

'Three hundred pounds?' I look at her in dismay. 'What, straight away?'

'Yeah. Actually, it's late. Just write me a cheque or something.'

'Fine,' I say airily. 'Three hundred quid coming up.'

I reach for my bag and write a cheque out straight away. Suze is so generous about the rent, I always pay my share of the bills, and sometimes add a bit extra. But still, I'm feeling cold as I hand it over. Three hundred pounds gone, just like that. And I've still got that bloody VISA bill to think of. Not a great month.

'Oh, and someone called,' adds Suze, and squints at a piece of paper. 'Erica Parsnip. Is that right?'

'Erica *Parsnip*?' Sometimes I think Suze's mind has been expanded just a little too often.

'Parnell. Erica Parnell from Endwich Bank. Can you call her.'

I stare at Suze, frozen in horror.

'She called here? She called this number?'

'Yes. This afternoon.'

'Oh shit.' My heart starts to thump. 'What did you say? Did you say I've got glandular fever?'

'What?' It's Suze's turn to stare. 'Of course I didn't say you've got bloody glandular fever!'

'Did she ask about my leg? Anything about my health at all?'

'No! She just said where were you? And I said you were at work—'

'Suze!' I wail in dismay.

'Well, what was I *supposed* to say?'

'You were supposed to say I was in bed with glandular fever and a broken leg!'

'Well, thanks for the warning!' Suze gazes at me, eyes narrowed, and crosses her legs into the lotus position. Suze has got the longest, thinnest, wiriest legs I've ever known. When she's wearing black leggings she looks just like a spider. 'What's the big deal anyway?' she says. 'Are you overdrawn?'

Am I overdrawn?

'Just a tad.' I shrug. 'It'll work itself out.'

There's silence and I look up, to see Suze tearing up my cheque.

'Suze! Don't be stupid!'

'Pay me back when you're in the black,' she says firmly.

'Thanks Suze,' I say, and give her a big hug. Suze has got to be the best friend I've ever had.

But there's a nagging feeling in my stomach which stays with me all evening and is still there when I wake up the next morning. A feeling I can't even shift by thinking about my Denny and George scarf. I lie in bed staring up at the ceiling and, for the first time in months, calculate how much I owe to everybody. The bank, VISA, my Harvey Nichols card, my Debenhams card, my Fenwicks card . . . And now Suze, too.

It's about . . . let's think . . . it's about six thousand pounds.

A cold feeling creeps over me as I contemplate this figure. How on earth am I going to find six thousand pounds? I could save six pounds a week for a thousand weeks. Or twelve pounds a week for five hundred weeks. Or . . . or sixty pounds a week for a hundred weeks. That's more like it. But how the hell am I going to find sixty pounds a week to save?

Or else I could bone up on lots of general knowledge and go on a game show. Or invent something really clever. Or I could . . . win the Lottery. At the thought, a lovely warm glow creeps over me, and I close my eyes and snuggle back down into bed. The Lottery is by far the best solution.

I wouldn't aim to win the jackpot of course – that's *completely* unlikely. But one of those minor prizes. There seem to be heaps of those going around. Say – a hundred thousand pounds. That would do. I could pay off all my debts, buy a car, buy a flat . . .

Actually – better make it two hundred thousand. Or a quarter of a million.

Or, even better, one of those shared jackpots. 'The five winners will each receive one point three million pounds.' (I love the way they say that. 'One point three.' As if that extra three hundred thousand pounds is a tiny, insignificant amount. As if you wouldn't notice whether it was there or not.)

One point three million should see me straight. And it's not being greedy, is it, to want to share your jackpot? Please God, I think, let me win the Lottery and I promise to share nicely.

And so, on the way down to my parents' house I stop off at a petrol station to buy a couple of lottery tickets. Choosing the numbers takes about half an hour. I know 44 always does well, and 42. But what about the rest? I write out a few series of numbers on a piece of paper and squint at them, trying to imagine them on the telly.

   1   6   9   16   23   44

No! Terrible! What am I thinking of? 1 never comes up, for a start. And 6 and 9 look wrong, too.

   3   14   21   25   36   44

That's a bit better. I fill in the numbers on the ticket.

5   11   18   27   28   42

I'm quite impressed by this one. It *looks* like a winner. I can just imagine Moira Stewart reading it out on the news. 'One ticket-holder, believed to live in south-west London, has won an estimated jackpot of ten million pounds.'

For a moment, I feel faint. What'll I do with ten million pounds? Where will I start?

Well, a huge party to begin with. Somewhere smart but cool, with loads of champagne and dancing and a taxi service so no-one has to drive. And going-home presents, like really nice bubble bath or something. (Does Calvin Klein do bubble bath? I make a mental note to check next time I'm in Boots.)

Then I'll buy houses for all my family and friends, of course. I lean against the lottery stand and close my eyes to concentrate. Suppose I buy twenty houses at £250,000 each. That'll leave me . . . five million. Plus about fifty thousand pounds on the party. And then I'll take everyone on holiday, to Barbados or somewhere. That'll cost about . . . a hundred thousand pounds, if we all fly Club.

So that's four million, eight hundred and fifty thousand. Oh! and I need six thousand to pay off all my credit cards and, overdraft. Plus three hundred for Suze. Call it seven thousand. So that leaves . . . four million, eight hundred and forty-three thousand.

Obviously, I'll do loads for charity. In fact, I'll probably set up a charitable foundation. I'll support all those unfashionable charities that get ignored, like skin diseases and home helps for the elderly. And I'll send a great big cheque to my old English teacher, Mrs James, so she can restock the school library. Perhaps they'll even rename it after me. The Bloomwood Library.

Oh, and three hundred for that swirly coat in

Whistles, which I *must* buy before they're all snapped up. So how much does that leave? Four million, eight hundred and forty-three thousand, minus—

'Excuse me.' A voice interrupts me and I look up dazedly. The woman behind is trying to get at the biro.

'Sorry,' I say, and politely make way. But the interruption has made me lose track of my calculations. Was it four million or five million?

Then, as I see the woman looking at my bit of paper covered in scribbled numbers, an awful thought strikes me. What if one of my rejected sets of numbers comes up? What if 1 6 9 16 23 44 comes up tonight and I haven't entered it? I'd hate myself, wouldn't I? All my life, I'd never forgive myself. I'd be like the guy who committed suicide because he forgot to post his pools coupon.

I quickly fill in tickets for all the combinations of numbers written on my bit of paper That's nine tickets in all. Nine quid – quite a lot of money, really. I almost feel bad about spending it. But then, that's nine times as many chances of winning, isn't it?

And I now have a very good feeling about 1 6 9 16 23 44. Why has that particular set of numbers leapt into my mind and stayed there? Maybe someone, somewhere, is trying to tell me something.

Brompton's Store

CUSTOMER ACCOUNTS

1 Brompton Street
London SW4 7TH

Ms Rebecca Bloomwood
Flat 2
4 Burney Rd
London SW6 8FD

2 March 2000

Dear Ms Bloomwood

Our records suggest that we have not received payment for your latest Brompton Gilt Card bill. If you have paid within the last few days, please ignore this letter.

Your outstanding bill is currently £235.76. The minimum payment is £43.00. You may pay by cash, cheque or on the enclosed bank giro credit slip. We look forward to receiving your payment.

Yours sincerely

John Hunter
Customer Accounts Manager

Brompton's Store
1 Brompton Street
London SW4 7TH

Ms Rebecca Bloomwood
Flat 2
4 Burney Rd
London SW6 8FD

2 March 2000

Dear Ms Bloomwood

There's never been a better time to spend!

For a limited time, we are offering EXTRA POINTS on all purchases over £50 made with the Brompton Gilt Card[*] – so take the opportunity now to add more points to your total and take advantage of some of our Pointholders' Gifts.

Some of the fantastic gifts we are offering include:

An Italian leather bag	**1,000 points**
A case of pink champagne	**2,000 points**
Two flights to Paris[**]	**5,000 points**

(Your current level is: 35 points)

And remember, during this special offer period, you will gain two points for every £5 spent. We look forward to welcoming you instore soon to take advantage of this unique offer.

Yours sincerely

Adrian Smith
Customer Services Manager

[*]excluding purchases at restaurants, pharmacy, newsstand and hairdresser
[**]certain restrictions apply – see enclosed leaflet

Four

When I arrive at my parents' house, they are in the middle of an argument. Dad is halfway up a stepladder in the garden, poking at the gutter on the side of the house, and Mum is sitting at the wrought-iron garden table, leafing through a Past Times catalogue. Neither of them even looks up when I walk through the patio doors.

'All I'm saying is that they should set a good example!' Mum is saying.

'And you think exposing themselves to danger is a good example, is it? You think that would solve the problem.'

'Danger!' says Mum derisively. 'Don't be so melodramatic, Graham. Is that the opinion you really have of British society?'

'Hi, Mum,' I say. 'Hi Dad.'

'Becky agrees with me. Don't you, darling?' says Mum, and points to a page of Past Times. 'Lovely cardigan,' she adds *sotto voce*. 'Look at that embroidery!'

'Of course she doesn't agree with you!' retorts my dad. 'It's the most ridiculous idea I've ever heard.'

'No it's not!' says Mum indignantly. 'Becky, you think it would be a good idea for the Royal Family to travel by public transport, don't you, darling?'

'Well . . .' I say cautiously. 'I hadn't really . . .'

'You think the Queen should travel to official engagements on the 93 bus?' scoffs Dad.

'And why not? Maybe then the 93 bus would become more efficient!'

'So,' I say, sitting down next to Mum. 'How are things?'

'You realize this country is on the verge of gridlock?' says Mum, as if she hasn't heard me. 'If more people don't start using public transport, our roads are going to seize up.'

My dad shakes his head.

'And you think the Queen travelling on the 93 bus would solve the problem. Never mind the security problems, never mind the fact that she'd be able to do far fewer engagements . . .'

'I didn't mean the Queen, necessarily,' retorts Mum, and pauses for a second. 'But some of those others. Princess Michael of Kent, for example. She could travel by tube every so often, couldn't she? These people need to learn about real life.'

The last time my mum travelled on the tube was about 1983.

'Shall I make some coffee?' I say brightly.

'If you ask me, this gridlock business is utter nonsense,' says my dad. He jumps down from the stepladder and brushes the dirt off his hands. 'It's all propaganda.'

'Propaganda?' exclaims my mum in outrage.

'Right,' I say hurriedly. 'Well, I'll go and put the kettle on.'

I walk back into the house, flick the kettle on in the kitchen and sit down at the table in a nice patch of sunshine. I've already forgotten what my mum and dad are arguing about. They'll just go round and round in circles and agree it's all the fault of Tony Blair. Anyway, I've got more important things to think about. I'm trying to figure out exactly how much I should give to Philip, my boss, after I win the Lottery. I can't leave him out, of course – but is cash a bit tacky? Would a present be better? Really nice cuff links, perhaps. Or one of those picnic hampers with all the plates inside. (Clare Edwards, obviously, will get nothing).

Sitting alone in the sunny kitchen, I feel as though I

have a little glowing secret inside me. I'm going to win the Lottery. Tonight, my life is going to change. God, I can't wait. Ten million pounds. Just think, tomorrow I'll be able to buy anything I want. Anything!

The newspaper's open in front of me at the property section and I carelessly pick it up to peruse expensive houses. Where shall I live? Chelsea? Notting Hill? Mayfair? *Belgravia*, I read. *Magnificent seven-bedroomed detached house with staff annexe and mature garden*. Well, that sounds all right. I could cope with seven bedrooms in Belgravia. My eye flicks complacently down to the price and stops still with shock. Six point five million pounds. That's how much they're asking. Six and a half million.

I feel stunned and slightly angry. Are they serious? I haven't got anything like six point five million pounds. I've only got about . . . four million left. Or was it five? Whatever it is, it's not enough. I stare at the page, feeling cheated. Lottery winners are supposed to be able to buy anything they want – but already I'm feeling poor and inadequate.

Crossly, I shove the paper aside and reach for a freebie brochure full of gorgeous white duvet covers at £100 each. That's more like it. When I've won the Lottery I'll only ever have crisp white duvet covers, I decide. And I'll have a white cast-iron bed and painted wooden shutters and a fluffy white dressing gown . . .

'So, how's the world of finance?' Mum's voice interrupts me and I look up. She's bustling into the kitchen, still holding her Past Times catalogue. 'Have you made the coffee? Chop chop, darling!'

'I was going to,' I say, and make a half-move from my chair. But, as I predicted, Mum's there before me. She reaches for a ceramic storage jar I've never seen before and spoons coffee into a new gold cafetière.

Mum's terrible. She's always buying new stuff for the kitchen – and she just gives the old stuff to Oxfam. New kettles, new toasters . . . We've already had three new rubbish bins this year – dark green, then chrome, and now yellow translucent plastic. I mean, what a waste of money.

'That's a nice skirt!' she says, looking at me as though for the first time. 'Where's that from?'

'DKNY,' I mumble back.

'Very pretty,' she says. 'Was it expensive?'

'Not really,' I say without pausing. 'About fifty quid.'

This is not strictly true. It was nearer a hundred and fifty. But there's no point telling Mum how much things really cost, because she'd have a coronary. Or, in fact, she'd tell my dad first – and then they'd both have coronaries, and I'd be an orphan.

So what I do is work in two systems simultaneously. Real Prices and Mum Prices. It's a bit like when everything in the shop is 20 per cent off, and you walk around mentally reducing everything, After a while, you get quite practised.

The only difference is, I operate a sliding-scale system, a bit like income tax. It starts off at 20 per cent (if it really cost £20, I say it cost £16) and rises up to . . . well, to 90 per cent if necessary. I once bought a pair of boots that cost £200, and I told Mum they were £20 in the sale. And she believed me.

'So, are you looking for a flat?' she says, glancing over my shoulder at the property pages.

'No,' I say sulkily, and flick over a page of my brochure. My parents are always on at me to buy a flat. Do they know how much flats cost? And I don't mean flats in Croydon.

'Apparently, Thomas has bought a very nice little starter home in Reigate,' she says, nodding towards our next-door neighbours. 'He commutes.' She says this with an air of satisfaction, as though she's telling me he's won the Nobel Peace Prize.

'Well, I can't afford a flat,' I say. 'Or a starter home.'

Not yet, anyway, I think. Not until eight o'clock tonight. Hee hee hee.

'Money troubles?' says Dad, coming into the

kitchen. 'You know, there are two solutions to money troubles?'

Oh God. Not this again. Dad's aphorisms.

'C.B.,' says Dad, his eyes twinkling, 'or M.M.M.'

He pauses for effect and I turn the page of my brochure, pretending I can't hear him.

'Cut Back,' says my dad, 'or Make More Money. One or the other. Which is it to be, Becky?'

'Oh, both, I expect,' I say airily, and turn another page of my brochure. To be honest, I almost feel sorry for Dad. It'll be quite a shock for him when his only daughter becomes a multimillionaire overnight.

After lunch, Mum and I go along to a craft fair in the local primary school. I'm really just going to keep Mum company, and I'm certainly not planning to buy anything – but when we get there, I find a stall full of amazing handmade cards, only £1.50 each! So I buy ten. After all, you always need cards, don't you? There's also a gorgeous blue ceramic plant holder with little elephants going round it – and I've been saying for ages we should have more plants in the flat. So I buy that, too. Only fifteen quid. Craft fairs are such a bargain, aren't they? You go along thinking they'll be complete rubbish – but you can always find *something* you want.

Mum's really happy, too, as she's found a pair of candlesticks for her collection. She's got collections of candlesticks, toast racks, pottery jugs, glass animals, embroidered samplers and thimbles. (Personally, I don't think the thimbles count as a proper collection, because she got the whole lot, including the cabinet, from an advert at the back of the *Mail on Sunday* magazine. But she never tells anybody that. In fact, I shouldn't have mentioned it.)

So anyway, we're both feeling rather pleased with ourselves, and decide to go for a cup of tea. Then, on the way out, we pass one of those really sad stalls which no-one is going near; the kind people glance at once, then quickly walk past. The poor guy behind it looks really sorry for himself, so I pause to have a look. And no wonder no-one's stopping. He's selling weird-shaped wooden bowls, and matching wooden cutlery. What on earth is the point of wooden cutlery?

'That's nice!' I say brightly, and pick one of the bowls up.

'Hand-crafted applewood,' he says. 'Took a week to make.'

Well, it was a waste of a week, if you ask me. It's shapeless, it's ugly, and the wood's a nasty shade of brown. But as I go to put it back down again, he looks so doleful I feel sorry for him and turn it over to look at the price, thinking if it's a fiver I'll buy it. But it's eighty quid! I show the price to Mum, and she pulls a little face.

'That particular piece featured in *Elle Decoration* last month,' says the man mournfully, and produces a cut-out page. And at his words, I freeze. *Elle Decoration*? Is he joking?

He's not joking. There on the page, in full colour, is a picture of a room, completely empty except for a suede bean bag, a low table, and a wooden bowl. I stare at it incredulously.

'Was it this exact one?' I ask, trying not to sound too excited. 'This exact bowl?' As he nods, my grasp tightens round the bowl. I can't believe it. I'm holding a piece of *Elle Decoration*. How cool is that? I suddenly feel incredibly stylish and trendy – and wish I was wearing white linen trousers and my hair slicked back like Yasmin Le Bon to match.

It just shows I've got good taste. Didn't I pick out this bowl – sorry, this *piece* – all by myself? Didn't I spot its quality? Already I can see our sitting room redesigned entirely around it, all pale and minimalist. Eighty quid. That's nothing for a timeless piece of style like this.

'I'll have it,' I say determinedly, and reach inside my

bag for my chequebook. The thing is, I remind myself, buying cheap is actually a false economy. It's much better to spend a little more and make a serious purchase that'll last a lifetime. And this bowl is quite clearly a classic. Suze is going to be *so* impressed.

When we get back home, Mum goes straight inside, but I stay in the driveway, carefully transferring my purchases from her car to mine.

'Becky! What a surprise!'

Oh God. It's Martin Webster from next door, leaning over the fence with a rake in his hand and a huge friendly smile on his face. Oh *God*. Martin has this way of always making me feel guilty, I don't know why.

Actually I do know why. It's because I know he was always hoping I would grow up and marry Tom, his son. And I haven't. The history of my relationship with Tom is: he asked me out once when we were both about sixteen and I said no, I was going out with Adam Moore. That was the end of it, and thank God for that. To be perfectly honest, I would rather marry Martin himself than marry Tom.

(That's not to say that I do really want to marry Martin. Or that I like older men or anything. It was just to make a point. Anyway, Martin's happily married.)

'Hi!' I say over-enthusiastically. 'How are you?'

'Oh, we're all doing well,' says Martin. 'You heard Tom's bought a house?'

'Yes,' I say. 'In Reigate. Fantastic!'

'It's got two bedrooms, shower room, reception room and open-plan kitchen,' he recites. 'Lime oak units in the kitchen.'

'Gosh,' I say. 'How fab.'

'Tom's thrilled with it,' says Martin. 'Janice!' he adds in a yell. 'Come and see who's here!'

A moment later, Janice appears on the front door step, wearing her floral apron.

'Becky!' she says. 'What a stranger you've become! How long is it?'

53

Oh God, now I feel guilty for not visiting my parents more often.

'Well,' I say, trying to give a nonchalant smile. 'You know. I'm quite busy with my job and everything.'

'Oh yes,' says Janice, giving an awe-stricken nod. 'Your Job.'

Somewhere along the line, Janice and Martin have got it into their heads that I'm this high-powered financial whiz-kid. I've tried telling them that really, I'm not – but the more I deny it, the more high-powered they think I am. It's a catch-22. So the upshot is, they now think I'm high-powered *and* modest.

Still, who cares? It's quite fun, pretending to be a financial genius.

'Yes, we've been quite busy lately,' I say coolly. 'What with the merger of SBG and Rutland.'

'Of course,' breathes Janice.

'You know, that reminds me,' says Martin. 'Becky, wait there. Back in two ticks.' He disappears before I can say anything, and I'm left awkwardly with Janice.

'So,' I say inanely. 'I hear Tom's got limed oak units in his kitchen!'

This is literally the only thing I can think of to say. I smile at Janice, and wait for her to reply. But instead, she's beaming at me delightedly. Her face is all lit up – and suddenly I realize I've made a huge mistake. I shouldn't have mentioned Tom's bloody starter home. I shouldn't have mentioned the limed oak units. Now Janice'll think I'm hankering after those units myself, won't she? She'll think I suddenly fancy Tom, now he's got a starter home to his name.

'It's limed oak and Mediterranean tiles,' she says proudly. 'It was a choice of Mediterranean or Farmhouse Quarry, and Tom chose Mediterranean.'

For an instant I consider saying I would have chosen Farmhouse Quarry. But that seems a bit mean.

'Lovely,' I say. 'And two bedrooms!'

Why can't I get off the subject of this bloody starter home?

'He wanted two bedrooms,' says Janice. 'After all, you never know, do you?' She smiles coyly at me, and ridiculously, I feel myself start to blush. Oh God. Why am I blushing? This is so stupid. Now she thinks I fancy Tom. She's picturing us together in the starter home, making supper together in the limed oak kitchen.

I should say something. I should say, 'Janice, I don't fancy Tom. He's too tall and his breath smells.' But how on earth can I?

'Well, do give him my love,' I hear myself saying instead.

'I certainly will,' she says, and pauses. 'Does he have your London number?'

Aarrgh!

'I think so,' I lie, smiling brightly. 'And he can always get me here if he wants.' Now everything I say sounds like some saucy *double entendre*. I can just imagine how this conversation will be reported back to Tom. 'She was asking *all* about your starter home. And she asked you to call her!'

Life would be a lot easier if conversations were rewindable and erasable, like videos. Or if you could instruct people to disregard what you just said, like in a courtroom. *Please strike from the record all references to starter homes and limed oak kitchens.*

Luckily, at that moment, Martin reappears, clutching a piece of paper.

'Thought you might cast your eye over this,' he says. 'We've had this with-profits fund with Flagstaff Life for fifteen years. Now we're thinking of transferring to their new unit-linked growth fund. What do you think?'

I don't know. What's he talking about, anyway? Some kind of savings plan? I run my eye over the piece of paper in what I hope looks like a knowledgeable fashion and nod several times.

'Yes,' I say vaguely. 'Well, I should think that's quite a good idea.'

'The company wrote to us, saying we might want a higher return in our retirement years,' says Martin. 'There's a guaranteed sum, too.'

'And they'll send us a carriage clock,' chimes in Janice. 'Swiss made.'

'Mmm,' I say, studying the letterhead intently.

Flagstaff Life, I'm thinking. I'm sure I've heard something about them recently. Which ones are Flagstaff Life? Oh yes! They're the ones who threw a champagne party at Soho Soho. And Elly got incredibly pissed and told David Salisbury from *The Times* that she loved him. It was a bloody good party, come to think of it. One of the best.

'D'you rate them as a company?' says Martin.

'Absolutely,' I say. 'They're very well regarded among the profession.'

'Well then,' says Martin, looking pleased. 'I think we should take their advice. Go for growth.'

'I would think the more growth you have, the better,' I say in my most professional-sounding voice. 'But that's just one view.'

'Oh well,' says Martin, and glances at Janice. 'If Becky thinks it's a good idea . . .'

'Well, I really wouldn't listen to me!' I say hurriedly.

'Listen to her!' says Martin with a little chuckle. 'The financial expert herself.'

'You know, Tom sometimes buys your magazine,' puts in Janice. 'Not that he's got much money now, what with the mortgage and everything . . . But he says your articles are very good! He says—'

'How nice!' I cut in. 'Well, look, I really must go. Lovely to see you. And love to Tom!'

I turn into the house so quickly, I bump my knee on the doorframe. Then I feel a bit bad, and wish I'd said goodbye nicely. But honestly! If I hear one more word about bloody Tom and his bloody kitchen, I'll go mad.

By the time I sit down in front of the National Lottery, however, I've forgotten all about them. We've had a nice supper – chicken provençale from Marks and Spencer, and a nice bottle of Pinot Grigio, which I brought. I know the chicken provençale comes from Marks and Spencer because I've bought it myself, quite a few times. I recognized the sun-dried tomatoes and the olives, and everything. Mum, of course, still pretended she'd made it from scratch, to her own recipe.

I don't know why she bothers. It isn't like anyone would care – especially when it's just me and Dad. And I mean, it's pretty obvious that there are never any raw ingredients in our kitchen. There are lots of empty cardboard boxes and lots of fully prepared meals – and nothing in between. But still Mum never ever admits she's bought a ready-made meal, not even when it's a pie in a foil container. My dad will eat one of those pies, full of plastic mushrooms and gloopy sauce, and then say, with a perfectly straight face, 'Delicious, my love.' And my mum will smile back, looking all pleased with herself.

But tonight it's not foil pie, it's chicken provençale. (To be fair, I suppose it almost does look home-made – except no-one would ever cut a red pepper up that small for themselves, would they? People have more important things to do.) So anyway, we've eaten it and we've drunk a fair amount of the Pinot Grigio, and there's an apple crumble in the oven – and I've suggested, casually, that we all go and watch telly. Because I know from looking at the clock that the National Lottery programme has already started. In a matter of minutes, it's all going to happen. Oh God, I cannot wait.

Luckily, my parents aren't the sort who want to make conversation about politics or talk about books. We've already caught up with all the family news, and I've told them how my work's going, and they've told me about their holiday in Corsica – so by now, we're grinding to a bit of a halt. We need the telly on, if only as a conversational sounding board.

So we all troop into the sitting room, and my dad lights the gas flame-effect fire and turns on the telly. And there it is! The National Lottery, in glorious Technicolor. The lights are shining, and Dale Winton is joshing with Tiffany from *EastEnders*, and every so often the audience gives an excited whoop. My stomach's getting tighter and tighter, and my heart's going thump-thump-thump. In a few minutes those balls are going to fall. In a few minutes I'm going to be a millionaire.

I lean calmly back on the sofa and think what I'll do when I win. At the very instant that I win, I mean. Do I scream? Do I keep quiet? Maybe I shouldn't tell anyone for twenty-four hours. Maybe I shouldn't tell anyone *at all*.

This new thought transfixes me. I could be a secret winner! I could have all the money and none of the pressure. If people asked me how I can afford so many designer clothes I'd just tell them I was doing lots of freelance work. Yes! And I could transform all my friends' lives anonymously, like a good angel. No-one would ever know. This is perfect!

I'm just working out how big a house I could manage to buy without everyone twigging, when a voice on the screen alerts me.

'Question to Number Three.'

What?

'My favourite animal is the flamingo because it's pink, fluffy, and has long legs.' The girl sitting on the stool excitedly unwinds a pair of long glossy legs, and the audience goes wild. I stare at her dazedly. What's going on? Why are we watching *Blind Date*?

'Now, this show used to be fun,' says Mum. 'But it's gone downhill.'

'You call this rubbish fun?' retorts my dad incredulously.

'Listen, Dad, actually, could we turn back to—'

'I didn't say it was fun *now*. I said—'

'Dad!' I say, trying not to sound too panicky. 'Could

we just go back to BBC1 for a moment?'

Blind Date disappears and I sigh with relief. The next moment, an earnest man in a suit fills the screen.

'What the police failed to appreciate,' he says in a nasal voice, 'is that the witnesses were not sufficiently—'

'Dad!'

'Where's the television guide?' he says impatiently. 'There's got to be something better than this.'

'There's the Lottery!' I almost scream. 'I want to watch the Lottery!'

'Why do you want to watch the Lottery? Have you got a ticket?'

For a moment I'm silenced. If I'm going to be a secret winner, I can't tell anyone I've bought a ticket. Not even my parents.

'No!' I say, giving a little laugh. 'I just want to see Martine McCutcheon.'

To my intense relief, it's back on, and Tiffany's singing a song. I relax into the sofa and glance at my watch.

I know strictly speaking that whether I watch it or not won't affect my chances of winning – but I don't want to miss the great moment, do I? You might think I'm a bit mad, but I feel that if I watch it, I can kind of communicate with the balls through the screen. I'll stare hard at them as they get tossed around, and silently urge on my winning numbers. It's a bit like supporting a team. *Team 1 6 9 16 23 44.*

Except the numbers never come out in order.

Team 44 1 23 6 9 16. Possibly. Or *Team 23 6 1 . . .*

Suddenly there's a round of applause and Martine McCutcheon's finished her song. Oh my God. It's about to happen. My life is about to change.

'The Lottery's become terribly commercialized, hasn't it?' says my mum, as Dale Winton leads Martine over to the red button. 'It's a shame, really.'

'What do you mean, it's *become* commercialized?' retorts my dad.

'People used to play the Lottery because they wanted to support the charities.'

'No they didn't! Don't be ridiculous! No-one gives a fig about the charities. This is all about self, self, self.' Dad gestures towards Dale Winton with the remote control and the screen goes dead.

'Dad!' I wail.

'So you think no-one cares about the charities?' says my mum into the silence.

'That's not what I said.'

'Dad! Put it back on!' I screech. 'Put-it-back-on!' I'm about to wrestle him for the remote control when he flicks it back on again.

I stare at the screen in utter disbelief. The first ball has already dropped. And it's 44. My number 44.

'. . . last appeared three weeks ago. And here comes the second ball . . . And it's number 1.'

I can't move. It's taking place, before my very eyes. I'm actually winning the Lottery. I'm winning the bloody Lottery!

Now that it's happening, I feel surprisingly calm. It's as if I've known, all my life, that this would happen. Sitting here silently on the sofa, I feel as though I'm in a fly-on-the-wall documentary about myself, narrated by Joanna Lumley or someone. 'Becky Bloomwood always secretly knew she would win the Lottery one day. But on the day it happened, even she couldn't have predicted . . .'

'And another low one. Number 3.'

What? My mind snaps to and I stare perplexedly at the screen. That can't be right. They mean 23.

'And number 2, last week's bonus ball.'

I feel cold all over. What the hell is going on? What *are* these numbers?

'And another low one! Number 4. A popular number – it's had twelve appearances so far this year. And finally . . . Number 5! Well I never! This is a bit of a first! Now, lining them up in order . . .'

No. This can't be serious. This has to be a mistake.

The winning lottery numbers cannot possibly be 1, 2, 3, 4, 5, 44. That's not a lottery combination, it's a . . . it's a sick joke.

And I was winning. I was *winning*.

'Look at that!' my mum's saying. 'Absolutely incredible! 1, 2, 3, 4, 5, 44.'

'And why should that be incredible?' replies Dad. 'It's as likely as any other combination.'

'It can't be!'

'Jane, do you know *anything* about the laws of probability?'

Quietly I get up and leave the room, as the National Lottery theme tune blares out of the telly. I walk into the kitchen, sit down at the table and bury my head in my hands. I feel slightly shaky, to tell you the truth. I was *so* convinced I was going to win. I was living in a big house and going on holiday to Barbados with all my friends, and walking into Agnès B and buying anything I wanted. It felt so real.

And now, instead, I'm sitting in my parents' kitchen, and I can't afford to go on holiday and I've just spent eighty quid on a wooden bowl I don't even like.

Miserably, I turn on the kettle, pick up a copy of *Woman's Journal* lying on the counter and flick through it – but even that doesn't cheer me up. Everything seems to remind me of money. Maybe my dad's right, I find myself thinking dolefully. Maybe Cut Back is the answer. Suppose . . . suppose I cut back enough to save sixty quid a week. I'd have £6,000 in a hundred weeks.

And suddenly my brain is alert. Six thousand quid. That's not bad, is it? And if you think about it, it can't be that hard to save sixty quid a week. It's only the same as a couple of meals out. I mean, you'd hardly notice it.

God, yes. That's what I'll do. Sixty quid a week, every week. Maybe I'll even pay it into a special account. It'll be fantastic! I'll be completely on top of my finances – and when I've paid off my bills I'll just keep saving. It'll become a habit to be frugal. Then at the end of every year I'll splash out on one classic investment like an Armani suit. Or maybe Christian Dior. Something really classy, anyway.

I'll start on Monday, I think excitedly, spooning chocolate Ovaltine into a cup. What I'll do is, I just won't spend *anything*. All my spare money will mount up, and I'll be rich. This is going to be so great.

Brompton's Store
CUSTOMER ACCOUNTS
1 Brompton Street
London SW4 7TH

Ms Rebecca Bloomwood
Flat 2
4 Burney Rd
London SW6 8FD

6 March 2000

Dear Ms Bloomwood

Thank you for your cheque for £43.00, received today.

Unfortunately, the cheque is unsigned. No doubt just an oversight on your part. I am therefore returning it to you and request that you sign it and return to us.

As you are no doubt aware, this payment is already late by eight days.

I look forward to receiving your signed cheque.

Yours sincerely

John Hunter
Customer Accounts Manager

Five

Frugality. Simplicity. These are my new watch-words. A new, uncluttered, Zen-like life, in which I spend nothing. Spend *nothing*. I mean, when you think about it, how much money do we all waste every day? No wonder I'm in a little bit of debt. And really, it's not my fault. I've merely been succumbing to the Western drag of materialism – which you have to have the strength of elephants to resist. At least, that's what it says in my new book.

You see, yesterday, when Mum and I went into Waterstone's to buy her paperback for the week, I sidled off to the self-help section, and bought the most wonderful book I've ever read. Quite honestly, it's going to change my life. I've got it now, in my bag. It's called *Controlling Your Cash* by David E. Barton, and it's fantastic. What it says is that we can all fritter away money without realizing it, and that most of us could easily cut our cash consumption by half in just one week.

In one week!

You just have to do things like make your own sandwiches instead of eating in restaurants and ride a bike to work instead of taking the tube. When you start thinking about it, you can save money everywhere. And as David E. Barton says, there are lots of free pleasures which we forget because we're so busy spending money, like parks and museums and the simple joy of a country walk.

It's all so easy and straighforward. And the best thing is, you have to start out by going shopping! The book says you should begin by itemizing every single purchase in a single normal spending day and plot it on a graph. It stresses that you should be honest and not suddenly curtail or alter your spending pattern – which is lucky, because it's Suze's birthday on Thursday and I've got to get her a present.

So on Monday morning, I stop off at Lucio's on the way into work and buy an extra large cappuccino and a chocolate muffin, just like I usually do. I have to admit I feel a bit sorrowful as I hand over my money, because this is my last ever cappuccino and my last ever chocolate muffin. My new frugality starts tomorrow – and cappuccinos aren't allowed. David E. Barton says if you have a coffee habit you should make it at home and take it into the office in a flask, and if you like eating snacks you should buy cheap cakes from the supermarket. 'The coffee merchants are fleecing you for what is little more than hot water and polystyrene,' he points out – and I suppose he's right. But I will miss my morning cappuccino. Still. I've promised myself I'll follow the rules of the book – and I will.

As I come out of the coffee shop, clutching my last ever cup, I realize I don't actually have a flask for coffee. But that's OK, I'll buy one. There are some lovely sleek chrome ones in Habitat. Flasks are actually quite trendy these days. I think Alessi might even do one. Wouldn't that be cool? Drinking coffee out of an Alessi flask. Much cooler than a takeaway cappuccino.

So I'm feeling quite happy as I walk along the street. When I get to Smith's I pop in and stock up on a few magazines to keep me going – and I also buy a sweet little silver notebook and pen to write down everything I spend. I'm going to be really rigorous about this, because David E. Barton says the very act of noting down purchases should have a curtailing effect. So when I get into work, I start my list.

Cappuccino	£1.50
Muffin	£1.00
Notebook	£3.99
Pen	£1.20
Magazines	£6.40

Which makes a grand total so far of . . . £14.09.

Gosh. I suppose that's quite a lot, bearing in mind it's only 9.40 in the morning.

But the notebook and pen don't count, do they? They're like course requirements. I mean, how on earth are you supposed to note down all your purchases without a notebook and pen? So I subtract both of those, and now my total comes to . . . £8.90. Which is much better.

Anyway, I'm at work now. I probably won't spend anything else all day.

Oh God, though. Somehow, spending nothing is absolutely impossible. First of all, Guy from Accounts comes round with yet another leaving present to give to. Then I have to go out and get some lunch. I'm very restrained with my sandwich – I choose egg and cress, which is the cheapest one at Boots, and I don't even like egg and cress.

David E. Barton says that when you make a real effort, particularly in the early stages, you should reward yourself – so I pick up some coconut bath oil from the Natural range as a little treat. Then I notice there are double Advantage points on the moisturizer I use.

I *love* Advantage points. Aren't they a wonderful invention? If you spend enough, you can get really good prizes, like a beauty day at a hotel. Last Christmas I was really canny – I let my points build up until I'd accumulated enough to buy my granny's Christmas present. What happened in fact was, I'd already built up 1653 points – and I needed 1800 to buy her a heated roller set. So I bought myself a great big bottle of

Samsara perfume, and that gave me 150 extra points on my card — and then I got the heated roller set absolutely free! The only thing is, I don't much like Samsara perfume — but I didn't realize that until I got home. Still, never mind.

The clever way to use Advantage points — as with all special offers — is to spot the opportunity and use it, because it may not come your way again. So I grab three pots of moisturizer and buy them. Double Advantage points! I mean, it's just free money, isn't it?

Then I have to get Suze's birthday present. I've already bought her a set of aromatherapy oils — but the other day I saw this gorgeous pink angora cardigan in Benetton, and I know she'd love it. I can always take the aromatherapy oils back or give them to someone for Christmas.

So I go into Benetton, and pick up the pink cardigan. I'm about to pay . . . when I notice they've got it in grey as well. The most perfect, soft, dove-grey angora cardigan, with little pearly buttons.

Oh *God*. You see, the thing is, I've been looking for a nice grey cardigan for ages. Honestly, I have. You can ask Suze, my mum, anybody. And the other thing is, I'm not actually *on* my new frugal regime yet, am I? I'm just monitoring myself.

David E. Barton says I should act as naturally as possible. So really, I *ought* to act on my natural impulses and buy it. It would be false not to. It would ruin the whole point.

And it only costs forty-five quid. And I can put it on VISA.

Look at it another way — what's forty-five quid in the grand scheme of things? I mean, it's nothing, is it?

So I buy it. The most perfect little cardigan in the world. People will call me the Girl in the Grey Cardigan. I'll be able to *live* in it. Really, it's an investment.

* * *

After lunch, I have to go and visit Image Store to choose a front cover picture for the next issue. This is my absolute favourite job – I can't understand why Philip always offloads it onto someone else. It basically means you get to go and sit drinking coffee all afternoon, looking at rows and rows of transparencies.

Because, of course, we don't have the editorial budget to create our own front covers. God no. When I first started out in journalism, I thought I'd be able to go to shoots, and meet models, and have a really glamorous time. But we don't even have a cameraman. All our sorts of magazines use picture libraries like Image Store, and the same images tend to go round and round. There's a picture of a roaring tiger that's been on at least three personal finance covers in the last year. Still, the readers don't mind, do they? They're not exactly buying the magazines to look at Kate Moss.

The good thing is that Elly's editor doesn't like choosing front covers either – and they use Image Store, too. So we always try to work it that we'll go together and have a good natter over the pics. Even better, Image Store is all the way over in Notting Hill Gate, so you can legitimately take ages getting there and back. Usually I don't bother going back to the office. Really, it's the perfect way to spend an afternoon. (A paid afternoon, that is. Obviously, I'd be thinking a bit differently if this was a Saturday.)

I get there before Elly and mutter 'Becky Bloomwood from *Successful Saving*', to the girl at reception, wishing I could say 'Becky Bloomwood from *Vogue*' or 'Becky Bloomwood from *Wall Street Journal*'. Then I sit on a squashy black leather chair, flicking through a catalogue of pictures of glossy happy families, until one of the trendy young men who works there comes and leads me to my own illuminated table.

'I'm Paul,' he says, 'and I'll be looking after you today. Do you know what you're looking for?'

'Well . . .' I say, and importantly pull out my

notebook. We had a meeting about the cover yesterday, and eventually decided on *Portfolio Management: getting the right balance*. Before your head falls off with boredom, let me just point out that last month, the coverline was *Deposit accounts: put to the test*.

Why can't we just *once* put self-tanning creams to the test instead? Oh well.

'I'm looking for pictures of scales,' I say, reading off my list. 'Or tightropes, unicycles . . .'

'Balancing images,' says Paul. 'No problem. Would you like a coffee?'

'Yes please,' I beam, and relax back in my chair. You see what I mean? It's so nice here. And I'm being paid to sit in this chair, doing nothing at all.

A few moments later, Elly appears with Paul, and I look at her in surprise. She's looking really smart, in an aubergine-coloured suit and high heels.

'So it's swimmers, boats, and European images,' says Paul to her.

'That's it,' says Elly, and sinks into the chair beside me.

'Let me guess,' I say. 'Something about floating currencies.'

'Very good,' says Elly. 'Actually, it's "Europe – sink or swim?"' She says it in an incredibly dramatic voice, and Paul and I both start giggling. When he's walked away, I look her up and down.

'So how come you're so smart?'

'I always look smart,' she parries. 'You know that.' Paul's already wheeling trolley-loads of transparencies towards us and she looks over at them. 'Are these yours or mine?'

She's avoiding the subject. What's going on?

'Have you got an interview?' I say, in a sudden flash of genius. She looks at me, flushes, then pulls a sheet of transparencies out of the trolley.

'Circus acts,' she says. 'People juggling. Is that what you wanted?'

'Elly! Have you got an interview? Tell me!'

There's silence for a while. Elly stares down at the sheet, then looks up.

'Yes,' she says and bites her lip. 'But—'

'That's fantastic!' I exclaim, and a couple of smooth-looking girls in the corner look up. 'Who for?' I say more quietly. 'It's not *Cosmo*, is it?'

We're interrupted by Paul who comes over with a coffee and puts it in front of Elly. 'Swimmers coming up,' he says, then grins and walks off.

'Who's it for?' I repeat. Elly applies for so many jobs, I lose track.

'It's Wetherby's,' she says, and a pink flush creeps over her face.

'Wetherby's Investments?' She gives a slight nod, and I frown in bemusement. Why is she applying to Wetherby's Investments? 'Have they got an in-house magazine or something?'

'I'm not applying to be a journalist,' she says in a low voice. 'I'm applying to be a fund manager.'

'*What?*' I say, appalled.

I know friends should be supportive of each other's life decisions and all that. But I'm sorry, a *fund manager?*

'I probably won't even get it,' she says, and looks away. 'It's no big deal.'

'But . . .'

I'm speechless. How can Elly even be thinking of becoming a fund manager? Fund managers aren't real people. They're the characters we laugh at on press trips.

'It's just an idea,' she says defensively. 'Maybe I just want to show Carol I can do something else. You know?'

'So it's like . . . a bargaining tool?' I hazard.

'Yes,' she says, and gives a little shrug. 'That's it. A bargaining tool.'

But she doesn't sound exactly convinced, and she's not nearly as chatty as usual during the rest of the afternoon. What's happened to her? I'm still puzzling over it as I make my way home from Image Store. I walk down to High Street Kensington, cross over the road and hesitate in front of Marks and Spencer.

The tube is to my right. The shops are to my left.

I must *ignore* the shops. I must practise frugality, go straight home and plot my expenditure graph. If I need entertainment, I can watch some nice free television and perhaps make some inexpensive, nutritious soup.

But there's nothing good on tonight, at least not until *EastEnders*. And I don't feel like soup. I really feel as if I need something to cheer me up. And besides – my mind's working fast – I'll be giving it all up tomorrow, won't I? It's like the beginning of Lent. This is my Shopping Pancake Day. I need to cram it all in before the fast begins.

With a surge of excitement I hurry towards the Barkers Centre. I won't go mad, I promise myself. Just one little treat to see me through. I've already got my cardigan – so not clothes . . . and I bought some new kitten heels the other day – so not that . . . although there are some nice Prada-y type shoes in Hobbs . . . Hmmm. I'm not sure.

I arrive at the cosmetics department of Barkers and suddenly I know. Makeup! That's what I need. A new mascara, and maybe a new lipstick. Happily, I start to wander around the bright, heady room, dodging sprays of perfume and painting lipsticks onto the back of my hand. I want a really pale lipstick, I decide. Sort of nudey beige/pink, and a lip-liner to go with it . . .

At the Clarins counter, my attention is grabbed by a big promotional sign.

> Buy two skincare products, and receive FREE beauty bag, containing trial-size cleanser, toner and moisturizer, Autumn Blaze lipstick, Extra Strength mascara and sample-size Eau Dynamisante. Stocks limited so hurry.

But this is fantastic! Do you know how much Clarins lipstick usually costs? And here they are, giving it away free! Excitedly, I start rooting through all the skincare products, trying to decide which two to buy. How about some neck cream? I've never used that before. And some of this revitalizing moisturiser. And then I'll get a free lipstick! It's a complete bargain.

'Hi,' I say to the woman in the white uniform. 'I'd like the neck cream and the revitalizing moisturiser. And the beauty bag,' I add, suddenly petrified that I might be too late; that the limited stocks might have run out.

But they haven't! Thank God. As my VISA card's processing, the woman hands me my shiny red beauty bag (which I have to admit is a bit smaller than I was expecting) and I excitedly open it up. And there, sure enough, is my free lipstick!

It's a kind of browny-red colour. A bit weird, actually. But if I mix it up a bit with some of my others and add a bit of lip gloss, it'll look really good.

By the time I get home, I'm exhausted. I open the door to the flat and Suze comes rushing up, like a puppy.

'What did you get?' she cries.

'Don't look!' I cry back. 'You're not allowed to look! It's your present.'

'My present!' Suze gets so overexcited about birthdays. Well, to be honest, so do I.

I hurry into my bedroom and hide the Benetton bag in the wardrobe. Then I unpack all the rest of my shopping and get out my little silver notebook to itemize my purchases. David E. Barton says this should be done *straightaway*, before items can be forgotten.

'D'you want a drink?' comes Suze's voice through the door.

'Yes please!' I shout back, writing in my book, and a moment later she comes in with a glass of wine.

'*EastEnders* in a minute,' she says.

'Thanks,' I say absently, and keep on writing. I'm

following the rules of the book exactly, taking out all my receipts and writing them all down, and I'm feeling really pleased with myself. It just shows, as David E. Barton says, that with a bit of application, anyone can gain control of their finances.

Come to think of it, I've bought quite a lot of moisturizer today, haven't I? To be honest, when I was at the Clarins counter, buying my revitalizing moisturizer, I forgot about all those pots I'd bought at Boots. Still, never mind. You always need moisturizer. It's a staple, like bread and milk, and David E. Barton says you should never scrimp on staples. And apart from that, I don't think I've done too badly. Of course I haven't added it all up yet, but . . .

OK. So here is my final and complete list:

Cappuccino	£1.50
Muffin	£1.00
~~Notebook~~	~~£3.99~~
~~Pen~~	~~£1.20~~
Magazines	£6.40
Egg and cress sandwich	99p
Coconut bath oil	£2.55
Boots moisturizers	£20.97
Two cardigans	£90
Evening Standard	35p
Clarins neck cream	£14.50
Clarins moisturizer	£32.50
Beauty bag	Free!
Banana smoothie	£2.00
Carrot cake	£1.20

And that comes to a grand total of £173.96

I stare at this figure in utter shock.

No, I'm sorry, that just can't be right. It *can't* be right. I can't have spent over £170 in one day.

I mean, it isn't even the weekend. I've been at work. I wouldn't have had *time* to spend that much. There has to be something wrong somewhere. Maybe I haven't added it up right. Or maybe I've entered something twice.

My eye runs more carefully down the list, and suddenly stops in triumph. 'Two cardigans'. I knew it! I only bought . . .

Oh yes. I did buy two, didn't I? Blast. Oh God, this is depressing. I'm going to go and watch *EastEnders*.

Endwich Bank
FULHAM BRANCH
3 Fulham Road
London SW6 9JH

Ms Rebecca Bloomwood
Flat 2
4 Burney Road
London SW6 8FD

6 March 2000

Dear Ms Bloomwood

Thank you for your answer-machine message of Sunday
5 March.

I am sorry to hear that your dog has died.

Nevertheless, I must insist that you make contact with
myself or my assistant Erica Parnell within the next few
days, in order to discuss your situation.

Yours sincerely

Derek Smeath
Manager

ENDWICH — BECAUSE WE CARE

Six

OK, I think firmly the next day. The thing is not to get freaked out by how much I happened to spend yesterday. It's water under the bridge. The point is, today is the beginning of my new frugal life. From now on, I'm just going to spend absolutely nothing. David E. Barton says you should aim to cut your expenditure by half in the first week but I reckon I can do much better than that. I mean, not wanting to be rude, but these self-help books are always for people with absolutely zero self-control, aren't they? And I gave up smoking easily enough. (Except socially, but that doesn't count.)

I feel quite exhilarated as I make myself a cheese sandwich and wrap it up in tinfoil. I've already saved a couple of quid, just by doing that! I haven't got a flask (must buy one at the weekend), so I can't take in coffee, but there's a bottle of Ame in the fridge so I decide I'll take that instead. It'll be healthier, too.

In fact, it makes you wonder why people buy shop-made sandwiches at all. Look how cheap and easy it is to make your own. And it's the same with curries. David E. Barton says instead of forking out for expensive takeaway meals you should learn how to make your own curries and stir-fries, for a fraction of the cost. So that's what I'm going to do this weekend, after I've been to a museum or maybe just walked along the river, enjoying the scenery.

As I walk along to the tube I feel pure and refreshed. Stern, almost. Look at all these people on the street, scurrying around, thinking about nothing but money.

Money, money, money. It's an obsession. But once you relinquish money altogether, it ceases to have any relevance. Already, I feel I'm in a completely different mindset. Less materialistic, more philosophical. More *spiritual*. As David E. Barton says, we all fail to appreciate each day just how much we already possess. Light, air, freedom, the companionship of friends . . . I mean, these are the things that matter, aren't they? Not clothes and shoes and fripperies.

It's almost frightening, the transformation that's already occurred within me. For example, I walk past the magazine kiosk at the tube station and idly glance over – but I don't feel the slightest desire to buy any of the magazines on offer. Magazines are irrelevant in my new life. (Plus I've already read most of them.)

So I get on the tube feeling serene and impervious, like a Buddhist monk. When I get off the tube at the other end, I walk straight past the discount shoe shop without even looking, and straight past Lucio's, too. No cappuccino today. No muffin. No spending at all – just straight to the office.

It's quite an easy time of the month for *Successful Saving*. We've only just put the latest issue of the magazine to bed, which basically means we can laze around for a few days doing nothing, before getting our act together for the next issue. Of course, we're meant to be starting on research for next month's article. In fact, I'm supposed to be making lots of phone calls to stockbrokers today, asking for their investment tips for the next six months.

But somehow the whole morning goes by and I haven't done anything, just changed the screensaver on my computer to three yellow fish and an octopus, and written out an expense claim form. To be honest, I can't really concentrate on proper work. I suppose I'm too exhilarated by my new pure self. I keep trying to work out how much I'll have saved by the end of the month and what I'll be able to afford in Jigsaw.

At lunchtime I take out my sandwich wrapped in

foil – and for the first time that day, I feel a bit depressed. The bread's gone all soggy, and some pickle's leaked out onto the foil, and it really doesn't look very appetizing at all. What I crave at that moment is Pret à Manger walnut bread and a chocolate brownie.

Don't think about it, I instruct myself firmly. Think how much money you're saving. So somehow I force myself to eat my soggy effort, and swig down some Ame. When I've finished, I throw away my foil, screw the top back on the Ame bottle and put it in our tiny office fridge. And that's about . . . five minutes of my lunch break gone.

So what am I supposed to do next? Where am I supposed to go?

I slump miserably at my desk. God, this frugality is hard going. I leaf dispiritedly through a few folders . . . then raise my head and stare out of the window, at all the busy Oxford Street shoppers clutching carrier bags. I want to get out there so desperately, I'm actually leaning forward in my chair, like a plant towards the light. I'm craving the bright lights and warm air; the racks of merchandise, even the bleep of the cash registers. But I can't go. This morning I told myself that I wouldn't go near the shops all day. I *promised* myself – and I can't break my own promise. Or at least, not so soon . . .

Then a brilliant thought occurs to me. I need to get a curry recipe for my home-made takeaway, don't I? David E. Barton says recipe books are a waste of money. He says you should use the recipes printed on the sides of food packets, or take books out of the library. But I've got an even better idea. I'll go into Smith's and *copy out* a curry recipe to make on Saturday night. That way, I can go into a shop – but I don't need to spend any money. Already I'm scrambling to my feet, reaching for my coat. Shops, here I come!

*　　*　　*

78

As I walk into Smith's I feel my whole body expand in relief. There's a thrill about walking into a shop – any shop – which you can't beat. It's partly the anticipation, partly the buzzy, welcoming atmosphere; partly just the lovely *newness* of everything. Shiny new magazines, shiny new pencils, shiny new protractors. Not that I've needed a protractor since I was eleven – but don't they look nice, all clean and unscratched in their packets? There's a new range of leopard-print stationery which I haven't seen before, and for a moment I'm almost tempted to linger. But instead I force myself to stride on past, down to the back of the shop where the books are stacked.

There's a whole array of Indian recipe books, and I pick up one at random, flicking over the pages and wondering what sort of recipe I should go for. I hadn't realized quite how complicated this Indian cookery is. Perhaps I should write down a couple, to be on the safe side.

I look around cautiously and take out my notebook and pen. I'm a bit wary, because I know Smith's don't like you copying down stuff out of their books. The reason I know this is because Suze once got asked to leave the Smith's in Victoria. She was copying out a page of the A-Z, because she'd forgotten hers – and they told her she had to either buy it or leave. (Which doesn't make any sense, because they let you read the magazines for free, don't they?)

So anyway, when I'm sure no-one's looking, I start copying out the recipe for 'Tiger prawn biriani'. I'm halfway through the list of spices when a girl in WH Smith uniform comes round the corner – so I quickly close the book and walk off a little, pretending I'm browsing. When I think I'm safe, I open it again – but before I can write anything down, an old woman in a blue coat says loudly,

'Is that any good, dear?'

'What?' I say.

'The book!' She gestures to the recipe book with her

umbrella. 'I need a present for my daughter-in-law, and she comes from India. So I thought I'd get a nice Indian recipe book. Is that a good one, would you say?'

'I really don't know,' I say. 'I haven't read it yet.'

'Oh,' she says, and starts to wander off. I ought to keep my mouth shut and mind my own business – but I just can't resist it, I have to clear my throat and say, 'Doesn't she have lots of Indian recipes already?'

'Who, dear?' says the woman, turning round.

'Your daughter-in-law!' Already, I'm regretting this. 'If she's Indian, doesn't she already know how to cook Indian food?'

'Oh,' says the old woman. She seems completely flummoxed. 'Well, what should I get, then?'

Oh God.

'I don't know,' I say. 'Maybe a book on . . . on something else?'

'That's a good idea!' she says brightly, and comes towards me. 'You show me, dear.'

Why me?

'Sorry,' I say. 'I'm in a bit of a hurry today.'

Quickly I stride off, feeling a bit bad. I reach the CD and video section, which is always quite empty, and hide behind a rack of Teletubbies videos. I glance around and check no-one's about, then open the book again. OK, turn to page 214, Tiger prawn biriani . . . I start copying again, and I've just got to the end of the list of spices, when a stern voice says in my ear,

'Excuse me?'

I'm so startled, my pen jerks off my notebook and, to my horror, makes a blue line, straight across a photograph of perfectly cooked basmati rice. Quickly I shift my hand, almost covering up the mark, and turn round innocently. A man in a white shirt and a name badge is looking at me disapprovingly.

'This isn't a public library, you know,' he says. 'You think we run a free information service?'

'I'm just browsing,' I say hurriedly, and make to close the book. But the man's finger comes out of nowhere and lands on the page before I can get it shut. Slowly he opens the book out again and we both stare at my blue biro line.

'Browsing is one thing,' says the man sternly. 'Defacing shop stock is another.'

'It was an accident!' I say. 'You startled me!'

'Hmm,' says the man, and gives me a hard stare. 'Were you actually intending to buy this book? Or any book?'

There's a pause – then, rather shamefacedly, I say, 'No.'

'I see,' says the man, tightening his lips. 'Well, I'm afraid this matter will have to go to the manageress. Obviously, we can't sell this book now, so it's our loss. If you could come with me and explain to her exactly what you were doing when the defacement occurred . . .'

Is he serious? Isn't he just going to tell me kindly that it doesn't matter and would I like a loyalty card? My heart starts to thud in panic. What am I going to do? Obviously, I can't buy the book, under my new frugal regime. But I don't want to go and see the manageress, either.

'Lynn?' the man's calling to an assistant at the pen counter. 'Could you page Glenys for me, please?'

He really *is* serious. He's looking all pleased with himself, as though he's caught a shoplifter. Can they prosecute you for making biro marks in books? Maybe it counts as vandalism. Oh God. I'll have a criminal record. I won't ever be able to go to America.

'Look, I'll buy it, OK?' I say breathlessly. 'I'll buy the bloody book.' I wrench it from the man's grasp and hurry off to the checkout before he can say anything else, my heart still thumping hard.

Standing at the next checkout is the old woman in the blue coat, and I try to avoid her eye. But she spots me, and calls triumphantly,

'I took your advice! I've got something I think she'll really like!'

81

'Oh good,' I reply, handing my recipe book over to be scanned.

'It's called *The Rough Guide to India*,' says the old woman, showing me the fat blue paperback. 'Have you heard of it?'

'Oh,' I say. 'Well, yes, but—'

'That's £24.99, please,' says the girl at my till.

What? I look at the girl in dismay. Twenty-five quid, just for recipes? Why couldn't I have picked up some cheap paperback? Damn. *Damn.* Very reluctantly, I take out my credit card and hand it over. Shopping is one thing – being forced into purchases against your will is something else. I mean, I could have bought some nice underwear with that twenty-five quid.

On the other hand, I think as I walk away, that's quite a lot of new points on my Club Card. The equivalent to . . . 50p! And now I'll be able to make loads of delicious, exotic curries and save all that wasted take-away money. Really, I've got to think of this book as an investment.

I don't want to boast – but apart from that one purchase, I do incredibly well over the next couple of days. The only things I buy are a really nice chrome flask to take coffee into the office (and some coffee beans and an electric grinder – because there's no point taking in crappy instant coffee, is there?). And some flowers and champagne for Suze's birthday.

But I'm allowed to get those, because, as David E. Barton says, you must treasure your friends. He says the simple act of breaking bread with friends is one of the oldest, most essential parts of human life. 'Do not stop giving your friends gifts,' he says. 'They need not be extravagant – use your creativity and try making them yourself.'

So what I've done is to buy Suze a half-bottle of champagne instead of a whole one – and instead of buying expensive croissants from the pâtisserie, I'm going to make them out of that special dough you get in tubes.

In the evening we're going out to Terrazza for supper with Suze's cousins Fenella and Tarquin – and, to be honest, it might be quite an expensive evening. But that's OK, because it counts as breaking bread with friends. (Except the bread at Terrazza is sun-dried tomato focaccia and costs £4.50 a basket.)

Fenella and Tarquin arrive at six o'clock on Suze's birthday, and as soon as she sees them, she starts squealing with excitement. I stay in my bedroom and finish my makeup, putting off the moment of having to go out and say hello. I'm not that keen on Fenella and Tarquin. In fact, I think they're a bit weird. For a start, they look weird. They're both very skinny – but in a pale, bony way – and have the same slightly protruding teeth. Fenella does make a bit of an effort with clothes and makeup, and doesn't look *too* bad. But Tarquin, frankly, looks just like a stoat. Or a weasel. Some bony little creature, anyway. They do strange things, too. They ride around on a tandem and wear matching jumpers knitted by their old nanny and have this stupid family language which no-one else can understand. Like they call sandwiches 'witchies'. And a drink is a 'titchy' (except if it's water, which is 'Ho'). Take it from me, it gets really irritating after a while.

But Suze loves them. She spent all her childhood summers with them in Scotland and she just can't see that they're a bit strange. The worst thing is, *she* starts talking about witchies and titchies when she's with them. It drives me mad.

Still, there's nothing I can do about it – they're here now. I finish brushing on my mascara and stand up, looking at my reflection. I'm pretty pleased with what I see. I'm wearing a really simple black top and black trousers – and, tied loosely round my neck, my gorgeous, *gorgeous* Denny and George scarf. God that was a good buy. It looks fantastic.

I linger a bit, then resignedly open my bedroom door.

'Hi, Bex!' says Suze, looking up with bright eyes. She's sitting cross-legged on the floor of the corridor, ripping open a present, while Fenella and Tarquin stand nearby, looking on. They're not wearing matching jumpers today, thank God, but Fenella's wearing a very odd red skirt made out of hairy tweed, and Tarquin's double-breasted suit looks as if it was tailored during the First World War.

'Hi!' I say, and kiss each of them politely.

'Oh, wow!' cries Suze, as she pulls out a picture in an old gilt frame. 'I don't believe it! I don't *believe* it!' She's looking from Tarquin to Fenella with shining eyes, and I look at the picture interestedly over her shoulder. But to be honest, I can't say I'm impressed. For a start it's really dingy – all sludgy greens and browns – and for another start, it just shows a horse standing still in a field. I mean, couldn't it have been jumping over a fence or rearing up or something? Or maybe trotting along in Hyde Park, ridden by a girl in one of those lovely *Pride and Prejudice* dresses.

'Happy Bad Day!' Tarquin and Fenella chime in unison. (That's another thing. They call birthdays bad days, ever since . . . Oh God. It really is too boring to explain.)

'It's absolutely gorgeous!' I say enthusiastically. 'Absolutely beautiful!'

'It is, isn't it?' says Tarquin earnestly. 'Just look at those colours.'

'Mmm, lovely,' I say, nodding.

'And the brushwork. It's exquisite. We were thrilled when we came across it.'

'It's a really wonderful picture,' I say. 'Makes you want to just . . . gallop off over the downs!'

What *is* this drivel I'm coming out with? Why can't I just be honest and say I don't like it?

'Do you ride?' says Tarquin, looking up at me in slight surprise.

I've ridden once. On my cousin's horse. And I fell off and vowed never to do it again. But I'm not going to admit that to Mr Horse of the Year.

'I used to,' I say, and give a modest little smile. 'Not very well.'

'I'm sure you'd get back into it,' says Tarquin, gazing at me. 'Have you ever hunted?'

Oh for God's sake. Do I *look* like Ms Country Life?

'Hey,' says Suze, fondly propping the picture against the wall. 'Shall we have a titchy before we go?'

'Absolutely!' I say, turning quickly away from Tarquin. 'Good idea.'

'Oooh yes,' says Fenella. 'Have you got any champagne?'

'Should have,' says Suze, and goes into the kitchen. At that moment the phone rings and I go to answer it.

'Hello?'

'Hello, may I speak to Rebecca Bloomwood?' says a strange woman's voice.

'Yes,' I say idly. I'm listening to Suze opening and shutting cupboard doors in the kitchen and wondering if we have actually got any champagne, apart from the dregs of the half-bottle we drank for breakfast . . . 'Speaking.'

'Ms Bloomwood, this is Erica Parnell from Endwich Bank,' says the voice, and I freeze.

Shit. It's the bank. Oh God, they sent me that letter, didn't they, and I never did anything about it.

What am I going to say? Quick, what am I going to say?

'Ms Bloomwood?' says Erica Parnell.

OK – what I'll say is, I'm fully aware that my overdraft is slightly larger than it should be, and I'm planning to take remedial action within the next few days. Yes, that sounds good. 'Remedial action' sounds very good. OK – go.

Firmly I tell myself not to panic – these people are human – and take a big breath. And then, in one seamless, unplanned movement, my hand puts down the receiver.

I stare at the silent phone for a few seconds, not quite able to believe what I've just done. *What* did I do that for? Erica Parnell knew it was me, didn't she? Any minute, she'll ring back. She's probably pressing redial now, and she'll be really angry . . .

Quickly I take the phone off the hook and hide it under a cushion. Now she can't get me. I'm safe.

'Who was that?' says Suze, coming into the room.

'No-one,' I say, feeling slightly shaky. 'Just a wrong . . . Listen, let's not have drinks here. Let's go out!'

'Oh,' says Suze. 'OK!'

'Much more fun,' I gabble, trying to head her away from the phone. 'We can go to some really nice bar and have cocktails, and then go on to Terrazza.'

What I'll do in future, I'm thinking, is screen all my calls. Or answer in a foreign accent. Or, even better, change the number. Go ex-directory.

'What's going on?' says Fenella, appearing at the door.

'Nothing!' I hear myself say. 'We're going out for a titchy and then on to sups.'

Oh, I don't believe it. I'm turning into one of them.

As we arrive at Terrazza, I'm feeling a lot calmer. Of course, Erica Parnell will have thought we were cut off by a fault on the line or something. She'll never have thought I put the phone down on her. I mean, we're two civilized adults, aren't we? Adults just don't *do* things like that.

And if I ever meet her – which I hope to God I never do – I'll just keep very cool and say, 'It was odd what happened, that time you phoned me, wasn't it?' Or even better, I'll accuse *her* of putting the phone down on *me* (in a joky way, of course).

Terrazza is full, buzzing with people and cigarette smoke and chatter, and as we sit down with our huge silver menus I feel myself relax even more. I love eating out. And I reckon I deserve a real treat, after being so frugal over the last few days. It hasn't been easy, keeping to such a tight regime, but somehow I've managed it. And I'm keeping to it so well! On Saturday I'm going to monitor my spending pattern again – and I'm sure it'll have gone down by at least 70 per cent.

'What shall we have to drink?' says Suze. 'Tarquin, you choose.'

'Oh look!' shrieks Fenella. 'There's Eddie Lazenby! I must just say hello.' She leaps to her feet and makes for a balding guy in a blazer, ten tables away. How she spotted him in this throng, I've no idea.

'Suze!' cries another voice, and we all look up. A blond girl in a tiny pastel-pink suit is heading towards our table, arms stretched out for a hug. 'And Tarkie!'

'Hello, Tory,' says Tarquin, getting to his feet. 'How's Mungo?'

'He's over there!' says Tory. 'You must come and say hello!'

How is it that Fenella and Tarquin spend most of their time in the middle of Perthshire – but the minute they set foot in London, they're besieged by long-lost friends?

'Eddie says hi,' announces Fenella, returning to the table. 'Tory! How are you? How's Mungo?'

'Oh, he's fine,' says Tory. 'But listen, have you heard? Caspar's back in town!'

'No!' everyone exclaims, and I'm almost tempted to join in. No-one has bothered to introduce me to Tory – but that's the way it goes with these people. You join the gang by osmosis. One minute you're a complete stranger, the next you're shrieking away with the rest of them, going, 'Did you *hear* about Venetia and Sebastian?'

'Look, we *must* order,' says Suze. 'We'll come and say hello in a minute, Tory.'

'OK, ciao,' says Tory, and she sashays off.

'Suze!' cries another voice, and a girl in a little black dress comes rushing up. 'And Fenny!'

'Milla!' they both cry. 'How are you? How's Benjy?'

Oh, God, it just doesn't stop. Here I am, staring at the menu – pretending to be really interested in the starters but really feeling like some utter loser that no-one wants to talk to – while bloody Fenella and Tarquin are Socialites of the Year. It's not fair. *I* want to table-hop, too. *I* want to bump into old friends I've known since babyhood. (Although to be honest, the only person I've known that long is Tom from next door, and he'll be in his limed oak kitchen in Reigate.)

But just in case, I lower my menu and gaze hopefully around the restaurant. Please, God, just once, let there be someone I recognize. It doesn't have to be anyone I like, or even know that well – just someone I can rush up to and go mwah mwah and shriek 'We must do lunch!' *Anyone*'ll do. Anyone at all . . .

And then, with a disbelieving thrill, I spot a familiar face, a few tables away! It's Luke Brandon, sitting at a table with a smartly dressed older man and woman.

Well, he's not exactly an old friend – but I know him, don't I? And it's not as if I've got much choice. And I *so* want to table-hop like the others.

'Oh look, there's Luke!' I shriek (quietly, so he doesn't hear). 'I simply *must* go and say hello!'

As the others look at me in surprise, I toss my hair back, leap to my feet and hurry off, full of a sudden exhilaration. I can do it, too! I'm table-hopping at Terrazza. I'm an It-girl!

It's only when I get within a few feet of his table that I slow down and wonder what I'm actually going to say to him.

Well . . . I'll just be polite. Say hello and – ah, genius! I can thank him again for his kind loan of twenty quid.

Shit, I did pay him back, didn't I?

Yes. Yes, I sent him that nice recycled card with poppies on it and a cheque. That's right. Now don't panic, just be cool and It.

'Hi!' I say as soon as I get within earshot of his table,

but the hubbub around us is so loud, he doesn't hear me. No wonder all Fenella's friends have got such screechy voices. You need about sixty-five decibels, just to be heard. 'Hi!' I try again, louder, but still no response. Luke is talking earnestly to the older man, and the woman's listening intently. None of them even glances up.

This is getting a bit embarrassing. I'm standing, marooned, being utterly ignored by the person I want to table-hop with. Nobody else ever seems to have this problem. Why isn't he leaping up, shrieking, 'Have you *heard* about Foreland Investments?' It's not fair. What shall I do? Shall I just creep away? Shall I pretend I was heading towards the Ladies?

A waiter barges past me with a tray, and I'm pushed helplessly forward, towards Luke's table – and at that moment, he looks up. He stares at me blankly as though he doesn't even know who I am, and I feel my stomach give a little flip of dismay. But I've got to go through with it now.

'Hi, Luke!' I say brightly. 'I just thought I'd say . . . hello!'

'Well, hello,' he says after a pause. 'Mum, Dad, this is Rebecca Bloomwood. Rebecca – my parents.'

Oh God. What have I done? I've table-hopped an intimate family gathering. Leave, quick.

'Hello,' I say, and give a feeble smile. 'Well, I won't keep you from—'

'So how do you know Luke?' enquires Mrs Brandon.

'Rebecca is a leading financial journalist,' says Luke, taking a sip of wine. (Is that really what he thinks? Cor, I must drop that into a conversation with Clare Edwards. And Philip, come to that.)

I grin confidently at Mr Brandon, feeling like a mover and a shaker. I'm a leading financial journalist hobnobbing with a leading entrepreneur at a leading London restaurant. How cool is that?

'Financial journalist, eh?' grunts Mr Brandon, and lowers his reading glasses to have a better look at me.

'So what do *you* think of the Chancellor's announcement?'

I'm never going to table-hop again. Never.

'Well,' I begin confidently, wondering if I could suddenly pretend to spot an old friend across the room.

'Dad, I'm sure Rebecca doesn't want to talk shop,' says Luke, frowning slightly.

'Quite right!' says Mrs Brandon, and smiles at me. 'That's a lovely scarf, Rebecca. Is it Denny and George?'

'Yes, it is!' I say brightly, full of relief at escaping the Chancellor's announcement. (What announcement?) 'I was so pleased, I got it last week in the sale!'

Out of the corner of my eye, I can see that Luke Brandon is staring at me with an odd expression. Why? Why is he looking so—

Oh fuck. How can I be so *stupid*?

'In the sale . . . for my aunt,' I continue, trying to think as quickly as I can. 'I bought it for my aunt, as a present. But she . . . died.'

There's a shocked silence and I look down. I can't quite believe what I've just said.

'Oh dear,' says Mr Brandon gruffly.

'Aunt Ermintrude died?' says Luke in a strange voice.

'Yes,' I reply, forcing myself to look up. 'It was terribly sad.'

'How awful!' says Mrs Brandon sympathetically.

'She was in hospital, wasn't she?' says Luke, pouring himself a glass of water. 'What was wrong with her?'

For an instant I'm silenced.

'It was . . . her leg,' I hear myself say.

'Her leg?' Mrs Brandon's staring at me anxiously. 'What was wrong with her leg?'

'It . . . swelled up and got septic,' I say after a pause. 'And they had to amputate it and then she died.'

'Christ,' says Mr Brandon, shaking his head. 'Bloody doctors.' He gives me a suddenly fierce look. 'Did she go private?'

'Ummm . . . I'm not sure,' I say, starting to back away. I can't take any more of this. Why didn't I just say she *gave* me the bloody scarf? 'Anyway, lovely to see you, Luke. Must dash, my friends will be missing me!'

I give a nonchalant kind of wave without quite looking Luke in the eye and then quickly turn round and walk back to Suze, my heart beating fast and my face flaming red. God, what a fiasco.

But I've managed to recompose myself by the time our food arrives. The food! I've ordered grilled scallops and as I take my first bite, I nearly swoon. After so many torturous days of cheap, functional food, this is like going to heaven. I feel almost tearful – like a prisoner returning to the real world, or children after the war, when rationing stopped. After my scallops I have steak *béarnaise* and chips – and when all the others say 'no thanks' to the pudding menu, I order chocolate mousse. Because who knows when I'm next going to be in a restaurant like this? There could be months ahead of cheese sandwiches and home-made coffee in a flask, with nothing to relieve the monotony.

It's a hard road, the one I've chosen. But it'll be worth it in the end.

While I'm waiting for my chocolate mousse, Suze and Fenella decide they simply must go and talk to Benjy, on the other side of the room. So they leap up, both lighting cigarettes as they do so, and Tarquin stays behind to keep me company. He doesn't seem quite as into table-hopping as the others. In fact, he's been pretty quiet all evening. I've also noticed that he's drunk more than any of us. Any moment I'm expecting his head to land on the table. Which would be fine by me.

For a while there's silence between us. To be honest, Tarquin is so weird, I don't feel any duty to talk to him. Then, suddenly, he says,

'Do you like Wagner?'

'Oh yes,' I say at once. I'm not sure I've ever heard any Wagner, but I don't want to sound uncultured, even in front of Tarquin. And I have been to the opera before – though I think that was Mozart.

'The Liebestod from *Tristan*,' he says, and shakes his head. 'The Liebestod.'

'Mmm,' I say, and nod in what I hope is an intelligent manner. I pour myself some wine, fill his glass up too, and look around to see where Suze has got to. Typical of her just to disappear off and leave me with her drunken cousin.

'Dah-dah-*dah*-dah, daaaah dah dah . . .'

Oh my God, he's singing. Not loudly, admittedly – but really intensely. And he's staring into my eyes as though he expects me to join in.

'Dah-dah-*dah*-dah . . .'

Now he's closed his eyes and is swaying. This is getting embarrassing.

'Da diddle-idy da-a-da-a daaaah dah . . .'

'Lovely,' I say brightly. 'You can't beat Wagner, can you?'

'*Tristan*,' he says. '*Und Isolde*.' He opens his eyes. 'You'd make a beautiful Isolde.'

I'd make a *what*? While I'm still staring at him, he lifts my hand to his lips and starts kissing it. For a few seconds I'm too shocked to move.

'Tarquin,' I say as firmly as I can, trying to pull my hand away. 'Tarquin, please . . .' I look up and desperately scan the room for Suze – and as I do so, meet the eye of Luke Brandon, making his way out of the restaurant. He frowns slightly, lifts his hand in farewell, then disappears out of the door.

'Your skin smells like roses,' murmurs Tarquin against my skin.

'Oh shut up!' I say crossly, and yank my hand out of his grasp so hard I get a row of teeth marks on my skin. 'Just leave me alone!'

I would slap him, but he'd probably take it as a come-on.

Just then, Suze and Fenella arrive back at the table, full of news about Binky and Minky – and Tarquin relapses into silence. For the rest of the evening, even when we say goodbye, he barely looks at me. Thank God. He must have got the message.

Seven

It doesn't seem he has, though, because on Saturday I receive a card of a Pre-Raphaelite girl looking coyly over her shoulder. Inside, Tarquin has written:

Many apologies for my uncouth behaviour. I hope to make it up to you. Tickets to Bayreuth – or, failing that, dinner?
Tarquin

Dinner with Tarquin. Can you imagine? Sitting opposite that stoaty head all evening. And what's he going on about, anyway? I've never heard of Bayreuth. Is it a new show or something? Or does he mean Beirut? Why would we want to go to Beirut, for God's sake?

Anyway, never mind, forget Tarquin. I've got more important things to think about today. This is my sixth day of Cutting Back – and, crucially, my first weekend. David E. Barton says this is often when one's frugal regime cracks, as the office routine is no longer there as a distraction and the day stretches empty, waiting to be filled with the familiar comfort of shopping.

But I'm too strong-willed to crack. I've got my day completely sussed – and I'm not going *near* any shops. This morning I'm going to visit a museum and then tonight, instead of wasting lots of money on an expensive takeaway, I'm cooking a home-made curry for me and Suze. I'm actually quite excited about it.

My entire budget for today is as follows:

Travel to museum:	free (I already have a travelcard)
Museum:	free
Curry:	£2.50. (David E. Barton says you can make a wonderful curry for four people for less than £5.00 — and there are only two of us).
Total daily expenditure:	£2.50

That's more like it. Plus I get to experience Culture instead of mindless materialism. I have chosen the Victoria & Albert Museum because I have never been to it before. In fact, I'm not even sure what they have in it. Statues of Queen Victoria and Prince Albert, or something?

Anyway whatever they have, it will be very interesting and stimulating, I'm sure. And above all, free!

As I come out of South Kensington tube, the sun's shining brightly and I stride along, feeling pleased with myself. Normally I waste my Saturday mornings watching *Live and Kicking* and getting ready to go to the shops. But look at this! I suddenly feel very grown-up and metropolitan, like someone in a Woody Allen film. I just need a long woolly scarf and some sunglasses and I'll look like Diane Keaton. (A young Diane Keaton, obviously, but without the seventies clothes.)

And on Monday, when people ask me how my weekend was, I'll be able to say, 'Actually, I went to the V&A.' No, what I'll say is, 'I caught an exhibition.' That sounds much cooler. (Why *do* people say they 'caught' an exhibition, by the way? It's not as though all the paintings were thundering past like bulls at Pamplona.) Then they'll say, 'Really? I didn't know you were into art, Rebecca.' And I'll say, smugly, 'Oh yes. I spend most of my free time at museums.' And they'll give me an impressed look and say . . .

Come to think of it, I've walked straight past the entrance. Silly me. Too busy thinking about the conversation between me and . . . actually, the person I realize I've pictured in this little scene is Luke Brandon. How weird. Why should that be? Because I table-hopped with him, I suppose. Anyway. Concentrate. Museum.

Quickly I retrace my steps and walk nonchalantly into the entrance hall, trying to look as though I come here all the time. Not like that bunch of Japanese tourists clustering round their guide. Ha! I think proudly, I'm no tourist. This is my heritage. *My* culture. I pick up a map carelessly as though I don't really need it, and look at a list of talks on things like 'Ceramics of the Yuan and Early Ming Dynasties.' Then, casually, I begin to walk through to the first gallery.

'Excuse me?' A woman at a desk is calling to me. 'Have you paid?'

Have I *what*? You don't have to pay to get into museums! Oh of course – she's just joking with me. I give a friendly little laugh, and carry on.

'Excuse me!' she says, in a sharper voice, and a bloke in security uniform appears out of nowhere. 'Have you paid for admission?'

'It's free!' I say in surprise.

'I'm afraid not,' she says, and points to a sign behind me. I turn to read it, and nearly keel over in astonishment.

Admission £5.00.

I feel quite faint with shock. What's happened to the world? They're *charging* for admission to a museum. This is outrageous. Everyone knows museums are supposed to be free. If you start charging for museums, no-one will ever go! Our cultural heritage will be lost to a whole generation, excluded by a punitive financial barrier. The nation will be dumbed down still further, and civilized society will face the very brink of collapse. Is that what you want, Tony Blair?

Plus, I don't have £5. I deliberately came out with no cash except £2.50 for my curry ingredients. Oh God, this is annoying. I mean, here I am, all ready for some culture. I *want* to go in and look at . . . well, whatever's in there – and I can't!

Now all the Japanese tourists are staring at me, as if I'm some sort of criminal. Go away! I think crossly. Go and look at some art.

'We take credit cards,' says the woman. 'VISA, Switch, American Express.

'Oh,' I say. 'Well . . .OK.'

'The season ticket is £15,' she says, as I reach for my purse, 'but it gives you unlimited access for a year.'

Unlimited access for a year! Now wait just a minute. David E. Barton says what you're supposed to do, when you make any purchase, is estimate the 'cost per use', which you get by dividing the price by the number of times you use it. Let's suppose that from now on I come to the V&A once a month. (I should think that's quite realistic.) If I buy a season ticket, that's only . . . £1.25 a visit.

Well, that's a bargain, isn't it? It's actually a very good investment, when you come to think of it.

'OK, I'll have the season ticket,' I say, and hand over my VISA card. Hah! Culture, here I come.

I start off really well. I look at my little map, and peer at each exhibit, and carefully read all the little cards.

Chalice made from silver, Dutch, 16th century
Plaque depicting Holy Trinity. Italian mid-15th century
Blue and white earthenware bowl, early 17th century

That bowl's really nice, I find myself thinking in sudden interest, and wonder how much it is. It looks quite expensive . . . I'm just peering to see if there's a price tag when I remember where I am. Of course. This isn't a shop. There aren't any prices here.

Which is a bit of a mistake, I think. Because it kind of takes the fun out of it, doesn't it? You wander round, just looking at things, and it all gets a bit boring after a while. Whereas if they put price tags on, you'd be far more interested. In fact, I think all museums should put prices on their exhibits. You'd look at a silver chalice or a marble statue or the *Mona Lisa* or whatever, and admire it for its beauty and historical importance and everything – and then you'd reach for the price tag and gasp, 'Hey, look how much this one is!' It would really liven things up.

I might write to the Victoria & Albert and suggest this to them. I am a season-ticket holder after all. They should listen to my opinion.

In the meantime, let's move on to the next glass case.

Carved goblet English, mid-15th century

God, I could die for a cup of coffee. How long have I been here? It must be . . .

Oh. Only fifteen minutes.

When I get to the gallery showing a history of fashion, I become quite rigorous and scholarly. In fact I spend longer there than anywhere else. But then the dresses and shoes come to an end and it's back to more statues and little fiddly things in cases. I keep looking at my watch, and my feet hurt . . . and in the end I sink down onto a sofa.

Don't get me wrong, I like museums. I do. And I'm really interested in Korean art. It's just that the floors are really hard, and I'm wearing quite tight boots, and it's hot so I've taken off my jacket but now it keeps slithering around in my arms. And it's weird, but I keep thinking I can hear the sound of a cash till. It must be in my imagination.

I'm sitting blankly, wondering if I can summon the energy to stand up again – when the group of Japanese

98

tourists comes into the gallery, and I feel compelled to get to my feet and pretend I'm looking at something. I peer vaguely at a piece of tapestry, then stride off down a corridor lined with exhibits of old Indian tiles. I'm just thinking that maybe we should get the Fired Earth catalogue and re-tile the bathroom, when I glimpse something through a metal grille and stop dead with shock.

Am I dreaming? Is it a mirage? I can see a cash register, and a queue of people, and a display cabinet with price tags . . .

Oh my God, I was right! It's a shop! There's a *shop*, right here in front of me!

Suddenly my steps have more spring in them; my energy has miraculously returned. Following the bleeping sound of the cash register, I hurry round the corner to the shop entrance, and pause on the threshold, telling myself not to raise my hopes; not to be disappointed if it's just bookmarks and tea towels.

But it's not. It's bloody fantastic! Why isn't this place better known? There's a whole range of gorgeous jewellery, and loads of really interesting books on art, and there's all this amazing pottery, and greetings cards, and . . .

Oh. But I'm not supposed to be buying anything today, am I? Damn.

This is awful. What's the point of discovering a new shop and then not being able to buy anything in it? It's not fair. Everyone else is buying stuff, everyone else is having fun. For a while I hover disconsolately beside a display of mugs, watching as an Australian woman buys a pile of books on sculpture. She's chatting away to the sales assistant, and suddenly I hear her say something about Christmas. And then I have a flash of pure genius.

Christmas shopping! I can do all my Christmas shopping here! I know March is a bit early – but why not be organized? And then when Christmas arrives I won't have to go near the horrible Christmas crowds. I can't believe I haven't thought of doing this before. And it's not breaking the rules – because I'd have to buy Christmas presents *some time*, wouldn't I? All I'm doing is shifting the buying process forward a bit. It makes perfect sense.

And so, about an hour later, I emerge happily with two carrier bags. I've bought a photograph album covered in William Morris print, an old-fashioned wooden jigsaw puzzle, a book of fashion photographs and a fantastic ceramic teapot. God, I *love* Christmas shopping. I'm not sure what I'll give to who – but the point is, these are all timeless and unique items that would enhance any home. (Or at least the ceramic teapot is, because that's what it said on the little leaflet.) So I reckon I've done really well.

In fact, this morning has been a great success. As I emerge from the exit of the museum, I feel incredibly content and uplifted. It just shows the effect that a morning of pure culture has on the soul. From now on, I decide, I'm going to spend every Saturday morning at a museum.

When I get back home, the second post is on the doormat and there's a square envelope addressed to me in writing I don't recognize. I rip it open as I lug my carrier bags to my room – and then stop in surprise. It's a card from Luke Brandon. How did he get my home address?

> *Dear Rebecca*, it says, *It was good to bump into you the other night, and I do hope you had an enjoyable evening. I now realize that I never thanked you for the prompt repayment of my loan. Much appreciated.*
> *With all best wishes – and, of course, deepest sympathy on the loss of your Aunt Ermintrude. (If it's any consolation, I can't imagine that scarf could suit anyone better than you.)*
> *Luke*

For a while I stare at it silently. I'm quite taken aback. Gosh, I think cautiously. It's nice of him to write, isn't it? A nice handwritten card like this, just to thank me for *my* card. I mean he didn't have to; he's not just being polite, is he? You don't have to send a thank-you card to someone just because they repaid your twenty quid.

Or do you? Maybe, these days, you do. Everyone seems to send cards for everything. I haven't got a clue what's done and what's not any more. (I *knew* I should have read that etiquette book I got in my stocking.) Is this card just a polite thank-you? Or is it something else? And if so . . . what?

Is he taking the piss?

Oh God, that's it. He knows Aunt Ermintrude doesn't exist. He's just pulling my leg to embarrass me.

But then . . . would he go to all the trouble of buying a card, writing in it and sending it, just to pull my leg?

Oh, I don't know. Who cares? I don't even like him, anyway.

Having been so cultured all morning, I deserve a bit of a treat in the afternoon, so I buy myself *Vogue* and a bag of Minstrels, and lie on the sofa for a bit. God, I've missed little treats like this. I haven't read a magazine for . . . well, it must be a week, except Suze's copy of *Harpers & Queen* yesterday. And I can't *remember* the last time I tasted chocolate.

But I can't spend too long enjoying myself, because I've got to go out and buy the stuff for our home-made curry. So after I've read my horoscope, I close *Vogue* and get out my new Indian recipe book. I'm quite excited, actually. I've never made curry before.

I've gone off the Tiger prawn recipe because it turns out Tiger prawns are very expensive. So what I'm going to make instead is chicken and mushroom balti. It all looks very cheap and easy, and I just need to write out my shopping list.

When I've finished I'm a bit taken aback. The list is

quite a lot longer than I'd thought it would be. I hadn't realized you needed so many spices just to make one curry. I've just looked in the kitchen, and we don't have a balti pan, or a grinder for grinding spices, or a blender for making the aromatic paste. Or a wooden spoon or any scales that work.

Still, never mind. What I'll do is quickly go to Peter Jones and buy all the equipment we need for the kitchen, and then I'll get the food and come back and start cooking. The thing to remember is, we only have to buy all this stuff once – and then we're fully equipped to make delicious curries every night. I'll just have to think of it as an investment.

By the time Suze arrives back from Camden Market that evening, I am dressed in my new stripy apron, grinding up roasted spices in our new grinder.

'Phew!' she says, coming into the kitchen. 'What a stink!'

'It's aromatic spices,' I say a bit crossly, and take a swig of wine. To be honest, this is all a bit more difficult than I'd thought. I'm trying to make something called balti masala mix, which we will be able to keep in a jar and use for months, but all the spices seem to be disappearing into the grinder and refusing to come back out. Where are they going?

'I'm absolutely starving,' says Suze, pouring herself a glass of wine. 'Will it be ready soon?'

'I don't know,' I say through clenched teeth, peering into the grinder. 'If I can just get these bloody spices out . . .'

'Oh well,' says Suze. 'I might just make some toast.' She pops a couple of pieces of bread in the toaster and then starts picking up all my little bags and pots of spices and looking at them.

'What's allspice?' she says, holding up a pot curiously. 'Is it all the spices, mixed together?'

'I don't know,' I say, banging the grinder on the counter. A tiny dusting of powder falls out and I stare at it angrily. What happened to a whole jarful that I could keep for months? Now I'll have to roast some more of the bloody things.

'Because if it is, couldn't you just use that and forget all the others?'

'No!' I say crossly. 'I'm making a fresh and distinct balti blend. OK?'

'OK,' says Suze, shrugging. 'You're the expert.'

Right, I think, taking another swig of wine. Start again. Coriander seeds, fennel seeds, cumin seeds, peppercorns . . . By this time, I've given up measuring, I'm just throwing everything in. They say cooking should be instinctive, anyway.

'What's this?' says Suze, looking at Luke Brandon's card on the kitchen table. 'Luke Brandon? How come he sent you a card?'

'Oh, you know,' I say, shrugging casually. 'He was just being polite.'

'Polite?' Suze wrinkles her brow, turning the card over in her hands. 'No way. You don't have to send a card to someone just because they returned your twenty quid.'

'Really?' My voice is slightly higher than usual – but that must be because of the roasting aromatic spices. 'I thought maybe that's what people did these days.'

'Oh no,' says Suze assuredly. 'What happens is, the money's lent, it's returned with a thank-you letter, and that's the end of the matter. This card – ' she waves it at me 'this – is something extra.'

This is why I love sharing a flat with Suze. She knows stuff like this, because she mixes in the right social circles. You know she once had dinner with the Duchess of Kent? Not that I'm boasting, or anything.

'So what do you think it means?' I say, trying not to sound too tense.

'I reckon he's being friendly,' she says, and puts the card back on the table.

Friendly. Of course, that's it. He's being friendly. Which is a good thing, of course. So why do I feel ever so slightly disappointed? I stare at the card, which has a face by Picasso on the front. What does that mean?

'Are those spices supposed to be going black, by the way?' says Suze, spreading peanut butter on her toast.

'Oh God!' I whip the balti pan off the stove and look at the blackened coriander seeds. This is driving me crazy. OK, tip them away and start again. Coriander seeds, fennel seeds, cumin seeds, peppercorns, bay leaves. That's the last of the bay leaves. This one had better not go wrong.

Somehow, miraculously it doesn't. Forty minutes later I actually have a curry bubbling away in my balti pan! This is fantastic! It smells wonderful, and it looks just like it does in the book – and I didn't even follow the recipe very carefully. It just shows, I have a natural affinity with Indian cookery. And the more I practise, the more accomplished I'll become. Like David E. Barton says, I'll be able to knock up a quick, delicious curry in the time it takes to call the delivery firm. And look how much money I've saved!

Triumphantly, I drain my basmati rice, take my ready-made naan breads out of the oven, and serve everything out onto plates. Then I sprinkle chopped fresh coriander over everything – and honestly, it looks like something out of *Marie-Claire*. I carry the plates through and put one in front of Suze.

'Wow!' she says. 'This looks fantastic!'

'I know,' I say proudly, sitting down opposite her. 'Isn't it great?'

I watch as she takes her first forkful – then put a forkful into my own mouth.

'Mmm! Delicious!' says Suze, chewing in relish. 'Quite hot,' she adds, after a while.

'It's got chilli powder in,' I say. 'And fresh chillies. But it's nice, though, isn't it?'

'It's wonderful!' says Suze. 'Bex, you're so clever! I could never make this in a million years!'

But as she's chewing, a slightly strange expression is coming over her face. To be honest, I'm feeling a bit breathless, too. This curry *is* quite hot. In fact it's bloody hot.

Suze has put down her plate and is taking a large slug of wine. She looks up, and I see her cheeks are red.

'OK?' I say, forcing myself to smile through the pain in my mouth.

'Yeah, great!' she says, and takes a huge bite of naan bread. I look down at my plate and resolutely take another forkful of curry. Immediately, my nose starts to run. Suze is sniffing too, I notice, but as I meet her eye she smiles brightly.

Oh God, this is hot. My mouth can't stand it. My cheeks are burning, and my eyes are starting to water. How much chilli powder did I put in this bloody thing? Only about one teaspoonful . . . or maybe it was two. I just kind of trusted my instincts and chucked in what looked about right. Well – so much for my instincts.

Tears start running down my face, and I give an enormous sniff.

'Are you OK?' says Suze in alarm.

'I'm fine!' I say, putting down my fork. 'Just . . . you know. A bit hot.'

But actually, I'm not OK. And it's not just the heat that's making tears run down my face. Suddenly I feel like a complete failure. I can't even get a quick and easy curry right. And look how much money I spent on it, with the balti pan and the apron and all the spices . . . Oh, it's all gone wrong, hasn't it? I haven't Cut Back at all. This week's been a complete disaster.

I give a huge sob, and put my plate on the floor.

'It's horrible!' I say miserably, and tears begin to stream down my face. 'Don't eat it, Suze. It'll poison you.'

'Bex! Don't be silly!' says Suze. 'It's fantastic!' She looks at me, then puts her own plate on the floor. 'Oh

105

Bex.' She shuffles across the floor, reaches up and gives me a hug. 'Don't worry. It's just a bit hot. But otherwise, it's brilliant! And the naan bread is delicious! Honestly. Don't get upset.'

I open my mouth to reply, and instead hear myself giving another huge sob.

'Bex, don't!' wails Suze, practically crying herself. 'It's delicious! It's the most delicious curry I've ever tasted.'

'It's not just the curry!' I sob, wiping my eyes. 'The point was, I was supposed to be Cutting Back. This curry was only supposed to cost £2.50.'

'But . . . why?' asks Suze perplexedly. 'Was it a bet, or something?'

'No!' I wail. 'It was because I'm in debt! And my dad said I should Cut Back or Make More Money. So I've been trying to Cut Back, but it hasn't worked . . .' I break off, shuddering with sobs. 'I'm just a complete failure.'

'Of course you're not a failure!' says Suze at once. 'Bex, you're the opposite of a failure. It's just . . .' She hesitates. 'It's just that maybe . . .'

'What?'

There's silence, then Suze says seriously, 'I think you might have chosen the wrong option, Becky. I don't think you're a Cut Back kind of person.'

'Really?' I sniff, and wipe my eyes. 'Do you think?'

'I think you should go for Make More Money instead.' Suze pauses thoughtfully. 'In fact, to be honest, I don't know why anyone would choose Cut Back. I think Make More Money is a *much* better option. If I ever had to choose, that's definitely the one I'd go for.'

'Yes,' I say slowly. 'Yes, maybe you're right. Maybe that's what I should do.' I reach down with a shaky hand and take a bite of warm naan bread – and Suze is right. Without the curry, it's delicious. 'But how shall I do it?' I say eventually. 'How shall I make more money?'

There is silence for a while, with both of us thoughtfully chewing on naan bread. Then Suze brightens.

'I know. Look at this!' She reaches for a magazine and flips to the classified ads at the back. 'Look what it says here. "Need extra money? Join the Fine Frames family. Make thousands, working from home in your spare time. Full kit supplied." You see? It's easy.'

Wow. I'm quite impressed, in spite of myself. Thousands. That's not bad.

'Yes,' I say shakily. 'Maybe I'll do that.'

'Or you could invent something,' says Suze.

'Like what?'

'Oh, anything,' she says confidently. 'You're really clever. You could think of something. Or . . . I know! Set up an Internet company. They're worth millions!'

You know, she's right. There's loads of things I could do to Make More Money. Loads of things! It's just a question of lateral thinking. Suddenly I feel a lot better. God, Suze is a good friend. I reach forward and give her a hug.

'Thanks, Suze,' I say. 'You're a star.'

'No problem,' she says, and hugs me back. 'So, you cut out this ad and start making your thousands . . .' She pauses. 'And I'll go and phone up for a takeaway curry, shall I?'

'Yes please,' I say in a small voice. 'A takeaway would be lovely.'

REBECCA BLOOMWOOD'S CUT-BACK PROJECT

HOME-MADE CURRY, SATURDAY 11 MARCH

PROPOSED BUDGET: £2.50

ACTUAL EXPENDITURE:

Balti pan	£15.00
Electric grinder	£14.99
Blender	£18.99
Wooden spoon	35p
Apron	£9.99
Two chicken breasts	£1.98
300g mushrooms	79p
Onion	29p
Coriander seeds	£1.29
Fennel seeds	£1.29
Allspice	£1.29
Cumin seeds	£1.29
Cloves	£1.39
Ground ginger	£1.95
Bay leaves	£1.40
Chilli powder	

OH GOD, FORGET IT.

PGNI First Bank Visa
7 Camel Square
Liverpool L1 5NP

Ms Rebecca Bloomwood
Flat 2
4 Burney Rd
London SW6 8FD

10 March 2000

Dear Ms Bloomwood

PGNI First Bank VISA Card No. 1475839204847586

Thank you for your letter of 3 March.

I can assure you that our computers are regularly checked, and that the possibility of a 'glitch', as you put it, is remote. Nor have we been affected by the Millennium bug. All accounts are entirely accurate.

You may write to Anne Robinson at *Watchdog* if you wish, but I am sure she will agree that you have no grounds for complaint.

Our records inform us that payment on your VISA account is now overdue. As you will see from your most recent VISA card statement, the minimum payment required is £105.40. I look forward to receiving your payment, as soon as possible.

Yours sincerely

Peter Johnson
Customer Accounts Executive

Eight

OK, so perhaps the Cutting Back didn't go that well. But it doesn't matter, because that's all in the past. That was negative thinking – now I'm seriously into positive thinking. Onward and upward. Growth and prosperity. M. M. M. It's the obvious solution, when you think about it. And you know what? Suze is absolutely right. Making More Money suits my personality far better than Cutting Back did. In fact, I'm already feeling much happier. Just the fact that I don't have to make any more grotty cheese sandwiches, or go to any more museums, has lifted a huge weight off my soul. And I'm allowed to buy all the cappuccinos I like, and start looking in shop windows again. Oh, the relief! I've even chucked *Controlling Your Cash* in the bin. I never did think it was any good.

The only small thing – tiny niggle – is I'm not quite sure how I'm going to do it. Make More Money, I mean. But now I've decided to go ahead with it, something will turn up. I'm sure of it.

When I get into work on Monday, Clare Edwards is already at her desk – surprise – and on the phone.

'Yes,' she's saying softly. 'I suppose the only answer is to plan ahead. Yes.'

When she sees me, to my surprise she blushes a faint pink and turns away slightly. 'Yes, I understand,' she whispers, scribbling in her notepad. 'And how has . . . response been so far?'

God knows why she's being so secretive. As if I'm interested in her tedious life. I sit down at my desk, briskly flip on my computer and open my diary. Oh

110

goody, I've got a press conference in the City. Even if it is some boring old pensions launch, at least it means a trip out of the office and, with any luck, a nice glass of champagne. Work can be quite fun, sometimes. And Philip isn't in yet, which means we can sit and gossip for a while.

'So, Clare,' I say, as she puts the phone down, 'how was your weekend?'

I look over, expecting to hear the usual thrilling account of what shelf she put up where with her boyfriend – but Clare doesn't even seem to have heard what I said.

'Clare?' I say, puzzled. She's staring at me with pink cheeks, as though I've caught her stealing pens from the stationery cupboard.

'Listen,' she says in a rush. 'That conversation you heard me having just now . . . could you not mention it to Philip?'

I stare at her in bemusement. What's she talking about? Oh wow – is she having an affair? But then, why should Philip care? He's her editor, not her—

Oh my God. She's not having an affair with *Philip*, is she?

'Clare, what's going on!' I say excitedly.

There's a long pause, as Clare blushes deep red. I can't believe this. A piece of office scandal at last! And involving Clare Edwards, of all people!

'Oh come on, Clare,' I whisper. 'You can tell me. I won't tell anyone.' I lean forward sympathetically. 'I might even be able to help.'

'Yes,' says Clare, rubbing her face. 'Yes, that's true. I could do with a bit of advice. The pressure's starting to get to me.'

'Start from the beginning,' I say calmly, just like an agony aunt. 'When did it all begin?'

'OK, I'll tell you,' whispers Clare, and looks nervously about. 'It was about . . . six months ago.'

'And what happened?'

'It all began on that Scottish press trip,' she says

slowly. 'I was away from home . . . I said yes without even thinking. I suppose I was flattered, more than anything else.'

'It's the old story,' I say wisely. God, I'm enjoying this.

'If Philip knew what I was doing, he'd go crazy,' she says despairingly. 'But it's just so easy. I use a different name – and no-one knows!'

'You use a different name?' I say, impressed, in spite of myself.

'Several,' she says, and gives a bitter little laugh. 'You've probably seen some of them around.' She exhales sharply. 'I know I'm taking a risk – but I can't stop. To be honest, you get used to the money.'

Money? Is she a *prostitute*?

'Clare, what exactly are you—'

'At first it was just a little piece on mortgages in the *Mail*,' she says, as though she hasn't heard me. 'I thought I could handle it. But then I was asked to do a full-length feature on life insurance in the *Sunday Times*. Then *Pension and Portfolio* got in on the act. And now it's about three articles every week. I have to do it all in secret, try to act normally . . .' She breaks off and shakes her head. 'Sometimes it gets me down. But I just can't say no any more. I'm hooked.'

I do not believe it. She's talking about work. Work! Only Clare Edwards could be such a disappointment. There I was, thinking she was having a steamy affair, ready to hear all the exciting details – and all the time it was just boring old . . .

Then something she's just said tweaks at my mind.

'Did you say the money was good?' I say casually.

'Oh yes,' she says. 'About three hundred quid a piece. That's how we could afford our flat.'

Three hundred quid!

Nine hundred quid a week! Bloody hell!

This is the answer. It's easy. I'll become a high-flying freelance journalist, just like Clare, and earn nine hundred quid a week. What I have to do is start networking and making contacts at events instead of always sitting at the back with Elly and giggling. I must shake hands firmly with all the finance editors of the nationals and wear my name badge prominently instead of putting it straight in my bag, and then phone them up discreetly when I get back to the office with ideas. And then I'll have £900 a week. Hah!

So when I arrive at the press conference, I pin my name badge on firmly, take a cup of coffee (no champagne – blast) and head towards Moira Channing of the *Daily Herald*.

'Hello,' I say, nodding in what I hope is a serious manner. 'Becky Bloomwood, *Successful Saving*.'

'Hello,' she says without interest, and turns back to the other woman in the group. 'So we had the second lot of builders back, and *really* read them the riot act.'

'Oh, Moira, you poor thing,' says the other woman. I squint at her badge and see that she's Lavinia Bellimore, Freelance. Well, there's no point impressing her – she's the competition.

Anyway, she doesn't give me a second glance. The two chat away about extensions and school fees, completely ignoring me – and after a bit I mutter, 'Good to meet you,' and creep away. God, I'd forgotten how unfriendly they are. Still, never mind. I'll just have to find someone else.

So after a bit I sidle up to a very tall guy on his own, and smile at him.

'Becky Bloomwood, *Successful Saving*,' I say.

'Geoffrey Norris, Freelance,' he says, and flashes his badge at me. Oh, for God's sake. The place is crawling with freelancers!

'Who do you write for?' I ask politely, thinking at least I might pick up some tips.

'It depends,' he says shiftily. His eyes keep darting backwards and forwards, and he's refusing to meet my eye. 'I used to be on *Monetary Matters*. But they sacked me.'

'Oh dear,' I say.

'They're bastards over there,' he says, and drains his coffee. 'Bastards! Don't go near them. That's my advice.'

'OK, I'll remember that!' I say brightly, edging away. 'Actually, I just have to . . .' And I turn, and walk quickly away. Why do I always find myself talking to weirdos?

Just then, a buzzer goes off, and people start to find their seats. Deliberately, I head for the second row, pick up the glossy brochure that's waiting for me on my seat, and take out my notebook. I wish I wore glasses; then I'd look even more serious. I'm just writing down Sacrum Asset Management Pension Fund Launch in capitals at the top of the page, when a man I've never seen before plonks himself down next to me. He's got dishevelled brown hair and smells of cigarettes, and is looking around with twinkling brown eyes.

'It's a joke, isn't it?' he murmurs, then meets my eye. 'All this gloss. All this show.' He gestures around. 'You don't fall for it, do you?'

Oh God. *Another* weirdo.

'Absolutely not,' I say politely and look for his name badge, but I can't see one.

'Glad to hear it,' says the man, and shakes his head. 'Bloody fat cats.' He gestures to the front, where three men in expensive suits are sitting down behind the table. 'You won't find *them* surviving on fifty quid a week, will you?'

'Well . . . no,' I say. 'More like fifty quid a minute.' The man gives an appreciative laugh.

'That's a good line. I might use that.' He extends his hand. 'Eric Foreman. *Daily World*.'

'*Daily World*?' I say, impressed in spite of myself. Gosh, the *Daily World*. I have to confess a little secret here – I really like the *Daily World*. I know it's only a tabloid, but it's so easy to read, especially if you're on a train. (My arms must be very weak or something, because holding *The Times* makes them ache after a while. And then all the pages get messed up. It's a

114

nightmare.) And some of the articles in the 'Female World' section are actually rather interesting.

But hang on – surely I've met the *Daily World*'s personal finance editor. Surely it's that drippy woman called Marjorie? So who's this guy?

'I haven't seen you around before,' I say casually. 'Are you new?'

Eric Foreman gives a chuckle.

'I've been on the paper for ten years. But this finance stuff isn't usually my scene.' He lowers his voice. 'I'm here to stir up a bit of trouble, as it goes. The editor's brought me on board for a new campaign we're running. "Can We Trust the Money Men?"'

He even *talks* in a tabloid voice.

'That sounds great,' I say politely.

'Could be, could be. As long as I can get past all this technical stuff.' He pulls a face. 'Never been good at figures.'

'I wouldn't worry,' I say kindly. 'You don't actually need to know very much. You'll soon pick up what's important.'

'Glad to hear it,' says Eric Foreman. He peers at my name badge. 'And you are . . .'

'Rebecca Bloomwood, *Successful Saving*,' I say, in my best networking manner.

'Glad to meet you, Rebecca,' he says, and fishes in his pocket for a business card.

'Oh, thanks,' I say, hastily reaching into my bag for my own business cards. Yes! I think triumphantly as I hand it over. I'm networking with the national newspapers! I'm swapping business cards!

Just then the microphones all come on with a screech of feedback, and a dark-haired girl at the podium clears her throat. Behind her is a lit-up screen, with the words SACRUM ASSET MANAGEMENT against a sunset.

I remember this girl now. She was really snotty to me at a press briefing last year. But Philip likes her, because she sends him a bottle of champagne every

115

Christmas, so I'll have to give this new pension plan a nice write-up.

'Ladies and gentlemen,' she says. 'My name is Maria Freeman, and I'm delighted to welcome you all to the launch of the Sacrum Asset Management Pension Series. This is an innovative range of products designed to combine flexibility and security with the powerful performance associated with Sacrum.'

A graph appears on the screen before us, with a wiggly red line rising and falling above a thinner black one.

'As Graph 1 shows,' says Maria Freeman confidently, pointing to the wiggly red line, 'our UK Enterprise Fund has consistently outperformed the rest of its particular sector.'

'Hmm,' murmurs Eric Foreman to me, frowning at his brochure. 'So, what's going on here, then? I heard a rumour that Sacrum Asset Management wasn't doing too well.' He jabs at the graph. 'But look at this. Outperforming the sector.'

'Yeah, right,' I murmur back. 'And what sector would that be? The Crap Investments Sector? The Lose All Your Money Sector?'

Eric Foreman looks at me and his mouth twists slightly.

'You think they've fiddled their figures?' he whispers.

'It's not exactly fiddling,' I explain. 'They just compare themselves to whoever's worse than themselves, and then call themselves the winners.' I point to the graph in the brochure. 'Look. They haven't actually specified what this so-called sector is.'

'Well blow me,' says Eric Foreman, and looks up at the Sacrum team sitting on the platform. 'They're canny bastards, aren't they?'

Really, this guy has no idea. I feel almost sorry for him.

Maria Freeman is droning on again, and I stifle a yawn. The trouble with sitting near the front is you have to pretend to look interested and be writing notes. 'Pensions,' I write, and draw a swirly line underneath.

Then I make the line into the stem of a vine and start drawing little bunches of grapes and leaves all the way along.

'In a moment I'll be introducing Mike Dillon, who heads up the investment team, and he'll be telling you a little about their methods. In the meantime, if there are any questions . . .'

'Yes,' says Eric Foreman. 'I've got a question.' I look up from my grapevine, slightly surprised.

'Oh yes?' Maria Freeman smiles sweetly at him. 'And you are . . .'

'Eric Foreman, *Daily World*. I'd like to know, how much do you all get paid?' He gestures with his hand along the table.

'What?' Maria Freeman turns pink – then regains her composure. 'Oh, you mean charges. Well, we'll be dealing with those . . .'

'I don't mean charges,' says Eric Foreman. 'I mean, how-much-do-you-get-paid? You, Mike Dillon.' He jabs at him with his finger. 'What are you on? Six figures, is it? And bearing in mind what a *disaster* the performance of Sacrum Asset Management was last year – shouldn't you be out on the streets?'

I'm absolutely gobsmacked. I've never seen anything like this at a press conference. Never!

There's a kerfuffle at the table, and then Mike Dillon leans forward towards his microphone.

'If we could get on with the presentation,' he says, 'and . . . and leave other questions for later.' He's looking decidedly uncomfortable.

'Just one more thing,' says Eric Foreman. 'What would you say to one of our readers who invested in your Safe Prospects plan and lost ten grand?' He glances briefly at me and winks. 'Show them a nice reassuring graph like that one, would you? Tell them you were "top of the sector?"'

Oh, this is fantastic! All the Sacrum people look like they want to die.

'A press release on the subject of Safe Prospects was

117

issued at the time,' says Maria and smiles icily at Eric. 'However, this press conference is restricted to the subject of the new pension series. If you could just wait until the presentation is over . . .'

'Don't worry,' says Eric Foreman comfortably. 'I won't be staying to hear the bullshit. I reckon I've got everything I need already.' He stands up and grins at me. 'Good to meet you, Rebecca,' he says. 'And thanks.' He extends his hand and I shake it, without quite knowing what I'm doing. And then, as everyone is turning in their seats and whispering, he makes his way along the row and out of the room.

'Ladies and gentlemen,' says Maria Freeman, two bright spots burning on her cheeks. 'Due to this . . . disturbance, we will have a short break before we resume. Please help yourself to tea and coffee. Thank you.' She turns off the microphone, climbs down from the podium and hurries over to the huddle of Sacrum Asset Management personnel.

'You should *never* have let him in!' I hear one of them saying.

'I didn't know who he was!' replies Maria defensively. 'He said he was a stringer for *Wall Street Journal*!'

Well, this is more like it! I haven't seen so much excitement since Alan Derring from the *Daily Investor* stood up at a Provident Assurance press conference and told everyone he was becoming a woman and wanted us all to call him Andrea.

I head towards the back to get another cup of coffee, and find Elly standing by the coffee table. Excellent. I haven't seen Elly for ages.

'Hi,' she grins. 'I like your new friend. Very entertaining.'

'I know!' I say delightedly. 'Isn't he cool?' I reach for a posh chocolate biscuit wrapped in gold foil, and give my cup to the waitress to be refilled. Then I take another couple of biscuits and pop them in my bag. (No point wasting them.)

Around us there is an excited buzz of conversation; the Sacrum people are still clustered at the front. This is great. We'll be able to natter for hours.

'So listen,' I say to Elly. 'Have you applied for any jobs recently?' I take a sip of coffee. 'Because I saw one for *New Woman* the other day in the *Media Guardian*, and I meant to ring you. It said it was essential to have experience on a consumer title, but I thought you could say—'

'Becky,' interrupts Elly in an odd voice, 'you know which job I've been going for.'

'What?' I stare at her. 'Not that fund manager job. But that wasn't serious. That was just a bargaining tool.'

'I took it,' she says, and I gaze at her in shock.

Suddenly a voice comes from the podium, and we both look up.

'Ladies and gentlemen,' Maria is saying. 'If you would like to resume your seats . . .'

I'm sorry, but I can't go and sit back down there. I *have* to hear about this.

'Come on,' I say quickly to Elly. 'We don't need to stay. We've got our press packs. Let's go and have lunch.'

There's a pause – and for an awful moment I think she's going to say No, she *wants* to stay and hear about personal pensions. But then she grins and takes my arm – and to the obvious dismay of the girl at the door, we waltz out of the room.

There's a Café Rouge around the corner, and we go straight in and order a bottle of white wine. I'm still in slight shock, to tell you the truth. Elly Granger is going to become a Wetherby's fund manager. She's deserting me. I won't have anyone to play with any more.

And how *can* she? She wanted to be beauty editor on *Marie-Claire*, for God's sake!

'So – what decided you?' I say cautiously as our wine arrives.

'Oh, I don't know,' she says, and sighs. 'I just kept thinking – where am I going? You know, I keep applying for all these glam jobs in journalism and never even getting an interview . . .'

'You would have got one eventually,' I say robustly. 'I know you would.'

'Maybe,' she says. 'Or maybe not. And in the meantime, I'm writing about all this boring financial stuff – and I suddenly thought, why not just sod it and *do* boring financial stuff? At least I'll have a proper career.'

'You were in a proper career!'

'No I wasn't, I was hopeless! I was paddling around with no aim, no game plan, no prospects—' Elly breaks off as she sees my face. 'I mean, I was quite different from you,' she adds hurriedly. 'You're much more sorted out than I was.'

Sorted out? Is she joking?

'So when do you start?' I say, to change the subject – because to be honest, I feel a bit thrown by all this. I don't have a game plan, I don't have prospects. Maybe I'm hopeless, too. Maybe I should rethink my career. Oh God, this is depressing. My job sounds so grand and exciting when I'm describing it to people like Martin and Janice next door. But now Elly's making me feel like a complete loser.

'Next week,' says Elly, and takes a swig of wine. 'I'm going to be based at the Silk Street office.'

'Oh, right,' I say miserably.

'And I've had to buy loads of new clothes,' she adds, and pulls a little face. 'They're all really smart at Wetherby's.'

New clothes? *New clothes?* Right, now I really am jealous.

'I went into Karen Millen and practically bought it out,' she says, eating a marinated olive. 'Spent about a thousand quid.'

'Blimey,' I say, feeling slightly awe-stricken. 'A thousand quid, all at once?'

'Well, I had to,' she says apologetically. 'And anyway, I'll be earning more now.'

'Really?'

'Oh yes,' she says, and gives a little laugh. 'Lots more.'

'Like . . . how much?' I ask, feeling tweaks of curiosity.

'I'm starting off on forty grand,' she says, and gives a careless shrug. 'After that, who knows? What they said is . . .'

And she starts talking about career structures and ladders and bonuses. But I can't hear a word, I'm too shell-shocked.

Forty grand?

Forty grand? But I only earn—

Actually, should I be telling you how much I earn? Isn't it one of those things like religion, you're not supposed to mention in polite company? Or maybe we're all allowed to talk about money these days. Suze would know.

Oh well, sod it. You know everything else, don't you? The truth is, I earn £21,000. And I thought that was a lot! I remember really well, when I moved jobs, I jumped from £18,000 to £21,000, and I thought I'd made the big time. I was so excited about it, I used to write out endless lists of what I would buy with all that extra money.

But now it sounds like nothing. I should be earning forty grand, like Elly, and buying all my clothes at Karen Millen. Oh, it's not fair. My life's a complete disaster.

As I'm walking back to the office, I feel pretty morose. Maybe I should give up journalism and become a fund manager too. Or a merchant banker. They earn a pretty good whack, don't they? Maybe I could join Goldman Sachs or somewhere. They earn about a million a year, don't they? God, that would be good. A million a year. I wonder how you get a job like that.

But on the other hand . . . do I really want to be a banker? I wouldn't mind the clothes-from-Karen-Millen part of it. In fact, I think I'd do that really well. But I'm not so sure about the rest. The getting-up-early-and-working-hideously-hard part. Not that I'm lazy or anything – but I quite like the fact that I can go and spend the afternoon at Image Store, or flick through the papers pretending to be doing research, and no-one gives me a hard time. It doesn't sound as if Elly will be doing much of that in her new job. In fact, it all sounds quite scary.

Hmm. If only there was some way that I could get all the nice clothes – but not have to do the scary work. One but not the other. If only there was a way . . . My eyes are automatically flicking into all the shop windows as I pass, checking out the displays – and suddenly I stop in my tracks.

This is a sign from God. It has to be.

I'm standing outside Ally Smith – which has some gorgeous full-length coats in the window – and there's a handwritten sign in the glass pane of the door. 'Wanted. Saturday sales assistants. Enquire within.'

I almost feel shaky as I stare at the sign. It's as though lightning has struck, or something. Why on *earth* haven't I thought of this before? It's pure genius. I'll get a Saturday job! I'll work in a clothes shop! That way, I'll make loads of extra money *and* I'll get a discount on all the clothes! And let's face it, working in a shop has got to be easier than becoming a fund manager, hasn't it? All you do is stand around and say 'Can I help you?' In fact, it'll be fun, because I can choose all my own clothes as I help the customers. I'll actually be getting *paid* to go shopping!

This is bloody fantastic, I think, striding into the shop with a friendly smile on my face. I *knew* something good was going to happen today. I just had a feeling about it.

* * *

Half an hour later, I come out with an even bigger smile on my face. I've got a job! I've got a Saturday job! I'm going to work from 8.30 to 5.30 every Saturday, and get £4.80 an hour, and 10 per cent off all the clothes! And after three months, it goes up to 20 per cent! All my money troubles are over.

Thank God it was a quiet afternoon. They let me fill in the application form on the spot, and Danielle, the manager, gave me an interview straight away. At first she looked a bit dubious – especially when I said I had a full-time job as a financial journalist and was doing this to get extra money and clothes. 'It'll be hard work,' she kept saying. 'You do realize that? It'll be very hard work.' But I think what changed her mind was when we started talking about the stock. I love Ally Smith stuff – so of course I knew the price of every single item in the shop and whether they have anything similar in Jigsaw or French Connection. Eventually Danielle gave me a funny look and said, 'Well, you obviously like clothes.' And then she gave me the job! I can't wait. I start this Saturday. Isn't it great?

As I arrive back at the office I feel exhilarated with my success. I look around – and suddenly this mundane office life seems far too boring and limited for a creative spirit like mine. I don't belong here, among fusty piles of press releases and grimly tapping computers. I belong out there, among the bright spotlights and cashmere cardigans of Ally Smith. Maybe I'll go into retail full time, I think, as I sit back down at my desk. Maybe I'll start my own chain of designer stores! God, yes. I'll be one of those people featured in articles about incredibly successful entrepreneurs. 'Becky Bloomwood was working as a financial journalist when she devised the innovative concept of Bloomwood Stores. Now a successful chain around the country, the idea came to her one day as she—'

The phone rings and I pick it up.

'Yes?' I say absently. 'Rebecca Bloomwood here.' I

nearly add, 'Of Bloomwood Stores', but maybe that's a tad premature.

'Ms Bloomwood, this is Derek Smeath from Endwich Bank.'

What? I'm so shocked, I drop the phone onto my desk with a clatter and have to scrabble around to pick it up. All the while, my heart's thumping like a rabbit. How does Derek Smeath know where I work? How did he get my number?

'Are you OK?' says Clare Edwards curiously.

'Yes,' I gulp. 'Yes, fine.'

And now she's looking at me. Now I can't just put the phone down and pretend it was a wrong number. I've got to talk to him. OK, what I'll do is be really brisk and cheerful and try and get rid of him as quickly as possible.

'Hi!' I say into the phone. 'Sorry about that! The thing is, I was just a bit busy with something else. You know how it is!'

'Ms Bloomwood, I've written you several letters,' says Derek Smeath. 'And to none of them have I had a satisfactory response.'

In spite of myself, I can feel my cheeks colouring. Oh God, he sounds really cross. This is horrible. What right has he got to come along and spoil my day?

'I've been very busy, I'm afraid,' I say. 'My . . . my aunt was very ill. I had to go and be with her. You understand.'

'I see,' he says. 'Nevetherless—'

'And then she died,' I add.

'I'm sorry to hear that,' says Derek Smeath. He doesn't *sound* sorry. 'But that doesn't alter the fact that your current account stands at a balance of . . .'

Has this man got no heart? As he starts talking about balances and overdrafts and agreements, I deliberately tune out so I don't hear anything that will upset me. I'm staring at the fake-wood grain on my desk, wondering if I could pretend to drop the receiver accidentally back down onto the phone. Oh God, this is awful. What am I going to do? *What am I going to do?*

'And if the situation is not resolved,' he's saying sternly, 'I'm afraid I will be forced to—'

'It's OK,' I hear myself interrupting. 'It's OK, because . . . I'm coming into some money soon.' Even as I say the words, I feel my cheeks flame guiltily. But I mean, what else am I supposed to do? I have to say *something*, otherwise he'll never leave me alone.

'Oh yes?'

'Yes,' I say, and swallow. 'The thing is, my . . . my aunt left me some money in her will.'

Which is kind of almost true. I mean, obviously Aunt Ermintrude would have left me some money. After all, I was her favourite niece, wasn't I? Did anyone else buy her Denny and George scarves? 'I'll get it in a couple of weeks,' I add, for good measure. 'A thousand pounds.'

Then I realize I should have made it £10,000 – that would have really impressed him. Oh well, too late now.

'You're saying that in two weeks' time you'll be paying a cheque for £1,000 into your account,' says Derek Smeath.

'Erm . . . yes,' I say after a pause. 'I suppose I am.'

'I'm glad to hear it,' he says. 'I've made a note of our conversation, Ms Bloomwood, and I'll be expecting the arrival of £1,000 into your account on Monday, 27 March.'

'Good,' I say boldly. 'Is that it?'

'For the moment. Goodbye, Ms Bloomwood.'

'Goodbye,' I say, and put the phone down.

Thank God. Got rid of him.

Brompton's Store

CUSTOMER ACCOUNTS
1 Brompton Street
London SW4 7TH

Ms Rebecca Bloomwood
Flat 2
4 Burney Rd
London SW6 8FD

10 March 2000

Dear Ms Bloomwood

Thank you for your prompt return of a signed cheque for £43.

Unfortunately, although this cheque is signed, it appears to be dated 14 February 2200. No doubt just an oversight on your part.

Brompton's Store cannot accept post-dated cheques as payment, and I am therefore returning it to you with the request that you return to us a signed cheque, dated with the date of signature.

Alternatively you can pay by cash or on the enclosed bank giro credit slip. A leaflet is enclosed for your information.

I look forward to receiving your payment.

Yours sincerely

John Hunter
Customer Accounts Manager

Nine

When I get home that night, there's a pile of post in the hall for me – but I ignore it because my package from Fine Frames has arrived! It cost me £100 to buy, which I suppose is quite expensive, but apparently it will give you a return of £300 in only a few hours. Inside the package there's a leaflet full of photographs of people who make fortunes from doing Fine Frames – and some of them make a hundred thousand a year! It makes me wonder what I'm doing, being a journalist.

So after supper, I sit down in front of *EastEnders* and open the kit. Suze is out tonight, so it's nice and easy to concentrate.

'Welcome to the best-kept secret in Britain . . .' says the leaflet. 'The Fine Frames home-working family! Join other members and earn £££ in the comfort of your own home. Our easy-to-follow instructions will aid you as you embark on the biggest money-making enterprise of your life. Perhaps you will use your earnings to buy a car, or a boat – or to treat someone special. And remember – the amount you earn is completely up to you!'

I'm utterly gripped. Why on earth haven't I done this before? This is a *fantastic* scheme! I'll work incredibly hard for two weeks, then pay off all my debts, go on holiday, buy loads of new clothes. God, I can't wait.

I start ripping at the packaging, and suddenly a pile of fabric strips falls onto the floor. Some are plain, and some are a flowered pattern. It's a pretty hideous pattern actually – but then, who cares? My job is just to make the frames and collect the money. I reach for the instructions and find them under a load of cardboard pieces. And sure enough, they're incredibly simple. What you have to do is glue wadding onto the cardboard frame, put the fabric over the top for that luxury upholstered effect, then glue braid along the back to hide the join. And that's it! It's completely simple and you get £2 a frame. There are 150 in the package – so if I do thirty a night for a week I'll have made three hundred quid just like that in my spare time!

OK, let's get started. Frame, wadding, glue, fabric, braid.

Oh God. Oh *God*. Who designed these bloody things? There just isn't enough fabric to fit over the frame and the wadding. Or at least you have to stretch it really hard – and it's such flimsy fabric, it rips. I've got glue on the carpet, and I've bent two of the cardboard frames from pulling them, and the only frame I've actually completed looks really wonky. And I've been doing it for . . .

I yawn, look at the time and feel a jolt of shock. It's 11.30, which means I've been working for three hours. And in that time I've made one dodgy-looking frame which I'm not sure they'll accept, and ruined two. I hate the sight of the bloody things. What do people want stupid upholstered photo frames for, anyway?

At that moment the door opens and Suze is back.

'Hi!' she says, coming into the sitting room. 'Nice evening?'

'Not really,' I begin disgruntledly. 'I've been making these things . . .'

'Well, never mind,' she says dramatically. 'Because guess what? You've got a secret admirer.'

'What?' I say, startled.

'Someone really likes you,' she says, taking off her coat. 'I heard it tonight. You'll never guess who!'

Luke Brandon pops into my mind before I can stop it. How ridiculous. And how would Suze have found

that out, anyway? Stupid idea. Very stupid.
Impossible.

She could have bumped into him at the cinema,
whispers my brain. She does know him after all,
doesn't she? And he could have said . . .

'It's my cousin!' she says triumphantly. 'Tarquin. He
really likes you.'

Oh for God's sake.

'He's got this secret little crush on you,' she continues happily. 'In fact, he's had one ever since he met
you!'

'It's not *that* secret . . .' I begin sarcastically – then,
as Suze looks up in surprise, I stop. After all, I don't
want to hurt her feelings.

'So you already know about it?' she says.

'Well,' I say and shrug. What can I say? I can't tell
her that her beloved cousin gives me the creeps. So
instead I start to pick at the fabric on the photo frame
in front of me, and a delighted smile spreads over
Suze's face.

'He's really keen on you!' she says. 'I said he should
just ring you and ask you out. You wouldn't mind,
would you?'

'Of course not,' I say feebly.

'Wouldn't that be great?' said Suze. 'If you two got
married. I could be bridesmaid!'

'Yes,' I say, and force myself to smile brightly.
'Lovely.'

What I'll do, I think, is agree to a date just to be
polite – and then cancel at the last moment. And hopefully Tarquin'll have to go back to Scotland or
something, and we can forget all about it.

But to be honest, I could really do without it. Now
I've got two reasons to dread the phone ringing.

However, to my relief, Saturday arrives and I haven't
heard a word from Tarquin. *Or* Derek Smeath.
Everyone's finally leaving me alone to get on with my
life!

On the slightly more negative side, I was planning to make 150 frames this week – but so far I've only made three, and none of them looks like the one in the picture. One doesn't have enough wadding in it, one doesn't quite meet at the corner, and the third has got a smear of glue on the front, which hasn't come off. I just can't understand why I'm finding it so difficult. Some people make hundreds of these things every week, without any effort. Mrs S. of Ruislip even takes her family on a cruise every year on her earnings. How come they can do it and I can't? It's really depressing. I mean, I'm supposed to be bright, aren't I? I've got a degree, for God's sake.

Still, never mind, I tell myself. It's my new job at Ally Smith today – so at least I'll be earning some extra money there.

I'm quite excited about it. Here starts a whole new career in fashion! I spend a long time choosing a cool outfit to wear on my first day – and eventually settle on black trousers from Jigsaw, a little cashmere (well, half cashmere) T-shirt and a pink wrap-around top which actually came from Ally Smith.

I'm quite pleased with the way I look, and am expecting Danielle to make some appreciative comment when I arrive at the shop, but she doesn't even seem to notice. She just says, 'Hi. The trousers and T-shirts are in the stock room. Pick out your size and change in the cubicle.'

Oh right. Now I come to think of it, all the assistants at Ally Smith do wear the same outfits. Almost like a . . . well, a uniform, I suppose. Reluctantly I get changed and look at myself – and, to tell you the truth, I'm disappointed. These grey trousers don't really flatter me, and the T-shirt's just plain boring. I'm almost tempted to ask Danielle if I can pick out another outfit to wear – but she seems a bit busy, so I don't. Maybe next week I'll have a little word.

But even though I don't like the outfit, I still feel a *frisson* of excitement as I come out onto the shop floor.

The spotlights are shining brightly; the floor's all shiny and polished; music's playing and there's a sense of anticipation in the air. It's almost like being a performer. I glance at myself in a mirror and murmur, 'How can I help you?' Or maybe it should be, '*Can* I help you?' I'm going to be the most charming shop assistant ever, I decide. People will come here just to be assisted by me, and I'll have a fantastic rapport with all the customers. And then I'll appear in the *Evening Standard* in some quirky column about favourite shops. Perhaps I'll even get my own TV show.

No-one's told me what to do yet, so – using my initiative, very good – I walk up to a woman with blond hair, who's tapping away at the till, and say,

'Shall I have a quick go?'

'What?' she says, not looking up.

'I'd better learn how to work the till, hadn't I? Before all the customers arrive?'

Then the woman does look up and, to my surprise, bursts into laughter.

'On the till? You think you're going to go straight onto the till?'

'Oh,' I say, blushing a little. 'Well I thought . . .'

'You're a beginner, darling,' she says. 'You're not going near the till. Go with Kelly. She'll show you what you'll be doing today.'

Folding jumpers. Folding bloody jumpers. That's what I'm here to do. Rush round after customers who have picked up cardigans and left them all crumpled, and fold them back up again. By eleven o'clock I'm absolutely exhausted – and, to be honest, not enjoying myself very much at all. Do you know how depressing it is to fold a cardigan in exactly the right Ally Smith way and put it back on the shelf, all neatly lined up – just to see someone casually pull it down again, look at it, pull a face and discard it? You want to scream at them, LEAVE IT ALONE IF YOU'RE NOT GOING TO BUY IT! I watched one girl even pick up a cardigan *identical* to the one she already had on! I mean, what is her problem?

And I'm not getting to chat to the customers, either. It's as if they see through you when you're a shop assistant. No-one's asked me a single interesting question like 'Does this shirt go with these shoes?'or 'Where can I find a really nice black skirt under £60?' I'd *love* to answer stuff like that. But the only questions I've been asked are, 'Is there a loo?' and 'Where's the nearest Midland cashpoint?' I haven't built up a single rapport with anyone.

Oh, it's depressing. The only thing that keeps me going is an end-of-stock reduced rack at the back of the shop. I keep sidling towards it and looking at a pair of zebra-print jeans, reduced from £180 to £90. I remember those jeans. I've even tried them on. And here they are, out of the blue – reduced. I just can't keep my eyes off them. They're even in size 12. My size.

I mean, I know I'm not really supposed to be spending money – but this is a complete one-off. They're the coolest jeans you've ever seen. And £90 is *nothing* for a pair of really good jeans. If you were in Gucci, you'd be paying at least £500. Oh God, I want them. I *want* them.

I'm just loitering at the back, eyeing them up for the hundredth time when Danielle comes striding up and I jump guiltily. But all she says is, 'Can you go on to fitting-room duty now? Sarah'll show you the ropes.'

No more folding jumpers! Thank God!

To my relief, this fitting-room lark is a lot more fun. Ally Smith has really nice fitting-rooms, with lots of space and individual cubicles, and my job is to stand at the entrance and check how many items people are taking in with them. It's really interesting to see what people are trying on. One girl's buying *loads* of stuff, and keeps saying how her boyfriend told her to go mad for her birthday, and he would pay.

Huh. Well, it's all right for some. Still, never mind,

at least I'm earning money. It's 11.30, which means I've earned . . . £14.40 so far. Well, that's not bad, is it? I could get some nice makeup for that.

Except that I'm not going to waste this money on makeup. Of course not – I mean that's not why I'm here, is it? I'm going to be really sensible. What I'm going to do is buy the zebra-print jeans – just because they're a one-off and it would be a crime not to – and then put all the rest towards my bank balance. I just can't *wait* to put them on. I get a break at 2.30, so what I'll do is nip to the reduced rail and take them to the staff room, just to make sure they fit, and . . .

Suddenly my face freezes. Hang on.

Hang on a moment. What's that girl holding over her arm? She's holding my zebra-print jeans! She's coming towards the fitting rooms. Oh my God. She wants to try them on. But they're mine!

'Hi!' she says brightly as she approaches.

'Hi,' I gulp, trying to stay calm. 'Ahm . . . how many items have you got?'

'Four,' she says, showing me the hangers. Behind me are tokens hanging on the wall, marked One Two, Three and Four. The girl's waiting for me to give her a token marked Four and let her in. But I can't.

I physically cannot let her go in there with my jeans.

'Actually,' I hear myself saying, 'you're only allowed three items.'

'Really?' she says in surprise. 'But . . .' She gestures to the tokens.

'I know,' I say. 'But they've just changed the rules. Sorry about that.' And I give her my best unhelpful-shop-assistant smile.

This is quite a power trip, actually. You can just stop people trying on clothes! You can ruin their lives!

'Oh, OK,' says the girl. 'Well, I'll leave out—'

'These,' I say, and grab the zebra-print jeans.

'No,' she says. 'Actually, I think I'll—'

"We have to take the top item,' I explain, and give the unhelpful smile again. 'Sorry about that.'

Thank *God* for bolshy shop assistants and stupid pointless rules. People are so used to them that this girl doesn't even question me. She just rolls her eyes, grabs the Three token and pushes her way past into the fitting-room, leaving me holding the precious jeans.

OK, now what? From inside the girl's cubicle, I can hear zips being undone and hangers being clattered. She won't take long to try on those three things. And then she'll be out, wanting the zebra-print jeans. Oh God. What can I do? For a few moments I'm frozen with indecision. Then the sound of a cubicle curtain being rattled back jolts me into action. Quickly, I stuff the zebra-print jeans out of sight behind the curtain and stand up again with an innocent look on my face.

A moment later, Danielle comes striding up, a clipboard in her hands.

'All right?' she says. 'Coping, are you?'

'I'm doing fine,' I say, and flash her a confident smile.

'I'm just rostering in breaks,' she says. 'If you could manage to last until three, you can have an hour then.'

'Fine,' I say in my positive, employee-of-the-month voice, even though I'm thinking *Three? I'll be starving!*

'Good,' she says, and moves off into the corner to write on her piece of paper, just as a voice says, 'Hi. Can I have those jeans now?'

Oh my God, it's the girl, back again. How can she have tried on all those other things so quickly? Is she bloody Houdini?

'Hi!' I say, ignoring the last bit of what she said. 'Any good? That black skirt's really nice. The way the splits go at the—'

'Not really,' she says, interrupting me, and shoves the lot back at me, all mussed up and off their hangers, I might add. 'It was really the jeans I wanted. Can I have them?'

My heart starts to thump hard.

'What jeans were they?' I say, wrinkling my brow

sympathetically. 'Blue ones? You can get them over there, next to the . . .'

'No!' says the girl impatiently. 'The zebra-print jeans I had a minute ago.'

'Oh,' I say blankly. 'Oh yes. I'm not sure where they went. Maybe someone else took them.'

'But I gave them to you! You were supposed to be looking after them.'

'Ah,' I say, and flash my shop-assistant smile. 'I'm afraid we can't be held responsible for property given to us to hold while customers are in the fitting rooms.'

'Oh for God's sake!' she says, looking at me as if I'm an imbecile. 'This is ridiculous! I gave them to you about thirty seconds ago! How can you have lost them?'

Shit. She's really angry. Her voice is getting quite loud, and people are starting to look.

'Is there a problem?' chimes in a syrupy voice, and I look up in horror. Danielle's coming over towards us, a sweet-but-menacing look on her face. OK, keep calm, I tell myself firmly. No-one can prove anything either way. And everyone knows the customer's always a troublemaker.

'I gave this assistant a pair of jeans to look after because I had four items, which is apparently too many,' the girl begins explaining.

'Four items?' says Danielle. 'But you're allowed four items in the fitting room.' And she turns to look at me with an expression which, frankly, isn't very friendly.

'*Are* you?' I say innocently. 'Oh God, I'm sorry. I thought it was three. I'm new,' I add apologetically.

'I *thought* it was four!' says the girl. 'I mean, you've got tokens with bloody "Four" written on them!' She gives an impatient sigh. 'So anyway, I gave her the jeans, and tried on the other things – and then I came out for the jeans, and they've gone.'

'Gone?' says Danielle sharply. 'Gone where?'

'I'm not sure,' I say, trying to look as baffled as the next person. 'Maybe another customer took them.'

'But you were holding them!' says the girl. 'So what – did someone just come up to you and whip them out of your fingers?'

Oh piss off. What's her problem, anyway? How can she be so obsessed with a bloody pair of *jeans*?

'Maybe you could get another pair from the rack,' I say, trying to sound helpful.

'There *isn't* another pair,' she says icily. 'They were from the reduced rail.'

'Rebecca, think!' says Danielle. 'Did you put them down somewhere?'

'I must have done,' I say vaguely. 'It's been so busy in here, I must have put them on the rail, and I suppose another customer must have walked off with them.' I give an apologetic little shrug as though to say 'Customers, eh?'

'Wait a minute!' says the girl sharply. 'What's that?'

I follow her gaze and freeze. The zebra-print jeans have rolled out from under the curtain. For a moment we all stare at them.

'Gosh!' I manage at last. 'There they are!'

'And what exactly are they doing down there?' asks Danielle.

'I don't know!' I say. 'Maybe they . . .' I swallow, trying to think as quickly as I can. 'Maybe . . .'

'You *took* them!' says the girl incredulously. 'You bloody took them! You wouldn't let me try them on, and then you hid them!'

'That's ridiculous!' I say, trying to sound convincing – but I can feel my cheeks flushing a guilty red. Oh God, *why* do I have to be someone who blushes? Why?

'You little—' The girl breaks off and turns to Danielle. 'I want to make an official complaint.'

'Rebecca,' says Danielle. 'Into my office, please.'

Hang on a minute. Isn't she going to back me up? Isn't she going to defend her staff to the public? What happened to a united front?

'Now!' she says sharply, and I jump in fright. As I walk slowly away to her office (broom cupboard, more like), I can see all the other staff looking at me and nudging each other. Oh God, how embarrassing. Still, it'll be OK. I'll just say sorry and promise not to do it again, and maybe offer to work overtime. Just as long as I don't get . . .

I don't believe it. She's fired me. I haven't even worked there for a day, and I've been kicked out. I was so shocked when she told me, I actually became almost tearful. I mean, apart from the incident with the zebra-print jeans, I thought I was doing really well. But apparently hiding stuff from customers is one of those automatic-firing things. (Which is really unfair, because she never told me that at the interview.)

As I get changed out of my grey trousers and T-shirt, there's a heavy feeling in my heart. My retail career is over before it's even begun. I was only given twenty quid for the hours I've done today – and Danielle said that was being generous. And when I asked if I could quickly buy some clothes using my staff discount, she looked at me as if she wanted to hit me.

It's all gone wrong. No job, no money, no discount, just twenty bloody quid. Miserably, I start to walk along the street, shoving my hands in my pockets. Twenty bloody quid. What am I supposed to do with—

'Rebecca!' My head jerks up and I find myself look-ing dazedly at a face which I know I recognize. But who is it? It's . . . it's . . . it's . . .

'Tom!' I exclaim in the nick of time. 'Hi there! What a surprise!'

Well, blow me down. Tom Webster, up in London. What's he doing here? Shouldn't he be in Reigate, grouting his Mediterranean tiles or something?

'This is Lucy,' he says proudly, and pulls forward a girl holding about sixty-five carrier bags. And I don't believe it. It's the girl who was buying all that stuff in Ally Smith. The girl whose boyfriend was paying. *Surely* she didn't mean . . .

'You're going out together?' I say stupidly. 'You and her?'

'Yes,' says Tom, and grins at me. 'Have been for some time now.'

But this doesn't make any sense. Why haven't Janice and Martin mentioned Tom's girlfriend? They've mentioned every other bloody thing in his life.

And fancy Tom having a girlfriend!

'Hi,' says Lucy.

'Hi there,' I say. 'I'm Rebecca. Next-door neighbour. Childhood friend. All that.'

'Oh *you're* Rebecca,' she says, and gives a swift glance at Tom.

What does that mean? Have they been talking about me? God, does Tom still fancy me? How embarrassing.

'That's me!' I say brightly, and give a little laugh.

'You know, I'm sure I've seen you somewhere before,' says Lucy thoughtfully – and then her eyes crinkle in recognition. 'You work at Ally Smith, don't you?'

'No!' I say, a little too sharply.

'Oh,' she says. 'I thought I saw you—'

God, I can't have it going back to my parents that I work in a shop. They'll think I've been lying about my entire life in London and that secretly I'm broke and living in a squalid bedsit.

'Research,' I say coolly. 'I'm a journalist, actually.'

'Rebecca's a financial journalist,' says Tom. 'Really knows her stuff.'

'Oh right,' says Lucy, and I give her a supercilious smile.

'Mum and Dad always listen to Rebecca,' says Tom. 'Dad was talking about it just the other day. Said you'd been very helpful on some financial matter. Switching funds or something.'

'I do what I can,' I say modestly, and give Tom a special, old-friends smile. Not that I'm jealous, or anything – but I do feel a little twinge seeing Tom smiling down at this Lucy character who, frankly, has very boring hair, even if her clothes are quite nice. Come to think of it, Tom's wearing quite nice clothes himself. Oh, what's going on? This is all wrong. Tom belongs in his starter home in Reigate, not prancing around expensive shops looking halfway decent.

'Anyway,' he says. 'We must get going.'

'Train to catch?' I say patronizingly. 'It must be hard, living so far out.'

'It's not so bad,' says Lucy. 'I commute to Wetherby's every morning and it only takes forty minutes.'

'You work for Wetherby's?' I say, aghast. Why am I *surrounded* by City high-flyers?

'Yes,' she says. 'I'm one of their political advisers.'

What? What does that mean? Is she really brainy, or something? Oh God, this gets worse and worse.

'And we're not catching our train just yet,' says Tom, smiling down at Lucy. 'We're off to Tiffany first. Choose a little something for Lucy's birthday next week.' He lifts a hand and starts twisting a lock of her hair round his finger.

I can't cope with this any more. It's not fair. Why haven't *I* got a boyfriend to buy me stuff in Tiffany's?

'Well, lovely to see you,' I gabble. 'Give my love to your mum and dad. Funny they didn't mention Lucy,' I can't resist adding, a little spitefully. 'I saw them the other day, and they didn't mention her once.'

I shoot an innocent look at Lucy. Hah! Now who's got the upper hand?

But she and Tom are exchanging looks again.

'They probably didn't want to—' begins Tom, and stops abruptly.

'What?' I say.

There's a long, awkward silence. Then Lucy says, 'Tom, I'll just look in this shop window for a second,' and walks off, leaving the two of us alone.

God, what drama! I'm obviously the Third Person in their relationship.

'Tom, what's going on?' I say, and give a little laugh.

But it's obvious, isn't it? He's still hankering after me. And Lucy knows it.

'Oh God,' says Tom, and rubs his face. 'Look, Rebecca, this isn't easy for me. But the thing is, Mum and Dad are aware of your . . . feelings for me. They didn't want to mention Lucy to you, because they thought you'd be . . .' He exhales sharply. 'Disappointed.'

What? Is this some kind of *joke*? I have never been more dumbfounded in all my life. For a few seconds I can't even move for astonishment.

'My feelings for *you*?' I stutter at last. 'Are you joking?'

'Look, it's pretty obvious,' he says, shrugging. 'Mum and Dad told me how the other day you kept on asking how I was, and all about my new house . . .' There's a slightly pitying look in his eye. Oh my God, I can't stand this. How can he think . . . 'I really like you, Becky,' he adds. 'I just don't . . .'

'I was being *polite*!' I roar. 'I don't *fancy* you!'

'Look,' he says. 'Let's just leave it, shall we?'

'But I *don't*!' I cry furiously. 'I never did fancy you! That's why I didn't go out with you when you asked me! When we were both sixteen, remember?'

I break off and look at him triumphantly – to see that his face hasn't moved a bit. He isn't listening. Or if he is, he's thinking that the fact I've dragged in our teenage past means I'm obsessed by him. And the more I try to argue the point, the more obsessed he'll think I am. Oh God, this is horrendous.

'OK,' I say, trying to gather together the remaining shreds of my dignity. 'OK, we're obviously not communicating here, so I'll just leave you to it.' I glance over at Lucy, who's looking in a shop window and obviously pretending not to be listening. 'Honestly, I'm not after your boyfriend,' I call. 'And I never was. Bye.'

And I stride off down the street, a nonchalant smile plastered stiffly across my face.

* * *

As I round the corner, however, the smile gradually slips, and I sit heavily down on a bench. In spite of myself, I feel humiliated. Of course, the whole thing's laughable. That Tom Webster should think I'm in love with *him*. Just serves me right for being too polite to his parents, and feigning interest in his bloody limed oak units. Next time I'll yawn loudly, or walk away. Or produce a boyfriend of my own. That would shut them all up, wouldn't it? And anyway, who cares what they think?

I know all this. I know I shouldn't care two hoots what Tom Webster or his girlfriend think. But even so . . . I have to admit, I feel a bit low. Why haven't I got a boyfriend? There isn't even anyone I fancy at the moment. The last serious boyfriend I had was Robert Hayman, and we split up three months ago. And I didn't even much like him. He used to call me 'Love' and jokingly put his hands over my eyes during the rude bits in films. Even when I told him not to, he still kept doing it. It used to drive me *mad*. Even remembering it now makes me feel all tense and scratchy.

But still, he was a boyfriend, wasn't he? He was someone to phone up during work, and go to parties with and use as ammunition against creeps. Maybe I shouldn't have chucked him. Maybe he was all right.

I give a gusty sigh, stand up and start walking along the street again. All in all, it hasn't been a great day. I've lost a job and been patronized by Tom Webster. And now I haven't got anything to do tonight. I thought I'd be too knackered after working all day, so I didn't bother to organize anything.

Still, at least I've got twenty quid.

Twenty quid. I'll buy myself a nice cappuccino and a chocolate brownie. And a couple of magazines.

And maybe something from Accessorize. Or some boots. In fact I really *need* some new boots — and I've seen some really nice ones in Hobbs with square toes and quite a low heel. I'll go there after my coffee, and look at the dresses, too. God, I deserve a treat, after today. And I need some new tights for work, and a nail file. And maybe a book to read on the tube . . .

By the time I join the queue at Starbucks, I feel happier already.

PGNI First Bank Visa
7 Camel Square
Liverpool L1 5NP

Ms Rebecca Bloomwood
Flat 2
4 Burney Rd
London SW6 8FD

15 March 2000

Dear Ms Bloomwood

PGNI First Bank VISA Card No. 1475839204847586

Thank you for your letter of 11 March.

Your offer of a free subscription to *Successful Saving* magazine is most kind, as is your invitation to dinner at the Ivy. Unfortunately, employees of PGNI First Bank are prohibited from accepting such gifts.

I look forward to receiving your outstanding payment of £105.40, as soon as possible.

Yours sincerely

Peter Johnson
Customer Accounts Executive

Ten

On Monday morning I wake early, feeling rather hollow inside. My gaze flits to the pile of unopened carrier bags in the corner of my room and then quickly flits away again. I know I spent too much money on Saturday. I know I shouldn't have bought two pairs of boots. I know I shouldn't have bought that purple dress. In all, I spent . . . Actually, I don't want to think about how much I spent. Think about something else, quick, I instruct myself. Something else. Anything'll do.

I'm well aware that at the back of my mind, thumping quietly like a drumbeat, are the twin horrors of Guilt and Panic.

Guilt Guilt Guilt Guilt.

Panic Panic Panic Panic.

If I let them, they'd swoop into my mind and take over. I'd feel completely paralysed with misery and fear. So the trick I've learned is simply not to listen. I close off the back of my mind – and then nothing worries me. It's simple self-defence. My mind is very well trained like that.

My other trick is to distract myself with different thoughts and activities. So I get up, switch the radio on, take a shower and get dressed. The thumping's still there at the back of my head, but gradually, gradually, it's fading away. As I go into the kitchen and make a cup of coffee, I can barely hear it any more. A cautious relief floods over me, like that feeling you get when a painkiller finally gets rid of your headache. I can relax. I'm going to be all right.

On the way out I pause in the hall to check my appearance in the mirror (Top: River Island, Skirt: French Connection, Tights: Pretty Polly Velvets, Shoes: Ravel) and reach for my coat (Coat: House of Fraser sale). Just then the post plops through the door, and I go to pick it up. There's a handwritten letter for Suze, and a postcard from the Maldives. And for me, there are two ominous-looking window envelopes. One from VISA, one from Endwich Bank.

For a moment, my heart stands still. Why another letter from the bank? And VISA. What do they want? Can't they just leave me alone?

Carefully I place Suze's post on the ledge in the hall and shove my own two letters in my pocket, telling myself I'll read them on the way to work. Once I get on the tube, I'll open them both and I'll read them, however unpleasant they are.

That really is my intention. Honestly. As I'm walking along the pavement, I promise my intention is to read the letters.

But then I turn into the next street – and there's a skip outside someone's house. A huge great yellow skip, already half full of stuff. Builders are coming in and out of the house, tossing old bits of wood and upholstery into the skip. Loads of rubbish, all jumbled up together.

And a little thought creeps into my mind.

My steps slow down as I approach the skip and I pause, staring intently at it as though I'm interested in the words printed on the side. I stand there, heart thumping, until the builders have gone back into the house and no-one's looking. Then, in one motion, I reach for the two letters, pull them out of my pocket, and drop them over the side, into the skip.

Gone.

As I'm standing there a builder pushes past me with two sacks of broken plaster, and heaves them into the skip. And now they really are gone. Buried beneath a layer of plaster, unread. No-one will ever find them.

Gone for good.

Quickly I turn away from the skip and begin to walk on again. Already my step's lighter and I'm feeling buoyant.

Before long, I'm feeling completely innocent; purged of guilt. I mean, it's not my fault if I never read the letters, is it? It's not my fault if I never got them, is it? As I bound along towards the tube station I honestly feel as though neither of those letters ever existed.

When I arrive at work, I switch on my computer, click efficiently to a new document and start typing my piece on pensions. Perhaps if I work really hard, it's occurred to me, Philip will give me a rise. I'll stay late every night and impress him with my dedication to the job, and he'll realize that I'm considerably under-valued. Perhaps he'll even make me associate editor, or something.

'These days,' I type briskly, 'none of us can rely on the government to take care of us in our old age. Therefore pension planning should be done as early as possible, ideally as soon as you are earning an income.'

'Morning, Clare,' says Philip, coming into the office in his overcoat. 'Morning Rebecca.'

Hah! Now is the time to impress him.

'Morning Philip,' I say, in a friendly-yet-professional manner. Then, instead of leaning back in my chair and asking him how his weekend was, I turn back to my computer and start typing again. In fact, I'm typing so fast that the screen is filled with lots of splodgy typos. It has to be said, I'm not the best typist in the world. But who cares? I look very businesslike, that's the point.

'The bwst ootion is oftwn yoor compaamy occu-patinoa Ischeme, bt if tehis is not posibsle, a wide vareiety of peronanlas penion lans is on ther markte, ranign from . . .' I break off, reach for a pension brochure and flip quickly through it, as though scanning for some crucial piece of information.

'Good weekend, Rebecca?' says Philip.

'Fine, thanks,' I say, glancing up from the brochure as though surprised to be interrupted while I'm at work.

'I was round your neck of the woods on Saturday,' he says. 'The Fulham Road. Trendy Fulham.'

'Right,' I say absently.

'It's the place to be, these days, isn't it? My wife was reading an article about it. Full of It-girls, all living on trust funds.'

'I suppose so,' I say vaguely.

'That's what we'll have to call you,' he says, and gives a little guffaw. 'The office It-girl.'

It-girl? What on earth is he talking about?

'Right,' I say, and smile at him. After all, he's the boss. He can call me whatever he—

Oh God, hang on a minute. Hang-on-a-minute. Philip hasn't got the idea that I'm rich, has he? He doesn't think I've got a trust fund or something ridiculous, does he?

'Rebecca,' says Clare, looking up from her telephone. 'I've got a call for you. Someone called Tarquin.'

Philip gives a little grin, as though to say, What else? and ambles off to his desk. I stare after him in frustration. This is all wrong. If Philip thinks I've got some kind of private income, he'll never give me a rise.

But what on earth could have given him that idea?

'Becky,' says Clare meaningfully, gesturing to my ringing phone.

'Oh,' I say. 'Yes, OK.' I pick up the receiver, and say, 'Hi. Rebecca Bloomwood here.'

'Becky,' comes Tarquin's unmistakable, reedy voice. He sounds rather nervous, as if he's been gearing up to this phone call for ages. Perhaps he has. 'It's so nice to hear your voice. You know, I've been thinking about you a lot.'

'Really?' I say, as unhelpfully as possible. I mean, I know he's Suze's cousin and everything, but honestly—

'I'd . . . I'd very much like to spend some more time in your company,' he says. 'May I take you out to dinner?'

Oh God. What am I supposed to say to that? It's such an innocuous request. I mean, it's not as if he's said, Can I sleep with you? or even Can I kiss you? If I say 'No' to dinner it's like saying, You're so unbearable, I can't even stand sharing a table with you for two hours.

Which is pretty near the truth – but I can't *say* that, can I? And Suze has been so sweet to me recently, and if I turn her darling Tarkie down flat, she'll be really upset.

'I suppose so,' I say, aware that I don't sound too thrilled – and also aware that maybe I should just come clean and say I Don't Fancy You. But somehow I can't face it. To be honest, it would be a lot easier just to go out to dinner with him. I mean, how bad can it be?

And anyway, I don't have to actually *go*. I'll call at the last moment and cancel. Easy.

'I'm in London until Sunday,' says Tarquin.

'Let's make it Saturday night, then!' I say brightly. 'Just before you leave.'

'Seven o'clock?'

'How about eight?' I suggest.

'OK,' he says. 'Eight o'clock.' And he rings off, without mentioning a venue. But since I'm not actually going to meet him, this doesn't really matter. I put the phone down, give an impatient sigh, and start typing again.

'The best option for many is to consult an independent financial adviser, who will be able to advise you on your own particular pension needs and recommend suitable products. New on the market this year is the . . .' I break off and reach for a brochure. Any old brochure. 'Sun Assurance "Later Years" Retirement Plan, which . . .'

'So, was that guy asking you out?' says Clare Edwards.

'Yes, he was, actually,' I say, looking up carelessly. In spite of myself, I feel a little flip of pleasure. Because Clare doesn't know what Tarquin's like, does she? For all she knows, he's incredibly good-looking and witty. 'We're going out on Saturday night.' I give her a non-chalant smile and start typing again.

'Oh, right,' she says, and snaps an elastic band round a pile of letters. 'You know, Luke Brandon was asking me if you had a boyfriend the other day.'

For an instant I can't move. Luke Brandon wants to know if I've got a boyfriend?

'Really?' I say, trying to sound normal. 'When . . . when was this?'

'Oh, just the other day,' she says. 'I was at a briefing at Brandon Communications, and he asked me. Just casually. You know.'

'And what did you say?'

'I said no,' said Clare, and gives me a little grin. 'You don't fancy him, do you?'

'Of course not,' I say, and roll my eyes.

But I have to admit, I feel quite cheerful as I turn back to my computer and start typing again. Luke Brandon. I mean, not that I like him or anything – but still. Luke Brandon. 'This flexible plan,' I type, 'offers full death benefits and a lump sum on retirement. For example, a typical man in his thirties who invested £100 a month . . .'

You know what? I suddenly think, stopping mid-sentence. This is boring. I'm better than this.

I'm better than sitting here in this crappy office, typing out the details from a brochure, trying to turn them into some kind of credible journalism. I deserve to do something more interesting than this. Or more well paid. Or both.

I stop typing and rest my chin on my hands. It's time for a new start. Why don't I do what Elly's doing? I'm not afraid of a bit of hard work, am I? Why don't I get my life in order, go to a City head-hunter and land myself a job which everyone will envy? I'll have a huge income and a company car and wear Karen Millen suits every day. And I'll never have to worry about money again.

I feel exhilarated. This is it! This is the answer to everything. I'll be a . . .

'Clare?' I say casually. 'Who earns the most in the City?'

'I don't know,' says Clare, frowning thoughtfully. 'Maybe futures brokers?'

That's it, then. I'll be a futures broker. Easy.

And it is easy. So easy, that ten o'clock the next morning sees me walking nervously up to the front doors of Willam Green, top City head-hunters. As I push the door open I glimpse my own reflection and feel a little thrill go through my stomach. Am I *really* doing this?

You bet I am. I'm wearing my smartest black suit, and tights and high heels, with an *FT* under my arm, obviously. And I'm carrying the briefcase with the combination lock which my mum gave me one Christmas and which I've never used. This is partly because it's really heavy and bumpy – and partly because I've forgotten the combination, so I can't actually open it. But it looks the part. And that's what counts.

Jill Foxton, the woman I'm meeting, was really nice on the phone when I told her about wanting to change careers, and sounded pretty impressed by all my experience. I quickly typed up a CV and e-mailed it through to her – and, OK, I embroidered it a bit, but that's what they expect, isn't it? It's all about selling yourself. And it worked, because she phoned back only about ten minutes after receiving it, and asked if I'd come in and see her, as she thought she had some interesting opportunities for me.

Interesting opportunities for me! I was so excited, I could barely keep still. I went straight in to Philip and told him I wanted to take tomorrow off to take my nephew to the zoo – and he didn't suspect a thing. He's going to be gobsmacked when he finds out I've turned overnight into a high-flying futures broker.

'Hi,' I say confidently to the woman at reception. 'I'm here to see Jill Foxton. It's Rebecca Bloomwood.'

'Of . . .'

Oh God. I can't say *Successful Saving*. It might get back to Philip that I've been looking for a new job.

'Of . . . just of nowhere, really,' I say and give a relaxed little laugh. 'Just Rebecca Bloomwood. I have a ten o'clock appointment.'

'Fine,' she says, and smiles. 'Take a seat.'

I pick up my briefcase and walk over to the black squashy chairs, trying not to give away how nervous I feel. I sit down, run my eye hopefully over the magazines on the coffee table (but there's nothing interesting, just things like *The Economist*), then lean back and look around. This foyer is pretty impressive, I have to admit. There's a fountain in the middle, and glass stairs rising in a curve, and what seems like several miles away I can see lots of state-of-the-art lifts. Not just one lift, or two, but about ten. Blimey. This place must be huge.

'Rebecca?' A blond girl in a pale trouser suit is suddenly in front of me. Nice suit, I think. Very nice suit.

'Hi!' I say. 'Jill!'

'No, I'm Amy,' she smiles. 'Jill's assistant.'

Wow. That's pretty cool. Sending your assistant to pick up your visitors, as if you're too grand and busy to do it yourself. Maybe that's what I'll get my assistant to do when I'm an important futures broker and Elly comes over for lunch. Or maybe I'll have a *male* assistant – and we'll fall in love! God, it would be just like a movie. The high-flying woman and the cute but sensitive . . .

'Rebecca?' I come to and see Amy staring at me curiously. 'Are you ready?'

'Of course!' I say gaily, and pick up my briefcase. As we stride off over the glossy floor, I surreptitiously run my gaze over Amy's trouser suit again – and find my eye landing on a discreet Emporio Armani label. I can't quite believe it. Emporio Armani! The *assistants* wear Emporio Armani! So what's Jill herself going to be in? Couture Dior? God, I love this place already.

We go up to the sixth floor and begin to walk along endless carpeted corridors.

'So you want to be a futures broker,' says Amy after a while.

'Yes,' I say. 'That's the idea.'

'And you already know a bit about it.'

'Well, you know,' I give a modest smile. 'I've written extensively on most areas of finance, so I do feel quite well equipped.'

'That's good,' says Amy, and gives me a smile. 'Some people turn up with no idea. Then Jill asks them a few standard questions, and . . .' She makes a gesture with her hand. I don't know what it means, but it doesn't look good.

'Right!' I say, forcing myself to speak in an easy tone. 'So – what sort of questions?'

'Oh, nothing to worry about!' says Amy. 'She'll probably ask you . . . oh, I don't know. Something like, "How do you trade a butterfly?" or "What's the difference between open outlay and OR?" Or "How would you calculate the expiry date of a futures instrument?" Really basic stuff.'

'Right,' I say, and swallow. 'Great.'

Something in me is telling me to turn and run – but we've already arrived at a pale blond-wood door.

'Here we are,' says Amy, and smiles at me. 'Would you like tea or coffee?'

'Coffee please,' I say, wishing I could say, 'A stiff gin, please.' Amy knocks on the door, opens it and ushers me in, and says, 'Rebecca Bloomwood.'

'Rebecca!' says a dark-haired woman behind the desk, and gets up to shake my hand.

To my slight surprise, Jill is not nearly as well dressed as Amy. She's wearing a blue, rather mumsy looking suit, and boring court shoes. But still, never mind, she's the boss. And her office is pretty amazing.

'It's very good to meet you,' she says, gesturing to a chair in front of her desk. 'And let me say straight away, I was extremely impressed by your CV.'

'Really?' I say, feeling relief creep over me. That can't be bad, can it? *Extremely impressed*. Maybe it won't matter if I don't know the answers to those questions.

'Particularly by your languages,' adds Jill. '*Very* good. You do seem to be one of those rare breeds, an all-rounder.'

'Well, my French is really only conversational,' I say modestly. '*Voici la plume de ma tante*, and all that!'

Jill gives an appreciative laugh, and I beam back at her.

'But Finnish!' she says, reaching for the cup of coffee on her desk. 'That's quite unusual.'

I keep smiling and hope we move off the subject of languages. To be honest, 'fluent in Finnish' went in because I thought 'conversational French' looked a bit bare on its own. After all, who speaks Finnish, for God's sake? No-one.

'And your financial knowledge,' she says, pulling my CV towards her. 'You seem to have covered a lot of different areas during your years in financial journalism.' She looks up. 'What attracts you to derivatives in particular?'

What? What's she talking about? Oh yes. Derivatives. They're futures, aren't they?

'Well,' I begin confidently – and am interrupted as Amy comes in with a cup of coffee.

'Thanks,' I say, and look up, hoping we've moved on to something else. But she's still waiting for an answer. 'I think futures *are* the future,' I say seriously. 'They're an extremely challenging area and I think . . .' What do I think? Oh God. Should I throw in a quick reference to butterflies or expiry dates or something? Probably better not. 'I think I'd be well suited to that particular field,' I say at last.

153

'I see,' says Jill Foxton, and leans back in her chair. 'The reason I ask, is there's a position we have in banking which I think might also suit you. I don't know what you would feel about that.'

A position in banking? Is she serious? Has she actually found me a job? I don't believe it!

'Well, that would be fine by me,' I say, trying not to sound too joyful. 'I mean, I'd miss the futures – but then, banking's good too, isn't it?'

Jill laughs. I think she thinks I'm joking or something.

'The client is a triple-A rated foreign bank, looking for a new recruit in the London arm of their debt financing division.'

'Right,' I say intelligently.

'I don't know whether you're familiar with the principles of European back-to-back arbitrage?'

'Absolutely,' I say confidently. 'I wrote an article on that very subject last year.'

What was that word, again? Arbi-something.

'Obviously I'm not trying to rush you into any decision,' she says, 'but if you do want a change of career, I'd say this would be perfect for you. There'd be an interview, of course, but I can't see any problems there.' She smiles at me. 'And we'll be able to negotiate you a very attractive package.'

'Really?' Suddenly I can't quite breathe. She's going to negotiate an attractive package. For me!

'Oh yes,' says Jill. 'Well, you must realize you're a bit of a one-off.' She gives me a confidential smile. 'You know, when your CV came through yesterday, I actually whooped! I mean, the *coincidence*!'

'Absolutely,' I say, beaming at her. God, this is fantastic. This is a bloody dream come true. I'm going to be a banker! And not just any old banker – a triple-A rated banker!

'So,' says Jill casually. 'Shall we go and meet your new employer?'

'What?' I say in astonishment, and a little smile spreads over her face.

'I didn't want to tell you until I'd met you – but the recruitment director of Bank of Helsinki is over here for a meeting with our managing director. I just know he's going to love you. We can have the whole thing wrapped up by this afternoon!'

'Excellent!' I say, and get to my feet. Hahaha! I'm going to be a banker!

It's only as we're halfway down the corridor that her words begin to impinge on my mind. Bank of Helsinki.

Bank of Helsinki. That doesn't mean . . . Surely she doesn't think . . .

'I can't wait to hear the two of you talking away in Finnish,' says Jill pleasantly, as we begin to climb a flight of stairs. 'It's not a language I know at all.'

Oh my God. *Oh my God. No.*

'But then, my languages have always been hopeless,' she adds comfortably. 'I'm not talented in that department. Not like you!'

I flash her a little smile, and keep walking, without missing a step. But my heart's thumping and I can hardly breathe. Shit. What am I going to do? *What the fuck am I going to do?*

We turn a corner and begin to walk calmly down another corridor. And I'm doing pretty well. As long as we just keep walking, I'm OK.

'Was Finnish a hard language to learn?' asks Jill.

'Not that hard,' I hear myself saying in a scratchy voice. 'My . . . my father's half-Finnish.'

'Yes, I thought it must be something like that,' says Jill. 'I mean, it's not the sort of thing you learn at school, is it?' And she gives a jolly little laugh.

It's all right for her, I think savagely. She's not the one being led to her death. Oh God, this is terrible. People keep passing us and glancing at me and smiling, as if to say, 'So that's the Finnish-speaker!'

Why did I put I was fluent in Finnish? *Why?*

'All right?' says Jill. 'Not nervous?'

'Oh no!' I say at once, and force a grin onto my face. 'Of course I'm not nervous!'

Maybe I'll be able to busk it, I think suddenly. I mean, the guy won't conduct the whole bloody interview in Finnish, will he? He'll just say 'Haållø' or whatever it is, and I'll say 'Haållø' back, and then before he can say anything else, I'll quickly say, 'You know, my technical Finnish is a bit rusty these days. Would you mind if we spoke in English?' And he'll say . . .

'Nearly there,' says Jill, and smiles at me.

'Good,' I say brightly, and clasp my sweaty hand more tightly round my briefcase handle. Oh God. Please save me from this. Please . . .

'Here we are!' she says, and stops at a door marked CONFERENCE ROOM. She knocks twice, then pushes it open. There's a roomful of people sitting round a table, and they all turn to look at me.

'Jan Virtanen,' she says. 'I'd like you to meet Rebecca Bloomwood.'

A bearded man rises from his chair, gives me a huge smile and extends his hand.

'Neiti Bloomwood,' he says cheerfully. 'On oikein hauska tavata. Pitääkö paikkansa että teillä on jonkinlainen yhteys Suomeen?'

I stare speechlessly at him, feeling my face turn red. Everyone in the room is waiting for me to answer.

'I . . . erm . . . erm . . . Haållø!' I lift my hand in a friendly little wave, and smile around the room.

But nobody smiles back.

'Erm . . . I've just got to . . .' I start backing away. 'Just got to . . .'

And I turn. And I run.

Eleven

As I arrive back down in the foyer, I'm panting slightly.
Which is not surprising, since I've just run about a
half-marathon along endless corridors, trying to get out
of this place. I descend the final flight of stairs
(couldn't risk the lifts in case the Finnish brigade suddenly turned up), then pause to catch my breath. I
straighten my skirt, transfer my briefcase from one
sweaty hand to the other, and begin to walk calmly
across the foyer towards the door, as though I've come
out of an utterly ordinary, utterly unspectacular meeting. I don't look right and I don't look left. I don't think
about the fact that I've just completely shredded any
chances I had of becoming a top City banker. All I can
think about is getting to that glass door and getting outside before anyone can . . .

'Rebecca!' comes a voice behind my head, and I
freeze. Shit. They've got me.

'Haållø!' I gulp, turning round. 'Haåll . . . Oh. Hell
. . . Hello.'

It's Luke Brandon.

It's Luke Brandon, standing right in front of me,
looking down at me with that strange stare he always
seems to have.

'This isn't the sort of place I would have expected to
find you,' he says. 'You're not after a City job, are you?'

And why shouldn't I be? Doesn't he think I'm clever
enough?

'Actually,' I say haughtily, 'I'm thinking of a change
of career. Maybe into foreign banking. Or futures
broking.'

'Really?' he says. 'That's a shame.'

A shame? What does that mean? Why is it a shame? As I look up at him, his dark eyes meet mine, and I feel a little flicker, deep inside me. Out of nowhere, Clare's words pop into my head. *Luke Brandon was asking me if you had a boyfriend.*

'What . . .' I clear my throat. 'What are *you* doing here, anyway?'

'Oh, I recruit from here quite often,' he says. 'They're very efficient. Soulless, but efficient.' He shrugs, then looks at my shiny briefcase. 'Have they fixed you up with anything yet?'

'I've . . . I've got a number of options open to me,' I say. 'I'm just considering my next move.'

Which to be honest, is straight out the door.

'I see,' he says, and pauses. 'Did you take the day off to come here?'

'Yes,' I say. 'Of course I did.'

What does he think? That I just sloped off for a couple of hours and said I was at a press conference?

Actually, that's not a bad idea. I might try that next time.

'So – what are you up to now?' he asks.

Don't say 'nothing'. *Never* say 'nothing'.

'Well, I've got some bits and pieces to do,' I say. 'Calls to make, people to see. That kind of thing.'

'Ah,' he says, nodding. 'Yes. Well. Don't let me keep you.' He looks around the foyer. 'And I hope it all works out for you, job-wise.'

'Thanks,' I say, giving him a businesslike smile.

And then he's gone, walking off towards the doors, and I'm left holding my clunky briefcase, feeling just a bit disappointed. I wait until he's disappeared, then wander slowly over to the doors myself and go out onto the street. And then I stop. To tell you the truth, I'm not quite sure what to do next. I'd kind of planned to spend the day ringing everyone up and telling them about my fab new job as a futures broker. Instead of which . . . Well, anyway. Let's not think about that.

But I can't stand still on the pavement outside William Green all day. People will start thinking I'm a piece of installation art or something. So eventually I begin walking along the street, figuring I'll arrive at a tube soon enough and then I can decide what to do. I come to a corner and I'm just waiting for the traffic to stop, when a taxi pulls up beside me.

'I know you're a very busy woman, with a lot to do,' comes Luke Brandon's voice, and my head jerks up in shock. There he is, leaning out of the taxi window, his dark eyes crinkled up in a little smile. 'But if you had the odd half-hour to spare – you wouldn't be interested in doing a little shopping, would you?'

This day is unreal. Completely and utterly unreal.

I get into the taxi, put my clunky briefcase on the floor and shoot a nervous look at Luke as I sit down. I'm already slightly regretting this. What if he asks me a question about interest rates? What if he wants to talk about the Bundesbank or American growth prospects? But all he says is, 'Harrods, please,' to the driver.

As we zoom off, I can't stop a smile coming to my face. This is so cool. I thought I was going to have to go home and be all miserable on my own – and instead, I'm on my way to Harrods, and someone else is paying. I mean, you can't get more perfect than that.

As we drive along, I look out of the window at the crowded streets. Although it's March, there are still a few SALE signs in the shop windows left over from January, and I find myself peering at the displays, wondering if there are any bargains I might have missed. We pause outside a branch of Lloyds Bank. I look idly at the window, and at the queue of people inside, and hear myself saying, 'You know what? Banks should run January sales. Everyone else does.'

There's silence and I look up, to see a look of amusement on Luke Brandon's face.

'Banks?' he says.

'Why not?' I say defensively. 'They could reduce

their charges for a month or something. And so could building societies. Big posters in the windows, "Prices Slashed" . . .' I think for a moment. 'Or maybe they should have April sales, after the end of the tax year. Investment houses could do it, too. "Fifty per cent off a selected range of funds."'

'A unit trust sale,' says Luke Brandon slowly. 'Reductions on all upfront charges.'

'Exactly,' I say. 'Everyone's a sucker for a sale. Even rich people.'

The taxi moves on again, and I gaze out at a woman in a gorgeous white coat, wondering where she got it. Maybe at Harrods. Maybe I should buy a white coat, too. I'll wear nothing but white, all winter. A snowy white coat and a white fur hat. People will start calling me the Girl in the White Coat.

When I look back again, Luke's writing something down in a little notebook. He looks up and meets my eye for a moment, then says,

'Rebecca, are you serious about leaving journalism?'

'Oh,' I say vaguely. To be honest, I'd forgotten all about leaving journalism. 'I don't know. Maybe.'

'And you really think banking would suit you better?'

'Who knows?' I say, feeling a bit rattled at his tone. It's all right for him. He doesn't have to worry about his career — he's got his own multimillion-pound company. I've only got my own multimillion-pound overdraft. 'Elly Granger is leaving *Investor's Weekly News*,' I add. 'She's joining Wetherby's as a fund manager.'

'I heard,' he says. 'But you're nothing like Elly Granger.'

Really? This comment intrigues me. If I'm not like Elly, who am I like, then? Someone really cool like Kristin Scott Thomas, maybe.

'You have imagination,' adds Luke. 'She doesn't.'

Wow! Now I really am gobsmacked. Luke Brandon thinks I have imagination? Gosh. That's good, isn't it.

That's quite flattering, really. *You have imagination.* Mmm, yes, I like that. Unless . . .

Hang on. It's not some polite way of saying I'm stupid, is it? Or a liar? Like 'creative accounting'. Perhaps he's trying to say that none of my articles are accurate.

Oh God, now I don't know whether to look pleased or not.

To cover up my embarrassment, I look out of the window. We've stopped at a traffic light, and a very large lady in a pink velour jogging suit is trying to cross the road. She's holding several bags of shopping and a pug dog, and she keeps losing grasp of one or other of them and having to put something down. It's so frustrating, I almost want to leap out and help her. Then, suddenly, she loses her grasp of one of the bags, and drops it on the ground. It falls open – and three huge tubs of ice-cream come out of it and start rolling down the road.

Don't laugh, I instruct myself. Be mature. Don't laugh. I clamp my lips together, but I can't stop a little giggle escaping.

I glance at Luke, and his lips are clamped together, too.

Then the woman starts chasing her ice-cream down the road, pug dog in tow, and that's it. I can't stop myself giggling. And when the pug dog reaches the ice-cream before the lady, and starts trying to get the lid off with its teeth, I think I'm going to die laughing. I look over at Luke, and I can't believe it. He's laughing helplessly too, wiping the tears from his eyes. God, I didn't think Luke Brandon *ever* laughed.

'Oh God,' I manage at last. 'I know you shouldn't laugh at people. But I mean . . .'

'That dog!' Luke starts laughing again. 'That bloody dog!'

'That outfit!' I give a little shudder as we start to move off again, past the pink woman. She's bending over the ice-cream, her huge pink bottom thrust up in

161

the air. 'I'm sorry, but pink velour jogging suits should be banned from this planet.'

'I couldn't agree more,' says Luke, nodding seriously. 'Pink velour jogging suits are hereby banned. Along with cravats.'

'And Y-fronts,' I say without thinking – then blush pink. How could I mention Y-fronts in front of Luke Brandon? 'And toffee-flavoured popcorn,' I quickly add.

'Right,' says Luke. 'So we're banning pink velour jogging suits, cravats, Y-fronts, toffee-flavoured popcorn . . .'

'And punters with no change,' comes the taxi driver's voice from the front.

'Fair enough,' says Luke, giving a little shrug. 'Punters with no change.'

'And punters who vomit. They're the worst.'

'OK . . .'

'And punters who don't know where the fuck they're going.'

Luke and I exchange glances and I begin to giggle again.

'And punters who don't speak the bloody language. Drive you crazy.'

'Right,' says Luke. 'So . . . most punters, in fact.'

'Don't get me wrong,' says the taxi driver. 'I've got nothing against foreigners . . .' He pulls up outside Harrods. 'Here we are. Going shopping, are you?'

'That's right,' says Luke, getting out his wallet.

'So – what're you after?'

I look at Luke expectantly. He hasn't told me what we're here to buy. Clothes? A new aftershave? Will I have to keep smelling his cheek? (I wouldn't mind that, actually.) Furniture? Something dull like a new desk?

'Luggage,' he says, and hands a tenner to the driver. 'Keep the change.'

Luggage! Suitcases and holdalls and stuff like that. As I wander round the department, looking at Louis

Vuitton suitcases and calfskin bags, I'm quite thrown. Quite shocked by myself. Luggage. Why on earth have I never considered luggage before?

I should explain. For years now, I've kind of operated under an informal shopping cycle. A bit like a farmer's crop rotation system. Except, instead of wheat–maize–barley–fallow, mine pretty much goes clothes–makeup–shoes–clothes. (I don't usually bother with fallow.) Shopping is actually very similar to farming a field. You can't keep buying the same thing – you have to have a bit of variety. Otherwise you get bored and stop enjoying yourself.

And I thought I had as much variety in my shopping life as anybody. I thought I had all the areas covered. To be honest, I was quite blasé about it. But look what I've been missing out on, all this time. Look what I've been denying myself. I feel quite shaky as I realize the opportunities I've just been throwing away over the years. Suitcases, weekend bags, monogrammed hat boxes . . . With weak legs, I wander into a corner and sit down on a carpeted pedestal, next to a red leather vanity case.

How can I have overlooked luggage for so long? How can I have just blithely led my life, *ignoring an entire retail sector*?

'So – what do you think?' says Luke, coming up to me. 'Anything worth buying?'

And now, of course, I feel like a fraud. Why couldn't he have wanted to buy a really good white shirt, or a cashmere scarf? Or even handcream? I would have been able to advise him authoritatively and even quote prices. But luggage. I'm a beginner at luggage.

'Well,' I say, playing for time. 'It depends. They all look great.'

'They do, don't they?' He follows my gaze around the department. 'But which one would you choose? If you had to buy one of these suitcases, which one would it be?'

It's no good. I can't bluff.

'To be honest,' I say, 'this isn't really my field.'

'What isn't?' he says, sounding incredulous. 'Shopping?'

'Luggage,' I explain. 'It's not an area I've put a lot of time into. I should have done, I know, but . . .'

'Well . . . never mind,' says Luke, his mouth twisting into a smile. 'As a non-expert. Which one would you choose?'

Well, that's different.

'Hmm,' I say, and get to my feet in a businesslike manner. 'Well, let's have a closer look.'

God, we have fun. We line up eight suitcases in a row, and give them marks for looks, heaviness, quality of lining, number of interior pockets and efficiency of wheels. (I test this by striding the length of the department, pulling the case behind me. By this time, the assistant has just given up and left us to it.) Then we look to see if they have a matching holdall and give that marks, too.

The prices don't seem to matter to Luke. Which is a bloody good thing, because they're absolutely astronomical – and at first sight, so scary they make me want to run away. But it's amazing how quickly £1,000 can start to seem like a very reasonable sum for a suitcase – especially since the Louis Vuitton monogrammed trunk costs about ten times as much. In fact, after a while I find myself thinking quite seriously that I too should really invest in a quality suitcase, instead of my battered old canvas bag.

But today is Luke's shopping trip, not mine. And strangely enough, it's almost more fun choosing for someone else than for yourself. In the end, we narrow it down to a dark green leather case, which has wonderful trundly wheels, or the palest beige calfskin case, which is a bit heavier, but has a stunning silk lining and is basically so beautiful I can't stop staring at it. It has a matching holdall and vanity case – and they're just as beautiful. God, if it were me, I'd . . .

But then, it's not up to me, is it? It's Luke who's buying the case. He's the one who's got to choose. We sit down on the floor, side by side, and look at them.

'The green one would be more practical,' says Luke eventually.

'Mmm,' I say noncommittally. 'I suppose it would.'

'It's lighter – and the wheels are better.'

'Mmm.'

'And that pale calfskin would probably scuff in a matter of minutes. Green's a more sensible colour.'

'Mmm,' I say, trying to sound as though I agree with him.

He gives me a quizzical look and says, 'Right. Well, I think we've made our choice, don't you?' And, still sitting on the floor, he calls over the assistant.

'Yes sir?' says the assistant, and Luke nods at him.

'I'd like to buy one of these pale beige suitcases, please.'

'Oh!' I say, and I can't stop a smile of delight spreading over my face. 'You're getting the one I liked best!'

'Rule of life,' says Luke, getting to his feet and brushing down his trousers. 'If you bother to ask someone's advice, then bother to listen to it.'

'But I didn't say which one . . .'

'You didn't have to,' says Luke, reaching out a hand to pull me to my feet. 'Your "Mmms" gave it all away.'

His hand is surprisingly strong round mine, and as he pulls me up, I feel a slight swooping in my stomach. He smells nice, too. Some expensive aftershave which I don't recognize. For a moment, neither of us says anything.

'Right,' says Luke at last. 'Well, I'd better pay for it, I suppose.'

'Yes,' I say, feeling ridiculously nervous. 'Yes, I suppose you had.'

He walks off to the checkout and starts talking to the assistant, and I perch next to a display of leather suit-carriers, suddenly feeling a bit awkward. I mean, the shopping's over now. What happens next?

Well, we'll just say goodbye politely, won't we? Luke'll probably have to get back to the office. He can't hang around shopping all day. And if he asks me what I'm doing next, I tell myself, I really will say I'm busy. I'll pretend I've got some important meeting arranged or something.

'All sorted out,' he says, coming back. 'Rebecca, I'm incredibly grateful to you for your help.'

'Great!' I say brightly. 'Well, I must be on my—'

'So I was wondering,' says Luke, before I can continue. 'Would you like some lunch?'

This is just turning into my perfect day. Shopping at Harrods – and lunch at Harvey Nichols. I mean, what could be better than that? We go straight up to the fifth-floor restaurant, and Luke orders a bottle of chilled white wine, and raises his glass in a toast.

'To luggage,' he says, and smiles.

'Luggage,' I reply happily, and take a sip. It's just about the most delicious wine I've ever tasted. Luke picks up his menu and starts to read it, and I pick mine up too – but to be honest, I'm not reading a word. I'm just sitting in a happy glow, like the Ready Brek kid. I'm looking around with relish at all the smart women coming in to have lunch here, and making notes of their outfits and wondering where that girl over there got her pink boots from. And now, for some reason, I'm thinking about that nice card Luke sent me. And I'm wondering whether it was just being friendly – or . . . or whether it was something else.

At this thought, my stomach flips so hard I almost feel sick, and very quickly I take another sip of wine. Well, a gulp, really. Then I put down my glass, count to five and say casually,

'Thanks for your card, by the way.'

'What?' he says, looking up. 'Oh, you're welcome.' He reaches for his glass and takes a sip of wine. 'It was nice to bump into you, that night.'

'It's a great place,' I say. 'Great for table-hopping.'

As soon as I've said this, I feel myself blush. But Luke just smiles, and says, 'Indeed.' Then he puts down his glass and says, 'Do you know what you want?'

'Ahm . . .' I say, glancing hurriedly at the menu. 'I think I'll just have . . . erm . . . fishcakes. And rocket salad.'

Damn, I've just spotted squid. I should have had that. Oh well, too late now.

'Good choice,' says Luke, smiling at me. 'And thanks again for coming along today. It's always good to have a second opinion.'

'No problem,' I say lightly, and take a sip of wine. 'Hope you enjoy the case.'

'Oh, it's not for me,' he says after a pause. 'It's for Sacha.'

'Oh right,' I say pleasantly. 'Who's Sacha? Your sister?'

'My girlfriend,' says Luke, and turns away to beckon to a waiter.

And I stare at him, unable to move.

His girlfriend. I've been helping him choose a suitcase for his girlfriend.

Suddenly I don't feel hungry any more. I don't want fishcakes and rocket salad. I don't even want to be here. My happy Ready Brek glow is fading away, and underneath I feel chilly and rather stupid. Luke Brandon's got a girlfriend. Of course he has. Some beautiful smart girl, called Sacha, who has manicured nails and travels everywhere with expensive cases. I'm a fool, aren't I? I should have known there'd be a Sacha somewhere on the scene. I mean, it's obvious.

Except . . . Except it's not that obvious. In fact, it's not obvious at all. Luke hasn't mentioned his girlfriend all morning. Why hasn't he? Why didn't he just *say* the suitcase was for her in the first place? Why did he let me sit on the floor beside him in Harrods and laugh as I marched up and down, testing the wheels? I wouldn't have behaved anything like that if I'd known we were buying a case for his girlfriend. And he must have known that. He must have known.

A cold feeling begins to creep over me. This is all wrong.

'All right?' says Luke, turning back to me.

'No,' I hear myself saying. 'No, it's not. You didn't tell me that case was for your girlfriend. You didn't even tell me you *had* a girlfriend.'

Oh God. I've done it now. I've been completely uncool. But somehow I don't care.

'I see,' says Luke after a pause. He picks up a piece of bread and begins to break it up with his fingers, then looks up. 'Sacha and I have been together a while now,' he says kindly. 'I'm sorry if I gave . . . any other impression.'

He's patronizing me. I can't bear it.

'That's not the point,' I say, feeling my cheeks flushing beetroot red. 'It's just . . . it's all wrong.'

'Wrong?' he says, looking amused.

'You should have told me we were choosing a case for your girlfriend,' I say doggedly, staring down at the table. 'It would have made things . . . different.'

There's silence and I raise my eyes, to see Luke looking at me as though I'm mad.

'Rebecca,' he says, 'you're getting this all out of proportion. I wanted your opinion on suitcases. End of story.'

'And are you going to tell your girlfriend you asked my advice?'

'Of course I am!' says Luke, and gives a little laugh. 'I expect she'll be rather amused.'

I stare at him in silence, feeling mortification creep over me. My throat's tight, and there's a pain growing in my chest. *Amused*. Sacha will be amused when she hears about me.

Well, of course she will. Who wouldn't be amused by hearing about the girl who spent her entire morning marching up and down Harrods, testing out suitcases for another woman? The girl who got completely the wrong end of the stick. The girl who was so stupid, she thought Luke Brandon might actually like her.

I swallow hard, feeling sick with humiliation. For the first time, I'm realizing how Luke Brandon sees me. How they all see me. I'm just the comedy turn, aren't I? I'm the scatty girl who gets things wrong and makes people laugh. The girl who didn't know SBG and Rutland Bank had merged. The girl no-one would ever think of taking seriously. Luke didn't bother telling me we were choosing a suitcase for his girlfriend because I don't matter. He's only buying me lunch because he hasn't got anything else to do – and probably because he thinks I might do something entertaining like drop my fork, which he can laugh about when he gets back to the office.

'I'm sorry,' I say in a wobbly voice, and stand up. 'I haven't got time for lunch after all.'

'Rebecca, don't be silly!' says Luke. 'Look, I'm sorry you didn't know about my girlfriend.' He raises his eyebrows quizzically, and I want to hit him. 'But we can still be friends, can't we?'

'No,' I say stiffly, aware that my voice is thick and my eyes smarting. 'No, we can't. Friends treat each other with respect. But you don't respect me, do you, Luke? You just think I'm a joke. A nothing. Well . . .' I swallow hard. 'Well, I'm not.'

And before he can say anything else I turn, and quickly make my way out of the restaurant, half blinded by disappointed tears.

PGNI First Bank Visa
7 Camel Square
Liverpool L1 5NP

Ms Rebecca Bloomwood
Flat 2
4 Burney Rd
London SW6 8FD

20 March 2000

Dear Ms Bloomwood

PGNI First Bank VISA Card No. 1475839204847586

Thank you for your payment of £10.00, received today.

As I think I have pointed out several times, the minimum payment required was in fact £105.40.

The balance currently overdue is therefore £95.40. I look forward to receiving your payment as soon as possible.

If satisfactory payment is not received within seven days, further action will have to be taken.

Yours sincerely

Peter Johnson
Customer Accounts Executive

BANK OF LONDON
London House
Mill Street EC3R 4DW

Ms Rebecca Boomwood
Flat 2
4 Burney Rd
London SW6 8FD

20 March 2000

Dear Ms Boomwood

Just think . . .

What kind of difference would a personal loan make to your life?

A new car, perhaps. Improvements to the home. A boat for those weekend breaks. Or maybe just peace of mind, knowing that all those bills can easily be taken care of.

Bank of London will offer loans for almost any purpose – so don't wait any longer! Turn your life into the lifestyle you deserve.

With a Bank of London Easifone Loan, you don't even have to fill in any forms. Simply call one of our friendly 24-hour operators on

0100 45 46 47 48

and let us do the rest.

Just think . . .

We look forward to hearing from you.

Yours sincerely

Sue Skepper
Marketing Executive

PS Why delay? Pick up the phone now – and dial 0100 45 46 47 48. It couldn't be easier.

Twelve

As I arrive home that afternoon, I feel weary and miserable. Suddenly, triple-A rated jobs in banking and Harrods with Luke Brandon seem miles away. Real life isn't swanning round Knightsbridge in a taxi, choosing £1,000 suitcases, is it? This is real life. Home to a tiny flat which still smells of curry, and a pile of nasty letters from the bank, and no idea what to do about them.

I put my key in the lock, and as I open the door, I hear Suze cry, 'Bex? Is that you?'

'Yes!' I say, trying to sound cheerful. 'Where are you?'

'Here,' she says, appearing at the door of my bedroom. Her face is all pink, and there's a shine in her eyes. 'Guess what! I've got a surprise for you!'

'What is it?' I say, putting down my briefcase. To be honest, I'm not in the mood for one of Suze's surprises. She'll just have moved my bed to a different place, or something. And all I want is to sit down and have a cup of tea and something to eat. I never did get any lunch.

'Come and see. No . . . no, shut your eyes, first. I'll lead you.'

'OK,' I say reluctantly. I close my eyes and allow her to take my hand. We start to walk along the corridor – and of course, as we near my bedroom door, I start feeling a little tingle of anticipation in spite of myself. I always fall for things like this.

'Dadaaa! You can look now!'

I open my eyes and look dazedly around my room, wondering what mad thing Suze has done now. At least she hasn't painted the walls or touched the curtains, and my computer's safely switched off. So what on earth can she have . . .

And then I see them. On my bed. Piles and piles of upholstered frames. All made up perfectly, with no wonky corners, and the braid glued neatly in place. I can't quite believe my eyes. There must be at least . . .

'I've done a hundred,' says Suze behind me. 'And I'm going to do the rest tomorrow! Aren't they fab?' I turn and stare incredulously at her.

'You . . . you did all these?'

'Yes!' she says proudly. 'It was easy, once I got into a rhythm. I did it in front of *Morning Coffee*. Oh, I wish you'd seen it. They had *such* a good phone-in, about men who dress up in women's clothes! There was this one guy—'

'Wait,' I say, trying to get my head round this. 'Wait. Suze, I don't understand. This must have taken you *ages*.' My eye runs disbelievingly over the pile of frames again. 'Why . . . why on earth did you—'

'Well, you weren't getting very far with them, were you?' says Suze kindly. 'I just thought I'd give you a helping hand.'

'A helping hand?' I echo weakly.

'I'll do the rest tomorrow, and then I'll ring up the delivery people,' says Suze. 'You know, it's a very good system. You don't have to post them, or anything. They just come and pick them up! And then they'll send you a cheque. It should come to about £284. Pretty good, huh?'

'Hang on.' I turn round. 'What do you mean, they'll send *me* a cheque?' Suze looks at me as though I'm stupid.

'Well, Bex, they are your frames.'

'But you made them! Suze, you should get the money!'

'But I did them for you!' says Suze, and stares at me. 'I did them so you could make your three hundred quid!'

I stare at her silently, feeling a sudden thickness in my throat. Suze made all these frames for me. Slowly I sit down on the bed, pick up one of the frames and run my finger along the fabric. It's absolutely perfect. You could sell it in Liberty's.

'Suze, it's your money. Not mine,' I say eventually. 'It's your project, now.'

'Well, that's where you're wrong,' says Suze, and a triumphant look spreads over her face. 'I've got my own project.'

She comes over to the bed, reaches behind the pile of made-up frames, and pulls something out. It's a photo frame – but it's nothing like a Fine Frame. It's upholstered in silver furry fabric, and the word ANGEL is appliqued in pink across the top, and there are little silver pom-poms at the corners. It's the coolest, kitschest frame I've ever seen.

'Do you like it?' she says, a bit nervously.

'I love it!' I say, grabbing it from her hands and looking more closely at it. 'Where did you get it?'

'I didn't get it anywhere,' she says. 'I made it.'

'What?' I stare at her. 'You . . . made this?'

'Yes. During *Neighbours*. It was awful, actually. Beth found out about Joey and Skye.'

I'm completely gobsmacked. How come Suze suddenly turns out to be so talented?

'So what do you reckon?' she says, taking the frame back and turning it over in her fingers. 'Could I sell these?'

Could she sell these?

'Suze,' I say quite seriously. 'You're going to be a millionaire.'

And we spend the rest of the evening getting very pissed and mapping out Suze's career as an Anita Roddick-style businesswoman. We get quite hysterical trying to decide if she should wear Chanel or Prada when she goes to meet the Queen – and by the time I get into bed, I've forgotten all about Luke Brandon and Bank of Helsinki and the rest of my disastrous day.

But the next morning, it all comes rushing back to me like a horror movie. I wake up feeling pale and shaky, and desperately wishing I could take a sickie. I don't want to go to work. I want to stay at home under the duvet, watching daytime telly and being a million-airess entrepreneur with Suze.

But it's the busiest week of the month, and Philip'll never believe I'm ill.

So, somehow, I haul myself out of bed and into some clothes and onto the tube. At Lucio's I buy myself an extra large cappuccino, and a muffin, *and* a chocolate brownie. I don't care if I get fat. I just need sugar and caffeine and chocolate, and as much as possible.

Luckily it's so busy, no-one's talking very much, so I don't have to bother telling everyone at the office what I did yesterday on my day off. Clare's tapping away at something and there's a pile of page proofs on my desk, ready for me to check. So after checking my e-mails – none – I scrunch miserably up in my chair, pick up the first one and start to read it.

'Balancing the risks and rewards of stock-market investment can be a dangerous business, especially for the novice investor.'

Oh God this is boring.

'While returns may be high in certain sectors of the market, nothing is ever guaranteed – and for the small-time investor . . .'

'Rebecca?' I look up, to see Philip approaching my desk, holding a piece of paper. He doesn't look very happy, and for one terrible moment I think he's spoken to Jill Foxton at William Green, has discovered every-thing, and is giving me my P45. But as he gets nearer, I see it's only some dull-looking press release.

'I want you to go to this instead of me,' he says. 'It's on Friday. I'd go myself, but I'm going to be tied up here with Marketing.'

'Oh,' I say, without enthusiasm, and take the piece of paper. 'OK. What is it?'

'Personal Finance Fair at Olympia,' he says. 'We always cover it.'

Yawn. Yawn yawn yawn . . .

'Barclays are giving a champagne lunchtime reception,' he adds.

'Oh right!' I say, with more interest. 'Well, OK. It sounds quite good. What exactly is it . . .'

I glance down at the paper, and my heart stops as I see the Brandon Communications logo at the top of the page.

'It's basically just a big fair,' says Philip. 'All sectors of personal finance. Talks, stands, events. Just cover whatever sounds interesting. I leave it up to you.'

'OK,' I say after a pause. 'Fine.'

I mean, what do I care if Luke Brandon might be there? I'll just ignore him. I'll show him about as much respect as he showed me. And if he tries to talk to me, I'll just lift my chin firmly in the air, and turn on my heel, and . . .

'How are the pages going?' says Philip.

'Oh, great,' I say, and pick the top one up again. 'Should be finished soon.' He gives a little nod and walks away, and I begin to read again.

'. . . for the small-time investor, the risks attached to such stocks may outweigh the potential of reward.'

Oh God this is boring. I can't even bring myself to focus on what the words mean.

'More and more investors are therefore demanding the combination of stockmarket performance with a high level of security. One option is to invest in a Tracker fund, which automatically "tracks" the top 100 companies at any time . . .'

Hmm. Actually, that gives me a thought. I reach for my Filofax, flip it open and dial Elly's new direct number at Wetherby's.

'Eleanor Granger,' comes her voice, sounding a bit far-off and echoey. Must be a dodgy line.

'Hi, Elly, it's Becky,' I say. 'Listen, whatever happened to Tracker bars? They're really yummy, aren't they? And I haven't eaten one for . . .'

There's a scuffly sort of sound on the line, and I gape at the receiver in surprise. In the distance, I can hear Elly saying, 'I'm sorry. I'll just be a . . .'

'Becky!' she hisses down the phone. 'I was on speaker phone! Our head of department was in my office.'

'Oh God!' I say, aghast. 'Sorry! Is he still there?'

'No,' says Elly, and sighs. 'God knows what he thinks of me now.'

'Oh well,' I say reassuringly. 'He's got a sense of humour, hasn't he?'

Elly doesn't reply.

'Oh well,' I say again, less certainly. 'Anyway, are you free for a drink at lunchtime?'

'Not really,' she says. 'Sorry, Becky, I've really got to go.' And she puts the phone down.

No-one likes me any more. Suddenly I feel a bit cold and shivery, and I scrunch up even more in my chair. Oh God, I hate today. I hate everything. I want to go hooome.

But by the time Friday arrives, I have to say I feel a lot more cheerful. This is primarily because:

1. It's Friday.

2. I'm spending all day out of the office.

3. Elly phoned yesterday and said sorry she was so abrupt, but someone else came into the office just as we were talking. *And* she's going to be at the Personal Finance Fair.

Plus

4. I have completely put the Luke Brandon incident from my mind. Who cares about him, anyway?

So as I get ready to go, I feel quite bouncy and positive. I put on my new grey cardigan over a short black shirt, and my new Hobbs boots – dark grey suede – and I have to say, I look bloody good in them. God, I love new clothes. If everyone could just wear new clothes every day, I reckon depression wouldn't exist any more.

As I'm about to leave, a pile of letters comes through the letterbox for me. Several of them look like bills, and one is yet another letter from Endwich Bank. But I have a clever new solution to all these nasty letters: I just put them in my dressing-table drawer and close it. It's the only way to stop getting stressed out about it. And it really does work. As I thrust the drawer shut and head out of the the front door, I've already forgotten all about them.

The conference is already buzzing by the time I get there. As I give my name to the press officer at reception, I'm given a big, shiny courtesy carrier bag with the logo of HSBC on the side. Inside this, I find an enormous press pack complete with a photo of all the conference organizers lifting glasses of champagne to each other (yeah right, like we're really going to use that in the magazine), a voucher for two drinks at the Sun Alliance Pimm's Stand, a raffle ticket to win £1,000 (invested in the unit trust of my choice) a big lollipop advertising Eastgate Insurance, and my name badge with PRESS stamped across the top. There's also a white envelope with the ticket to the Barclays champagne reception inside, and I put that carefully in my bag. Then I fasten my name badge prominently on my lapel and start to walk around the arena.

Normally, of course, the rule is to throw away your name badge as soon as you're given it. But the great thing about being PRESS at one of these events is that people fall over themselves to ply you with free stuff. A lot of it's just boring old leaflets about savings plans, but some of them are giving out free gifts and snacks, too. So after an hour, I've accumulated two pens, a paperknife, a mini box of Ferrero Rocher chocolates, a helium balloon with Save & Prosper on the side, and a T-shirt with a cartoon on the front, sponsored by some mobile phone company. And I've had two free cappuccinos, a *pain au chocolat*, some scrumpy (from Somerset Savings), a mini pack of Smarties and my Pimm's from Sun Alliance. (I haven't written a single note in my notebook, or asked a single question – but never mind. I can always just copy some stuff out of the press pack.)

I've seen that some people are carrying quite neat little silver desk clocks, and I wouldn't mind one of those, so I'm just wandering along, trying to work out what direction they're coming from, when a voice says,

'Becky!'

I look up – and it's Elly! She's standing at the Wetherby's display with a couple of guys in suits, waving at me to come over.

'Hi!' I say delightedly. 'How *are* you?'

'Fine!' she says, and beams at me. 'Really getting along well.' And she does look the part, I have to say. She's wearing a bright red suit (Karen Millen, no doubt), and some really nice square-toed shoes, and her hair's been tied back. The only thing I don't go for is the earrings. Why is she suddenly wearing pearl earrings? Maybe it's just to blend in with the others.

'God, I can't believe you're actually one of them!' I say, lowering my voice slightly. 'I'll be interviewing you next!' I tilt my head earnestly, like Martin Bashir on *Panorama*. '"Ms Davies, could you tell me the aims and principles of Wetherby's Investments?"'

Elly gives a little laugh – then reaches into a box beside her.

'I'll give you this,' she says, and hands me a brochure.

'Oh thanks,' I say ironically, and stuff it into my bag. I suppose she has to look good in front of her colleagues.

'It's actually quite an exciting time at Wetherby's,' continues Elly. 'You know we're launching a whole new range of funds next month? I think there are five altogether. UK Growth, UK Prospects, European Growth, European Prospects, and . . .'

Why is she telling me this, exactly?

'Elly . . .'

'And US Growth!' she finishes triumphantly. There isn't a flicker of humour in her eyes.

'Right,' I say after a pause. 'Well, that sounds . . . fab!'

'I could arrange for our PR people to give you a call, if you like,' she says. 'Fill you in a bit more.'

What?

'No,' I say hurriedly. 'No, it's OK. So, erm . . . what are you doing afterwards? Do you want to go for a drink?'

'No can do,' she says apologetically. 'I'm going to look at a flat.'

'Are you moving?' I say in surprise. Elly lives in the coolest flat in Camden, with two guys who are in a band and get her into loads of free gigs and stuff. I can't think why she'd want to move.

'Actually, I'm buying,' she says. 'I'm looking around Streatham, Tooting . . . I just want to get on the first rung of that property ladder.'

'Right,' I say feebly. 'Good idea.'

'You should do it yourself, you know, Becky,' she says. 'You can't hang around in a student flat for ever. Real life has to begin some time!' She glances at one of her men in suits, and he gives a little laugh.

It's not a student flat, I think indignantly. And anyway, who defines 'real life'? Who says 'real life' is property ladders and hideous pearl earrings? 'Shit-boring tedious life', more like.

'Are you going to the Barclays champagne reception?' I say as a last gasp, thinking maybe we can go and get pissed together and have some fun. But she pulls a little face, and shakes her head.

'I might pop in,' she says, 'but I'll be quite tied up here.'

'OK,' I say. 'Well I'll . . . I'll see you later.'

I move away from the stand, and slowly start walking towards the corner where the champagne reception's being held, feeling slightly dispirited. In spite of myself, a part of me starts wondering if maybe Elly's right and I'm wrong. Maybe I should be talking about property ladders and growth funds, too. Oh God, maybe there's something wrong with me. I'm missing the gene which makes you grow up and buy a flat in Streatham and start visiting Homebase every weekend. Everyone's moving on without me, into a world I don't understand.

But as I get near the entrance to the champagne reception, I feel my spirits rising. Whose spirits *don't* rise at the thought of free champagne? It's being held in a huge tent, and there's a huge banner, and a band playing music, and a girl in a sash at the entrance, handing out Barclays keyrings. When she sees my badge, she gives me a wide smile, hands me a white glossy press pack, and says, 'Bear with me a moment.' Then she walks off to a little group of people, murmurs in the ear of a man in a suit and comes back. 'Someone will be with you soon,' she says. 'In the meantime, let me get you a glass of champagne.'

You see what I mean about being PRESS? Everywhere you go, you get special treatment. I accept a glass of champagne, stuff the white press pack into my carrier bag and take a sip. Oh, it's delicious. Icy cold and sharp and bubbly. Maybe I'll stay here for a couple of hours, I think, just drinking champagne until there's none left. They won't dare chuck me out, I'm PRESS. In fact, maybe I'll—

'Rebecca. Glad you could make it.'

I look up and feel myself freeze. The man in the suit was Luke Brandon. Luke Brandon's standing in front of me, looking straight at me, with an expression I can't quite read. And suddenly I feel sick. All that stuff I planned about playing it cool and icy isn't going to work – because just seeing his face, I feel hot with humiliation, all over again.

'Hi,' I mutter, looking down. Why am I even saying Hi to him?

'I was hoping you'd come,' he says in a low, serious voice. 'I very much wanted to—'

'Yes,' I interrupt. 'Well, I . . . I can't talk, I've got to mingle. I'm here to work, you know.'

I'm trying to sound dignified, but there's a wobble in my voice, and I can feel my cheeks slowly turning red as he keeps gazing at me. So I turn away before he can say anything else, and march off towards the other side of the tent. I don't quite know where I'm heading, but I've just got to keep walking until I find someone to talk to.

The trouble is, I can't see anyone I recognize. It's all just groups of bank-type people laughing loudly together and talking about golf. They all seem really tall and broad-shouldered, and I can't even catch anyone's eye. God, this is embarrassing. I feel like a six-year-old at a grown-ups' party. In the corner I spot Moira Channing from the *Daily Herald*, and she gives me a half-flicker of recognition – but I'm certainly not going to talk to her. OK, just keep walking, I tell myself. Pretend you're on your way somewhere. Don't panic.

Then I see Luke Brandon on the other side of the tent. His head jerks up as he sees me, and he starts heading towards me. Oh God, quick. Quick. I've *got* to find somebody to talk to.

Right, how about this couple standing together? The guy's middle-aged, the woman's quite a lot younger, and they don't look as if they know too many people, either. Thank God. Whoever they are, I'll just ask them how they're enjoying the Personal Finance Fair and whether they're finding it useful, and pretend I'm making notes for my article. And when Luke Brandon arrives, I'll be too engrossed in conversation even to notice him. OK, go.

I take a gulp of champagne, approach the man and smile brightly.

'Hi there,' I say. 'Rebecca Bloomwood, *Successful Saving.*'

'Hello,' he says, turning towards me and extends his hand. 'Derek Smeath from Endwich Bank. And this is my assistant, Erica.'

Oh my God.

I can't speak. I can't shake his hand. I can't run. My whole body's paralysed.

'Hi!' says Erica, giving me a friendly smile. 'I'm Erica Parnell.'

'Yes,' I say, after a huge pause. 'Yes, hi.'

Please don't recognize my name. Please don't recognize my name.

'Are you a journalist, then?' she says, looking at my name badge and frowning. 'Your name seems quite familiar.'

'Yes,' I manage. 'Yes, you . . . you might have read some of my articles.'

'I expect I have,' she says, and takes an unconcerned sip of champagne. 'We get all the financial mags in the office. Quite good, some of them.'

Slowly the circulation is returning to my body. It's going to be OK, I tell myself. They don't have a clue who I am.

'You journalists have to be expert on everything, I suppose,' says Derek, who has given up trying to shake my hand and is swigging his champagne instead.

'Yes, we do really,' I reply, and risk a smile. 'We get to know all areas of personal finance – from banking to unit trusts to life assurance.'

'And how do you acquire all this knowledge?'

'Oh, we just pick it up along the way,' I say smoothly.

You know what? This is quite fun, now that I've relaxed. *You don't know who I am!* I feel like chanting. *You don't know who I am!* And Derek Smeath isn't at all scary in the flesh. In fact he's rather cosy and friendly, like some nice sitcom uncle.

'I've often thought,' says Erica Parnell, 'that they should do a fly-on-the-wall documentary about a bank.' She gives me an expectant look and I nod vigorously.

'Good idea!' I say. 'I think that would be fascinating.'

'You should *see* some of the characters we get in! People who have absolutely no idea about their finances. Don't we, Derek?'

'You'd be amazed,' says Derek. 'Utterly amazed. The lengths people go to, just to avoid paying off their over-drafts! Or even talking to us!'

'Really?' I say, as though astonished.

'You wouldn't believe it!' says Erica. 'I sometimes wonder—'

'Rebecca!' A voice booms behind me and I turn round in shock to see Philip, clutching a glass of cham-pagne and grinning at me. What's he doing here?

'Hi,' he says. 'Marketing cancelled the meeting, so I thought I'd pop along after all. How's it all going?'

'Oh, great!' I say, and take a gulp of champagne. 'This is Derek, and Erica . . . this is my editor, Philip Page.'

'Endwich Bank, eh?' says Philip, looking at Derek Smeath's name badge. 'You must know Martin Gollinger, then.'

'We're not head office, I'm afraid,' says Derek, giving a little laugh. 'I'm the manager of our Fulham branch.'

'Fulham!' says Philip. 'Trendy Fulham.'

And suddenly a warning bell goes off in my head. Dong-dong-dong! I've got to do something. I've got to say something; change the subject. But it's too late. I'm the spectator on the mountain, watching the trains collide in the valley below.

'Rebecca lives in Fulham,' Philip's saying. 'Who do you bank with, Rebecca? You're probably one of Derek's customers!' He laughs loudly at his own joke, and Derek laughs politely, too.

But I can't laugh. I'm frozen to the spot, watching Erica Parnell's face as it changes. As realization slowly dawns. She meets my eye, and I feel something icy drip down my spine.

'Rebecca Bloomwood,' she says, in quite a different voice. 'I *thought* I knew that name. Do you live in Burney Road, Rebecca?'

'That's clever!' says Philip. 'How did you know that?' And he takes another swig of champagne.

Shut up, Philip, I think frantically. Shut *up*.

'So you do?' Her voice is sweet but sharp. Oh God, now Philip's looking at me, waiting for me to answer.

'Yes,' I say, in a strangled voice, aware that my cheeks are flaming.

'Derek, have you realized who this is?' says Erica pleasantly. 'This is Rebecca Bloomwood, one of our customers. I think you spoke to her the other day. Remember?' Her voice hardens. 'The one with the dead dog?'

There's silence. I don't dare look at Derek Smeath's face. I don't dare look at anything except the floor.

'Well, there's a coincidence!' says Philip. 'More champagne, anyone?'

'Rebecca Bloomwood,' says Derek Smeath. He sounds quite faint. 'I don't believe it.'

'Yes!' I say, desperately slugging back the last of my champagne. 'Hahaha! It's a village. Well, I must be off and interview some more—'

'Wait!' says Erica, her voice like a dagger. 'We were hoping to have a little meeting with you, Rebecca. Weren't we, Derek?'

'Indeed we were,' says Derek Smeath. I look up and meet his gaze – and feel a sudden trickle of fear. This man isn't like a cosy sitcom uncle any more. He's like a scary exam invigilator, who's just caught you cheating. 'That is,' he adds, pointedly, 'assuming your legs are both intact and you aren't suffering from any dreaded lurgy?'

'What's this?' says Philip cheerfully.

'How *is* the leg, by the way?' says Erica sweetly.

'Fine,' I mumble. 'Fine, thanks.' Stupid bitch.

'Good,' says Derek Smeath. 'So we'll say Monday at 9.30, shall we?' He looks at Philip. 'You don't mind if Rebecca joins us for a quick meeting on Monday morning, do you?'

'Of course not!' says Philip.

'And if she doesn't turn up,' says Derek Smeath, 'we'll know where to find her, won't we?' He gives me a sharp look, and I feel my stomach contract in fright.

'Rebecca'll turn up!' says Philip. 'Or if she doesn't, there'll be trouble!' He gives me a joky grin, lifts his glass and wanders off. Oh God, I think in panic. Don't leave me alone with them.

'Well, I'll look forward to seeing you,' says Derek Smeath. He pauses, and gives me a beady look. 'And if I remember rightly from our telephone conversation the other day, you'll be coming into some funds by then.'

Oh shit. I thought he'd have forgotten about that.

'That's right,' I say after a pause. 'Absolutely. My aunt's money. Well remembered! My aunt left me some money recently,' I explain to Erica Parnell.

Erica Parnell doesn't look impressed.

'Good,' says Derek Smeath. 'Then I'll expect you on Monday.'

'Fine,' I say, and smile even more confidently at him. 'Looking forward to it already!'

$\mathcal{O}\,\mathcal{C}\,\mathcal{T}\,\mathcal{A}\,\mathcal{G}\,\mathcal{O}\,\mathcal{N}$

flair . . . style . . . vision

Financial Services Department
8th floor
Tower House
London Road
Winchester SO44 3DR

Ms Rebecca Blomwood   *Charge Card Number 7854 4567*
Flat 2
4 Burney Rd
London SW6 8FD

20 March 2000

Dear Ms Blomwood

FINAL REMINDER

Further to my letter of 3rd March, there is still an outstanding balance of £245.57 on your Octagon Charge Card. Should payment not arrive within the next seven days, your account will be frozen and further action will be taken.

I was glad to hear that you have found the Lord and accepted Jesus Christ as your saviour; unfortunately this has no bearing on the matter.

I look forward to receiving your payment shortly.

Yours sincerely

Grant Ellesmore
Customer Finance Manager

Thirteen

Oh God. This is bad. I mean – I'm not just being paranoid, am I? This is really bad.

As I sit on the tube on my way home, I stare at my reflection – outwardly calm and relaxed. But inside, my mind's scurrying around like a spider, trying to find a way out. Round and round and round, legs flailing, no escape . . . OK, stop. Stop! Calm down and let's go through the options one more time.

Option One: Go to meeting and tell the truth.

I can't. I just can't. I *can't* go along on Monday morning and admit that there isn't £1,000 from my aunt and there never will be. What will they do to me? They'll get all serious, won't they? They'll sit me down and start going through all my expenditure and . . . Oh God, I feel sick at the thought of it. I can't do it. I can't go. End of story.

Option Two: Go to meeting and lie.

So – what – tell them the £1,000 is absolutely on its way, and that further funds will be coming through soon. Hmmm. Possible. The trouble is, I don't think they'll believe me. So they'll still get all serious, sit me down, give me a lecture. No. No way.

Option Three: Don't go to meeting.

But if I don't, Derek Smeath will phone Philip and they'll start talking. Maybe the whole story will come out, and he'll find out I didn't actually break my leg. Or have glandular fever. And after that I won't ever be able to go back into the office. I'll be unemployed. My life will be over at the age of twenty-five. But then, maybe that's a price worth paying.

Option Four: Go to meeting with cheque for £1,000.

Perfect. Waltz in, hand over the cheque, say 'Will there be anything else?' and waltz out again. Perfect.

But how do I get £1,000 before Monday morning? How?

Option Five: Run away.

Which would be very childish and immature. Not worth considering.

I wonder where I could go? Maybe abroad somewhere. Las Vegas. Yes, and I could win a fortune at the casinos. A million pounds or something. Even more, perhaps. And then – yes – then I'd fax Derek Smeath, saying I'm closing my bank account due to his lack of faith in me.

God yes! Wouldn't that be great? 'Dear Mr Smeath, I was a little surprised at your recent implication that I have insufficient funds to cover my overdraft and indeed by your sarcastic manner. As this cheque for £1.2 million shows, I have ample funds at my disposal – which I will shortly be moving to one of your competitors. Perhaps they will treat me with more respect. PS I am copying this letter to your superiors.'

I love this idea so much, I wallow in it for a while, amending the letter over and over in my head. 'Dear Mr Smeath, as I tried to inform you discreetly at our last encounter, I am in fact a millionairess. If only you had trusted me, things might have been different.'

God, he'll be sorry, won't he? That'll teach him. He'll probably phone up and apologize. Try and grovel for my business and say he hadn't meant to offend me. But it'll be too late. *Far* too late. Hah! Hahahaha . . .

Oh blast. Missed my stop.

When I get home, Suze is sitting on the floor, surrounded by glossy magazines.

'Hi!' she says brightly. 'Guess what? I'm going to be in *Vogue*!'

'What?' I say disbelievingly. 'Were you spotted on the streets or something?' Then I realize I shouldn't sound quite so surprised. I mean, Suze has got an excellent figure. She could easily be a model. But still . . . *Vogue*!

'Not me, silly!' she says. 'My frames.'

'Your *frames* are going to be in *Vogue*?' Now I really am disbelieving.

'In the June issue! I'm going to be in a piece called "Just relax – designers who are bringing the fun back into interiors". It's cool, isn't it? The only thing is, I've only made two frames so far, so I need to make a few more in case people want to buy them.'

'Right,' I say, trying to get my head round all this. 'So – how come *Vogue* are doing a piece about you? Did they . . . hear about you?'

How can they have *heard* about her? I'm thinking. I mean, she only started making frames four days ago!

'No silly!' she says, and laughs. 'I phoned up Lally. Have you met Lally?' I shake my head. 'Well, she's fashion editor of *Vogue* now, and she spoke to Perdy, who's the interiors editor, and Perdy phoned me back – and when I told her what my frames were like, she just went wild.'

'Gosh,' I say. 'Well done.'

'She told me what to say in my interview, too,' Suze adds, and clears her throat importantly. 'I want to create spaces for people to enjoy, not admire. There's a bit of the child in all of us. Life's too short for minimalism.'

'Oh right,' I say. 'Great!'

'No, wait, there was something else, too.' Suze frowns thoughtfully. 'Oh yes, my designs are inspired by the imaginative spirit of Gaudi. I'm going to phone up Charlie now,' she adds happily. 'I'm *sure* he's something on *Tatler*.'

'Great,' I say again.

And it is great.

I'm really glad for Suze. Of course I am.

But there's a part of me that's thinking – how come

everything happens so easily for her? I bet she's never had to face a nasty bank manager in her life. And I bet she never will have to, either. Dispiritedly, I sink down onto the floor and begin to flip through a magazine.

'By the way,' says Suze, looking up from the phone. 'Tarquin rang about an hour ago, to arrange your date.' She grins wickedly. 'Are you looking forward to it?'

'Oh,' I say dully. 'Of course I am.'

I'd forgotten all about it, to be honest. But it's OK – I'll just wait until tomorrow afternoon and say I've got period pain. Easy. No-one ever questions that, especially not men.

'Oh yes,' says Suze, gesturing to a *Harpers & Queen* open on the floor. 'And look who I came across just now in the Hundred Richest Bachelors list! Oh hi, Charlie,' she says into the phone. 'It's Suze! Listen . . .'

I look down at the open *Harpers & Queen* and freeze. Luke Brandon is staring out of the page at me, an easy smile on his face. *Number 31,* reads the caption. *Age 32. Estimated wealth: £10 million. Scarily intelligent entrepreneur. Lives in Chelsea; currently dating Sacha de Bonneville, daughter of the French billionaire.*

I don't want to know this. Why would I be interested in who Luke Brandon is dating? Savagely I flip the page backwards and start reading about Number 17, who sounds much nicer. *Dave Kington. Age 28. Estimated wealth: £20 million. Former striker for Manchester United, now management guru and sportswear entrepreneur. Lives in Hertfordshire, recently split from girlfriend, model Cherisse.*

And anyway, Luke Brandon's boring. Everyone says so. All he does is work. Obsessed by money, probably.

Number 16. Ernest Flight. Age 52. Estimated wealth: £22 million. Chairman and major shareholder of the Flight Foods Corporation. Lives in Nottinghamshire, recently divorced from third wife Susan.

I don't even think he's that goodlooking. Too tall.

And he probably doesn't go to the gym or anything. Too busy. He's probably hideous underneath his clothes.

Number 15. Tarquin Cleath-Stuart. Age 26. Estimated wealth: £25 million. Landowner since inheriting huge family estate at age of 19. V. publicity-shy. Lives in Perthshire and London with old nanny; currently single.

Anyway, what kind of man buys luggage as a present? I mean, a *suitcase*, for God's sake, when he had the whole of Harrods to choose from. He could have bought his girlfriend a necklace, or some clothes. Or he could have . . . He could have . . .

Hang on a moment, what was that?

What was that?

No. That can't be – Surely that's not—

Oh my God.

And suddenly I can't breathe. I can't move. My entire frame is concentrated on the blurry picture in front of me. Tarquin Cleath-Stuart? Tarquin Suze's-Cousin? *Tarquin?*

Tarquin . . . has . . . 25 . . . million . . . pounds?

I think I'm going to pass out, if I can ever ungrip my hand from this page. I'm staring at the fifteenth-richest bachelor in Britain – and I know him.

Not only do I know him, he's asked me out on a date.

I'm having dinner with him tomorrow night.

OH-MY-GOD.

I'm going to be a millionairess. A multimillionairess. I knew it. Didn't I know it? I *knew* it. Tarquin's going to fall in love with me and ask me to marry him and we'll get married in a gorgeous Scottish castle just like in *Four Weddings* (except with nobody dying on us). And I'll have £25 million.

And what will Derek Smeath say *then*? Hah!

Hah!

'D'you want a cup of tea?' says Suze, putting down the phone. 'Charlie's such a poppet. He's going to feature me in Britain's Up-And-Coming-Talent.'

'Excellent,' I say vaguely, and clear my throat. 'Just . . . just looking at Tarquin here.'

I have to check. I have to check there isn't some other Tarquin Cleath-Stuart, some cousin I don't know about. Please God, please let me be going out with the rich one.

'Oh yes,' says Suze casually. 'He's always in those things.' She runs her eyes down the text and shakes her head. 'God, they always exaggerate everything. £25 million!'

My heart stops.

'Hasn't he got £25 million, then?' I say carelessly.

'Oh no!' She laughs as though the idea's ridiculous. 'The estate's worth about . . . Oh, I don't know. £18 million.'

£18 million. Well, that'll do. That'll do nicely.

'These magazines!' I say, and roll my eyes sympathetically.

'Earl Grey?' says Suze, getting up. 'Or normal?'

'Earl Grey,' I say, even though I actually prefer Typhoo. Because I'd better start acting posh, hadn't I, if I'm going to be the girlfriend of someone called Tarquin Cleath-Stuart.

Rebecca Cleath-Stuart.

Becky Cleath-Stuart.

Hi, it's Rebecca Cleath-Stuart here. Yes, Tarquin's wife. We met at . . . Yes, I was wearing Chanel. How clever of you!

'By the way,' I add, 'did Tarquin say where I should meet him?'

'Oh, he's going to come and pick you up,' says Suze.

But of course he is. The fifteenth-richest bachelor in Britain doesn't just meet you at a tube station, does he? He doesn't just say, 'See you under the big clock at Waterloo'. He comes and picks you up.

Oh, this is it. This is it! My new life has finally begun.

*   *   *

I have never spent so long on getting ready for a date in my life. Never. The process starts at eight on Saturday morning when I look at my open wardrobe and realize that I don't have a *single* thing to wear – and only ends at 7.30 that evening when I give my lashes another layer of mascara, spray myself in Coco Chanel and walk into the sitting room for Suze's verdict.

'Wow!' she says, looking up from a frame she is upholstering in distressed denim. 'You look . . . bloody amazing!'

And I have to say, I agree. I'm wearing all black – but expensive black. The kind of deep, soft black you fall into. A simple sleeveless dress from Whistles, the highest of Jimmy Choos, a pair of stunning uncut amethyst earrings. And please don't ask how much it all cost, because that's irrelevant. This is investment shopping. The biggest investment of my life.

I haven't eaten anything all day so I'm nice and thin, and for once my hair has fallen perfectly into shape. I look . . . well, I've never looked better in my life.

But of course, looks are only part of the package, aren't they? Which is why I cannily stopped off at Waterstone's on the way home and bought a book on Wagner. I've been reading it all afternoon, while I waited for my nails to dry, and have even memorized a few little passages to throw into the conversation.

I'm not sure what else Tarquin is into, apart from Wagner. Still, that should be enough to keep us going. And anyway, I expect he's planning to take me somewhere really glamorous with a jazz band, so we'll be too busy dancing cheek to cheek to make conversation.

The doorbell rings and I give a little start. I have to admit, my heart is pounding with nerves. But at the same time I feel strangely cool. This is it. Here begins my new multimillion-pound existence. Luke Brandon, eat your heart out.

'I'll get it,' says Suze, grinning at me, and disappears out into the hall. A moment later I hear her saying, 'Tarkie!'

'Suze!'

I glance at myself in the mirror, take a deep breath and turn to face the door, just as Tarquin appears. His head is as bony as ever, and he's wearing another of his ancient, odd-looking suits. But somehow none of that seems to matter any more. In fact, I'm not really taking in the way he looks. I'm just staring at him. Staring and staring at him, unable to speak; unable to frame any thought at all except: twenty-five million pounds.

Twenty-five million pounds. The sort of thought that makes you feel dizzy and elated, like a fairground ride. I suddenly want to run around the room, yelling 'Twenty-five million! Twenty-five million!' throwing banknotes up in the air as if I were in some Hollywood comedy caper.

But I don't. Of course I don't. I say, 'Hi Tarquin,' and give him a dazzling smile.

'Hi, Becky,' he says. 'You look wonderful.'

'Thanks,' I say, and look bashfully down at my dress.

'D'you want to stay for a titchy?' says Suze, who is looking on fondly – as if she's my mother and this is senior prom night and I'm dating the most popular boy in school.

'Ermm . . . no, I think we'll just get going,' says Tarquin, meeting my eye. 'What do you think, Becky?'

'Absolutely,' I say. 'Let's go.'

Fourteen

A taxi is chugging outside in the road, and Tarquin ushers me inside. To be honest, I'm a bit disappointed it isn't a chauffeur-driven limousine – but still. This is pretty good, too. Being whisked off in a taxi by one of Britain's most eligible bachelors to . . . who knows where? The Savoy? Claridges? Dancing at Annabel's? Tarquin hasn't told me yet where we're going.

Oh God, maybe it'll be one of those mad places where everything is served under a silver dome and there's a million knives and forks and snooty waiters looking on, just waiting to catch you out. But that's OK. As long as I don't panic. Just keep calm and remember the rules. Right. What are they, again? Cutlery: start from the outside and work your way in. Bread: do not slice your bread roll but break into little bits and butter each one individually. Tomato ketchup: do not ask for under any circumstances.

What if it's lobster? I've never eaten a lobster in my life. Shit. It's going to be lobster, isn't it? And I won't know what to do and it'll be hideously embarrassing. Why haven't I ever eaten lobster? Why? It's all my parents' fault. They should have taken me to expensive restaurants from an early age so I would develop a non-chalant *savoir-faire* with tricky food.

'I thought we'd just have a nice quiet supper,' says Tarquin, looking over at me.

'Lovely,' I say. 'Nice quiet supper. Perfect.'

Thank God. That probably means we're not heading for lobster and silver domes. We're going to some tiny tucked-away place that hardly anyone knows about.

Some little private club where you have to knock on an anonymous-looking door in a back street, and you get inside and it's packed with celebrities sitting on sofas, behaving like normal people. Yes! And maybe Tarquin knows them all!

But of course he knows them all. He's a multi-millionaire, isn't he?

I look out of the window and see that we're driving past Harrods. And for just a moment, my stomach tightens painfully as I remember the last time I was here. Bloody suitcases. Bloody Luke Brandon. Huh. In fact, I wish he was walking along the road right now, so I could give him a careless, I'm-with-the-fifteenth-richest-man-in-Britain wave.

'OK,' says Tarquin suddenly to the taxi driver. 'You can drop us here.' He grins at me. 'Practically on the doorstep.'

'Great,' I say, and reach for the door.

Practically on the doorstep of where? As I get out I look around, wondering where on earth we're going. We're at Hyde Park Corner. What's at Hyde Park Corner? I turn round slowly, and glimpse a sign – and suddenly I realize what's going on. We're going to the Lanesborough!

Wow. How classy is that? Dinner at the Lanesborough. But naturally. Where else would one go on a first date?

'So,' says Tarquin, appearing at my side. 'I just thought we could get a bite to eat and then . . . see.'

'Sounds good,' I say, as we start walking.

Excellent! Dinner at the Lanesborough and then on to some glam nightclub. This is all shaping up wonderfully.

We walk straight past the entrance to the Lanesborough, but I'm not fazed by that. Everyone knows VIPs always go in through the back to avoid the paparazzi. Not that I can actually see any paparazzi – but it probably becomes a habit. We'll duck into some back alley, and walk through the kitchens while the

197

chefs pretend they can't see us, and then emerge in the foyer. This is so cool.

'I'm sure you've been here before,' says Tarquin apologetically. 'Not the most original choice.'

'Don't be silly!' I say, as we stop and head towards a pair of glass doors. 'I simply adore . . .'

Hang on, where are we? This isn't the back entrance to anywhere. This is . . .

Pizza on the Park.

Tarquin's taking me to Pizza Express. I don't believe it. The fifteenth-richest man in the country is taking me to bloody Pizza Express.

'. . . pizza,' I finish weakly. 'Love the stuff.'

'Oh good!' says Tarquin. 'I thought we probably didn't want anywhere too flashy.'

'Oh no.' I pull what I think is a very convincing face. 'I hate flashy places. Much better to have a nice quiet pizza together.'

'That's what I thought,' says Tarquin, turning to look at me. 'But now I feel rather bad. You've dressed up so nicely . . .' He pauses doubtfully, gazing at my outfit. (As well he might. I didn't go and spend a fortune in Whistles just to be taken to Pizza Express.) 'I mean, if you wanted to, we could go somewhere a bit smarter. The Lanesborough's just around the corner . . .'

He raises his eyes questioningly, and I'm about to say, 'Oh, yes please!' when suddenly, in a blinding flash, I realize what's going on. This is a test, isn't it? It's like choosing out of three caskets in a fairytale. Everyone knows the rules. You *never* choose the gold shiny one. Or even the quite impressive silver one. What you're supposed to do is choose the dull little lead one, and then there's a flash of light and it turns into a mountain of jewels. So this is it. Tarquin's testing me, to see whether I like him for himself or if I'm only after him for his money.

Which, frankly, I find rather insulting. I mean, who does he think I am?

'No, let's stay here,' I say, and touch his arm briefly. 'Much more relaxed. Much more . . . fun.'

Which is actually quite true. And I do like pizza. And that yummy garlic bread. Mmm. You know, now I come to think about it, this is quite a good choice.

As the waiter hands us our menus, I give a cursory flash down the list, but I already know what I want. It's what I always have when I go to Pizza Express – Fiorentina. The one with spinach and an egg. I know it sounds weird, but honestly, it's delicious.

'Would you like an aperitif?' says the waiter, and I'm about to say what I usually do, which is, Oh, let's just have a bottle of wine, when I think sod it. I'm having dinner with a multimillionaire here. I'm bloody well going to have a gin and tonic.

'A gin and tonic,' I say firmly, and look at Tarquin, daring him to look taken aback. But he grins at me, and says,

'Unless you wanted champagne?'

'Oh,' I say, completely thrown.

'I always think champagne and pizza is a good combination,' he says, and looks at the waiter. 'A bottle of Moët, please.'

Well this is more like it. This is a lot more like it. Champagne and pizza. And Tarquin is actually being quite normal.

The champagne arrives and we toast each other and take a few sips. I'm really starting to enjoy myself. Then I spot Tarquin's bony hand edging slowly towards mine on the table. And in a reflex action – completely without meaning to – I whip my fingers away, pretending I have to scratch my ear. A flicker of disappointment passes over his face and I find myself giving a really fake, embarrassed cough and looking intently at a picture on the wall to my left.

Oh God. What did I have to go and do that for? If I'm going to marry the guy, I've got to do a lot more than hold his hand.

I can do this, I tell myself firmly. I *can* be attracted to him. It's just a matter of self-control and possibly also getting very drunk. So I lift my glass and take several huge gulps. I can feel the bubbles surging into my head, singing happily, 'I'm going to be a millionaire's wife! I'm going to be a millionaire's wife!' And when I look back at Tarquin, he already seems a bit more attractive (in a stoaty kind of way). Alcohol is obviously going to be the key to our marital happiness.

My head is filled with a happy vision of our wedding day. Me in some wonderful designer dress; my mum and dad looking on proudly. No more money troubles ever. *Ever.* The fifteenth-richest man in the country. A house in Belgravia. Mrs Tarquin Cleath-Stuart. Just imagining it, I feel almost faint with longing.

Oh God, it could all be mine. It *can* be mine.

I smile as warmly as I can at Tarquin, who hesitates – then smiles back. Phew. I haven't wrecked things. It's all still on. Now we just need to discover that we're utter soulmates with loads of things in common.

'I love the—' I say.

'Do you—'

We both speak at once.

'Sorry,' I say. 'Do carry on.'

'No *you* carry on,' says Tarquin.

'Oh,' I say. 'Well . . . I was just going to say again how much I love the picture you gave Suze.' No harm in complimenting his taste again. 'I *love* horses,' I add for good measure.

'Then we should go riding together,' says Tarquin. 'I know a very good livery near Hyde Park. Not quite the same as in the country, of course . . .'

'What a wonderful idea!' I say. 'That would be such fun!'

There's no way anyone's getting me on a horse. Not even in Hyde Park. But that's OK, I'll just go along with the plan, and then on the day, say I've twisted my ankle or something.

'Do you like dogs?' asks Tarquin.

'I love dogs,' I say confidently.

Which is sort of true. I wouldn't actually like to *have* a dog – too much hard work and hairs everywhere. But I like seeing labradors running across the park. And the Andrex puppy. That kind of thing.

We lapse into silence, and I take a few sips of champagne.

'Do you like *EastEnders*?' I ask eventually. 'Or are you a . . . a *Coronation Street* person?'

'I've never watched either, I'm afraid,' says Tarquin apologetically. 'I'm sure they're very good.'

'Well . . . they're OK,' I say. 'Sometimes they're really good, and other times . . .' I tail off a bit feebly, and smile at him. 'You know.'

'Absolutely,' exclaims Tarquin, as though I've said something really interesting.

There's another awkward silence. This is getting a bit sticky.

'Are there good shops, where you live in Scotland?' I say at last. Tarquin pulls a little face.

'I wouldn't know. Never go near shops if I can help it.'

'Oh right,' I say, and take a deep gulp of champagne. 'No, I . . . I hate shops too. Can't *stand* shopping.'

'Really?' says Tarquin in surprise. 'I thought all girls loved shopping.'

'Not me!' I say. 'I'd far rather be . . . out on the moors, riding along. With a couple of dogs running behind.'

'Sounds perfect,' says Tarquin, smiling at me. 'We'll have to do it some time.'

This is more like it! Common interests. Shared pursuits.

And OK, maybe I haven't been completely honest, maybe they aren't exactly my interests at the moment. But they could be. They *can* be. I can easily get to like dogs and horses, if I have to.

'Or . . . or listening to Wagner, of course,' I say casually. Ha! Genius!

'Do you really like Wagner?' says Tarquin. 'Not everyone does.'

'I *adore* Wagner,' I insist. 'He's my favourite composer.' OK, quick – what did that book say? 'I love the . . . er . . . sonorous melodic strands which interweave in the Prelude.'

'The Prelude to what?' says Tarquin interestedly.

Oh shit. Is there more than one Prelude? I take a gulp of champagne, playing for time, desperately trying to recall something else from the book. But the only other bit I can remember is 'Richard Wagner was born in Leipzig.'

'All the Preludes,' I say at last. 'I think they're all . . . fab.'

'Right,' says Tarquin, looking a bit surprised. Oh God. That wasn't the right thing to say, was it? Change the subject. Change the subject.

Luckily, at that moment a waiter arrives with our garlic bread, and we can get off the subject of Wagner. And Tarquin orders some more champagne. Somehow, I think we're going to need it.

Which means that by the time I'm halfway through my Fiorentina, I've drunk almost an entire bottle of champagne and I'm . . . Well, frankly, I'm completely pissed. My face is tingling and my eyes are sparkling, and my arm gestures are a lot more erratic than usual. But this doesn't matter. In fact, being pissed is a *good* thing – because it means I'm also delightfully witty and lively and am more or less carrying the conversation single-handedly. Tarquin is also pissed, but not as much as me. He's got quieter and quieter, and kind of thoughtful. And he keeps gazing at me.

As I finish my last scraps of pizza and lean back pleasurably, he stares at me silently for a moment, then reaches into his pocket and produces a little box.

'Here,' he says. 'This is for you.'

I have to admit, for one heartstopping moment I think . . . This Is It! He's Proposing! (Funnily enough, the very next thought that flashes into my mind is Thank God I'll Be Able To Pay Off My Overdraft. Hmmm. When he proposes for real, I must make sure to think something a bit more romantic.)

But of course, he's not proposing, is he? He's just giving me a little present.

I knew that.

So I open it and find a leather box, and inside is a little gold brooch in the shape of a horse. Lots of fine detail; beautifully crafted. A little green stone (emerald?) for the eye.

Really not my kind of thing.

'It's gorgeous,' I breathe in awe. 'Absolutely . . . stunning.'

'It's rather jolly, isn't it?' says Tarquin. 'Thought you'd like it.'

'I *adore* it.' I turn it over in my fingers (hallmark – good) then look up at him and blink a couple of times with misty eyes. God I'm drunk. I think I'm actually *seeing* through champagne. 'This is so thoughtful of you,' I murmur.

Plus I don't really wear brooches. I mean, where are you supposed to put them? Slap bang in the middle of a really nice top? I mean, come on. And they always leave great brooch-holes everywhere.

'It'll look lovely on you,' says Tarquin after a pause – and suddenly I realize he's expecting me to put it on.

Aaargh! It'll ruin my lovely Whistles dress! And who wants a horse galloping across their tits, anyway?

'I *must* put it on,' I say, and open the clasp. Gingerly I thread it through the fabric of my dress and clasp it shut, already feeling it pulling the dress out of shape. How stupid do I look now?

'It looks wonderful,' says Tarquin, meeting my gaze. 'But then . . . you always look wonderful.'

My stomach gives a flip as I see him leaning forward. He's going to try and hold my hand again, isn't he? And probably kiss me. I glance at Tarquin's lips – parted and slightly moist – and give an involuntary shudder. Oh God. I'm not quite ready for this. I mean, obviously I *do* want to kiss Tarquin, of course I do. In fact, I find him incredibly attractive. It's just . . . I think I need some more champagne first.

'That scarf you were wearing the other night,' says Tarquin. 'It was simply stunning. I looked at you in that, and I thought . . .'

Now I can see his hand edging towards mine.

'My Denny and George scarf?' I cut in brightly, before he can say anything else. 'Yes, that's lovely, isn't it? It was my aunt's, but she died. It was really sad, actually.'

Just keep talking, I think. Keep talking brightly and gesture a lot.

'But anyway, she left me her scarf,' I continue hurriedly. 'So I'll always remember her through that. Poor Aunt Ermintrude.'

'I'm really sorry,' says Tarquin, looking taken aback. 'I had no idea.'

'No. Well . . . her memory lives on through her good works,' I say, and give him a little smile. 'She was a very charitable woman. Very . . . giving.'

'Is there some sort of foundation in her name?' says Tarquin. 'When my uncle died—'

'Yes!' I say gratefully. 'Exactly that. The . . . the Ermintrude Bloomwood Foundation for . . . violinists,' I improvise, catching sight of a poster for a musical evening. 'Violinists in Malawi. That was her cause.'

'Violinists in Malawi?' echoes Tarquin.

'Oh absolutely!' I hear myself babbling. 'There's a desperate shortage of classical musicians out there. And culture is so enriching, whatever one's material circumstances.'

I can't *believe* I'm coming out with all this rubbish. I glance apprehensively up at Tarquin – and to my complete disbelief, he's looking really interested.

'So, what exactly is the foundation aiming to do?' he asks.

Oh God. What am I getting myself into, here?

'To . . . to fund six violin teachers a year,' I say, after a pause. 'Of course, they need specialist training, and special violins to take out there. But the results will be very worthwhile. They're going to teach people how to make violins, too, so they'll be self-sufficient and not dependent on the West.'

'Really?' Tarquin's brow is furrowed. Have I said something that doesn't make sense?

'Anyway.' I give a little laugh. 'That's enough about me and my family. Have you seen any good films, recently?'

This is good. We can talk about films, and then the bill will come, and then—

'Wait a moment,' says Tarquin. 'Tell me – how's the project going, so far?'

'Oh,' I say. 'Ahm . . . quite well. Considering. I haven't really kept up with its progress recently. You know, these things are always—'

'I'd really like to contribute something,' he says, interrupting me.

What?

He'd like to *what*?

'Do you know who I should make the cheque payable to?' he says, reaching into his jacket pocket. 'Is it the Bloomwood Foundation?'

And as I watch, paralysed in astonishment, he brings out a Coutts chequebook.

A pale grey Coutts chequebook.

The fifteenth-richest man in the country.

'I'm . . . I'm not sure,' I hear myself say, as though from a great distance. 'I'm not sure of the *exact* wording.'

'Well, I'll make it payable to you, then, shall I?' he says. 'And you can pass it on.' Briskly he starts to write:

Pay Rebecca Bloomwood
The sum of
Five . . .

Five hundred pounds. It must be. He wouldn't just give five poxy . . .

Thousand pounds,
T. A. J. Cleath-Stuart

I can't believe my eyes. Five thousand pounds, on a cheque, addressed to me. Five thousand pounds which belongs to Aunt Ermintrude and the violin teachers of Malawi.

If they existed.

'Here you are,' says Tarquin, and hands me the cheque – and as though in a dream, I find myself reaching out towards it.

Pay Rebecca Bloomwood the sum of five thousand pounds.

I read the words again, slowly – and feel a wave of relief so strong, it makes me want to burst into tears. The sum of five thousand pounds. More than my overdraft and my VISA bill put together. This cheque would solve all my problems, wouldn't it? It would solve all my problems in one go. And, OK, I'm not exactly violinists in Malawi – but Tarquin would never know the difference, would he? He'd never check up. Or if he did, I could come up with some story.

Anyway, what's £5,000 to a multimillionaire like Tarquin? He probably wouldn't even notice whether I paid it in or not. A poxy £5,000, when he's got £25 million! If you work it out as a fraction of his wealth it's . . . well, it's laughable, isn't it? It's the equivalent of about fifty pence to normal people. I'm talking about pinching fifty pence. Why am I even hesitating?

'Rebecca?'

Tarquin is staring at me, and I realize my hand is still inches away from the cheque. *Come on, take it*, I instruct myself firmly. *It's yours. Take the cheque and put it in your bag.* With a heroic effort, I stretch out my hand further, willing myself to close my fingers around the cheque. I'm getting closer . . . closer . . . almost there . . . my fingers are trembling with the effort . . .

It's no good, I can't. I just can't do it. I can't take his money.

'I can't take it,' I say in a rush. I pull my hand away and feel myself flushing. 'I mean . . . I'm not actually sure the foundation is accepting money yet.'

'Oh, right,' says Tarquin, looking slightly taken aback.

'I'll tell you who to make a cheque payable to when I've got more details,' I say, and take a deep gulp of champagne. 'You'd better tear that up.'

As he slowly rips the paper, I can't look. I stare into my champagne glass, feeling like crying. Five thousand pounds. It would have changed my life. It would have solved everything. Tarquin reaches for the box of matches on the table, sets the scraps of paper alight in the ashtray, and we both watch as they briefly flame.

Then he puts down the matches, smiles at me and says,

'Do excuse me a minute.'

He gets up from the table and heads off towards the back of the restaurant, and I take another gulp of champagne. Then I lean my head in my hands and give a sigh. Oh well, I think, trying to be philosophical. Maybe I'll win £5,000 in a raffle or something. Maybe Derek Smeath's computer will go haywire and he'll be forced to cancel all my debts and start again. Maybe some utter stranger really *will* pay off my VISA bill for me by mistake.

Maybe Tarquin will come back from the loo and ask me to marry him.

I raise my eyes, and they fall with an idle curiosity on the Coutts chequebook which Tarquin has left on the table. That's the chequebook of the fifteenth-richest man in the country. Wow. I wonder what it's like inside? He probably writes enormous cheques all the time, doesn't he? He probably spends more money in a day than I spend in a year.

On impulse, I pull the chequebook towards me and

open it. I don't know quite what I'm looking for – really, I'm just hoping to find some excitingly huge amount. But the first stub is only for £30. Pathetic! I flip on a bit, and find £520. Payable to Arundel & Son, whoever they are. Then, a bit later on, there's one for £7,515 to American Express. Well, that's more like it. But I mean, really, it's not the most exciting read in the world. This could be anybody's chequebook. This could practically be mine.

I close it and push it back towards his place, and glance up. As I do so, my heart freezes. Tarquin is staring straight at me.

He's standing by the bar, being directed to the other side of the restaurant by a waiter. But he isn't looking at the waiter. He's looking at me. As our eyes meet, my stomach gives a little lurch. Oh damn.

Damn. What exactly did he see?

Quickly I pull my hand back from his chequebook and take a sip of champagne. Then I look up and pretend to spot him for the first time. I give a bright little smile, and after a pause he smiles back. Then he disappears off again and I sink back into my chair, my heart thumping.

OK, don't panic, I instruct myself. Just behave naturally. He probably didn't even see you. And even if he did – it's not the hugest crime in the world, is it, looking at his chequebook? If he asks me what I was doing, I'll say I was . . . checking he'd filled in his stub correctly. Yes. That's what I'll say I was doing if he mentions it.

But he doesn't. He comes back to the table, silently pockets his chequebook, and says politely, 'Have you finished?'

'Yes,' I say. 'Yes, I have, thanks.'

I'm trying to sound as natural as possible – but I'm aware my voice sounds guilty, and my cheeks are hot.

'Right,' he says. 'Well, I've paid the bill . . . so shall we go?'

And that's it. That's the end of the date. With impeccable courtesy, Tarquin ushers me to the door of Pizza on the Park, hails a taxi and pays the driver the fare back to Fulham. I don't dare ask him if he'd like to come back or go for a drink somewhere else. There's a coldness about my spine which stops me uttering the words. So we kiss each other on the cheek and he tells me he had a delightful evening, and I thank him again for a lovely time.

And I sit in the taxi all the way back to Fulham with a jumpy stomach, wondering what exactly he saw.

As the taxi pulls in front of our house, I say goodnight to the taxi driver and reach for my keys. I'm thinking that I'll go and run a hot bath and sit in it, and calmly try to work out exactly what happened back there. Did Tarquin really see me looking through his chequebook? Maybe he just saw me pushing it back towards his place in a helpful manner. Maybe he saw nothing at all.

But then why did he suddenly become all stiff and polite? He must have seen something; suspected something. And then he'll have noticed the way I flushed and couldn't meet his eye. Oh God, why do I always have to look so guilty? I wasn't even *doing* anything. I was just curious. Is that such a crime?

Perhaps I should have quickly said something – made some joke about it. Turned it into a lighthearted, amusing incident. But what kind of joke can you make about leafing through someone's private chequebook? Oh God, I'm so *stupid*. Why did I ever touch the bloody thing? I should have just sat, quietly sipping my drink.

But in my defence . . . he left it on the table, didn't he? He can't be that secretive about it. And I don't *know* that he saw me looking through it, do I? Maybe he didn't. Maybe I'm just paranoid.

As I put my key into the lock, I'm actually feeling quite positive. OK, so Tarquin wasn't that friendly just now – but he might have been feeling ill or something.

Or maybe he just didn't want to rush me. What I'll do is, tomorrow I'll send a nice chatty note to him, saying thanks again, and suggesting we go and see some Wagner together. Excellent idea. And I'll mug up a bit about the Preludes, so that if he asks me which one again, I'll know exactly what to say. Yes! This is all going to be fine. I need never have worried.

I swing the door open, unbuttoning my coat – and then my heart gives a flip. Suze is waiting for me in the hall. She's sitting on the stairs, waiting for me – and there's a funny expression on her face.

'Oh Bex,' she says, and shakes her head reproachfully. 'I've just been speaking to Tarquin.'

'Oh right,' I say, trying to sound natural, but aware that my voice is a frightened squeak. I turn away, take my coat and slowly unwind my scarf, playing for time. What exactly has he said to her?

'I don't suppose there's any point asking you *why*?' she says after a pause.

'Well,' I falter, feeling sick. God, I could do with a cigarette.

'I'm not *blaming* you, or anything. I just think you should have . . .' She shakes her head and sighs. 'Couldn't you have let him down more gently? He sounded quite upset. The poor thing was really keen on you, you know.'

This isn't quite making sense. Let him down more gently?

'What exactly . . .' I lick my dry lips. 'What exactly did he say?'

'Well, he was only really phoning to tell me you'd left your umbrella behind,' says Suze. 'Apparently one of the waiters came rushing out with it. But of course I asked him how the date had gone . . .'

'And . . . and what did he say?'

'Well,' says Suze, and gives a little shrug. 'He said you'd had a really nice time – but you'd pretty much made it clear you didn't want to see him again.'

'Oh.'

I sink down onto the floor, feeling rather weak. So that's it. Tarquin did see me leafing through his chequebook. I've ruined my chances with him completely.

But he didn't tell Suze what I'd done. He protected me. Pretended it was my decision not to carry things on. He was a gentleman.

In fact – he was a gentleman all evening, wasn't he? He was kind to me, and charming, and polite. And all I did, all throughout the date, was tell him lies.

Suddenly I want to cry.

'I just think it's such a shame,' says Suze. 'I mean, I know it's up to you and everything – but he's such a sweet guy. And he's had a crush on you for ages! You two would go perfectly together.' She gives me a wheedling look. 'Isn't there any chance you might go out with him again?'

'I . . . I honestly don't think so,' I say in a scratchy voice. 'Suze . . . I'm a bit tired. I think I'll go to bed.'

And without meeting her eye I get up and slowly walk down the corridor to my room.

BANK OF LONDON
London House
Mill Street EC3R 4DW

Ms Rebecca Boomwood
Flat 2
4 Burney Rd
London SW6 8FD

23 March 2000

Dear Ms Boomwood

Thank you very much for your application for a Bank of London
Easifone Loan.

Unfortunately 'buying clothes and makeup' was not deemed a
suitable purpose for such a substantial unsecured loan, and
your application has been turned down by our credit team.

Thank you very much for considering Bank of London.

Yours sincerely

Margaret Hopkins
Loans adviser

Endwich Bank
FULHAM BRANCH
3 Fulham Road
London SW6 9JH

Ms Rebecca Bloomwood
Flat 2
4 Burney Rd
London SW6 8FD

24 March 2000

Dear Ms Bloomwood

I am writing to confirm our meeting at 9.30 am on Monday, 27 March, here at our Fulham office. Please ask for me at reception.

I look forward to seeing you then.

Yours sincerely

Derek Smeath
Manager

ENDWICH – BECAUSE WE CARE

Fifteen

I have never in my life felt as terrible as I do when I wake up the next morning. Never.

The first thing I feel is pain. Exploding sparks of pain as I try to move my head; as I try to open my eyes; as I try to work out a few basics like: Who am I? What day is it? Should I be somewhere else by now?

For a while I lie quite still, panting with the exertion of just being alive. In fact, my face is growing scarlet and I'm almost starting to hyperventilate, so I force myself to slow down and breathe regularly. *In . . . out, in . . . out.* And then surely everything will come back to me and I will feel better. *In . . . out, in . . . out.*

OK . . . Rebecca. That's right. I'm Rebecca Bloomwood, aren't I? *In . . . out, in . . . out.*

What else? Dinner. I had dinner somewhere last night. *In . . . out, in . . . out.*

Pizza. I had pizza. And who was I with, again? *In . . . out. In . . .*

Tarquin.

Out.

Oh God. Tarquin.

Leafing through chequebook. Everything ruined. All my own fault.

A familiar wave of despair floods over me and I close my eyes, trying to calm my throbbing head. At the same time, I remember that last night, when I went back to my room, I found the half-bottle of malt whisky which Scottish Prudential once gave me, still sitting on my dressing table. I opened it up – even though I don't like whisky – and drank . . . well, certainly a few

214

toothmugfuls. Which might possibly explain why I'm feeling so ill now.

Slowly I struggle to a sitting position and listen for sounds of Suze, but I can't hear anything. The flat's empty. It's just me.

Me and my thoughts.

Which, to be honest, I can't endure. My head's pounding and I feel pale and shaky – but I've got to get moving; distract myself. I'll go out, have a cup of coffee somewhere quiet and try to get myself together.

Somehow I manage to get out of bed, stagger to my chest of drawers and stare at myself in the mirror. I don't like what I see. My skin's green, my mouth is dry and my hair's sticking to my skin in clumps. But worst of all is the expression in my eyes: a blank, miserable self-loathing. Last night I was given a chance – a fantastic opportunity on a silver platter. And I threw it in the bin. God, I'm a disaster. I don't deserve to live.

I head to the King's Road, to lose myself in the anonymous bustle. The air's crisp and fresh, and as I stride along it's almost possible to forget about last night. Almost, but not quite.

I go into Aroma and order a large cappuccino, and try to drink it normally. As if everything's fine and I'm just another girl out on a Sunday for some shopping. But I can't do it. I can't escape my thoughts. They're churning round in my head, like a record that won't stop, over and over and over.

If only I hadn't picked up his chequebook. If only I hadn't been so *stupid*. It was all going so well. He really liked me. We were holding hands. He was planning to ask me out again. Oh God, if only I could go back; if only I could play the evening again . . .

Don't think about it. Don't think about what could have been. It's too unbearable. If I'd played it right, I'd probably be sitting here drinking coffee with Tarquin, wouldn't I? I'd probably be well on my way to becoming the fifteenth-richest woman in the country.

Instead of which . . . what?

I have debts up to my eyeballs. I have a meeting with my bank manager on Monday morning. I have no idea what I'm going to do. No idea at all.

Miserably I take a sip of coffee and unwrap my little chocolate. I'm not in the mood for chocolate, but I stuff it into my mouth anyway.

The worst thing – the very worst thing of all – is that I was actually starting to quite like Tarquin. Maybe he isn't God's gift in the looks department, but he's very kind, and quite funny, in his own way. And that brooch – it's really quite sweet.

And the way he didn't tell Suze what he'd seen me doing. And the way he *believed* me when I told him I liked dogs and Wagner and bloody violinists in Malawi. The way he was so completely, utterly unsuspicious.

Oh God, now I really am going to start crying.

Roughly I brush at my eyes, drain my cup and stand up. Out on the street I hesitate, then begin walking briskly again. Maybe the breeze will blow these unbearable thoughts out of my head. Maybe I'll feel better in a while.

But I stride and stride, and I still feel no better. My head's aching and my eyes are red and I could really do with a drink or something. Just a little something, to make me feel a bit better. A drink, or a cigarette, or . . .

I look up, and I'm in front of Octagon. My favourite shop in the whole world. Three floors of clothes, accessories, furnishings, gifts, coffee shops, juice bars and a florist which makes you want to fill your entire home with flowers.

I've got my purse with me.

Just something small, to cheer me up. A T-shirt or something. Or even some bubble bath. I *need* to buy myself something. I won't spend much. I'll just go in, and . . .

I'm already pushing my way through the doors. Oh God, the relief. The warmth, the light. This is where I belong. This my natural habitat.

Except that even as I'm heading towards the T-shirts, I'm not quite as happy as I should be. I look through the racks, trying to recreate the excitement I usually feel at buying myself a little treat – but somehow today I feel a bit empty. Still, I choose a cropped top with a silver star in the middle, and put it over my arm, telling myself I feel better already. Then I spot a rack of dressing gowns. I could do with a new dressing gown, as a matter of fact.

As I finger a lovely white waffle robe, I can hear a little voice at the back of my head, like a radio turned down low. *Don't do it. You're in debt. Don't do it. You're in debt.*

Yes, well, maybe I am.

But quite frankly, what does it matter now? It's too late to make any difference. I'm already in debt; I might as well be more in debt. Almost savagely, I pull the dressing gown down from the rack and put it over my arm. Then I reach for the matching waffle slippers. No point buying one without the other.

The checkout point is directly to my left, but I ignore it. I'm not done yet. I head for the escalators and go up to the home-furnishing floor. Time for a new duvet set. White, to match my new dressing gown. And a pair of bolster cushions, and a fake-fur throw.

Every time I add something to my pile, I feel a little whoosh of pleasure, like a firework going off. And for a moment, everything's all right. But then, gradually, the light and sparkles disappear, and I'm left with cold dark blackness again. So I look feverishly around for something else. A huge scented candle. A set of Jo Malone shower gel and moisturizer. A bag of hand-made potpourri. As I add each one, I feel a whoosh – and then blackness. But the whooshes are getting shorter and shorter each time. Why won't the pleasure stay? Why don't I feel happier?

'Can I help you?' says a voice, interrupting my thoughts. A young assistant, dressed in the Octagon outfit of white shirt and linen trousers, has come up and is looking at my pile of stuff on the floor. 'Would you like me to hold some of these while you continue shopping?'

'Oh,' I say blankly, and look down at the stuff I've accumulated. It's actually quite a lot by now. 'No, don't worry. I'll just . . . I'll just pay for this lot.'

Somehow, between us, we manage to lug all my shopping across the beechwood floor to the stylish granite checkout point in the middle, and the assistant begins to scan everything through. The bolster cushions have been reduced – which I hadn't realized – and while she's checking the exact price, a queue begins to form behind me.

'That'll be £370.56,' she says at last, and smiles at me. 'How would you like to pay?'

'Erm . . . Switch card,' I say, and reach for my purse. As she's swiping it, I eye up my carrier bags and wonder how I'm going to get all this stuff home.

But immediately my thoughts bounce away. I don't want to think about home. I don't want to think about Suze, or Tarquin, or last night. Or any of it.

'I'm sorry,' says the girl apologetically, 'but there's something wrong with your card. It won't authorize the purchase.' She hands it back to me. 'Do you have anything else?'

'Oh,' I say, slightly flustered. 'Well . . . here's my VISA card.'

How embarrassing. And anyway, what's wrong with my card? It looks all right to me. I must complain to the bank about this.

The bank. Meeting tomorrow, with Derek Smeath. Oh God. Don't think about it. Quick, think about something else. Look at the floor. Glance about the shop. There's quite a big line of people behind me now, and I can hear coughing and clearing of throats. Everyone's waiting for me. As I meet the eye of the woman behind me, I smile awkwardly.

'No,' says the girl. 'This one's no good either.'

'What?' I whip round in shock. How can my VISA card be no good? It's my *VISA* card, for God's sake. Accepted all over the world. What's going on? It doesn't make any sense. It doesn't make any—

My thoughts stop mid-stream, and a nasty chill feeling begins to creep over me. All those letters. Those letters I've been putting in my dressing-table drawer. Surely they can't have . . .

No. Don't say they've cancelled my card. They can't have done.

My heart starts to thump in panic. I know I haven't been that great at paying my bills – but I need my VISA card. I *need* it. They can't just cancel it, just like that. Suddenly I feel rather shaky.

'There are other people waiting,' says the girl, gesturing to the queue. 'So if you aren't able to pay . . .'

'Of course I'm able to pay,' I say stiffly, aware that my cheeks are now flaming red. With trembling hands I scrabble in my purse and eventually produce my silver Octagon charge card. It was buried under all the others, so I can't have used it for a while. 'Here,' I say. 'I'll put it all on this.'

'Fine,' says the girl curtly, and swipes the card.

It's only as we're waiting silently for the authorization that I begin to wonder whether I've actually paid off my Octagon account. They sent me a nasty letter a while ago, didn't they? Something about an outstanding balance. But I'm sure I paid it off, ages ago. Or at least, some of it. Didn't I? I'm sure I—

'I'm just going to have to make a quick call,' says the assistant, staring at her machine. She reaches for the phone next to the till, and dials a number.

'Hi,' she says. 'Yes, if I can give you an account number . . .'

Behind me, somebody sighs loudly. I can feel my face growing hotter and hotter. I don't dare look round. I don't dare move.

'I see,' says the assistant eventually, and puts down the phone. She looks up – and at the sight of her face, my stomach gives a lurch. Her expression isn't apologetic, or polite any more. It's plain unfriendly.

'Our financial services department would like you to contact them urgently,' she says curtly. 'I'll give you the number.'

'Right,' I say, trying to sound relaxed. As though this is a fairly normal request. 'OK. Well, I'll do that. Thanks.' I hold my hand out for my charge card. I'm not interested in my shopping any more. All I want to do is get out of here as quickly as possible.

'I'm sorry, I'm afraid your account's been frozen,' says the assistant without lowering her voice. 'I'm going to have to retain your card.'

I stare at her in disbelief, feeling my face prickling with shock. Behind me there's an interested rustle as everybody hears this and starts nudging each other.

'So, unless you have another means of paying . . .' she adds, looking at my heap of stuff on the counter. My waffle robe. My new duvet set. My scented candle. A huge, conspicuous pile of stuff. Stuff I don't need. Stuff which I can't pay for. Suddenly the sight of it all makes me feel sick.

Numbly I shake my head. I feel as if I've been caught stealing.

'Elsa,' calls the assistant. 'Will you deal with this, please? The customer isn't going to make the purchase after all.' She gestures to the pile of stuff, and the other assistant moves it along the counter, out of the way, her face deliberately blank.

'Next, please.'

The woman behind me steps forward, avoiding my eye in embarrassment, and slowly I turn away. I have never felt so humiliated in all my life. The whole floor seems to be looking at me – all the customers, all the sales assistants, all whispering and nudging. *Did you see? Did you see what happened?*

With wobbling legs I walk away, not looking right or left. This is a nightmare. I just have to get out, as quickly as possible. I have to get out of the shop and onto the street and go . . .

Go where? Home, I suppose.

But I can't go back and face Suze and hear her going on about how sweet Tarquin is. Or even worse, risk bumping into him. Oh God. The very thought makes me feel sick.

What am I going to do? Where am I going to go?

Shakily, I begin to walk along the pavement, looking away from the mocking window displays. What can I do? Where can I go? I feel empty; almost lightheaded with panic.

I pause at a corner, waiting for a traffic light to change and look blankly at a display of cashmere jumpers to my left. And suddenly, at the sight of a scarlet Pringle golfing jumper, I feel tears of relief springing to my eyes. There's one place I can go. One place I can always go.

Home to my mum and dad.

Sixteen

When I turn up at my parents' house that afternoon
with no warning, saying I want to stay for a few days,
I can't say they seem shocked, or even surprised.

In fact, so unsurprised do they seem, that I begin to
wonder if they've been expecting this eventuality all
along, ever since I moved to London. Have they been
waiting every week for me to arrive on the doorsteps
with no luggage and red eyes? They're certainly behaving as calmly as a hospital casualty team operating
an emergency procedure that was rehearsed only last
week.

Except that surely the casualty team wouldn't keep
arguing about the best way to resuscitate the patient?
After a few minutes, I feel like going outside, letting
them decide on their plan of action, and ringing the
bell again.

'You go upstairs and have a nice hot bath,' says
Mum, as soon as I've put down my handbag. 'I expect
you're exhausted!'

'She doesn't have to have a bath if she doesn't want
to!' retorts Dad. 'She might want a drink! D'you want a
drink, darling?'

'Is that *wise*?' says Mum, shooting him a meaningful
What If She's An Alkie? look, which presumably I'm
not supposed to notice.

'I don't want a drink, thanks,' I say. 'But I'd love a
cup of tea.'

'Of course you would!' says Mum. 'Graham, go and
put the kettle on.' And she gives him another meaningful look. As soon as he's disappeared into the

kitchen, she comes close to me and says, in a lowered voice,

'Are you feeling all right, darling? Is anything . . . wrong?'

Oh God, there's nothing like your mother's sympathetic voice when you're feeling down, to make you want to burst into tears.

'Well,' I say, in a slightly wobbly voice. 'Things have been better. I'm just . . . in a bit of a difficult situation at the moment. But it'll be all right in the end.' I give a small shrug and look away.

'Because . . .' She lowers her voice even more. 'Your father isn't as old-fashioned as he seems. And I know that if it were a case of us looking after a . . . a Little One, while you pursued your career . . .'

What?

'Mum, don't worry!' I exclaim sharply. 'I'm not pregnant!'

'I never said you were,' she says and flushes a little. 'I just wanted to offer you our support.'

Bloody hell, what are my parents like? They watch too many soap operas, that's their trouble. In fact, they were probably *hoping* I was pregnant. By my wicked married lover whom they could then murder and bury under the patio.

And what's this 'offer you our support' business, anyway? My mum would never have said that before she started watching Ricki Lake every afternoon.

'Well, come on,' she says. 'Let's sit you down with a nice cup of tea.'

And so I follow her into the kitchen, and we all sit down with a nice cup of tea. And I have to say, it is very nice. Hot strong tea and a chocolate bourbon biscuit. Perfect. I close my eyes and take a few sips, and then open them again, to see both my parents gazing at me with naked curiosity all over their faces. Immediately my mother changes her expression to a smile, and my father gives a little cough – but I can tell, they are *gagging* to know what's wrong.

'So,' I say cautiously, and both their heads jerk up. 'You're both well, are you?'

'Oh yes,' says my mother. 'Yes, *we're* fine.'

There's another silence.

'Becky?' says my father gravely, and both Mum and I swivel to face him. 'Are you in some kind of trouble we should know about? Only tell us if you want to,' he adds hastily. 'And I want you to know – we're there for you.'

That's another bloody Ricki Lake-ism, too. My parents should really get out more.

'Are you all right, darling?' says Mum gently – and she sounds so kind and understanding that, in spite of myself, I find myself putting down my cup with a shaky hand and saying, 'To tell you the truth, I am in a spot of bother. I didn't want to worry you, so I haven't said anything before now . . .' I can feel tears gathering in my eyes.

'What is it?' says Mum in a panicky voice. 'Oh God, you're on drugs, aren't you?'

'No, I'm not on drugs!' I exclaim. 'I'm just . . . It's just that I . . . I'm . . .' I take a deep gulp of tea. This is even harder than I thought it would be. Come on, Rebecca, just *say* it.

I close my eyes and clench my hand tightly around my mug.

'The truth is . . .' I say slowly.

'Yes?' says Mum.

'The truth is . . .' I open my eyes. 'I'm being stalked. By a man called . . . called Derek Smeath.'

There's silence apart from a long hiss as my father sucks in breath.

'I knew it!' says my mother in a sharp, brittle voice. 'I knew it! I knew there was something wrong!'

'We all knew there was something wrong!' says my father, and rests his elbows heavily on the table. 'How long has this been going on, Becky?'

'Oh, ahm . . . months now,' I say, staring into my tea. 'It's just . . . pestering, really. It's not serious or anything. But I just couldn't deal with it any more.'

'And who is this Derek Smeath?' says Dad. 'Do we know him?'

'I don't think so. I came across him . . . I came across him through work.'

'Of course you did!' says Mum. 'A young, pretty girl like you, with a high-profile career . . . I knew this was going to happen!'

'Is he another journalist?' says Dad and I shake my head.

'He works for Endwich Bank. He does things like . . . like phone up and pretend he's in charge of my bank account. He's really convincing.'

There's silence while my parents digest this and I eat another chocolate bourbon.

'Well,' says Mum at last. 'I think we'll have to phone the police.'

'No!' I exclaim, spluttering crumbs all over the table. 'I don't want the police! He's never threatened me or anything. In fact, he's not really a stalker at all. He's just a pain. I thought if I disappeared for a while . . .'

'I see,' says Dad, and glances at Mum. 'Well, that makes sense.'

'So what I suggest,' I say, meshing my hands tightly in my lap, 'is that if he rings, you say I've gone abroad and you don't have a number for me. And . . . if anyone else rings, say the same thing. Even Suze.'

'Are you sure?' says Mum, wrinkling her brow. 'Wouldn't it be better to go to the police?'

'No!' I say quickly. 'That would only make him feel important. I just want to vanish for a bit.'

'Fine,' says Dad. 'As far as we're concerned, you're not here.'

He reaches across the table and clasps my hand. And as I see the worry on his face, I hate myself for what I'm doing. I feel so guilty that, for a moment, I feel I might just burst into tears, and tell them everything, truthfully.

But . . . I can't do it. I simply can't tell my kind,

225

loving parents that their so-called successful daughter with her so-called top job is in fact a disorganized, deceitful mess, up to her eyeballs in debt.

And so we have supper (Waitrose Cumberland Pie) and watch an Agatha Christie adaptation together, and then I go upstairs to my old bedroom, put on an old nightie and go to bed. And when I wake up the next morning I feel more happy and well rested than I have for weeks.

Above all, staring at my old bedroom ceiling, I feel safe. Cocooned from the world; wrapped up in cotton wool. No-one can get me here. No-one even *knows* I'm here. I won't get any nasty letters and I won't get any nasty phone calls and I won't get any nasty visitors. It's like a sanctuary. All responsibility has been lifted from my shoulders. I feel as if I'm fifteen again, with nothing to worry about but my homework. (And I haven't even got any of that.)

It's at least nine o'clock before I rouse myself and get out of bed, and as I do so, it occurs to me that miles away in London, Derek Smeath is expecting me to arrive for a meeting in half an hour. A slight twinge passes through my stomach and for a moment I consider phoning up the bank and giving some excuse. But even as I'm considering it, I know I'm not going to do it. I don't even want to acknowledge the bank's existence. I want to forget all about it.

None of it exists any more. Not the bank, not VISA, not Octagon. All eliminated from my life, just like that.

The only call I make is to the office, because I don't want them sacking me in my absence. I phone at 9.20 – before Philip gets in – and get Mavis on reception.

'Hello, Mavis?' I croak. 'It's Rebecca Bloomwood here. Can you tell Philip I'm ill?'

'You poor thing!' says Mavis. 'Is it bronchitis?'

'I'm not sure,' I croak. 'I've got a doctor's appointment later. I must go. Bye.'

And that's it. One phone call, and I'm free. No-one

suspects anything – why should they? I feel light with relief. It's so easy to escape. So simple. I should have done this long ago.

At the back of my mind, like a nasty little gremlin, is the knowledge that I won't be able to stay here for ever. That sooner or later things will start to catch up with me.

But the point is – not yet. Not for a long time. And in the meantime, I'm not even going to think about it. I'm just going to have a nice cup of tea and watch *Morning Coffee* and blank my mind out completely.

When I go into the kitchen, Dad's sitting at the table, reading the paper. There's the smell of toast in the air, and Radio Four in the background. Just like when I was younger and lived at home. Life was simple then. Life was so easy. No bills, no demands, no threatening letters. An enormous wave of nostalgia overcomes me, and I turn away to fill the kettle, blinking slightly.

'Interesting news,' says Dad, jabbing at the *Daily Telegraph*.

'Oh yes?' I say, putting a teabag in a mug. 'What's that?'

'Scottish Prime have taken over Flagstaff Life.'

'Oh right,' I say vaguely. 'Right. Yes, I think I'd heard that was going to happen.'

'All the Flagstaff Life investors are going to receive huge windfall payments. The biggest ever, apparently.'

'Gosh,' I say, trying to sound interested. I reach for a copy of *Good Housekeeping*, flick it open and begin to read my horoscope.

But something's niggling at my mind. Flagstaff Life. Why does that sound familiar? Who was I talking to about . . .

'Martin and Janice next door!' I exclaim suddenly. 'They're with Flagstaff Life! Have been for fifteen years.'

'Then they'll do very well,' says Dad. 'The longer you've been with them, the more you get, apparently.'

He turns the page with a rustle, and I sit down at the

table with my cup of tea and *Good Housekeeping* open at an article on making Easter cakes. It's not fair, I find myself thinking resentfully. Why can't I get a windfall payment? Why doesn't Endwich Bank get taken over? Then they could pay me a windfall big enough to wipe out my overdraft. And preferably sack Derek Smeath at the same time.

'Any plans for the day?' says Dad, looking up.

'Not really,' I say, and take a sip of tea.

Any plans for the rest of my life? Not really.

In the end, I spend a pleasant, unchallenging morning helping Mum sort out a pile of clothes for a jumble sale, and at 12.30 we go into the kitchen to make a sandwich. As I look at the clock, the fact that I was supposed to be at Endwich Bank three hours ago flickers through my mind – but very far off, like a distant sound. My whole London life seems remote and unreal now. *This* is where I belong. Away from the madding crowd; at home with Mum and Dad, having a relaxed uncomplicated time.

After lunch I wander out into the garden with one of Mum's mail-order catalogues, and go and sit on the bench by the apple tree. A moment later, I hear a voice from over the garden fence, and look up. It's Martin from next door. Hmmm. I'm not feeling very well disposed towards Martin at the moment.

'Hello, Becky,' he says softly. 'Are you all right?'

'I'm fine thanks,' I say shortly. *And I don't fancy your son*, I feel like adding. But then, they'd probably think I was in denial, wouldn't they?

'Becky,' says Janice, appearing beside Martin, holding a garden trowel. She gives me an awe-stricken look. 'We heard about your . . . *stalker*,' she whispers.

'It's criminal,' says Martin fiercely. 'These people should be locked up.'

'If there's anything we can do,' says Janice. 'Anything at all. You just let us know.'

'I'm fine, really,' I say, softening slightly towards

them. 'I just want to stay here for a while. Get away from it all.'

'Of course you do,' says Martin. 'Wise girl.'

'I was saying to Martin this morning,' says Janice, 'you should hire a bodyguard.'

'Can't be too careful,' says Martin. 'Not these days.'

'The price of fame,' says Janice, sorrowfully shaking her head. 'The price of fame.'

'Well anyway,' I say, trying to get off the subject of my stalker. 'How are you?'

'Oh we're both well,' says Martin. 'I suppose.' To my surprise there's a slightly forced cheerfulness to his voice. There's a pause, and he glances at Janice, who frowns, and shakes her head slightly.

'Anyway, you must be pleased with the news,' I say brightly. 'About Flagstaff Life.'

There's silence.

'Well,' says Martin. 'We would have been.'

'No-one could have known,' says Janice, giving a little shrug. 'It's just one of those things. Just the luck of the draw.'

'What is?' I say puzzledly. 'I thought you were getting some huge great windfall.'

'It appears . . .' Martin rubs his face. 'It appears not in our case.'

'But . . . but why?'

'Martin phoned them up this morning,' says Janice. 'To see how much we would be getting. They were saying in the papers that long-term investors would be getting *thousands*. But . . .' She glances at Martin.

'But what?' I say, feeling a twinge of alarm.

'Apparently we're no longer eligible,' says Martin awkwardly. 'Since we switched our investment. Our old fund would have qualified, but . . .' He coughs. 'I mean, we will get *something* – but it'll only be about £100.'

I stare at him blankly.

'But you only switched—'

'Two weeks ago,' he says. 'That's the irony. If we'd

229

just held on a little bit longer . . . Still, what's done is done. No point whingeing about it.' He gives a resigned shrug, and smiles at Janice, who smiles back.

And I look away and bite my lip.

Because a nasty cold feeling is creeping over me. They took the decision to switch their money based on my advice, didn't they? They asked me if they should switch funds, and I said go ahead. But now I come to think of it . . . hadn't I already heard a rumour about this takeover? Oh God. Did I already know? Could I have stopped this?

'We could never have known these windfalls would happen,' says Janice, and puts her hand comfortingly on his arm. 'They keep these things secret right up until the last minute, don't they, Becky?'

My throat's too tight to answer. I can remember exactly now. It was Alicia who first mentioned the takeover. The day before I came down here. And then Philip said something about it in the office. Something about with-profits holders doing well. Except . . . I wasn't really listening. I think I was doing my nails at the time.

'Twenty thousand pounds, they reckon we would have got if we'd stayed,' says Martin gloomily. 'Makes you sick to think about it. Still, Janice is right. We couldn't have known. Nobody knew.'

Oh God. This is all my fault. It's all my fault. If I'd just used my brain and *thought* for once in my life . . .

'Oh Becky, don't look so upset!' says Janice. 'This isn't your fault! You didn't know! Nobody knew! None of us could have—'

'I knew,' I hear myself saying miserably.

There's a flabbergasted silence.

'What?' says Janice faintly.

'I didn't *know*, exactly,' I say, staring at the ground. 'But I heard a sort of rumour about it a while ago. I should have said something when you asked me. I should have warned you to wait. But I just . . . didn't think. I didn't remember.' I force myself to look up and meet Martin's astonished gaze. 'I . . . I'm really sorry. It's all my fault.'

There's silence, during which Janice and Martin glance at each other and I hunch my shoulders, loathing myself. Inside, I can hear the phone ringing, and footsteps as someone goes to answer it.

'I see,' says Martin eventually. 'Well . . . not to worry. These things happen.'

'Don't blame yourself, Becky,' says Janice kindly. 'It was our decision to switch funds, not yours.'

'And remember, you've been under a lot of pressure yourself recently,' adds Martin, putting a sympathetic hand on my arm. 'What with this dreadful stalking business.'

Now I really think I'm going to cry. I don't deserve these people's kindness. I've just lost them £20,000, through being too bloody lazy to keep up with events I'm supposed to know about. I'm a financial journalist, for God's sake.

And suddenly, standing there in my parents' garden, I'm plunged to the lowest ebb of my life. What have I got going for me? Nothing. Not one thing. I can't control my money, I can't do my job and I haven't got a boyfriend. I've hurt my best friend, I've lied to my parents – and now I've ruined my neighbours. I should just give up and go to a Buddhist monastery or something.

'Becky?'

My father's voice interrupts us all, and I look up in surprise. He's striding across the lawn towards us, a perturbed look on his face.

'Becky, don't be alarmed,' he says, 'but I've just had that Derek Smeath chap on the phone.'

'What?' I say, feeling my face drain in horror.

'The stalker?' exclaims Janice, and Dad gives a sober nod.

'Quite an unpleasant fellow, I would say. He was really quite aggressive towards me.'

'But how does he know Becky's here?' says Janice.

'Obviously just taking pot luck,' says Dad. 'I was very civil, simply told him you weren't here and that I had no idea where you were.'

'And . . . and what did he say?' I say in a strangled voice.

'Came out with some nonsense about a meeting you'd set up with him.' Dad shakes his head. 'The chap's obviously deluded.'

'You should change your number,' advises Martin. 'Go ex-directory.'

'But where was he phoning from?' says Janice, her voice rising in alarm. 'He could be anywhere!' She starts looking agitatedly around the garden as though expecting him to jump out from behind a bush.

'Exactly,' says Dad. 'So, Becky, I think maybe you should come inside now. You never know with these characters.'

'OK,' I say numbly. I can't quite believe this is happening. I look at Dad's kind, concerned face and suddenly feel like crumpling into tears. Oh *why* didn't I tell him and Mum the truth? Why did I let myself get into this situation?

'You look quite shaken up, dear,' says Janice, and pats me on the shoulder. 'You go and have a nice cup of tea.'

'Yes,' I say. 'Yes, I think I will.'

And Dad leads me off gently towards the house, as though I'm some kind of invalid.

This is all getting out of hand. Now, not only do I feel like an utter failure, I don't feel safe any more either. I don't feel cocooned and secure; I feel exposed and edgy. I sit on the sofa next to Mum, drinking tea and watching *Countdown*, and every time there's a sound outside, I jump with nerves.

What if Derek Smeath's on his way here? How long would it take him to drive here from London? An hour and a half? Two, if the traffic's bad?

He wouldn't do that. He's a busy man.

But he *might*.

Or send the bailiffs round. Oh God. Threatening men in leather jackets. My stomach is squeezed tight with fear. I'm beginning to feel as though I genuinely do have a stalker.

As the advert break begins, Mum reaches for a catalogue full of gardening things. 'Look at this lovely birdbath,' she says. 'I'm going to get one for the garden.'

'Great,' I mutter, unable to concentrate.

'They've got some super windowboxes, too,' she says. 'You could do with some nice windowboxes in your flat.'

'Yes,' I say. 'Maybe.'

'Shall I put you down for a couple? They're not expensive.'

'No, it's OK.'

'You can pay by cheque, or VISA . . .' she says, flipping over the page.

'No, really, Mum,' I say, my voice sharpening slightly.

'You could just phone up with your VISA card, and have them delivered—'

'Mum, stop it!' I cry. 'I don't want them, OK?'

Mum gives me a surprised, slightly reproving look, and turns to the next page of her catalogue. And I gaze back at her, full of a choking panic. My VISA card doesn't work. My Switch card doesn't work. Nothing works. And she has no idea.

Don't think about it. Don't think about it. I grab for an ancient copy of the *Radio Times* on the coffee table, and begin to leaf through it blindly.

'It's a shame about poor Martin and Janice, isn't it?' says Mum, looking up. 'Fancy switching funds two weeks before the takeover! Such bad luck!'

'I know,' I mumble, staring down at a page of listings. I don't want to be reminded about Martin and Janice.

'It seems a terrible coincidence,' says Mum, shaking her head. 'That the company should launch this new

233

fund just before the takeover. You know, there must be a lot of people who did exactly what Martin and Janice did, who have lost out. Dreadful, really.' She looks at the television. 'Oh look, it's starting again.'

The cheery *Countdown* music begins to play, and a round of applause rattles noisily from the television. But I'm not listening to it, or even paying any attention to the vowels and consonants. I'm thinking about what Mum has just said. A terrible coincidence – but it wasn't exactly a coincidence, was it? The bank actually wrote to Janice and Martin, suggesting that they switch funds. They even offered an incentive, didn't they? A carriage clock.

Why did they do that?

Suddenly I feel alert. I want to see the letter from Flagstaff Life – and find out exactly how long before the takeover they sent it.

'"ENDING",' says Mum, staring at the screen. 'That's six. Ooh, there's an S. Can you have "ENDINGS"?'

'I'm just . . . popping next door,' I say, getting to my feet. 'I won't be a minute.'

As Martin opens the front door, I see that he and Janice have also been sitting in front of the telly, watching *Countdown*.

'Hi,' I say sheepishly. 'I was just wondering – could we have a quick chat?'

'Of course!' says Martin. 'Come on in! Would you like a sherry?'

'Oh,' I say, a little taken aback. I mean, not that I'm against drinking, obviously – but it isn't even five o'clock yet. 'Well – OK then.'

'Never too early for a sherry!' says Martin.

'I'll have another one, thanks, Martin,' comes Janice's voice from the sitting room.

Blow me down. They're a pair of alcoholics!

Oh God, perhaps this is my fault too. Perhaps their financial mishap has driven them to seek solace in alcohol and daytime television.

'I was just wondering,' I say nervously as Martin pours dark brown sherry into a schooner. 'Just out of interest, could I have a look at that letter you got from Flagstaff Life, asking you to switch funds? I was wondering when they sent it.'

'It arrived the very day we saw you,' says Martin. 'Why do you want to see it?' He raises his glass. 'Your good health.'

'Cheers,' I say, and take a sip. 'I'm just wondering—'

'Come into the living room,' he interrupts, and ushers me through from the hall. 'Here you are, my love,' he adds, and gives Janice her sherry. 'Bottoms up!'

'Sssh,' she replies. 'It's the numbers game! I need to concentrate.'

'I thought I might do a little investigation into this,' I whisper to Martin as the *Countdown* clock ticks round. 'I feel so bad about it.'

'Fifty times 4 is 200,' says Janice suddenly. 'Six minus 3 is 3, times 7 is 21 and add it on.'

'Well done, love!' says Martin, and roots about in a carved oak sideboard. 'Here's the letter,' he says. 'So – do you want to write an article or something?'

'Possibly,' I say. 'You wouldn't mind, would you?'

'Mind?' He gives a little shrug. 'No, I wouldn't think so.'

'Sssh!' says Janice. 'It's the *Countdown* Conundrum.'

'Right,' I whisper. 'Well I'll just . . . I'll just take this, shall I?'

'Explicate!' yells Janice. 'No, Exploited!'

'And . . . thanks for the sherry.' I take a huge gulp, shuddering slightly at its sticky sweetness, then put my glass down and tiptoe out of the room.

Half an hour later, sitting in my bedroom, I've read the letter from Flagstaff Life several times and I'm sure there's something fishy about it. How many investors must have switched funds after receiving this crappy carriage clock offer – and missed out on their windfall?

More to the point, how much money must Flagstaff Life have saved? Suddenly I really want to know. And more than that, I really want to write about it. For the first time in my life, I'm actually *interested* in a financial story.

And I don't just want to write it up for crappy *Successful Saving*, either.

Eric Foreman's card is still in my purse, with his direct telephone number printed at the top, and I take it out. I stare at it for a moment, then go to the phone and quickly punch in the number before I can change my mind.

'Eric Foreman, *Daily World*,' comes his voice, booming down the line.

Oh God. Am I really doing this?

'Hi,' I say nervously. 'I don't know if you remember me. Rebecca Bloomwood from *Successful Saving*. We met at the Sacrum Asset Management press conference.'

'That's right, so we did,' he says cheerfully. 'How are you, my love?'

'I'm fine,' I say, and clench my hand tightly around the receiver. 'Absolutely fine. Ahm . . . I was just wondering, are you still running your series on "Can we Trust the Money Men?"'

'We are, as it goes,' says Eric Foreman. 'Why?'

'It's just . . .' I swallow. 'It's just, I think I've got a story that might interest you.'

Seventeen

I have never before worked so hard on an article.
Never.

Mind you, I've never before been asked to write one
so quickly. At *Successful Saving*, we get a whole
month to write our article – and we complain about
that. When Eric Foreman said, 'Can you do it by
tomorrow?' I thought he was joking at first. I jauntily
replied, 'Of course!' and nearly added, 'In fact, I'll have
it with you in five minutes' time!' Then, *just* in time, I
realized he was serious. Crikey.

So I'm round at Martin and Janice's first thing the next
morning with a Dictaphone, writing down exactly all
the information on their investment and trying to get in
lots of heart-wrenching details, as advised by Eric.

'We need human interest,' he told me over the
phone. 'None of your dull financial reporting here.
Make us feel sorry for them. Make us weep. A hard-
working, ordinary couple, who thought they could rely
on a few savings to see them through their old age.
Ripped off by the fat cats. What kind of house do these
people live in?'

'Ahmm . . . a four-bedroomed detached house in
Surrey.'

'Well, for Christ's sake don't put that in!' he boomed.
'I want honest, poor and proud. Never demanded a
penny off the state, saved to provide for themselves.
Trusted a respectable financial institution. And all it
did was kick them in the face.' He paused, and it
sounded as if he might be picking his teeth. 'That kind
of thing. Think you can manage it?'

'I . . . ahm . . . yes! Of course!' I stuttered.

Oh God, I thought as I put down the phone. Oh God, what have I got myself into?

But it's too late to change my mind now. So the next thing is to persuade Janice and Martin that they don't mind appearing in the *Daily World*. The trouble is, it's not exactly the *Financial Times*, is it? Or even the normal *Times*. (Still, as I remind them, it could be a lot worse. It could be the *Sun* – and they'd end up sandwiched between a topless model and a blurred paparazzi shot of Posh Spice.)

Luckily, however, they're so bowled over that I'm making all this effort on their behalf, they don't seem to care which newspaper I'm writing for. And when they hear that a photographer's coming over at midday to take their picture, you'd think the Queen was coming to visit.

'My hair!' says Janice in dismay, staring into the mirror. 'Have I time to get Maureen in to give me a blow-dry?'

'Not really. And it looks lovely,' I say reassuringly. 'Anyway, they want you as natural as possible. Just . . . honest, ordinary people.' I glance around the living room, trying to pick up poignant details to put into my article.

An anniversary card from their son stands proudly on the well-polished mantelpiece. But this year there will be no celebration for Martin and Janice Webster.

'I must phone Phyllis!' says Janice. 'She won't believe it!'

'You weren't ever a soldier, or anything?' I say thoughtfully to Martin. 'Or a . . . a fireman? Anything like that. Before you became a travel agent.'

'Not really, love,' says Martin, wrinkling his brow. 'Just the Cadets at school.'

'Oh, right,' I say, brightening. 'That might do.'

Martin Webster fingers the cadet badge he was so proud to wear as a youth. His life has been one of hard work and service for others. Now, in his retirement

238

years, he should be enjoying the rewards he deserves.

But the fat cats have conned him out of his nest egg. The Daily World *asks . . .*

'I've photocopied all the documents for you,' says Martin. 'All the paperwork. I don't know if it'll be any use . . .'

'Oh, thanks,' I say, taking the pile of pages from him. 'I'll have a good read through these.'

When honest Martin Webster received a letter from Flagstaff Life, inviting him to switch investment funds, he trusted the money men to know what was best for him.

Two weeks later he discovered they had tricked him out of a £20,000 windfall.

'My wife is ill as a result of all this,' he said. 'I'm so worried.'

Hmmm.

'Janice?' I say, looking up casually. 'Do you feel all right? Not . . . unwell, or anything?'

'A bit nervous, to be honest, dear,' she says, looking round from the mirror. 'I'm never very good at having my picture taken.'

'My nerves are shot to pieces,' said Mrs Webster in a ragged voice. 'I've never felt so betrayed in all my life.'

'Well, I think I've got enough now,' I say, getting up and switching off my Dictaphone. 'I might have to *slightly* digress from what's on the tape – just to make the story work. You don't mind, do you?'

'Of course not!' says Janice. 'You write what you like, Becky! We trust you.'

'So what happens now?' says Martin.

'I'll have to go and talk to Flagstaff Life,' I say. 'Get them to give their defence.'

'What defence?' says Martin. 'There is no defence for what they did to us!'

'I know,' I say and grin at him. 'Exactly.'

As I go back home and up to my bedroom, I'm full of happy adrenalin. All I need to do is get a quote from Flagstaff Life, and I can start writing the piece. I haven't got long: it needs to be finished by two o'clock if it's going to make tomorrow's edition. God, this is exciting. Why has work never seemed so exciting before?

Briskly I reach for the phone and dial Flagstaff's number – only to be told by the switchboard operator that all press enquiries are dealt with out-of-house. She gives me a number, which seems rather familiar, and I frown at it for a moment, then punch it in.

'Hello,' says a smooth voice. 'Brandon Communications.'

Oh God, of course. Suddenly I feel a bit shaky. The word 'Brandon' has hit me right in the stomach like a punch. I'd forgotten all about Luke Brandon. To be honest, I'd forgotten all about the rest of my life. And frankly, I don't want to be reminded of it.

But it's OK – I don't have to speak to him personally, do I?

'Hi!' I say. 'It's Rebecca Bloomwood here. Ermm . . . I just wanted to talk to somebody about Flagstaff Life.'

'Let me check . . .' says the voice. 'Yes, that's Luke Brandon's client. I'll just put you through to his assistant . . .' And the voice disappears before I can say anything.

Oh God.

Oh God, I can't do this. I can't speak to Luke Brandon. My questions are jotted down on a piece of paper in front of me, but as I stare at them I'm not reading them. I'm remembering the humiliation I felt that day in Harrods. That horrible plunge in my stomach when I heard the patronizing note in his voice and suddenly realized what he thought of me. A joke. A nothing.

OK, I *can* do this, I tell myself firmly. I can do it. I'll just be very stern and businesslike and ask my questions, and—

'Rebecca!' comes a voice in my ear. 'How are you! It's Alicia here.'

'Oh,' I say in surprise. 'I thought I was going to speak to Luke. It's about Flagstaff Life.'

'Yes, well,' says Alicia. 'Luke Brandon is a very busy man. I'm sure I can answer any questions you have.'

'Oh, right,' I say, and pause. 'But they're not your client, are they?'

'I'm sure that won't matter in this case,' she says, and gives a little laugh. 'What did you want to know?'

'Right,' I say, and look at my list. 'Was it a deliberate policy for Flagstaff Life to invite their investors to move out of with-profits just before they announced windfalls? Some people lost out a lot, you know.'

'Right . . .' she says. 'Thanks, Camilla, I'll have smoked salmon and lettuce.'

'What?' I say.

'Sorry, yes, I am with you,' she says. 'Just jotting it down . . . I'll have to get back to you on that, I'm afraid.'

'Well, I need a response soon!' I say. 'My deadline's in a few hours.'

'Got that,' says Alicia. Suddenly her voice goes muffled. 'No, smoked salmon. OK then, Chinese chicken. Yes.' The muffle disappears. 'So, Rebecca, any other questions? Tell you what, shall I send you our latest press pack? That's bound to answer any other queries. Or you could fax in your questions.'

'Fine,' I say curtly. 'Fine, I'll do that.' And I put the phone down.

For a while I stare straight ahead in brooding silence. Stupid patronizing cow. Can't even be bothered to take my questions seriously.

Then gradually it comes to me that this is the way I always get treated when I ring up press offices. No-one's ever in any hurry to answer my questions, are they? People are always putting me on hold, saying they'll ring me back and not bothering. I've never minded before – I've rather enjoyed hanging on to a phone, listening to 'Greensleeves' (at least it beats working). I've never cared before whether people took me seriously or not.

But today, I do care. Today what I'm doing *does* seem important, and I *do* want to be taken seriously.

Well, I'll show her, I think fiercely. I'll show them all, Luke Brandon included. Show them that I, Rebecca Bloomwood, am not a joke.

With a sudden determination I reach for my dad's typewriter. I feed in some paper, switch on my Dictaphone, take a deep breath and begin to type.

REBECCA BLOOMWOOD
THE PINES
43 ELTON ROAD
OXSHOTT
SURREY

FAX MESSAGE FOR   ERIC FOREMAN
                     DAILY WORLD

FROM   REBECCA BLOOMWOOD

28 March 2000

Dear Eric

I enclose my 950-word article on Flagstaff Life and the lost windfalls. I do
hope you like it.

With best wishes

Rebecca Bloomwood
Financial Journalist

Eighteen

The next morning, I wake at six in the morning. It's pathetic, I know, but I'm as excited as a little kid on Christmas Day (or as me on Christmas Day, to be perfectly honest).

I lie in bed, telling myself to be grown-up and laid back and not think about it – but I just can't resist it. My mind is swimming with images of all the piles of newspapers in all the newsagents', all over the country. Of all the copies of the *Daily World* being dropped on people's doormats this morning; all the people who are going to be opening their papers, yawning, wondering what's in the news.

And what are they going to see?

They're going to see my name! Rebecca Bloomwood in print in the *Daily World*! My first national byline. 'By Rebecca Bloomwood.' Doesn't that sound cool? 'By Rebecca Bloomwood.'

I know the piece has gone in, because Eric Foreman phoned me up yesterday afternoon and told me the editor was really pleased with it. And they've got it on a colour page – so the picture of Janice and Martin will be in full colour. Really high profile. I can't quite believe it. The *Daily World*!

Even as I'm lying here, it occurs to me, there's already a whole pile of *Daily World*s at the newsagent in the parade of shops round the corner. A whole pile of pristine, unopened copies. And the newsagent opens at . . . what time? Six, I seem to remember. And now it's five past six. So in *theory*, I could go and buy one right now if I wanted to. I could just get up, slip on some clothes, go down to the newsagent and buy one.

Not that I would, of course. I'm not quite so sad and desperate that I'm going to rush down as soon as the shop's opened, just to see my name. I mean, what do you take me for? No, what I'll do is just saunter down casually later on – perhaps at eleven or midday – pick up the paper and flip through it in mild interest and then saunter home again. I probably won't even bother to buy a copy. I mean – I've seen my name in print before, haven't I? It's hardly a big deal. No need to make a song and dance about it.

I'm going to turn over now and go back to sleep. I can't think why I'm awake so early. Must be the birds or something. Hmm . . . close my eyes, plump up my pillow, think about something else . . . I wonder what I'll have for breakfast when I get up?

But I've never seen my name in the *Daily World*, have I? says a little voice in my head. I've never seen it in a national newspaper.

Oh God, this is killing me. I can't wait any longer, I've *got* to see it.

Abruptly I get out of bed, throw on my clothes and tiptoe down the stairs. As I close the door, I feel just like the girl in that Beatles song about leaving home. Outside the air is fresh and crisp, and the road is completely quiet. Gosh, it's nice being up early. Why on earth don't I get up at six more often? I should do this every day. A power walk before breakfast, like people do in New York. Burn off loads of calories and then return home to an energizing breakfast of oats and freshly squeezed orange juice. Perfect. This will be my new regime.

But as I reach the little parade of shops, my heart begins to thump, and without quite meaning to, I slow my walk to a funereal pace. Now that I'm here, I'm starting to feel a bit nervous. I'm not actually sure I want to see my name in print at all. Maybe I'll just buy myself a Mars Bar and go home again. Or a Mint Aero, if they've got them.

Cautiously, I push at the door and wince at the 'ping!' as it opens. I really don't want to draw attention to myself this morning. What if the guy behind the counter has read my article and thinks it's rubbish? Oh God, this is nerve-racking. I should never have become a journalist. I should have become a beautician, like I always wanted to. Maybe it's not too late. I'll retrain, open my own boutique . . .

'Hello, Becky!'

I look up, and feel my face jerk in surprise. Martin Webster's standing at the counter, holding a copy of the *Daily World*. 'I just happened to be awake,' he explains sheepishly. 'Thought I'd just come down, have a little look . . .'

'Oh,' I say. 'Erm . . . me too.' I give a nonchalant shrug. 'Since I was awake anyway . . .'

My eye falls on the newspaper and I feel my stomach flip over. Oh God. I'm going to expire with nerves. Please, just kill me quickly.

'So – what . . . what's it like?' I say in a strangled voice.

'Well,' says Martin, gazing at the page as though perplexed. 'It's certainly big.' He turns the paper round to face me, and I nearly keel over. There, in full colour, is a picture of Martin and Janice staring miserably up at the camera, below the headline COUPLE CHEATED BY FAT CATS AT FLAGSTAFF LIFE.

Shaking slightly, I take the paper from Martin. My eye skips across the page to the first column of text . . . and there it is! 'By Rebecca Bloomwood.' That's my name! That's me!

There's a ping at the door of the shop, and we both look round. And there, to my utter astonishment, is Dad.

'Oh,' he says, and gives an embarrassed little cough. 'Your mother wanted me to buy a copy. And since I was awake anyway . . .'

'So was I,' says Martin quickly.

'Yes, so was I,' I say.

'Well,' says Dad. 'So – is it in?'

'Oh yes,' I say, 'it's in.' I turn the paper round so he can see it.

'Gosh,' he says. 'It's big, isn't it?'

'The photo's good, don't you think?' says Martin enthusiastically. 'Brings out the flowers in our curtains beautifully.'

'Yes, the photo's great,' I agree.

I'm not going to demean myself by asking what he thought of the article itself. If he wants to compliment my writing, he will. If he doesn't – then it really doesn't matter. The point is, *I'm* proud of it.

'And Janice looks very nice, I thought,' says Martin, still gazing at the photograph.

'Very nice,' agrees Dad. 'If a little mournful.'

'You see, these professionals, they know how to light a shot,' says Martin. 'The way the sunlight falls just here, on her—'

'What about my article?' I wail piteously. 'Did you like that?'

'Oh, it's very good!' says Martin. 'Sorry, Becky, I should have said! I haven't read it all yet, but it seems to capture the situation exactly. Makes me out to be quite a hero!' He frowns. 'Although I never did fight in the Falklands, you know.'

'Oh well,' I say hurriedly. 'That's neither here nor there, really.'

'So you wrote all this yesterday?' says Dad. 'On my typewriter?' He seems astounded.

'Yes,' I say smugly. 'It looks good, doesn't it? Have you seen my byline? "By Rebecca Bloomwood".'

'Janice'll be thrilled,' says Martin. 'I'm going to buy two copies.'

'I'm going to buy three,' says Dad. 'Your granny will love to see this.'

'And I'll buy one,' I say. 'Or two, perhaps.' I carelessly reach for a handful and plonk them on the counter.

'Six copies?' says the assistant. 'Are you sure?'

'I need them for my records,' I say, and blush slightly.

When we get home, Mum and Janice are both waiting at our front door, desperate to see a copy.

'My hair!' wails Janice as soon as she sees the picture. 'It looks terrible! What have they done to it?'

'No it doesn't, love!' protests Martin. 'You look very nice.'

'Your curtains look lovely, Janice,' says Mum, looking over her shoulder.

'They do, don't they?' says Martin eagerly. 'That's just what I said.'

I give up. What kind of family have I got, that are more interested in curtains than top financial journalism? Anyway, I don't care. I'm mesmerized by my byline. 'By Rebecca Bloomwood.' 'By Rebecca Bloomwood.'

After everyone's peered at the paper, Mum invites Janice and Martin round to ours for breakfast, and Dad goes and puts on some coffee. There's a rather festive air to the proceedings, and everyone keeps laughing a lot. I don't think any of us can quite believe that Janice and Martin are in the *Daily World*. (And me, of course. 'By Rebecca Bloomwood'.)

At ten o'clock, I slope off and ring up Eric Foreman. Just casually, you know. To let him know I've seen it.

'Looks good, doesn't it?' he says cheerfully. 'The editor's really going for this series, so if you come up with any more stories like this just give me a shout. I like your style. Just right for the *Daily World*.'

'Excellent,' I say, although I'm not quite sure whether that's a compliment or not.

'Oh, and while I'm at it,' he adds, 'you'd better give me your bank details.'

My stomach gives a nasty lurch. Why does Eric Foreman want my bank details? Shit, is he going to check that my own finances are in order or something? Is he going to run a credit check on me?

'Everything's done by transfer these days,' he's saying. 'Four hundred quid. That all right?'

What? What's he—

Oh my God, he's going to *pay* me. But of course he is. Of course he is!

'That's fine,' I hear myself say. 'No problem. I'll just ahm . . . give you my account number, shall I?'

Four hundred quid! I think dazedly as I scrabble for my chequebook. Just like that! I can't quite believe it.

'Excellent,' says Eric Foreman, writing the details down. 'I'll sort that out for you with Accounts.' Then he pauses. 'Tell me, would you be in the market for writing general features? Human interest stories, that kind of thing?'

Would I be in the market? Is he kidding?

'Sure,' I say, trying not to sound too thrilled. 'In fact . . . I'd probably prefer it to finance.'

'Oh right,' he says. 'Well, I'll keep an eye out for bits that might suit you. As I say, I think you've got the right style for us.'

'Great,' I say. 'Thanks.'

As I put the phone down, there's a huge smile on my face. I've got the right style for the *Daily World*! Ha! At last I've found my niche!

The phone rings again, and I pick it up, wondering if it's Eric Foreman offering me some more work already.

'Hello, Rebecca Bloomwood,' I say in a businesslike voice.

'Rebecca,' says Luke Brandon's curt voice – and my heart freezes. 'Could you please tell me what the fuck is going on?'

Shit.

Shit, he sounds really angry. For an instant I'm paralysed. My throat feels dry; my hand is sweaty round the receiver. Oh God. What am I going to say? What am I going to say to him?

But hang on a minute. *I* haven't done anything wrong.

249

'I don't know what you mean,' I say, playing for time. Keep calm, I tell myself. Calm and cool.

'Your tawdry effort in the *Daily World*,' he says scathingly. 'Your one-sided, unbalanced, probably libellous little story.'

For a second I'm so shocked I can't speak. Tawdry? Libellous?

'It's not tawdry!' I splutter at last. 'It's a good piece. And it's certainly not libellous. I can prove everything I said.'

'And I suppose getting the other side of the story would have been inconvenient,' he snaps. 'I suppose you were too busy writing your purple prose to approach Flagstaff Life and ask for their version of events. You'd rather have a good story than spoil it by trying to give a balanced picture.'

'I *tried* to get the other side of the story!' I exclaim furiously. 'I phoned your stupid PR company up yesterday and told them I was writing the piece!'

There's silence.

'Who did you speak to?' says Luke.

'Alicia,' I reply. 'I asked her a very clear question about Flagstaff's policy on switching funds, and she told me she'd get back to me. I *told* her I had an urgent deadline.'

Luke gives an impatient sigh.

'What the fuck were you doing, speaking to Alicia? Flagstaff's my client, not hers.'

'I know! I said that to her! But she said you were a very busy man and she could deal with me.'

'Did you tell her you were writing for the *Daily World*?'

'No,' I say, and feel myself flush slightly red. 'I didn't specify who I was writing for. But I would have told her if she'd asked me. She just didn't bother. She just assumed I couldn't possibly be doing anything important.' In spite of myself, my voice is rising in emotion. 'Well, she was wrong, wasn't she? You were all wrong. And maybe now you'll start treating everybody with respect. Not just the people you *think* are important.'

I break off, panting slightly, and there's a bemused silence.

'Rebecca,' says Luke at last, 'if this is about what happened between us that day – if this is some kind of petty revenge—'

God, I'm really going to explode now.

'Don't you bloody insult me!' I yell. 'Don't you bloody try and make out this is some kind of personal thing! It's got nothing to do with that! It's your company's incompetence that's to blame! I was completely professional. I gave you every chance to put your side of the story. *Every* chance. And if you blew it, that's not my fault.'

And without giving him the chance to reply, I slam the phone down.

I'm feeling quite shaky as I go back into the kitchen. To think I ever liked Luke Brandon. To think I table-hopped with him. To think I let him lend me twenty quid. He's just an arrogant, self-centred, chauvinistic—

'Telephone!' says Mum. 'Shall I get it?'

Oh God. It'll be him again, won't it? Ringing back to apologize. Well, he needn't think I'm that easily won round. I stand by every word I said. And I'll tell him so. In fact, I'll add that—

'It's for you Becky,' says Mum.

'Fine,' I say coolly, and make my way to the telephone. I don't hurry; I don't panic, I feel completely in control.

'Hello?' I say.

'Rebecca? Eric Foreman here.'

'Oh!' I say in surprise. 'Hi!'

'Bit of news about your piece.'

'Oh yes?' I say, trying to sound calm. But my stomach's churning. What if Luke Brandon's spoken to him? What if I *did* get something wrong? Oh shit, I did check all the facts, didn't I?

'I've just had *Morning Coffee* on the phone,' he says. 'You know, the TV programme? Rory and Emma. They're interested in your story.'

'What?' I say stupidly.

'There's a new series they're doing on finance. "Managing your Money." They get some financial expert in every week, tell the viewers how to keep tabs on their dosh.' Eric Foreman lowers his voice. 'Frankly, they're running out of stuff to talk about. They've done mortgages, store cards, pensions, all the usual cobblers . . .'

'Right,' I say, trying to sound intelligent. But as his words slowly sink in, I'm feeling a bit dazed. Rory and Emma have read my article? Rory and Emma themselves? I have a sudden vision of them holding the paper together, jostling for a good view.

But of course, that's silly, isn't it? They'd have a copy each.

'So, anyway, they want to have you on the show tomorrow morning,' Eric Foreman's saying. 'Talk about this windfall story, warn their viewers to take care. You interested in that kind of thing? If not, I can easily tell them you're too busy.'

'No!' I say quickly. 'No. Tell them I'm . . .' I swallow. 'I'm interested.'

As I put down the phone, I feel faint. I can't quite believe it. I'm going to be on television.

Rebecca Bloomwood
c/o William Green Recruitment
39 Farringdon Square
London EC4 7TD

27 March 2000

Hyvä Rebecca Bloomwood

Oli erittäin hauska tavata teidät viime viikolla,
vaikka tapaaminen jäikin lyhyeksi. Olitte selvästi
hermostunut, mikä on aivan ymmärrettävää. Siitä
huolimatta minä ja kollegani ihailimme tavalli-
suudesta poikkeavaa luonteenlaatuanne. Olemme
varmoja, että teistä olisi yhtiöllemme paljon hyötyä,
ja mielellämme tapaisimme teidät uudestaan, ehkä
lounaan merkeissä.

Haluaisin onnitella teitä suurenmoisesta artikkelis-
tanne **«Daily World»** -lehdessä. Olette selvästi
taitava ilmaisemaan ajatuksianne, ja on suuri ilo
päästä pian keskustelemaan kanssanne äidinkielel-
läni. Toivoisin että ottaisitte minuun yhteyttä yllä
mainitulla osoitteella.

Parhain terveisin

Ystävällisesti

Jan Virtanen

Nineteen

The car to take me to the television studios arrives promptly at 7.30 the next morning. As the doorbell rings, Mum, Dad and I all jump, even though we've been waiting in a tense silence for ten minutes.

'Well,' says Dad gruffly, glancing at his watch. 'They're here, anyway.'

Ever since I told him about the arrangements yesterday, Dad's been predicting that the car won't turn up and that he'll have to drive me to the studios himself. He even worked out a route last night, and phoned up Uncle Malcolm as a standby. (To be honest, I think he was quite looking forward to it.)

'Oh Becky,' says Mum in a trembling voice. 'Good luck, darling.' She looks at me, then shakes her head. 'Our little Becky, on television. I can't believe it.'

I start to get up, but Dad puts out a restraining arm.

'Now before you answer the door, Becky,' he says. 'You are sure, aren't you? About the risk you're taking.' He glances at Mum, who bites her lip.

'I'll be fine!' I say, trying to sound as soothing as possible. 'Honestly, Dad, we've been over it all.'

Last night, it suddenly occurred to Dad that if I went on the telly, my stalker would know where I was. At first he was adamant I'd have to call the whole thing off – and it took an awful lot of persuasion to convince him and Mum I'd be perfectly safe in the TV studios. They were even talking about hiring a bodyguard, can you believe it? I mean, what on earth would I look like, turning up with a bodyguard?

Actually, I'd look pretty cool and mysterious,

wouldn't I? Damn. That might have been quite a good idea.

The doorbell rings again and I leap to my feet.

'Well,' says Dad. 'You just be careful.'

'I will, don't worry!' I say, picking up my bag. I walk to the door calmly, trying not to give away how excited I feel. But inside I feel as light as a bubble.

I just can't believe how well everything's going. Not only am I going to be on the telly – but everyone's being so nice to me! Yesterday I had several phone conversations with an assistant producer of *Morning Coffee*, who's a really sweet girl called Zelda. We went over exactly what I was going to say on the programme, then she fixed up for a car to come and pick me up – and when I told her I was at my parents' house with none of my clothes handy, she thought for a bit, then said I could choose something to wear from the wardrobe. I mean, how cool is that? Choosing any outfit I like from the wardrobe! I expect they'll let me keep it afterwards, too.

As I open the front door, my stomach gives an excited leap. There, waiting in the drive, is a portly, middle-aged man in a blue blazer and cap, standing next to a shiny saloon car. My own private chauffeur! This just gets better and better.

'Miss Bloomwood?' says the driver.

'Yes,' I say, unable to stop myself grinning at him in delight. I'm about to reach for the door handle – but he gets there before me, opens the car door with a flourish and stands to attention, waiting for me to get in. God, this is like being a film star or something!

I glance back towards the house and see Mum and Dad standing on the front step, both looking utterly gobsmacked.

'Well – bye then!' I say, trying to sound casual, as though I always ride around in a chauffeur-driven car. 'See you later!'

'Becky, is that you?' comes a voice from next door, and Janice appears on the other side of the hedge in her dressing gown. Her eyes grow large as they take in the car and she glances at Mum, who raises her shoulders, as though to say, 'I know, isn't it unbelievable?'

'Morning, Janice,' says Dad.

'Morning, Graham,' says Janice dazedly. 'Oh Becky! I've never seen anything like it. In all the years . . . If Tom could only see you . . .' She breaks off and looks at Mum. 'Have you taken any photographs?'

'We haven't!' says Mum in dismay. 'It didn't even occur to us. Graham, quick – go and get the camera.'

'No, wait, I'll get our camcorder!' says Janice. 'It won't take me two ticks. We could have the car arriving in the drive, and Becky walking out of the front door . . . and maybe we could use *The Four Seasons* as the soundtrack, and then cut straight to—'

'No!' I say hastily, seeing a flicker of amusement pass across the face of the driver. God, this is embarrassing. And I was doing so well at looking nonchalant and professional. 'We haven't got time for any pictures. I have to get to the studios!'

'Yes,' says Janice, suddenly looking anxious. 'Yes, you don't want to be late.' She glances fearfully at her watch as though afraid the programme might already have started. 'It's on at eleven, isn't it?'

'Eleven o'clock the programme starts,' says Dad. 'Set the video for five to, that's what I've been telling people.'

'That's what we'll do,' says Janice. 'Just in case.' She gives a little sigh. 'I shan't dare to go to the loo, all morning, just in case I miss it!'

There's an awed silence as I get into the car. The driver closes the door smartly, then walks around to the driver's door. I press the button to lower my window and grin out at Mum and Dad.

'Becky, darling, what will you do afterwards?' says Mum. 'Come back here or go back to the flat?'

Immediately I feel my smile falter, and look down, pretending to fiddle with the window controls. I don't want to think about afterwards.

In fact, I can't even visualize afterwards. I'm going to be on the telly . . . and that's as far as it goes. The rest of my life is shut securely away in a box at the back of my head and I don't want to remember it's there.

'I . . . I'm not sure,' I say. 'I'll see what happens.'

'They'll probably take you out to lunch afterwards,' says Dad knowledgeably. 'These showbiz types are always having lunch with each other.'

'Liquid lunches,' puts in Janice, and gives a little laugh.

'At the Ivy,' says Mum. 'That's where all the actors meet up, isn't it?'

'The Ivy's old hat!' retorts Dad. 'They'll take her to the Groucho Club.'

'The Groucho Club!' says Janice, clasping her hands. 'Isn't that where Kate Moss goes?'

This is getting ridiculous.

'We'd better go,' I say, and the driver nods.

'Good luck, sweetheart,' calls Dad. I close the window and lean back, and the car purrs out of the drive.

For a while, we drive in silence. I keep casually glancing out of the window to see if anyone's looking at me in my chauffeur-driven car and wondering who I am (that new girl on *EastEnders*, perhaps). Although we're whizzing along the dual carriageway so fast, I probably look like a blur.

'So,' says the driver after a while. 'You're appearing on *Morning Coffee*, are you?'

'Yes, I am,' I say, and immediately feel a joyful smile plaster itself over my face. God, I must *stop* this. I bet Jeremy Paxman doesn't start grinning inanely every time someone asks him if he's appearing on *University Challenge*. He probably just gives a little sneer, as if to say *Of course I'm appearing on* University Challenge, *you brainless little* . . .

'So what're you on for?' says the driver, interrupting my thoughts.

I'm about to reply, 'To be famous and maybe get

257

some free clothes' when I realize what he means.

'A financial story,' I say coolly. 'I wrote a piece in the *Daily World*, and the producers read it, and wanted me on the show.'

'Been on television before?'

'No,' I admit, slightly reluctantly. 'No, I haven't.'

We pull up at some lights and the driver turns round in his seat to survey me.

'You'll be fine,' he says. 'Just don't let the nerves get to you.'

'Nerves?' I say, and give a little laugh. 'I'm not nervous! I'm just . . . looking forward to it.'

'Glad to hear it,' says the driver, turning back. 'You'll be OK, then. Some people, they get onto that sofa, thinking they're fine, relaxed, happy as a sandboy . . . then they see that red light, and it hits them that 2.5 million people around the country are all watching them. Makes some people start to panic. Don't know why.'

'Oh,' I say after a slight pause. 'Well . . . I'm nothing like them! I'll be fine!'

'Good,' says the driver.

'Good,' I echo, a little less certainly, and look out of the window.

I'll be fine. Of course I will. I've never been nervous in my life before, and I'm certainly not going to start . . .

2.5 million people.

Gosh. When you think about it – that is quite a lot, isn't it? 2.5 million people, all sitting at home, staring at the screen. Staring at my face. Waiting for what I'm going to say next.

Oh God. OK, don't think about it. The important thing is just to keep remembering how well prepared I am. I rehearsed for ages in front of the mirror last night and I know what I'm going to say practically by heart.

It all has to be at a very basic and simple level, Zelda said – because apparently 76 per cent of the *Morning Coffee* audience are housewives looking after toddlers, who have very short attention spans. She kept apologizing for what she called the 'dumbing down effect' and saying a financial expert like myself must feel really frustrated by it – and of course, I agreed with her.

But to be honest, I'm quite relieved. In fact, the more dumbed-down the better, as far as I'm concerned. I mean, writing a *Daily World* article with all my notes to hand was one thing, but answering tricky questions on live TV is quite another. (A scary thought, actually – not that I told Zelda that. I don't want her to think I'm a total durr-brain.)

So anyway, I'm going to start off by saying, 'If you were offered a choice between a carriage clock and £20,000, which would you choose?' Rory or Emma will reply: '£20,000, of course!' and I'll say, 'Exactly. Twenty thousand pounds'. I'll pause briefly, to let that figure sink into the audience's mind – and then I'll say, 'Unfortunately, when Flagstaff Life offered their customers a carriage clock to transfer their savings, they didn't tell them that if they did so, they would *lose* a £20,000 windfall!'

That sounds quite good, don't you think? Rory and Emma will ask a few very easy questions like 'What can people do to protect themselves?', and I'll give nice simple answers. And right at the end, just to keep it light, we're going to talk about all the different things you could buy with £20,000.

Actually, that's the bit I'm looking forward to most of all. I've already thought of loads of things. Did you know, with £20,000 you could buy fifty-two Gucci watches, *and* have enough left over for a bag?

The *Morning Coffee* studios are in Maida Vale, and as we draw near to the gates, familiar from the opening credits of the show, I feel a dart of excitement. I'm actually here. I'm actually going to be on television!

The doorman waves us through the barrier; we pull up outside a pair of huge double doors, and the driver opens the door for me. As I get out my legs are shaking slightly, but I force myself to walk confidently up the steps, into the reception hall, and up to the desk.

'I'm here for *Morning Coffee*,' I say, and give a little laugh as I realize what I've just said. 'I mean . . .'

'I know what you mean,' says the receptionist, kindly but wearily. She looks my name up on a list, jabs a number into her phone, and says, 'Jane? Rebecca Bloomwood's here.' Then she gestures to a row of squashy chairs and says, 'Someone will be with you shortly.'

I walk over to the seating area and sit down opposite a middle-aged woman with lots of wild dark hair and a big amber necklace round her neck. She's lighting up a cigarette, and even though I don't really smoke any more, I suddenly feel as though I could do with one myself.

Not that I'm nervous or anything. I just fancy a cigarette.

'Excuse me,' calls the receptionist. 'This is a no-smoking area.'

'Damn,' says the woman in a raspy voice. She takes a long drag, then stubs the cigarette out on a saucer and smiles at me conspiratorially. 'Are you a guest on the show?' she says.

'Yes,' I say. 'Are you?'

The woman nods. 'Promoting my new novel, *Blood Red Sunset*.' She lowers her voice to a thrilling throb. 'A searing tale of love, greed and murder, set in the ruthless world of South American money launderers.'

'Gosh,' I say. 'That sounds really—'

'Let me give you a copy,' interrupts the woman. She reaches into a Mulberry holdall by her side and pulls out a vividly coloured hardback book. 'Remind me of your name?'

Remind her?

'It's Rebecca,' I say. 'Rebecca Bloomwood.'

'To Becca,' the woman says aloud, as she scrawls inside the front page. 'With love and great affection.'

She signs with a flourish and hands the book to me.

'Gosh,' I say. 'Thanks . . .' quickly I look at the cover 'Elisabeth.'

Elisabeth Plover. To be honest, I've never heard of her.

'I expect you're wondering how I came to know such a lot about such a violent, dangerous world,' says Elisabeth. She leans forward and gazes at me with huge green eyes. 'The truth is, I lived with a money launderer for three long months. I loved him, I learned from him . . . and then I betrayed him.' Her voice dies to a trembling whisper. 'I still remember the look he gave me as the police dragged him away. He knew what I'd done. He knew I was his Judas Iscariot. And yet, in a strange kind of way, I think he loved me for it.'

'Wow,' I say, impressed in spite of myself. 'Did all this happen in South America?'

'Hove,' she says, after a slight pause. 'But money launderers are the same the world over.'

'Rebecca?' says a voice, before I can think of a reply to this, and we both look up to see a girl with smooth dark hair, in jeans and a black polo-neck, walking swiftly towards us. 'I'm Zelda. We spoke yesterday?'

'Zelda!' exclaims Elisabeth, getting to her feet. 'How have you been, my darling?' She holds out her arms, and Zelda stares at her.

'I'm sorry,' she says, 'have we—' She stops as her gaze falls on my copy of *Blood Red Sunset*. 'Oh yes, that's right. Elisabeth Plummer. One of the researchers will be down for you in a minute. Meanwhile, do help yourself to coffee.' She flashes her a smile, then turns to me. 'Rebecca, are you ready?'

'Yes!' I say eagerly, leaping up from my chair. (I have to admit, I feel quite flattered that Zelda's come down to get me herself. I mean, she obviously doesn't come down for everyone.)

'Great to meet you,' says Zelda, shaking my hand. 'Great to have you on the show. Now, as usual, we're completely frantic – so if it's OK by you, I thought we'd

261

just head straight off to hair and makeup and we can talk on the way.'

'Absolutely,' I say, trying not to sound too excited. 'Good idea.'

Hair and makeup! This is so cool!

'There's been a slight change of plan which I need to fill you in on,' says Zelda. 'Nothing to worry about . . . Any word from Bella yet?' she adds to the receptionist.

The receptionist shakes her head, and Zelda mutters something which sounds like 'Stupid cow'.

'OK, let's go,' she says, heading off towards a pair of swing doors. 'I'm afraid it's even more crazy than usual today. One of our regulars has let us down, so we're searching for a replacement, and there's been an accident in the kitchen . . .' She pushes through the swing doors and now we're striding along a green-carpeted corridor buzzing with people. 'Plus we've got Heaven Sent 7 in today,' she adds over her shoulder. 'Which means the switchboard gets jammed with fans calling in, and we have to find dressing-room space for seven enormous egos.'

'Right,' I say nonchalantly. But suddenly I can't quite breathe. Heaven Sent 7? But I mean . . . they're really famous! And I'm appearing on the same show as them! I'll get to meet them and everything, won't I? Maybe we'll all go out for a drink afterwards and become really good friends. They're all a bit younger than me, but that won't matter. I'll be like their older sister.

Or maybe I'll *go out* with one of them! God, yes. That nice one with the dark hair. Nathan. (Or is it Ethan? Whatever he's called.) He'll catch my eye after the show, and quietly ask me out to dinner without the others. We'll go to some tiny little restaurant, and at first it'll be all quiet and discreet, but then the press will find out and we'll become one of those really famous couples who go to premières all the time. And I'll wear . . .

'OK, here we are,' says Zelda, and I look up dazedly. We're standing in the doorway of a room lined with mirrors and spotlights. Three people are sitting in chairs in front of the mirrors, wearing capes and having makeup applied by trendy-looking girls in jeans; another is having her hair blow-dried. Music is playing in the background, there's a friendly level of chatter, and in the air are the mingled scents of hairspray, face-powder and coffee.

It's basically my idea of heaven.

'So,' says Zelda, leading me towards a girl with red hair. 'Chloe will do your makeup, and then we'll pop you along to wardrobe. OK?'

'Fine,' I say, unable to stop a delighted grin spreading over my face as I take in Chloe's collection of makeup. There's about a zillion brushes, pots and tubes littered over the counter in front of us, all really good brands like Chanel and MAC.

God, what a great job. I always knew I should have become a makeup artist.

'Now, about your slot,' continues Zelda as I sit down on a swivel chair. 'As I say, we've gone for a rather different format from the one we talked about previously . . .'

'Zelda!' comes a man's voice from outside. 'Bella's on the line for you!'

'Oh shit,' says Zelda. 'Look, Rebecca, I've got to go and take this call, but I'll come back as soon as I can. OK?'

'Fine!' I say happily, as Chloe drapes a cape round me and pulls my hair back into a wide towelling band. In the background, the radio's playing my favourite song by Lenny Kravitz. This couldn't be more perfect.

'I'll just cleanse and tone, and then give you a base,' says Chloe. 'If you could shut your eyes . . .'

I close my eyes, and after a few seconds, feel a cool, creamy liquid being massaged into my face. It's the most delicious sensation in the world. I could sit here all day.

'So,' says Chloe after a while. 'What are you on the show for?'

'Errm . . . finance,' I say vaguely. 'A piece on finance.'

To be honest, I'm feeling so relaxed, I can hardly remember what I'm doing here.

'Oh yeah,' says Chloe, efficiently smoothing foundation over my face. 'They were talking earlier about some financial thing.' She reaches for a palette of eyeshadows, blends a couple of colours together, then picks up a brush. 'So, are you a financial expert, then?'

'Well,' I say, and give a modest little shrug. 'You know.'

'Wow,' says Chloe, starting to apply eyeshadow to my eyelids. 'I don't understand the first thing about money.'

'Me neither!' chimes in a dark-haired girl from across the room. 'My accountant's given up trying to explain it all to me. As he says the word "tax-year", my mind glazes over.'

I'm about to reply sympathetically, 'Me too!' and launch into a nice girly chat. But just in time I realize that might not sound too good. I am supposed to be a financial expert, after all.

'It's all quite simple, really,' I say instead, and flash a confident little smile. 'Once you get the hang of the three basic principles.'

'Really?' says the dark-haired girl, and pauses, hairdrier in hand. 'What are they, then?'

'Oh,' I say, clearing my throat. 'Erm, well, the first one is . . .' I pause, and rub my nose. God, my mind's completely blank.

'Sorry, Rebecca,' says Chloe, 'I'm going to have to interrupt.' Thank goodness for that. 'Now, I was thinking a raspberry red for the lips. Is that OK by you?'

What with all this chatting, I haven't really been paying attention to what she's been doing to my face. But as I look at my reflection properly, I can't quite believe it. My eyes are huge; I've suddenly got amazing cheekbones . . . honestly, I look like a different person. Why on earth don't I wear makeup like this every day?

'Wow!' I breathe. 'That's fantastic!'

'It's easier because you're so calm,' observes Chloe, reaching into a black vanity case. 'We get some people in here, really trembling with nerves. Even celebrities. We can hardly do their makeup.'

'Really?' I say, and lean forward, ready to hear some insider gossip. But Zelda's voice interrupts us.

'Sorry about that, Rebecca!' she exclaims. 'Right, how are we doing? Makeup looks good. What about hair?'

'It's nicely cut,' says Chloe, picking up a few strands of my hair and dropping them back down again, just like Nicky Clarke on a makeover. 'I'll just give it a blow-dry for sheen.'

'Fine,' says Zelda. 'And then we'll get her along to wardrobe.' She glances at something on her clipboard, then sits down on a swivel chair next to me. 'OK, so Rebecca, we need to talk about your item.'

'Excellent,' I say, matching her businesslike tone. 'Well, I've prepared it all just as you wanted. Really simple and straightforward.'

'Yup,' says Zelda. 'Well, that's the thing. We had a talk at the meeting yesterday, and you'll be glad to hear, we don't need it too basic, after all.' She smiles. 'You'll be able to get as technical as you like! Graphs . . . figures . . .'

'Oh right,' I say, taken aback. 'Well . . . good! That's great! Although I might still keep it fairly low—'

'We want to avoid talking down to the audience. I mean, they're not morons!' Zelda lowers her voice slightly. 'Plus we had some new audience research in yesterday – and apparently 80 per cent feel patronized by some or all of the show's content. Basically, we need to redress that balance. So we've had a complete change of plan for your item!' She beams at me. 'What we thought is, instead of a simple interview, we'd have more of a high-powered debate.'

'A high-powered debate?' I echo, trying not to sound as alarmed as I feel.

'Absolutely!' says Zelda. 'What we want is a really heated discussion! Opinions flying, voices raised. That kind of thing.'

Opinions? But I don't have any opinions.

'So is that OK?' says Zelda, frowning at me. 'You look a bit—'

'I'm fine!' I force myself to smile brightly. 'Just . . . looking forward to it! A high-powered debate. Great!' I clear my throat. 'And . . . and who will I be debating with?'

'A representative from Flagstaff Life,' says Zelda triumphantly. 'Head-to-head with the enemy. It'll make great television!'

'Zelda!' comes a voice from outside the room. 'Bella again!'

'Oh, for Christ's sake!' says Zelda, leaping up. 'Rebecca, I'll be back in a sec.'

'Fine,' I manage. 'See you in a minute.'

'OK,' says Chloe cheerfully. 'While she's gone, let me put on that lipstick.' She reaches for a long brush and begins to paint in my lips, and I stare at my reflection, trying to keep calm; trying not to panic. But my heart's thumping hard and my throat's so tight, I can't swallow. I've never felt so frightened in all my life.

I can't talk in a high-powered debate! I just can't do it. I don't have any opinions, I don't have any facts, I don't know anything . . .

Oh God, *why* did I ever want to be on television?

'Rebecca, could you try to keep your lips still?' says Chloe with a puzzled frown. 'They're really shaking.'

'Sorry,' I whisper, staring at my reflection like a frozen rabbit. She's right, I'm trembling all over. Oh God, this is no good. I've got to calm down. Think Zen. Think happy thoughts.

In an effort to distract myself, I focus on the reflection in the mirror. In the background I can see Zelda standing in the corridor, talking into a phone with a furious expression on her face.

'Yup,' I can hear her saying curtly. 'Yup. But the

point is, Bella, we pay you a retainer to *be* available. What the fuck am I supposed to do now?' She looks up, sees someone, and lifts a hand in greeting. 'OK, Bella, I do see that . . .'

A blond woman and two men appear in the corridor, and Zelda nods to them apologetically. I can't see their faces, but they're all wearing smart overcoats and holding briefcases, and one of the men has a folder bulging with papers. The blond woman's coat is rather nice, I find myself thinking. *And* she's got a ponyskin Fendi baguette. I wonder who she is.

'Yup,' Zelda's saying. 'Yup. Well, if *you* can suggest an alternative phone-in subject . . .'

She raises her eyebrows at the blond woman, who shrugs and turns away to look at a poster on the wall. And as she does so, my heart nearly stops dead.

Because I recognize her. It's Alicia. It's Alicia from Brandon Communications, standing five yards away from me.

I almost want to laugh at the incongruity of it. What's she doing here? What's Alicia Bitch Long-legs doing here, for God's sake?

One of the men turns round to say something to her – and as I see his face, I think I recognize him, too. He's another one of the Brandon C lot, isn't he? One of those young, eager, baby-faced types.

But what on earth are they all doing here? What's going on? Surely it can't be—

They can't all be here because of—

No. Oh no. Suddenly I feel rather cold.

'Luke!' comes Zelda's voice from the corridor, and my stomach starts to churn. '*So* glad you could make it. We always love having you on the show. You know, I had no idea you represented Flagstaff Life, until Sandy said . . .'

In the mirror, I can see my face draining of colour.

This isn't happening. Please tell me this isn't happening.

'The journalist who wrote the piece is already here,'

Zelda's saying, 'and I've primed her on what's happening. I think it's going to make really great television, the two of you arguing away!'

She starts moving down the corridor, and in the mirror I see Alicia and the eager young man begin to follow her. Then the third overcoated man starts to come into view. And although my stomach's churning painfully, I can't stop myself. I slowly turn my head as he passes the door.

I meet Luke Brandon's grave, dark eyes and he meets mine, and for a few still seconds, we just stare at each other. Then abruptly he looks away and strides off down the corridor. And I'm left, gazing helplessly at my painted reflection, feeling sick with panic.

POINTS FOR TELEVISION INTERVIEW

SIMPLE AND BASIC FINANCIAL ADVICE

1. Prefer clock/twenty grand? Obvious.
2. Flagstaff Life ripped off innocent customers. Beware.

Ermm . . .

3. Always be very careful with your money.
4. Don't put it all in one investment but diversify.
5. Don't lose it by mistake
6. Don't

THINGS YOU CAN BUY WITH £20,000

1. Nice car eg small BMW
2. Pearl and diamond necklace from Asprey's plus big diamond ring
3. 3 couture evening dresses eg from John Galliano
4. Steinway grand piano
5. 5 gorgeous leather sofas from the Conran shop
6. 52 Gucci watches, plus bag
7. Flowers delivered every month for forty-two years
8. 55 pedigree labrador puppies
9. 80 cashmere jumpers
10. 666 Wonderbras
11. 454 pots Helena Rubinstein moisturizer
12. 800 bottles of champagne
13. 2,860 Fiorentina pizzas
14. 15,384 tubes of Pringles
15. 90,909 packets of Polos
16.

Twenty

By 11.25 I'm sitting on a brown upholstered chair in the green room. I'm dressed in a midnight-blue Jasper Conran suit, sheer tights and a pair of suede high heels. What with my makeup and blown-dry hair, I've never looked smarter in my life. But I can't relish my appearance. I can't enjoy any of it. All I can think of is the fact that in fifteen minutes, I've got to sit on a sofa and discuss high-powered finance with Luke Brandon on live television.

The very thought of it makes me feel like crying. Or laughing. I mean, it's like some kind of sick joke. Luke Brandon against me. Luke Brandon, with his genius IQ and bloody photographic memory – against me. He'll walk all over me. He'll *massacre* me.

'Darling, have a croissant,' says Elisabeth Plover, who's sitting opposite me, munching a *pain au chocolat*. 'They're simply sublime. Every bite like a ray of golden Provençal sun.'

'No thanks,' I say. 'I . . . I'm not really hungry.'

I don't understand how she can eat. I honestly feel as though I'm about to throw up at any moment. How on earth do people appear on television every day? How does Fiona Phillips do it? No wonder they're all so thin.

'Coming up!' comes Rory's voice from the television monitor in the corner of the room, and both our heads automatically swivel round to see the screen filled with a picture of a beach at sunset. 'What is it like, to live with a gangster and then, risking everything, betray him? Our next guest has written an explosive

270

novel based on her dark and dangerous background . . .'

'. . . And we introduce a new series of in-depth discussions,' chimes in Emma. The picture changes to one of pound coins raining onto the floor, and my stomach gives a nasty flip. '*Morning Coffee* turns the spotlight on the issue of financial scandal, with two leading industry experts coming head-to-head in debate.'

Is that me? Oh God, I don't want to be a leading industry expert. I want to go home and have a nice cup of tea.

'But first!' says Rory cheerily. 'Scott Robertson's getting all fired up in the kitchen.'

The picture switches abruptly to a man in a chef's hat grinning and brandishing a blow-torch. I stare at him for a few moments, then look down again, clenching my hands tightly in my lap. I can't quite believe that soon it'll be me up on that screen. Sitting on the sofa. Trying to think of something intelligent to say.

To distract myself, I unscrew my crappy piece of A4 paper for the thousandth time and read through my paltry notes. Maybe it won't be so bad, I find myself thinking hopefully, as my eyes circle the same few sentences again and again. Maybe I'm worrying about nothing. We'll probably keep the whole thing at the level of a casual chat. Keep it simple and friendly. After all . . .

'Good morning, Rebecca,' comes a voice from the door. Slowly I look up – and as I do so, I feel my heart sink. Luke Brandon is standing in the doorway. He's wearing an immaculate dark suit, his hair is shining, and his face is bronze with makeup. And there isn't an ounce of friendliness in his face. His jaw is tight; his eyes are hard and businesslike. As they meet mine, they don't even flicker.

For a few moments we gaze at each other without speaking. I can hear my heart beating loudly in my ears; my face feels hot beneath all the makeup. Then, summoning all my inner resources, I force myself to say calmly,

'Hello, Luke.'

There's an interested silence as he walks into the room. Even Elisabeth Plover seems intrigued by him.

'I know that face,' she says, leaning forward. 'I know it. You're an actor, aren't you? Shakespearian, of course. I believe I saw you in *Lear* three years ago.'

'I don't think so,' says Luke shortly.

'You're right!' says Elisabeth, slapping the table. 'It was *Hamlet*. I remember it well. The desperate pain, the guilt, the final tragedy . . .' She shakes her head solemnly. 'I'll never forget that voice of yours. Every word was like a stab wound.'

'I'm sorry to hear it,' says Luke eventually, and looks at me. 'Rebecca—'

'Luke, here are the final figures,' interrupts Alicia, hurrying into the room and handing him a piece of paper. 'Hello, Rebecca,' she adds, giving me a snide look. 'All prepared?'

'Yes, I am, actually,' I say, crumpling my A4 paper into a ball in my lap. 'Very well prepared.'

'Glad to hear it,' says Alicia, raising her eyebrows. 'It should be an interesting debate.'

'Yes,' I say defiantly. 'Very.'

God she's a cow.

'I've just had John from Flagstaff on the phone,' adds Alicia to Luke in a lowered voice. 'He was very keen that you should mention the new Foresight Savings Series. Obviously, I told him—'

'This is a damage limitation exercise,' says Luke curtly. 'Not a bloody plug-fest. He'll be bloody lucky if he . . .' He glances at me and I look away as though I'm not remotely interested in what he's talking about. Casually I glance at my watch and feel a leap of fright as I see the time. Ten minutes. Ten minutes to go.

'OK,' says Zelda, coming into the room. 'Elisabeth, we're ready for you.'

'Marvellous,' says Elisabeth, taking a last mouthful of *pain au chocolat*. 'Now, I do *look* all right, don't I?'

She stands up and a shower of crumbs falls off her skirt.

'You've got a piece of croissant in your hair,' says Zelda, reaching up and removing it. 'Other than that – what can I say?' She catches my eye and I have a hysterical desire to giggle.

'Luke!' says the baby-faced guy, rushing in with a mobile phone. 'John Bateson on the line for you. And a couple of packages have arrived . . .'

'Thanks, Tim,' says Alicia, taking the packages and ripping them open. She pulls out a bunch of papers and begins scanning them quickly, marking things every so often in pencil. Meanwhile, Tim sits down, opens a laptop computer and starts typing.

'Yes, John, I do see your bloody point,' Luke's saying in a low, tight voice. 'But if you would listen to me for just one moment—'

'Tim,' says Alicia, looking up. 'Can you quickly check the return on the Flagstaff Premium Pension over the last three, five and ten?'

'Absolutely,' says Tim, and starts tapping at his computer.

'Tim,' says Luke, looking up from the phone. 'Can you print out the Flagstaff Foresight draft press release for me asap? Thanks.'

I can't quite believe what I'm seeing. They've practically set up an office, here in the *Morning Coffee* green room. An entire office of Brandon Communications staff complete with computers and modems and phones . . . pitted against me and my crumpled piece of A4.

As I watch Tim's laptop efficiently spewing out pages, and Alicia handing sheets of paper to Luke, a cold feeling starts to creep over me. I mean, let's face it. I'll never beat this lot, will I? I haven't got a chance. I should just give up now. Tell them I'm ill or something. Run home and hide under my duvet.

'OK, everyone?' says Zelda, poking her head round the door. 'On in seven minutes.'

'Fine,' says Luke.

'Fine,' I echo in a wobbly voice.

'Oh, and Rebecca, there's a package for you,' says Zelda. She comes into the room and hands me a large, square box. 'I'll be back in a minute.'

'Thanks, Zelda,' I say in surprise and, with a sudden lift of spirits, begin to rip the box open. I've no idea what it is or who it's from – but it's got to be something helpful, hasn't it? Special last-minute information from Eric Foreman, maybe. A graph, or a series of figures that I can produce at the crucial moment. Or some secret document that Luke doesn't know about.

Out of the corner of my eye I can see that all the Brandonites have stopped what they're doing, and are watching, too. Well, that'll show them. They're not the only ones to get packages delivered to the green room. They're not the only ones to have resources. Finally I get the sticky tape undone and open the flaps of the box.

And as everyone watches, a big red helium balloon, with GOOD LUCK emblazoned across it, floats up to the ceiling. There's a card attached to the string, and, without looking anyone in the eye, I rip it open.

Immediately, I wish I hadn't.

'Good luck to you, good luck to you, whatever you're about to do,' sings a tinny electronic voice.

I slam the card shut and feel my cheeks flame red. God, how embarrassing. From the other side of the room I can hear little sniggers, and I look up to see Alicia smirking. She whispers something into Luke's ear, and an amused expression spreads across his face.

He's laughing at me. They're all laughing at Rebecca Bloomwood and her singing balloon. For a few moments I can't move for mortification. My face is hot; my throat feels tight; I've never felt less like a leading industry expert in my life.

Then, on the other side of the room, I hear Alicia murmur some malicious little comment and give a snort of laughter – and deep inside me, something snaps. Sod them, I think suddenly. Sod them all. They're probably only jealous, anyway. They wish they had balloons, too.

Defiantly, I open the card again to read the message. 'No matter if it rain or shine, we all know that you'll be fine,' sings the card's tinny voice at once. 'Hold your head up, keep it high – all that matters is you try.'

To Becky, I read. *With love and thanks for all your wonderful help. We're so proud to know you. From your friends Janice and Martin.*

I stare down at the card, reading the words over and over, and feel my eyes grow foolishly hot. Janice and Martin *have* been good friends over the years – even if their son is a bit of a prat. They've always been kind to me, even when I gave them such disastrous advice. I owe this to them. And I'm bloody well not going to let them down.

I blink a few times, take a deep breath and look up to see Luke Brandon gazing at me, his eyes dark and expressionless.

'Friends,' I say coolly. 'Sending me their good wishes.'

Carefully I place the card on the coffee table, making sure it stays open so it'll keep singing, then pull my balloon down from the ceiling and tie it to the back of my chair.

'OK,' comes Zelda's voice from the door. 'Luke and Rebecca. Are you ready?'

'Couldn't be readier,' I say calmly, and walk past Luke to the door.

Twenty-One

As we stride along the corridors to the set, neither Luke nor I say a word. I dart a glance at him as we turn a corner – and his face is even steelier than it was in the green room.

Well, that's fine. I can do steely, too. I can do hard and businesslike. Firmly I lift my chin and begin to take longer strides, pretending to be Alexis Carrington in *Dynasty*.

'So, do you two already know each other?' says Zelda, who's walking along between us.

'We do, as it happens,' says Luke shortly.

'In a business context,' I say, equally shortly. 'Luke's always trying to promote some pathetic financial product or other. And I'm always trying to avoid his calls.'

Zelda gives an appreciative laugh and I see Luke's eyes flash angrily. But I really don't care. I don't care how angry he gets. In fact, the angrier he gets, the better I feel.

'So – Luke, you must have been quite pissed off at Rebecca's article in the *Daily World*,' says Zelda.

'I wasn't pleased,' says Luke.

'He phoned me up to complain, can you believe it?' I say airily. 'Can't cope with the truth, eh Luke? Can't cope with seeing what's under the PR gloss? You know, perhaps you should change jobs.'

There's silence and I turn to look at Luke. He looks so furious, I think for a terrifying moment that he's going to hit me. Then his face changes and in an icily calm voice, he says,

'Let's just get on the fucking set and get this little charade over with, shall we?'

Zelda raises her eyebrows at me and I grin back. I've never seen Luke so rattled before.

'OK,' says Zelda as we approach a set of double swing doors. 'Here we are. Keep your voices down when we go in.'

She pushes open the doors and ushers us in, and for a moment my cool act falters. I feel all shaky and awed, like Laura Dern in *Jurassic Park* when she saw the dinosaurs for the first time. Because there it is, in real life. The real live *Morning Coffee* set. With the sofa and all the plants and everything, all lit up by the brightest, most dazzling lights I've ever seen in my life.

This is just unreal. How many zillion times have I sat at home, watching this on the telly? And now I'm actually going to be part of it. I can't quite believe it.

'We've got a couple of minutes till the commercial break,' says Zelda, leading us across the floor, across a load of trailing cables. 'Rory and Emma are still with Elisabeth in the library set.'

She gestures to us to sit down on opposite sides of the coffee table, and, gingerly, I do so. The sofa's harder than I was expecting, and kind of . . . different. Everything's different. God, this is weird. The lights are so bright on my face, I can hardly see anything, and I'm not quite sure how to sit. A girl comes and threads a microphone cable under my shirt and clips it to my lapel. Awkwardly, I lift my hand to push my hair back, and immediately Zelda comes hurrying over.

'Try not to move too much, OK, Rebecca?' she says. 'We don't want to hear a load of rustling.'

'Right,' I say. 'Sorry.'

Suddenly my voice doesn't seem to be working properly. I feel as though a wad of cotton wool's been stuffed into my throat. I glance up at a nearby camera and, to my horror, see it zooming towards me.

'OK, Rebecca,' says Zelda, hurrying over again, 'one

more golden rule – don't look at the camera, all right? Just behave naturally!'

'Fine,' I say huskily.

Behave naturally. Easy-peasy.

'Thirty seconds till the news bulletin,' she says, looking at her watch. 'Everything OK, Luke?'

'Fine,' says Luke calmly. He's sitting on his sofa as though he's been there all his life. Typical. It's all right for men, they don't care what they look like.

I shift on my seat, tug nervously at my skirt and smooth my jacket down. They always say that television puts ten pounds on you, which means my legs will look really fat. Maybe I should cross them the other way. Or not cross them at all? But then maybe they'll look even fatter.

'Hello!' comes a high-pitched voice from across the set before I can make up my mind. My head jerks up, and I feel an excited twinge in my stomach. It's Emma March in the flesh! She's wearing a pink suit and hurrying towards the sofa, closely followed by Rory, who looks even more square-jawed than usual. God, it's weird seeing celebrities in real life. They don't look quite real, somehow.

'Hello!' Emma says cheerfully, and sits down on the sofa. 'So you're the finance people, are you? Gosh, I'm dying for a wee.' She frowns into the lights. 'How long is this slot, Zelda?'

'Hi there!' says Rory and shakes my hand. 'Roberta.'

'It's Rebecca!' says Emma, and rolls her eyes at me sympathetically. 'Honestly, he's hopeless.' She wriggles on the sofa. 'Gosh, I really need to go.'

'Too late now,' says Rory.

'But isn't it really unhealthy not to go when you need to?' Emma wrinkles her brow anxiously. 'Didn't we have a phone-in on it once? That weird girl phoned up who only went once a day. And Dr James said . . . what did he say?'

'Search me,' says Rory cheerfully. 'These phone-ins always go over my head. Now I'm warning you,

Rebecca,' he adds, turning to me, 'I can never follow any of this finance stuff. Far too brainy for me.' He gives me a wide grin and I smile weakly back.

'Ten seconds,' calls Zelda from the side of the set, and my stomach gives a tweak of fear. Over the loud-speakers I can hear the *Morning Coffee* theme music, signalling the end of a commercial break.

'Who starts?' says Emma, squinting at the autocue. 'Oh, me.'

So this is it. I feel almost lightheaded with fear. I don't know where I'm supposed to be looking; I don't know when I'm supposed to speak. My legs are trembling and my hands are clenched tightly in my lap. The lights are dazzling my eyes; a camera's zooming in on my left, but I've got to try to ignore it.

'Welcome back!' says Emma suddenly to the camera. 'Now, which would you rather have? A carriage clock or £20,000?'

What? I think in shock. But that's *my* line. That's what I was going to say.

'The answer's obvious, isn't it?' continues Emma blithely. 'We'd all prefer the £20,000.'

'Absolutely!' interjects Rory with a cheerful smile.

'But when some Flagstaff Life investors received a letter inviting them to move their savings recently,' says Emma, suddenly putting on a sober face, 'they didn't realize that if they did so, they would lose out on a £20,000 windfall. Rebecca Bloomwood is the journalist who uncovered this story – Rebecca, do you think this kind of deception is commonplace?'

And suddenly everyone's looking at me, waiting for me to reply. The camera's trained on my face; the studio's silent.

2.5 million people, all watching at home.

Oh God. I can't breathe.

'Do you think investors need to be cautious?' prompts Emma.

'Yes,' I manage, in a strange, woolly voice. 'Yes, I think they should.'

'Luke Brandon, you represent Flagstaff Life,' says Emma, turning away. 'Do you think—'

Shit, I think miserably. That was pathetic. Pathetic! What's happened to my voice, for God's sake? What's happened to all my prepared answers?

Now I'm not even listening to Luke's reply. Come on, Rebecca. Focus your mind. Concentrate.

'What you must remember,' Luke's saying smoothly, 'is that nobody's *entitled* to a windfall. This isn't a case of deception!' He smiles at Emma. 'This is simply a case of a few investors being a little too greedy for their own good. They believe they've missed out – so they're deliberately stirring up bad publicity for the company. Meanwhile, there are thousands of people who *have* benefited from Flagstaff Life.'

What? What's he saying?

'I see,' says Emma, nodding her head. 'So, Luke, would you agree that—'

'Wait a minute!' I hear myself interrupting. 'Just . . . just wait a minute. Mr Brandon, did you just call the *investors* greedy?'

'Not all,' says Luke. 'But some, yes.'

I stare at him in disbelief, my skin prickling with outrage. An image of Janice and Martin comes into my mind – the sweetest, least greedy people in the world – and for a few moments I'm so angry, I can't speak.

'The truth is, the majority of investors with Flagstaff Life have seen record returns over the last five years,' Luke's continuing to Emma, who's nodding intelligently. 'And that's what they should be concerned with. Good quality investment. Not flash-in-the-pan windfalls. After all, Flagstaff Life was originally set up to provide—'

'Correct me if I'm wrong, Luke,' I cut in, forcing myself to speak calmly. 'Correct me if I'm wrong – but I believe Flagstaff Life was originally set up as a mutual company? For the *mutual benefit* of all its members. Not to benefit some at the expense of others.'

'Absolutely,' replies Luke without flickering. 'But

that doesn't entitle every investor to a £20,000 windfall, does it?'

'Maybe not,' I say, my voice rising slightly. 'But
surely it entitles them to believe they won't be misled
by a company they've put their money with for fifteen
years? Janice and Martin Webster trusted Flagstaff Life.
They trusted the advice they were given. And look
where that trust got them!'

'Investment is a game of luck,' says Luke blandly.
'Sometimes you win—'

'It wasn't luck!' I hear myself crying furiously. 'Of
course it wasn't luck! Are you telling me it was complete coincidence that they were advised to switch
their funds two weeks before the windfall announce-
ments?'

'My clients were simply making available an offer
that they believed would add value to their customers'
portfolios,' says Luke, giving me a tight smile. 'They
have assured me that they were simply wishing to
benefit their customers. They have assured me that—'

'So you're saying your clients are incompetent,
then?' I retort. 'You're saying they had all the best
intentions – but cocked it up?'

Luke's eyes flash in anger and I feel a thrill of exhilaration.

'I fail to see—'

'Well, we could go on debating all day!' says Emma,
shifting slightly on her seat. 'But moving on to a
slightly more—'

'Come on, Luke,' I say, cutting her off. 'Come *on*. You
can't have it both ways.' I lean forward, ticking points
off on my hand. 'Either Flagstaff Life were incompetent, or they were deliberately trying to save money.
Whichever it is, they're in the wrong. The Websters
were loyal customers and they should have got that
money. In my opinion, Flagstaff Life deliberately
encouraged them out of the with-profits fund to stop
them receiving the windfall. I mean, it's obvious, isn't
it?'

I look around for support and see Rory gazing blankly at me.

'It all sounds a bit technical for me,' he says with a little laugh. 'Bit complicated.'

'OK, let's put it another way,' I say quickly. 'Let's . . .' I close my eyes, searching for inspiration. 'Let's . . . suppose I'm in a clothes shop!' I open my eyes again. 'I'm in a clothes shop, and I've chosen a wonderful cashmere Nicole Farhi coat. OK?'

'OK,' says Rory cautiously.

'I love Nicole Farhi!' says Emma, perking up. 'Beautiful knitwear.'

'Exactly,' I say. 'OK, so imagine I'm standing in the checkout queue, minding my own business, when a sales assistant comes up to me and says, "Why not buy this other coat instead? It's better quality than this one – and I'll throw in a free bottle of perfume." I've got no reason to distrust the sales assistant, so I think, wonderful, and I buy the other coat.'

'Right,' says Rory, nodding. 'With you so far.'

'But when I get outside,' I say carefully. 'I discover that this other coat isn't Nicole Farhi, and isn't real cashmere. I go back in – and the shop won't give me a refund.'

'You were ripped off!' exclaims Rory, as though he's just discovered gravity.

'Exactly,' I say. 'I was ripped off. And the point is – so were thousands of Flagstaff Life customers. They were persuaded out of their original choice of investment, into a fund which left them £20,000 worse off.' I pause, marshalling my thoughts. 'Perhaps Flagstaff Life didn't break the law. Perhaps they didn't contravene any regulations. But there's a natural justice in this world, and they didn't just break that, they shattered it. Those customers deserved that windfall. They were loyal, long-standing customers, and they deserved it. And if you're honest, Luke Brandon, you *know* they deserved it.'

I finish my speech breathlessly and look at Luke.

He's staring at me with an unreadable expression on his face – and in spite of myself, I feel my stomach give a nervous flip. I swallow, and try to shift my gaze away from his – but somehow I can't move my head. It's as though our eyes are glued together.

'Luke?' says Emma. 'Do you have a response to Rebecca's point?'

Luke doesn't respond. He's staring at me, and I'm staring back, feeling my heart thump like a rabbit.

'Luke?' repeats Emma slightly impatiently. 'Do you have—'

'Yes,' says Luke. 'Yes I do. Rebecca . . .' He shakes his head, almost smiling to himself, then looks up again at me. 'Rebecca, you're right.'

There's a sudden still silence around the studio.

I open my mouth, but I can't make a sound.

Out of the corner of my eye, I see Rory and Emma glancing at each other, puzzled.

'Sorry, Luke,' says Emma. 'Do you mean—'

'She's right,' says Luke, and gives a shrug. 'Rebecca's absolutely right.' He reaches for his glass of water, leans back on his sofa and takes a sip. 'If you want my honest opinion, those customers deserved that windfall. I very much wish they *had* received it.'

This can't be happening. Luke's agreeing with me. How can he be agreeing with me?

'I see,' says Emma, sounding a bit affronted. 'So, you've changed your position, then?'

There's a pause, while Luke stares thoughtfully into his glass of water. Then he looks up and says,

'My company is employed by Flagstaff Life to maintain their public profile. But that doesn't mean that personally I agree with everything they do – or even that I know about it.' He pauses. 'To tell you the truth, I had no idea any of this was going on until I read about it in Rebecca's article in the *Daily World*. Which, by the way, was a fine piece of investigative journalism,' he adds, nodding to me. 'Congratulations.'

I stare back helplessly, unable even to mutter 'Thank

you'. I've never felt so wrong-footed in all my life. I want to stop, and bury my head in my hands and think all of this through slowly and carefully – but I can't, I'm on live television. I'm being watched by 2.5 million people, all around the country.

Shit, I hope my legs look OK.

'If I were a Flagstaff customer and this had happened to me, I'd be very angry,' Luke continues. 'There *is* such a thing as customer loyalty; there *is* such a thing as playing straight. And I would hope that any client of mine, whom I represent in public, would abide by both of those principles.'

'I see,' says Emma and turns to the camera. 'Well – this is quite a turn-around! Luke Brandon, here to represent Flagstaff Life, now says that what they did was wrong. Any further comment, Luke?'

'To be honest,' says Luke, with a wry smile, 'I'm not sure I'll be representing Flagstaff Life any more after this.'

'Ah,' says Rory, leaning forward intelligently. 'And can you tell us why that is?'

'Oh, honestly, Rory!' says Emma impatiently. She rolls her eyes and Luke gives a little snort of laughter.

Suddenly everyone's laughing, and I join in too, slightly hysterically. I catch Luke's eye and feel something flash in my chest, then quickly look away again.

'Right, well, anyway,' says Emma abruptly, pulling herself together and smiling at the camera. 'That's it from the finance experts – but, coming up after the break – the return of hot-pants to the catwalk . . .'

'. . . and cellulite creams – do they really work?' adds Rory.

'Plus our special guests – Heaven Sent 7 – singing live in the studio.'

The theme music blares out of the loudspeakers and both Emma and Rory leap to their feet.

'Wonderful debate,' says Emma, hurrying off. 'Sorry, I'm *dying* for a wee.'

'Excellent stuff,' adds Rory earnestly. 'Didn't

understand a word – but great television.' He slaps Luke on the back, raises his hand to me and then hurries off the set.

And all at once it's over. All finished. It's just me and Luke, sitting opposite each other on the sofas, with bright lights still shining in our eyes and microphones still clipped to our lapels. I feel slightly shell-shocked. Slightly dizzy.

Did all that really just happen?

'So,' I say eventually, and clear my throat.

'So,' echoes Luke, with a tiny smile. 'Well done.'

'Thanks,' I say, and bite my lip awkwardly in the silence.

I'm wondering if he's in big trouble now. If attacking one of your clients on live TV is the PR equivalent of hiding clothes from the customers.

If he really changed his mind because of my article. Because of me.

But I can't ask that. Can I?

The silence is growing louder and louder and at last I take a deep breath.

'Did you—'

'I was—'

We both speak at once.

'No,' I say, flushing red. 'You go. Mine wasn't . . . You go.'

'OK,' says Luke, and gives a little shrug. 'I was just going to ask if you'd like to have dinner tonight.'

I stare at him, taken aback.

What does he mean, have dinner? Does he mean—

'To discuss a bit of business,' he continues. 'I very much liked your idea for a unit trust promotion along the lines of the January sales.'

My what?

What idea? What's he . . .

Oh God, *that.* Is he serious? That was just one of my stupid, speak-aloud, brain-not-engaged moments.

'I think it could be a good promotion for a particular client of ours,' he's saying, 'and I was wondering whether you'd like to consult on the project. On a free-lance basis, of course.'

Consult. Freelance. Project.

I don't believe it. He's serious.

'Oh,' I say, and swallow, inexplicably disappointed. 'Oh, I see. Well, I . . . I suppose I might be free tonight.'

'Good,' says Luke. 'Shall we say the Ritz?'

'If you like,' I say offhandedly, as though I go there all the time.

'Good,' says Luke again, and his eyes crinkle into a smile. 'I look forward to it.'

And then – oh God. To my utter horror, before I can stop myself, I hear myself saying bitchily, 'What about Sacha? Doesn't she have plans for you tonight?'

Even as the words hit the air, I feel myself redden. Oh shit. What did I say that for?

There's a long silence during which I want to slink off somewhere and die.

'Sacha left, a week ago,' says Luke finally, and my head pops up.

'Oh,' I say feebly. 'Oh dear.'

'No warning – she packed up her suitcase and went.' Luke looks up. 'Still – it could be worse.' He gives a deadpan shrug. 'At least I didn't buy the holdall as well.'

Oh God, now I'm going to giggle. I mustn't giggle. I *mustn't*.

'I'm really sorry,' I manage at last.

'I'm not,' says Luke, gazing at me seriously, and the laughter inside me dies away. I stare back at him nervously and feel my heart begin to pound.

'Rebecca! Luke!'

Our heads jerk round to see Zelda approaching the set, clipboard in hand.

'Fantastic!' she exclaims. 'Just what we wanted. Luke, you were great. And Rebecca . . .' She comes and sits next to me on the sofa and pats my shoulder. 'You were so wonderful, we were thinking – how would you like to stand in as our phone-in expert later in the show?'

'What?' I stare at her. 'But . . . but I can't! I'm not an expert on anything.'

'Hahaha, very good!' Zelda gives an appreciative laugh. 'The great thing about you, Rebecca, is you've got the common touch. We see you as finance guru meets girl-next-door. Informative but approachable. Knowledgeable but down-to-earth. The financial expert people really want to talk to. What do you think, Luke?'

'I think Rebecca will do the job perfectly,' says Luke. 'I can't think of anyone better qualified. I also think I'd better get out of your way.' He stands up and smiles at me. 'See you later, Rebecca. Bye, Zelda.'

I watch in a daze as he picks his way across the cable-strewn floor towards the exit, half wishing he would look back.

'Right,' says Zelda, and squeezes my hand. 'Let's get you sorted.'

Twenty-Two

I was made to go on television. That's the truth. I was absolutely *made* to go on television.

We're sitting on the sofas again, Rory and Emma and me, and Anne from Leeds is falteringly admitting over the line that she's never once sent in a tax return.

I glance at Emma and smile, and she twinkles back. I'm one of the team. One of the gang. I've never felt so warm and happy in all my life.

What's really weird is that when it was me being interviewed, I felt all tongue-tied and nervous – but now I'm on the other side of the sofa, I'm in my element. God, I could do this all day. I don't even mind the bright lights any more. They feel normal. And I've practised the most flattering way to sit in front of the mirror (knees together, feet crossed at the ankle) – and I'm sticking to it.

'I've started doing some cleaning,' says Anne, 'and I never gave it a second thought. But now my employer's asked me if I've paid any tax. I mean, it didn't even occur to me.'

'Oh dear,' says Emma, and glances at me. 'Anne's obviously in a bit of a spot.'

'Absolutely,' I say sympathetically. 'Well the first thing to know, Anne, is that you may not have to pay any tax at all, if you're below the threshold. And the second thing is, you've still got plenty of time to get a tax return in and sort everything out.'

That's the other really weird thing. God knows how – but *I know the answers to all the questions*. I know about mortgages, and I know about life assurance, and

I know about pensions. I know this stuff! A few minutes ago, Kenneth from St Austell asked what the annual contribution limit for an ISA is – and I answered £5,000 without even thinking about it. It's almost as if some part of my mind has carefully been storing every single bit of information I've ever written in *Successful Saving*, and now, when I need it, it's all there. Ask me anything! Ask me . . . the rules on capital gains tax for home owners. Go on, ask me.

'If I were you, Anne,' I finish, 'I'd contact your local Inland Revenue office and ask them for their advice. And don't be scared!'

'Thanks,' says Anne's crackly voice. 'Thanks a lot, Rebecca.'

'Well, I hope that helps you, Anne,' says Emma, and smiles at the camera. 'Now we're going to Davina for the news and weather – but then, since so many of you are ringing in, we'll be coming back to this phone-in on "Managing your Money".'

'Lots of people with money problems out there,' chimes in Rory.

'Absolutely,' says Emma. 'And we want to help. So whatever your query, however big or small, please call in for Rebecca Bloomwood's advice, on 0333 4567.' She freezes for a moment, smiling at the camera, then relaxes back in her chair as the light goes off. 'Well, this is going very well!' she says brightly, as a make-up girl hurries up and touches up her face with powder. 'Isn't it, Zelda?'

'Fantastic!' says Zelda, appearing from out of the gloom. 'The lines haven't been this busy since we did "I'd like to meet a Spice Girl".' She looks curiously at me. 'Have you ever done a course in television presenting, Rebecca?'

'No,' I say honestly. 'I haven't. But . . . I've watched a lot of telly.'

Zelda roars with laughter.

'Good answer! OK, folks, we're back in thirty.'

Emma smiles at me and consults the piece of paper

in front of her, and Rory leans back and examines his nails. They're treating me like a fellow professional, I think joyfully. They're treating me like one of them.

I've never felt so completely and utterly happy. Never. Not even that time I found a Vivienne Westwood bustier for £60 in the Harvey Nichols sale. (I wonder where that is, actually. I must get round to wearing it some time.) This beats everything. Life is perfect.

I lean back, full of contentment and am idly looking around the studio when an oddly familiar figure catches my eye. I peer harder, and my skin starts to prickle in horror. There's a man standing in the gloom of the studio – and honestly, I must be hallucinating or something, because he looks exactly like—

'And . . . welcome back,' says Rory and my attention snaps back to the set. 'This morning's phone-in is on financial problems, big and small. Our guest expert is Rebecca Bloomwood and our next caller is Fran from Shrewsbury. Fran?'

'Yes,' says Fran. 'Hi. Hi, Rebecca.'

'Hi there, Fran,' I say, smiling warmly. 'And what seems to be the trouble?'

'I'm in a mess,' says Fran. 'I . . . I don't know what to do.'

'Are you in debt, Fran?' says Emma gently.

'Yes,' says Fran, and gives a shaky sigh. 'I'm overdrawn, I owe money on all my credit cards, I've borrowed money off my sister . . . and I just can't stop spending. I just . . . love buying things.'

'What sort of things?' says Rory interestedly.

'I don't know, really,' says Fran after a pause. 'Clothes for me, clothes for the kids, things for the house, just rubbish, really. Then the bills arrive . . . and I throw them away.'

Emma gives me a significant look, and I raise my eyebrows back.

'Rebecca?' she says. 'Fran's obviously in a bit of a spot. What should she be doing?'

'Well, Fran,' I say kindly. 'The first thing you've got to do is be brave, and confront your problem. Contact the bank and tell them you're having trouble managing. They're not monsters! They want to help.' I turn directly to the camera and look earnestly into the lens. 'Running away won't solve anything, Fran. The longer you leave it, the worse it'll get.'

'I know,' comes Fran's wobbly voice. 'I know you're right. But it's not easy.'

'I know,' I say sympathetically. 'I know it's not. Just hang in there, Fran.'

'Rebecca,' says Emma. 'Would you say this a common problem?'

'I'm afraid it is,' I reply, turning back to her. 'Sadly, a lot of people out there simply don't put financial security first.'

'Oh dear,' says Emma, shaking her head sorrowfully. 'That's not good.'

'But it's never too late,' I continue. 'As soon as they turn that corner, and wake up to their responsibilities, their lives are transformed.'

I make a confident sweeping gesture with my arm, and as I do so, my gaze takes in the whole studio. And . . . Oh my God it's him.

I'm not hallucinating.

It's really him. Standing at the corner of the set, wearing a security badge and sipping something in a polystyrene cup as though he belongs here. Derek Smeath is standing here in the *Morning Coffee* studios, ten yards away from me.

Derek Smeath of Endwich Bank.

But it . . . it can't be.

But it is. It's Derek Smeath. I don't understand. What's he doing here?

Oh God, and now he's staring straight at me.

My heart begins to pound, and I swallow hard, trying to keep control of myself.

'Rebecca?' Emma says, and I force myself to turn my attention back to the show. I can't even remember what

291

we're talking about. 'So you think Fran should go and see her bank manager?'

'I . . . ahm . . . that's right,' I say, my cheeks suddenly burning red.

What am I going to do? He's staring right at me. I can't escape.

'So,' says Emma. 'You think that once Fran faces up to reality, she'll be able to get her life in order.'

'That's right,' I say like an automaton, and force myself to smile brightly at Emma. But underneath, my confident happiness is evaporating. Derek Smeath is here. I can't block him out of my vision; I can't forget about him.

And now all the parts of my life I'd so carefully buried at the back of my mind are starting to worm their way out again. I don't want to remember any of them — but I've got no choice. Here they come, wriggling into my mind, one piece of horrible reality after another.

'Well,' says Rory. 'Let's all hope Fran takes Rebecca's very good advice.'

My row with Suze. My disastrous date with Tarquin. A nasty cold feeling starts trickling down my spine.

'Now our next caller,' says Emma, 'is John from Luton. John?'

'Hi, Rebecca,' comes a voice down the line. 'Thing is, I was given an insurance policy when I was a child, but I've lost all the papers. And now I'd like to get hold of the dosh, know what I mean?'

My VISA card, cancelled. My Octagon card, confiscated in front of that whole crowd. God, that was humiliating.

OK, stop it. Concentrate. Concentrate.

'This is actually quite a common problem,' I hear myself saying. 'Do you remember which company the policy was with?'

'No,' says John. 'Not a clue.'

My bank account. Thousands of pounds of debt. Derek Smeath.

Oh God. I feel sick. I want to run and hide some-where.

'Well, you still should be able to trace it,' I continue, forcing myself to keep smiling. 'You could start with an agency which specializes in this sort of thing. I can check this for you, but I think their name is . . .'

My whole terrible, disorganized life. It's all there, isn't it? Waiting for me, like a great big spider. Just waiting to pounce, as soon as this phone-in ends.

'We're out of time, I'm afraid,' says Emma, as I come to an end. 'Many thanks to our financial expert, Rebecca Bloomwood, and I'm sure we'll all be heeding her wise words. Coming up after the break, the results of our makeover in Newcastle and Heaven Sent 7, live in the studio.'

There's a frozen pause – then everyone relaxes.

'Right,' says Emma, consulting her piece of paper. 'Where are we next?'

'Good work, Rebecca,' says Rory cheerfully. 'Excellent stuff.'

'Oh Zelda!' says Emma, leaping up. 'Could I have a quick word? That was fab, Rebecca,' she adds. 'Really fab.'

Suddenly they're both gone. And I'm left alone on the set, exposed and vulnerable, desperately avoiding Derek Smeath's eye and thinking as quickly as I can.

Maybe I could slip out at the back.

Or maybe I could stick it out here on the sofa. Just sit here until he gets bored and leaves. I mean, he won't dare to come onto the actual set, will he?

Maybe I could *pretend to be someone else*. God, yes. I mean, with all this makeup on, I practically look like someone else, anyway.

Anyway – it suddenly occurs to me – who's to say he's even noticed me? He's probably here for some completely other reason. He's probably going to appear on the show or something. Exactly. Nothing to do with me. So I'll just get up and walk briskly past, and it'll all be fine.

'Excuse me, love,' says a man in jeans, coming onto the set. 'I need to shift this sofa along.'

'Oh, right,' I say, leaping up. As I do, I mistakenly catch the eye of Derek Smeath again. He's still looking right at me. He's waiting for me.

Oh God.

OK, it'll be fine – just keep walking. Just keep walking and pretend you don't recognize him.

Deliberately avoiding his gaze, I stand up, take a deep breath and walk briskly across the set. My pace doesn't falter; my expression doesn't waver. My eyes are fixed firmly on the double doors, and I'm doing well. Just a few more steps now. Just a few more . . .

'Miss Bloomwood.' His voice hits the back of my head like a bullet and for an instant I consider ignoring it. Possibly even diving for the doors. But Zelda and Emma are standing nearby. They'll have heard him calling my name. I can't get out of it.

So I turn round, and give what I think is a very convincing double-take, as though recognizing him for the first time.

'Oh, hello, it's *you*!' I say brightly. 'What a surprise. How are you?'

A technician gestures to us to keep our voices down, and Derek Smeath firmly ushers me out of the studio, into a foyer area. He turns to me and I give him a confident smile. Perhaps we can keep it all at a social level.

'Miss Bloomwood—'

'Lovely weather we're having,' I say. 'Don't you think?'

'Miss Bloomwood, our meeting,' says Derek Smeath tightly.

Oh God. I was hoping he might have forgotten about that.

'Our meeting,' I echo thoughtfully. 'Erm . . .' Then I have a sudden inspiration. 'That's right. It's tomorrow, isn't it? I'm really looking forward to it.'

Derek Smeath looks as though he's going to explode.

'It is not tomorrow! It was on Monday morning. And you failed to turn up!'

'Oh,' I say. 'Oh, *that* meeting. Yes, sorry about that. I meant to come, honestly. It's just . . . It's just that . . .'

But I can't think of a single good excuse. I've used them all up. So I tail off feebly, and bite my lip, feeling like a naughty child.

'Miss Bloomwood,' says Derek Smeath wearily. 'Miss Bloomwood . . .' He rubs his face with his hand, then looks up. 'Do you know quite how long I have been writing letters to you? Do you know how long I've been trying to get you into the bank for a meeting?'

'Ahm . . . I'm not quite—'

'Six months,' says Derek Smeath, and pauses. 'Six long months of excuses and prevarication. Now, I'd just like you to think about what that means for me. It means endless letters. Numerous phone calls. Hours of time and effort on my part and that of my assistant, Erica. Resources which, quite frankly, could be better spent elsewhere.' He gestures sharply with his polystyrene cup and some coffee slops out of the side onto the floor. 'Then finally I pin you down to a cast-iron appointment. Finally I think you're taking your situation seriously . . . And you don't turn up. You disappear completely. I telephone your home to find out where you are – and get accused most unpleasantly of being some kind of stalker!'

'Oh yes,' I say, and pull an apologetic face. 'Sorry about that. It's just my dad, you know. He's a bit weird.'

'I'd all but given up on you,' says Derek Smeath, his voice rising. 'I'd all but given up. And then I'm passing a television shop this morning – and what should I see, on six different screens, but the missing, vanished Rebecca Bloomwood, advising the nation. And what are you advising them on?' He begins to shake with laughter. (At least, I think it's laughter.) 'Finance! *You* are advising the British public . . . on finance!'

I stare at him crossly. It's not *that* funny.

'Look, I'm very sorry I couldn't make the last meeting,' I say, trying to sound businesslike. 'Things were a bit difficult for me at that time. But if we could reschedule . . .'

'Reschedule!' cries Derek Smeath, as though I've just cracked a hysterical joke. 'Reschedule!'

I gaze at him indignantly. He's not taking me seriously at all, is he? He's not even listening to what I'm saying. I'm telling him I want to come in for a meeting – I actually *want* to – and he's just treating me like a joke. He's treating me like some sort of comedy act.

And no wonder, interrupts a tiny voice inside me. *Look at the way you've behaved. Look at the way you've treated him. Frankly it's a wonder he's being civil to you at all.*

I look up at his face, still crinkled in laughter . . . and feel rather chastened.

Because the truth is, he could have been a lot nastier to me than he has been. He could have taken my card away a long time ago. Or sent the bailiffs round. Or had me blacklisted. He's actually been very nice to me, one way or another.

'Listen,' I say quickly. 'Please. Give me another chance. I really want to sort my finances out. I want to repay my overdraft. But I need you to help me. I'm . . .' I swallow. 'I'm asking you to help me, Mr Smeath.'

There's a long pause. Derek Smeath looks around for a place to put his coffee cup, takes a white handkerchief out of his pocket and rubs his brow with it. Then he puts it away and gives me a long look.

'You're serious,' he says at last.

'Yes.'

'You'll really make an effort?'

'Yes. And . . .' I bite my lip. 'And I'm very grateful for all the allowances you've made for me. I really am.'

Suddenly I feel almost tearful. I want to be good. I want to get my life in order. I want him to tell me what to do.

'All right,' says Derek Smeath at last. 'Let's see what we can sort out. You come into the office tomorrow, 9.30 sharp and we'll have a little chat.'

'Thanks,' I say, my whole body subsiding in relief. 'Thank you so much. I'll be there. I promise.'

'You'd better be,' he says. 'No more excuses.' Then a faint smile passes over his features. 'By the way,' he adds, gesturing to the set. 'I thought you did very well up there. Spot on with all your advice.'

'Oh,' I say in surprise. 'Well . . . thanks. That's really . . .' I clear my throat. 'How did you get into the studio, anyway? I thought they had quite tight security.'

'They do,' replies Derek Smeath. 'But my daughter works in television.' He smiles fondly. 'She used to work on this very show.'

'Really?' I say incredulously.

God, how amazing. Derek Smeath has got a daughter. He's probably got a whole family, come to that. A wife, and everything. Who would have thought it?

'I'd better go,' he says, and drains his polystyrene cup. 'This was a bit of an unscheduled detour.' He gives me a severe look. 'And I'll see you tomorrow.'

'I'll be there,' I say quickly, as he walks off towards the exit. 'And . . . and thanks. Thanks a lot.'

As he disappears, I sink down onto a nearby chair. I can't quite believe I've just had a pleasant, civilized conversation with Derek Smeath. With Derek Smeath! And he seems quite a sweetheart. He's been so nice and kind to me, and his daughter works in television . . . I mean, who knows, maybe I'll get to know her, too. Maybe I'll become friends with the whole family. Wouldn't that be great? I'll start going to dinner at their house, and his wife will give me a warm hug when I arrive, and I'll help her with the salad and stuff . . .

'Rebecca!' comes a voice from behind me, and I turn round to see Zelda approaching, still clutching her clipboard.

'Hi,' I say happily. 'How's it going?'

'Great,' she says, and pulls up a chair. 'Now, I want to have a little talk.'

'Oh,' I say. 'OK. What about?'

'We thought you did tremendously well today,' says Zelda, crossing one jeaned leg over the other. '*Tremendously* well. I've spoken to Emma and Rory and our senior producer' – she pauses for effect – 'and they'd all like to see you back on the show.'

I stare at her in disbelief.

'You mean . . .'

'Not every week,' says Zelda. 'But fairly regularly. We thought maybe three times a month. Do you think your work would allow you to do that?'

'I . . . I don't know,' I say dazedly. 'I expect it would.'

'Excellent!' says Zelda. 'We could probably plug your magazine as well, keep them happy.' She scribbles something on a piece of paper and looks up. 'Now, you don't have an agent, do you? So I'll have to talk money directly with you.' She pauses, and looks down at her clipboard. 'What we're offering, per slot, is . . .'

Twenty-Three

I put my key in the lock and slowly open the door of
the flat. It feels like about a million years since I was
here last, and I feel like a completely different person.
I've grown up. Or changed. Or something.

'Hi,' I say cautiously into the silence, and drop my
bag onto the floor. 'Is anyone—'

'Bex!' gasps Suze, appearing at the door of the sitting
room. She's wearing tight black leggings and holding a
half-made denim photograph frame in one hand. 'Oh
my God! Where've you *been*? What have you been
doing? I saw you on *Morning Coffee* and I couldn't
believe my eyes! I tried to phone in and speak to you,
but they said I had to have a financial problem. So I
said, OK, how should I invest half a million? but they
said that wasn't really—' She breaks off. 'Bex, where
have you been? What happened?'

I don't reply straight away. I'm gazing at the pile of
letters addressed to me on the table. White, official-
looking envelopes, brown window envelopes,
envelopes marked menacingly, 'Final Reminder'. The
scariest pile of letters you've ever seen.

Except somehow . . . they don't seem quite so scary
any more.

'I was at my parents' house,' I say, looking up. 'And
then I was on television.'

'But I phoned your parents! They said they didn't
know where you were!'

'I know,' I say, flushing slightly. 'They were . . . pro-
tecting me from a stalker.' I look up, to see Suze staring
at me in utter incomprehension. Which I suppose is

299

fair enough. 'Anyway,' I add defensively, 'I left you a message on the machine, saying not to worry, I was fine.'

'I know,' wails Suze, 'but that's what they always do in films. And it means the baddies have got you and you've got a gun jammed against your head. Honestly, I thought you were dead! I thought you were, like, cut up into a million pieces somewhere.'

I look at her face again. She isn't kidding. She really was worried. Suddenly I feel awful. I should never have vanished like that. It was completely thoughtless and irresponsible and selfish.

'Oh Suze.' On impulse, I hurry forward and hug her tightly. 'I'm really sorry. I never meant to worry you.'

'It's OK,' says Suze, hugging me back. 'I was worried for a bit – but then I knew you must be all right when I saw you on the telly. You were fantastic, by the way.'

'Really?' I say, a tiny smile flickering round the corners of my mouth. 'Did you really think so?'

'Oh yes!' says Suze. 'Much better than whatshisface. Luke Brandon. God, he's arrogant.'

'Yes,' I say after a tiny pause. 'Yes, I suppose he is. But he was actually quite nice to me afterwards.'

'Really?' says Suze indifferently. 'Well, you were brilliant, anyway. Do you want some coffee?'

'Love some,' I say, and she disappears into the kitchen.

I pick up my letters and bills and begin slowly to leaf through them. Once upon a time, this lot would have sent me into a blind panic. In fact, they would have gone straight into the bin, unread. But you know what? Today I don't feel a flicker of fear. Honestly, how could I have been so silly about my financial affairs? How could I have been so cowardly? This time I'm just going to face up to them properly. I'm going to sit down with my chequebook and my latest bank statements, and sort methodically through the whole mess.

Staring at the clutch of envelopes in my hand, I feel suddenly very grown-up and responsible. Far-sighted and sensible. I'm going to sort my life out and keep my finances in order from now on. I've completely and utterly changed my attitude towards money.

Plus . . .

OK, I wasn't actually going to tell you this. But *Morning Coffee* are paying me absolute loads. *Loads.* You won't believe it, but for every single phone-in I do, I'm going to get—

Oh, I'm all embarrassed now. Let's just say it's . . . it's quite a lot. Heehee!

I just can't stop smiling about it. I've been floating along, ever since they told me. So the point is, I'll easily be able to pay all these bills off now. My VISA bill, and my Octagon bill, and the money I owe Suze – and everything! Finally, *finally* my life is going to be sorted.

'So, why did you just disappear like that?' asks Suze, coming back out of the kitchen and making me jump. 'What was wrong?'

'I don't really know,' I say, with a sigh, putting the letters back down on the hall table. 'I just had to get away and think. I was all confused.'

'Because of Tarquin?' says Suze at once, and I feel myself stiffen apprehensively.

'Partly,' I say after a pause, and swallow. 'Why? Has he . . .'

'I know you're not that keen on Tarkie,' says Suze wistfully, 'but I think he still really likes you. He came round a couple of nights ago, and left you this letter.'

She gestures to a cream envelope stuck in the mirror. With slightly trembling hands I take it. Oh God, what's he going to say? I hesitate, then rip it open and a ticket falls onto the floor.

'The opera!' says Suze, picking it up. 'Tonight!' She looks up. 'God, it's lucky you came back today, Bex.'

My dear Rebecca. I'm reading incredulously.
Forgive my reticence in contacting you before.
But the more time passes, the more I realize how

much I enjoyed our evening together and how
much I would like to repeat it.

I enclose a ticket for Die Meistersinger *at the*
Opera House. I shall be attending in any case
and if you were able to join me, I would be
delighted.

Yours very sincerely
Tarquin Cleath-Stuart

I stare at the letter, completely confused. What does
this mean? That Tarquin didn't see me leafing through
his chequebook after all? That he did see – but has
decided to forgive me? That he's a complete schizoid?

'Oh Bex, you must go!' says Suze, reading over my
shoulder. 'You've got to go. He'll be devastated if you
don't. I really think he likes you.'

'I can't go,' I say, thrusting the letter down. 'I've got
a business meeting tonight.'

'Well that's OK!' says Suze. 'You can cancel it.'

'I . . . I can't. It's quite important.'

'Oh,' says Suze, crestfallen. 'But what about poor
Tarkie? He'll be sitting there, waiting for you, all
excited . . .'

'You go instead,' I suggest. 'You go.'

'Really?' Suze pulls a face and glances down at the
ticket. 'I suppose I could. I quite like opera. But
honestly . . .' She looks up. 'Who's your business meeting with, anyway?'

'It's . . . it's with Luke Brandon,' I say, trying to sound
unconcerned. But it's no good, I can feel myself starting to blush.

'Luke Brandon?' says Suze, puzzled. 'But what—'
She stares at me, and her expression slowly changes.
'Oh no. Bex! Don't tell me . . .'

'It's just a business meeting,' I say, avoiding her eye.
'That's all. Two businesspeople meeting up and talking
about business. In a . . . in a business situation. That's
all.'

And I hurry off to my room.

*　*　*

Business meeting. Clothes for a business meeting. OK, let's have a look.

I pull all my outfits out of the wardrobe and lay them on the bed. Blue suit, black suit, pink suit. Hopeless. Pin-striped suit? Hmmm. Maybe overdoing it. Cream suit . . . too weddingy. Green suit . . . isn't that bad luck or something?

'So what are you going to wear?' says Suze, looking in through my open bedroom door. 'Are you going to buy something new?' Her face lights up. 'Hey, shall we go shopping?'

'Shopping?' I say distractedly. 'Ahm . . . maybe.'

Normally, of course, I'd jump at the chance of a shopping trip. Leap at it. But somehow today . . . Oh, I don't know. I almost feel too tense to go shopping. Too keyed up. I don't think I'd be able to give it my full attention.

'Bex, did you hear me?' says Suze in surprise. 'I said, "Shall we go shopping?"'

'Yes, I know.' I glance up at her, then reach for a black top and look at it critically. 'Actually, I think I'll take a rain-check.'

'You mean . . .' Suze pauses. 'You mean you *don't* want to go shopping?'

'Exactly.'

There's silence, and I look up, to see Suze staring at me.

'I don't understand,' she says, and she sounds quite upset. 'Why are you being all weird?'

'I'm not being weird!' I give a little shrug. 'I just don't feel like shopping.'

'Oh God, there's something wrong, isn't there?' wails Suze. 'I knew it. Maybe you're really ill.' She hurries into the room and reaches for my head. 'Have you got a temperature? Does anything hurt?'

'No!' I say, laughing. 'Of course not!'

'Have you had a bump on the head?' She wiggles her hand in front of my face. 'How many fingers?'

'Suze, I'm fine,' I say, thrusting her hand aside. 'Honestly. I'm just . . . not in a shopping mood.' I hold a grey suit up against myself. 'What do you think of this?'

'Honestly, Bex, I'm worried about you,' says Suze, shaking her head. 'I think you should get yourself checked out. You're so . . . different. It's frightening.'

'Yes well.' I reach for a white shirt and smile at her. 'Maybe I've changed.'

It takes me all afternoon to decide on an outfit. There's a lot of trying on, and mixing and matching, and suddenly remembering things at the back of my wardrobe (I *must* wear those purple jeans some time). But eventually I plump for simple and straightforward. My nicest black suit (Jigsaw sale, two years ago), a white T-shirt (M&S) and knee-high black suede boots (Dolce & Gabbana, but I told Mum they were from BHS. Which was a mistake, because then she wanted to get some for herself, and I had to pretend they'd all sold out). I put it all on, screw my hair up into a knot, and stare at myself in the mirror.

'Very nice,' says Suze admiringly from the door. 'Very sexy.'

'Sexy?' I feel a lollop of dismay. 'I'm not going for sexy! I'm going for businesslike.'

'Can't you be both at once?' suggests Suze. 'Businesslike *and* sexy?'

'I . . . No,' I say after a pause, and look away. 'No, I don't want to.'

I don't want Luke Brandon to think I've dressed up for him, is what I really mean. I don't want to give him the slightest chance to think I've misconstrued what this meeting is about. Not like last time.

With no warning, a surge of fresh humiliation goes through my body as I remember that awful moment in Harvey Nichols. I shake my head hard, trying to clear it; trying to calm my beating heart. Why the hell did I agree to this bloody dinner, anyway?

'I just want to look as serious and businesslike as possible,' I say, and frown sternly at my reflection.

'I know, then,' says Suze. 'You need some accessories. Some businesswoman-type accessories.'

'Like what? A Filofax?'

'Like . . .' Suze pauses thoughtfully. 'OK, I've got an idea. Wait there—'

I arrive at the Ritz that evening five minutes after our agreed time of 7.30, and as I reach the entrance to the restaurant, I see Luke there already, sitting back looking relaxed and sipping something that looks like a gin and tonic. He's wearing a different suit from the one he was wearing this morning, I can't help noticing, and he's put on a fresh, dark green shirt. He actually looks . . . Well. Quite nice. Quite goodlooking.

Not that businessy, in fact.

And, come to think of it, this restaurant isn't very businessy, either. It's all chandeliers and gold garlands and soft pink chairs, and the most beautiful painted ceiling, all clouds and flowers. The whole place is sparkling with light, and it looks . . .

Well actually, the word that springs to mind is 'romantic'.

Oh God. My heart starts thumping with nerves, and I glance quickly at my reflection in a gilded mirror. I'm wearing the black Jigsaw suit and white T-shirt and black suede boots as originally planned. But now I also have a crisp copy of the *Financial Times* under one arm, a pair of tortoiseshell glasses (with clear glass) perched on my head, my clunky executive briefcase in one hand and – Suze's *pièce de résistance* – an AppleMac laptop in the other.

Maybe I overdid it.

I'm about to back away and see if I can quickly deposit the briefcase in the cloakroom (or, to be honest, just put it down on a chair and walk away), when Luke looks up, sees me, and smiles. Damn. So I'm forced to go forward over the plushy carpet, trying to look as relaxed as possible, even though one arm is clamped tightly to my side, to stop the *FT* falling on the floor.

'Hello,' says Luke as I arrive at the table. He stands up to greet me, and I realize that I can't shake his hand, because I'm holding the laptop. Flustered, I plonk my briefcase on the floor, transfer the laptop to the other side – nearly dropping the *FT* as I do so – and, with slightly reddened cheeks, hold out my hand.

A flicker of amusement passes over Luke's face and he solemnly shakes my hand. He gestures to a chair, and watches politely as I put the laptop on the table-cloth, all ready for use.

'That's an impressive machine,' he says. 'Very . . . high-tech.'

'Yes,' I reply, and give him a brief, cool smile. 'I often use it to take notes at business meetings.'

'Ah,' says Luke, nodding. 'Very organized of you.'

He's obviously waiting for me to switch it on, so experimentally I press the return key. This, according to Suze, should make the screen spring to life. But nothing happens.

Casually, I press the key again – and still nothing. I jab at it, pretending my finger slipped by accident – and *still* nothing. Shit, this is embarrassing. Why do I ever listen to Suze?

'Is there a problem?' says Luke.

'No!' I say at once, and snap the lid shut. 'No, I've just . . . On second thoughts, I won't use it today.' I reach into my bag for a notebook. 'I'll jot my notes down in here.'

'Good idea,' says Luke mildly. 'Would you like some champagne?'

'Oh,' I say, slightly thrown. 'Well . . . OK.'

'Excellent,' says Luke. 'I hoped you would.'

He glances up, and a beaming waiter scurries forward with a bottle. Gosh, Krug.

But I'm not going to smile, or look pleased or anything. I'm going to stay thoroughly cool and professional. In fact, I'm only going to have one glass, before moving on to still water. I need to keep a clear head, after all.

While the waiter fills my champagne flute, I write down, 'Meeting between Rebecca Bloomwood and Luke Brandon' in my notebook. I look at it appraisingly, then underline it twice. There. That looks very efficient.

'So,' I say, looking up, and raise my glass. 'To business.'

'To business,' echoes Luke and gives a wry smile. 'What little I've got left of it.'

'Really?' I stare at him, puzzled – and then the penny drops. 'You mean – after what you said on *Morning Coffee*? Has it got you into trouble?'

He nods and I feel a pang of sympathy for him.

I mean, Suze is right – Luke is pretty arrogant. But I actually thought it was really good of him to stick his neck out like that and say publicly what he really thought about Flagstaff Life. And now, if he's going to be ruined as result, well, it just seems all wrong.

'Have you lost everything?' I say quietly, and Luke laughs.

'I wouldn't go that far. But we've had to do an awful lot of explaining to our other clients this afternoon.' He grimaces. 'It has to be said, insulting one of your major clients on live television isn't exactly normal PR practice.'

'Well, I think they should respect you!' I retort. 'For actually saying what you think! I mean, so few people do that these days. It could be like . . . your company motto. "We tell the truth".'

I take a gulp of champagne and look up into silence. Luke's gazing at me, an odd expression on his face.

'Rebecca, you have the uncanniest knack of hitting the nail right on the head,' he says at last. 'That's exactly what some of our clients have said. It's as though we've given ourselves a seal of integrity.'

'Oh,' I say, feeling rather pleased with myself. 'Well, that's good. So you're not ruined.'

'I'm not ruined,' agrees Luke, and gives a little smile. 'Just slightly dented.'

A waiter appears from nowhere and replenishes my glass, and I take a sip. When I look up, Luke's staring at me again.

'You know, Rebecca, you're an extremely perceptive person,' he says. 'You see what other people don't.'

'Oh well.' I wave my champagne glass airily. 'Didn't you hear Zelda? I'm finance guru meets girl-next-door.' I meet his eye and we both start to laugh.

'You're informative meets approachable.'

'Knowledgeable meets down-to-earth.'

'You're intelligent, meets charming, meets bright, meets . . .' Luke tails off, staring down into his drink, then looks up.

'Rebecca, I want to apologize,' he says. 'I've been wanting to apologize for a while. That lunch in Harvey Nichols . . . you were right. I didn't treat you with the respect you deserved. The respect you deserve.'

He breaks off into silence and I stare down at the tablecloth, feeling my cheeks flaming. It's all very well for him to say this *now*, I'm thinking furiously. It's all very well for him to book a table at the Ritz and order champagne and expect me to smile and say, 'Oh, that's OK.' But underneath all the bright banter, I still feel wounded by that whole episode. And after my success this morning, I'm in fighting mood.

'My piece in the *Daily World* had nothing to do with that lunch,' I say without looking up. 'Nothing. And for you to insinuate that it did . . .'

'I know,' says Luke, and sighs. 'I should never have said that. It was a . . . a defensive, angry remark on a day when, frankly, you had us all on the hop.'

'Really?' I can't help a pleased little smile coming to my lips. 'I had you all on the hop?'

'Are you joking?' says Luke. 'A whole page in the *Daily World* on one of our clients, completely out of the blue?'

Ha. I quite like that idea, actually. The whole of

Brandon C thrown into disarray by Janice and Martin Webster.

'Was Alicia on the hop?' I can't resist asking.

'She was hopping as fast as her Manolos would let her,' says Luke drily. 'Even faster when I discovered she'd actually spoken to you the day before.'

Ha!

'Good,' I hear myself saying childishly – then wish I hadn't. Top businesswomen don't gloat over their enemies being told off. I should have simply nodded, or said 'Ah,' meaningfully.

'So – did I have you on the hop, too?' I say, giving a careless little shrug.

There's silence, and after a while I look up. Luke's gazing at me with an unsmiling expression which makes my heart start to thud.

'You've had me on the hop for quite a while, Rebecca,' he says quietly. He holds my eyes for a few seconds while I stare back, unable to breathe – then looks down at his menu. 'Shall we order?'

The meal seems to go on all night. We talk and talk and eat, and talk, and eat some more. The food is so delicious I can't say no to anything, and the wine is so delicious I abandon my plan of drinking a businesslike single glass and then sticking to water. By the time I'm toying listlessly with chocolate *feuillantine* with lavender honey ice-cream and caramelized pears, it's about midnight, and my head is starting to droop.

'How's the chocolate thing?' says Luke, finishing a mouthful of cheesecake.

'Nice,' I say, and push it towards him. 'Not as good as the lemon mousse, though.'

That's the other thing – I'm absolutely stuffed to the brim. I couldn't decide between all the scrummy-sounding puddings, so Luke said we should order all the ones we liked the sound of. Which was most of them. So now my stomach feels as though it's the size of a Christmas pudding, and just as heavy.

I honestly feel as if I'll never ever be able to get out of this chair. It's so comfortable, and I'm so warm and cosy, and it's all so pretty, and my head's spinning just enough to make me not want to stand up. Plus . . . I don't want it all to stop. I don't want the evening to end. I've had *such* a good time. The amazing thing is how much Luke makes me laugh. You'd think he'd be all serious and boring and intellectual, but really, he's not. In fact, come to think of it, we haven't talked about that unit trust thingy once.

A waiter comes and clears away all our pudding dishes, and brings us each a cup of coffee. I lean back in my chair, close my eyes and take a few delicious sips. Oh God, I could stay here for ever. I'm actually feeling really sleepy by now – partly because I was so nervous last night about *Morning Coffee*, I hardly slept at all.

'I should go,' I say eventually, and force myself to open my eyes. 'I should go back to . . .' Where do I live, again? 'Fulham. To Fulham.'

'Right,' says Luke, after a pause, and takes a sip of coffee. He puts his cup down and reaches for the milk. And as he does so, his hand brushes against mine – and stops still. At once I feel my whole body stiffen. My cheeks start to burn, and my heart starts to beat in apprehension.

OK, I'll admit it – I kind of put my hand in his way. Just to see what would happen. I mean, he could easily move his hand back if he wanted to, couldn't he? Pour his milk, make a joke, say goodnight.

But he doesn't. Very slowly, he closes his hand over mine.

And now I really can't move. His thumb starts to trace patterns on my wrist, and I can feel how warm and dry his skin is. I look up and meet his gaze, and feel a little jolt inside me. I can't tear my eyes away from his. I can't move my hand. I'm completely transfixed.

'That chap I saw you with in Terrazza,' he says after

310

a while, his thumb still drawing leisurely pictures on my skin. 'Was he anything . . .'

'Just . . . you know.' I try to give a careless laugh, but I'm feeling so nervous it comes out as a squeak. 'Some multimillionaire or other.'

Luke stares intently at me for a second – then looks away.

'Right,' he says, as though closing the subject. 'Well. Perhaps we should get you a taxi.' I feel a thud of disappointment, and try not to let it show. 'Or maybe . . .' He stops.

There's an endless pause. I can't quite breathe. Maybe what? What?

'I know them pretty well here,' says Luke at last. 'If we wanted to . . .' He meets my eyes. 'I expect we could stay.'

I feel an electric shock go through my body.

'Would you like to?'

Unable to speak, I nod my head. Oh God. Oh God, this is the most exciting thing I've ever done.

'OK, wait here,' says Luke. 'I'll go and see if I can get rooms.' He gets up and I stare after him in a daze, my hand cold and bereft.

Rooms. Rooms, plural. So he didn't mean . . .

He doesn't want to . . .

Oh God. What's *wrong* with me?

We travel up in the lift in silence with a smart porter. I glance a couple of times at Luke's face, but he's staring impassively ahead. In fact, he's barely said a word since he went off to ask about staying. I feel a bit chilly inside – in fact, to be honest, I'm half wishing they hadn't had any spare rooms for us after all. But it turns out there was a big cancellation tonight – and it also turns out that Luke is some big-shot client of the Ritz. When I commented on how nice they were being to us, he shrugged, and said he often puts up business contacts here.

Business contacts. So is that what I am? Oh, it

doesn't make any sense. I wish I'd gone home after all.

We walk along an opulent corridor in complete silence – then the porter swings open a door and ushers us into a spectacularly beautiful room, furnished with a big double bed and plushy chairs. He places my briefcase and AppleMac on the luggage rail, then Luke gives him a note and he disappears.

There's a pause. I've never felt more awkward in my life.

'Well,' says Luke. 'Here you are.'

'Yes,' I say, in a voice which doesn't sound like mine. 'Thanks . . . thank you. And for dinner.' I clear my throat. 'It was delicious.'

We seem to have turned into complete strangers.

'Well,' says Luke again, and glances at his watch. 'It's late. You'll probably be wanting to . . .' He stops, and there's a sharp, waiting silence.

My heart's thudding in my chest; my hands are twisted in a nervous knot. I don't dare look at him.

'I'll be off, then,' says Luke at last. 'I hope you have a—'

'Don't go,' I hear myself say, and blush furiously. 'Don't go yet. We could just . . .' I swallow. 'Talk, or something.'

I look up and meet his eyes, and something fearful starts to pound within me. Slowly he walks towards me, until he's standing just in front of me. I can just smell the scent of his aftershave, and hear the crisp cotton rustle of his shirt as he moves. My whole body's prickling with anticipation. Oh God, I want to touch him. But I daren't. I daren't move anything.

'We could just talk, or something,' he echoes, and slowly lifts his hands until they cup my face. 'We could just talk. Or something.'

And then he kisses me.

His mouth is on mine, gently parting my lips, and I feel a white-hot dart of excitement. His hands are running down my back and cupping my bottom; fingering under the hem of my skirt. Then he pulls me tightly towards him, and suddenly I'm finding it hard to breathe.

And it's pretty obvious we're not going to do much talking at all.

Twenty-Four

Mmmm.

Bliss.

Lying in the most comfortable bed in the world, feeling all dreamy and smiley and happy, letting the morning sunlight play on my closed eyelids. Stretching my arms above my head, then collapsing contentedly onto an enormous mound of pillows. Oh, I feel good. I feel . . . sated. Last night was absolutely . . .

Well, let's just say it was . . .

Oh, come on. You don't need to know *that*. Anyway, can't you use your imagination? Of course you can.

I open my eyes, sit up and reach for my cup of room-service coffee. Luke's in the shower, so it's just me alone with my thoughts. And I don't want to sound all pretentious here – but I do feel this is a pretty significant day in my life.

It's not just Luke – although the whole thing was . . . well, amazing, actually. God, he really knows how to . . .

Anyway. Not the point. The point is, it's not just Luke – and it's not just my new job with *Morning Coffee* (even though every time I remember it, I feel a leap of disbelieving joy).

No, it's more than that. It's that I feel like a completely new person. I feel as though I've . . . I've grown up. I've matured. I'm moving on to a new stage in life – with a different outlook, and different priorities. When I look back at the frivolous way I used to think – well, it makes me want to laugh, really. The new

Rebecca is so much more serious and level-headed. So much more responsible. It's as though the tinted glasses have fallen off and suddenly I can see what's really important in the world and what's not.

I've even been thinking this morning that I might go into politics or something. Luke and I discussed politics a bit last night, and I have to say, I came up with lots of interesting views. I could be a young, intellectual MP, and be interviewed about lots of important issues on television. I'd probably specialize in health, or education, or something like that. Maybe foreign affairs.

Casually I reach for the remote control and switch on the television, thinking I might watch the news. I flick a few times, trying to find BBC1, but the TV seems stuck on rubbish cable channels. Eventually I give up, leave it on one called QVT or something, and lean back down on my pillows.

The truth, I think, taking a sip of coffee, is that I'm quite a serious-minded person. That's probably why Luke and I get on so well.

Mmmm, Luke. Mmmm, that's a nice thought. I wonder where he is.

I sit up in bed, and am just considering going into the bathroom to surprise him, when a woman's voice from the television attracts my attention.

'. . . offering genuine NK Malone sunglasses. In tortoiseshell, black and white, with that distinctive NKM logo in brushed chrome.'

That's interesting, I think idly. NK Malone sunglasses. I've always quite wanted a pair of those.

'Buy all three pairs . . .' the woman pauses '. . . and pay, not £400. Not £300. But £200! A saving of at least 40 per cent off the recommended retail price.'

I stare at the screen, riveted.

But this is incredible. *Incredible.* Do you know how much NK Malone sunglasses usually cost? At least a hundred and forty quid. Each! Which means you're saving . . .

'Send no money now,' the woman is saying. 'Simply call this number . . .'

My heart beating fast, I scrabble for the notebook on my bedside table and scribble down the number. This is an absolute dream come true. NK Malone sunglasses. I can't quite believe it. And three pairs! I'll never have to buy sunglasses again. People will call me the Girl in the NK Malone shades. (And those Armani ones I bought last year are all wrong now. Completely out of date.) Oh, this is *such* an investment.

With shaking hands I dial the number – and get through immediately! I would have thought everyone would be on the line, it's such a good deal. I give my name and address, thank the woman very much indeed, then put down the receiver, a joyful smile plastered across my face. This day is perfect. Absolutely perfect. And it's only nine o'clock!

Happily I snuggle back down under the covers and close my eyes. Maybe Luke and I will spend all day here, in this lovely room. Maybe we'll have oysters and champagne sent up. (I hope not, actually, because I hate oysters.) Maybe we'll . . .

Nine o'clock, interrupts a little voice in my mind. I frown for a second, shake my head, then turn over to get rid of it. But it's still there, prodding annoyingly at my thoughts.

Nine o'clock. Nine . . .

And I sit bolt upright in bed, my heart thumping in dismay. Oh my God.

Nine-thirty.

Derek Smeath.

I promised to be there. I *promised*. And here I am, with half an hour to go, all the way over at the Ritz. Oh God. What am I going to do?

I switch off the TV, bury my head in my hands, and try to think calmly and rationally. OK, if I got going straight away, I might make it. If I got dressed as quickly as possible, and ran downstairs and jumped in a taxi – I might just make it. Fulham's not that far away.

And I could be a quarter of an hour late, couldn't I? We could still have the meeting. It could still happen.

In theory, it could still happen.

'Hi,' says Luke, putting his head round the bathroom door. He's got a white towel wrapped round his body, and a few drops of water are glistening on his shoulders. I never even noticed his shoulders last night, I think, staring at them. God, they're bloody sexy. In fact, all in all, he's pretty damn . . .

'Rebecca? Is everything OK?'

'Oh,' I say, starting slightly. 'Yes, everything's great. Lovely! Oh, and guess what? I just bought the most wonderful . . .'

And then for some reason I stop myself, mid-stream. I'm not exactly sure why.

'Just . . . having breakfast,' I say instead, and gesture to the room-service tray. 'Delicious.'

A faintly puzzled look passes over Luke's face, and he disappears back into the bathroom. OK, quick, I tell myself. What am I doing to do? Am I going to get dressed and go? Am I going to make the meeting?

But my hand's already reaching for my bag as though it's got a will of its own; I'm pulling out a business card and punching a number into the phone.

Because, I mean, we don't actually *need* to have a meeting, do we?

And I'd probably never make it in time, anyway.

And he probably won't even mind. He's probably got loads of other stuff he'd prefer to be doing instead. In fact, he probably won't even *notice*.

'Hello?' I say into the phone, and feel a tingle of pleasure as Luke comes up behind me and begins to nuzzle my ear. 'Hello, yes. I'd . . . I'd like to leave a message for Mr Smeath.'

317

Rebecca Bloomwood
c/o William Green Recruitment
39 Farringdon Square
London EC4 7TD

5 April 2000

Hyvä Rebecca Bloomwood

Saanen jälleen kerran onnitela teitä hienosta
suorituksestanne – tällä kertaa **«Morning Coffee»** –
ohjelmassa. Arvostelukykynne ja näkemyksenne
tekivät minuun syvän vaikutuksen ja uskon, että
teistä olisi suurta hyötyä täällä Helsingin Pankissa.

Olette todennäköisesti saanut lukemattomia työtar-
jouksia – teidän lahjoillanne voisi hyvin saada
minkä tahansa toimen **«Financial Timesista.»**
Pyydän teitä kuitenkin vielä kerran harkitsemaan
vaatimatonta yhtiötämme.

Parhaiten teille ehkä sopisi viestintävirkailijan
paikka, joka meillä on tällä hetkellä avoinna.
Toimen edellinen haltija erotettiin hiljattain hänen
luettuaan töissä **«Playboyta.»**

Parhain terveisin

Ystävällisesti

Jan Virtanen

Fine Frames Ltd
The happy homeworking family

230a Burnside Road
Leeds L6 4ST

Ms Rebecca Bloomwood
Flat 2
4 Burney Rd
London SW6 8FD

7 April 2000

Dear Rebecca

I write to acknowledge receipt of 136 completed Fine Frames ('Sherborne' style – blue). Thank you very much for your fine work. A cheque for £272 is enclosed, together with an application form for your next frame-making pack.

Our quality control manager, Mrs Sandra Rowbotham, has asked me to inform you that she was extremely impressed with the quality of your first batch. Novices rarely come up to the exacting standards of the Fine Frames Quality Promise – it is clear you have a natural gift for frame-making.

I would therefore like to invite you to come and demonstrate your technique at our next Framemakers' Convention, to be held in Wilmslow on June 21. This is an occasion when all the members of the Fine Frames home-working family gather under one roof, with a chance to exchange frame-making tips and anecdotes. It's a lot of fun, believe me!

We very much look forward to hearing from you.

Happy frame-making!

Malcolm Headley
Managing Director

P.S. Are you the same Rebecca Bloomwood who gives advice on *Morning Coffee*?

Endwich Bank
FULHAM BRANCH
3 Fulham Road
London SW6 9JH

Ms Rebecca Bloomwood
Flat 2
4 Burney Road
London SW6 8FD

10 April 2000

Dear Ms Bloomwood

Thank you for your answer-machine message of Sunday, 9 April.

I am sorry to hear you are still suffering from acute agoraphobia.

Bearing in mind the relatively healthy state of your current account at the present time, I suggest that we might postpone our meeting for the moment.

However, be assured that I shall be keeping a close eye on the situation and will be in touch, should matters change in any way.

With best wishes

Yours sincerely

Derek Smeath
Manager

PS I enjoyed your performance on *Morning Coffee*.

ENDWICH — BECAUSE WE CARE